Marti Talbott's

Highlander Series

Book 2

(Maree, Gillie, Jessup & Glenna)

By

Marti Talbott

-

Editor: *Frankie Sutton*

Author's note: All of Marti Talbott's Books are clean.

MAREE

CHAPTER I

Maree loved children. She was always the first to visit when a little one was born, and the first to offer to care for the child of a nervous mother, or one who just needed time alone. Everyone loved Maree. She was a pretty girl at fifteen, saw herself as a wife and mother someday and almost always had a smile on her face.

She lived inside the wall of the MacGreagor village, where several paths began at the courtyard, led to old and new cottages, and connected at a vegetable and herb garden in the back. The Keep, where her laird and mistress lived, was a two-story structure, and a moat outside the wall provided fresh water and protection from enemies. A squeaky drawbridge across the moat was lowered each morning and the first to use it were the hunters, mounted on the horses that were normally kept in stables, inside the wall. The women and children walked across the bridge to the loch each morning to bathe, and the men, after a hard day's work, bathed in the same loch in the afternoon.

Maree's special talent was telling stories and on this day, she sat on a log in front of her cottage surrounded by no fewer than ten children, ranging in ages from four to nine. Her stories always had a happy ending and taught a good lesson.

"There once was a lassie named Leah," she began, "who was very lonely. She had eight brothers, all older and no sisters at all. There were lots of other lassies in the village, but they already had friends. So one day she decided to..." Maree stopped. On the path behind the children stood a man wearing a Cameron plaid and when she looked up, she noticed how handsome he was.

His name was Yule Cameron and he had never been to the MacGreagor hold before. It was very different from his home, especially the structure of it, and he wanted to learn what the people were like. If they were anything like the pretty one telling a story to the children, he would be very envious of Kevin's oldest son, Sween; very envious indeed.

"Please continue," Yule said. "I too want to know what the lonely lassie did."

Maree was embarrassed by his attention and thought to rid herself of the uncomfortable audience. "I would, but I make all the children sit down when I tell stories." She expected him to go away. Instead, he sat down. Now what was she to do?

At nineteen, Kevin's oldest son, Sween MacGreagor, had no time for such nonsense and rarely, if ever, noticed Maree. Still, his father wanted him to be hospitable to Yule, and he really had no choice but to reluctantly sit down as well.

Maree smiled at him, but Sween dismissed her with a half-hearted nod. She was not impressed and neither was Yule, she noticed, but she quickly turned her attention to the children waiting breathlessly for the rest of her story. "So the lassie thought of a way to get all the other lassies to notice her. She put a spot of ash right on the tip of her nose." The children laughed and Yule smiled. For some odd reason, he was making Maree nervous and she wasn't sure she could finish the rest of the story. His eyes were a wonderful shade of brown and his dark hair was thick and wavy. She decided not to look at him ever again.

Most women loved children, Yule knew, but this one seemed to worship them. In the short time he had been there, two more little ones came and before they sat down, they both gave Maree a hug and a kiss on the cheek. Each caress made her close her eyes and drink in the love the children had for her. He almost wished he were a child again, so he too could get that close.

Yule and Sween were the same age and his laird, Blair Cameron, wanted to someday make Yule his third in command. It was an important position, full of responsibilities as well as honor. Should something happen to his laird and the second in command, he would hold the lives of the Cameron Clan in his hands. For that reason, Laird Cameron sent Yule to learn from the MacGreagors.

Before he came, Yule thought he might find a wife among the MacGreagor women. The most beautiful woman he had ever seen was Bridget and she was married to his friend, Blair. Some time ago, Yule decided beauty might not be such a good thing; Blair always had to glare at men who paid his wife too much attention. Instead of beautiful, pretty would be far more welcome to Yule and Maree was all that and more. She had golden hair and blue eyes, much to his liking. He smiled twice more at her story and when she was finished; he got up and reached out his hand to help her stand.

Maree stared at his hand. She would have to take it soon; it was unthinkable to refuse, but for some reason she hesitated. She looked into his eyes finally, took his hand and stood up. His touch was even more exciting than his eyes. The children scattered and she didn't even notice.

"You tell a fine story, I am Yule Cameron." He expected Sween to introduce her, but Sween walked away. Perhaps that was a good thing.

"I am Maree."

Her hand was still in his and he marveled at how different if felt than when he gave a hand up to other women. He finally let go and clasped his hands behind his back. "I will be here for seven days at least. Perhaps we will meet again. Do you tell stories every day?"

"Most days, but I fear if you come to hear them often, the people will think you daft."

"You are right, of course. May I walk you home?"

Maree giggled. "You already have, I live in this cottage."

"I see." He lifted his hand to his forehead and rubbed his brow. "I am not doing this very well, am I?"

"Doing what?"

"I am hoping to spend time with you while I am here, but I do not know how to ask. What does a MacGreagor do when he wants to learn about a lass?"

"Well, I like to take walks and ride a horse, when someone will take me. Kevin does not like the lasses to go riding alone. He worries about us."

"As well he should. I will ask his permission to take you riding tomorrow after the noon meal. Are you willing?"

She was delighted and quickly nodded. She loved to ride and few had time to take her.

He started to walk away and then thought better of it. "Would you like to take a walk now? I seem to be free at the moment."

"I would like that very much."

*

Her name was Steppen and she was finally six-years-old. The color of her MacGreagor plaid was predominantly blue, the pleats were crooked and her wide leather belt was so loose, it barely kept her long skirt held up. She wore a white shirt and a small stretch of cloth over one shoulder, just like the grownup women.

She had light brown eyes and very light blonde hair, with a lock in the front that would not stay out of her face, no matter how many times she pushed it away. Being six opened a whole new world to her. She could go anywhere inside the wall by herself now, and she wanted to see everything. First, she stopped to hug Maree and listen to her story, and then she was off. She wasn't sure exactly how to start her exploration, but soon decided to go all the way to the drawbridge, and work her way around the inside of the wall until her circle was complete.

Her world consisted only of the MacGreagor hold. It was a pleasant place with a meadow outside the wall, and a path that led through the trees to another clearing where the MacGreagors rested their dead. She never wanted to see the graveyard, but she wanted desperately to play in the meadow. Steppen had hardly ever been outside the wall except to bathe or swim.

When she reached the lowered bridge, she took a peek at the

moat. The children were not allowed to go across the bridge alone until they were ten. They must also know how to swim and swimming did not come easy to her. She sighed. Ten would probably never come anyway; it took all her life just to get to six. Steppen looked beyond the bridge to the road and the forest. The road was straight and she had only been down it once. That was when her father took her for a ride on his horse. It was the happiest day of her life and remembering it made her smile.

Next, she looked at the wall and had a question -- who the devil planted flowers by the wall?

She was amazed her parents let her live so long. They were always fussing and fuming about something she did. At least they had not taken her to see Laird Kevin. Kevin would never hurt a child, but he could, and would, punish her by making her clean something. That meant chores. Long ago, she pledged to avoid chores at all costs.

"Hello, wee one."

She jumped about a mile high and then looked at the giant's big shoes. They weren't her father's shoes…that she knew for certain. She let her eyes drift up his very long leg with leather straps that laced up to his knee, then over his blue kilt and up to his wide leather belt. Her neck was starting to hurt already and she was only half way there. It occurred to her she could run, but if the giant's arms were as long as his legs, she doubted she would get very far. She looked at his shirt, raised her eyes to his neck and at last, found his face. "Who the devil are you?"

He smiled. "My name is Connor, what is your name?"

She sighed. "They call me all sorts of names."

The little girl was about to fall over looking up at him, so Connor took pity and knelt down on one knee. "You mean you have more than one name?"

"Depends."

"On what?"

"On how much trouble I am in." She put her hands on her hips with her thumbs going the wrong way. "Do you have children?"

"I have two. The first is Justin and the second is Danny."

Steppen patted Connor's arm. "Who the devil planted all those flowers?"

"I do not know, perhaps Anna planted them."

"Oh, so you know our mistress. I like her, she smiles a lot. My mother does not smile, save at my father. You got a wife yet?"

"I do, she is Rachel and she is Anna's sister."

"Oh, then you know everyone. Well, I got to go. I am six and you know what that means."

He didn't know what six meant, but she was off and running before Connor had a chance to ask. He stood up and then realized she still didn't tell him her name.

*

Yule and Maree strolled down the path toward the drawbridge, intending to go across and walk down the road. Compared to other clans, the MacGreagor land was long rather than wide, with good hunting, ample forests, and many clearings and streams. There was only one problem with it in the eyes of most -- it bordered England to the south. Yet that was a good two days away and rarely did the MacGreagors have trouble with the English.

The young couple crossed the courtyard and were about to cross the bridge, when Yule looked back and noticed several little children following them. He stopped, turned around, spread his legs apart and clasped his hands behind his back. Three of the little boys did the same, although they were not well practiced at the non-threatening pose, and had to adjust themselves a couple of times to get it right. Yule smiled.

Maree was thrilled when she saw them. She knelt down and opened her arms. Yet, she had not braced herself well enough for the onslaught, and was grateful when Yule put his hand on her back to keep her from falling over. It was a good feeling. Maree had a hug and a kiss for each child, and then reminded them they were not to cross the bridge.

Yule helped her stand and then watched the little ones turn back. "They love you very much."

"And I love them. Children make me feel life in a way nothing else can." As soon as they crossed the bridge, both looked back to make sure the children obeyed.

*

When Steppen saw it, she was mesmerized. She was behind the very first cottage and couldn't take her eyes off of it. The thing had five arms, it was slowly spinning and she had never seen anything like it. The arms were made of very thin wood, connected somehow right smack dab at the end of a long stick, and the stick was planted in the ground just like a flower. She looked at her hand and then looked back. Nope, they were not arms, they were hands and each was slanted. Very carefully, she extended her first finger and touched it.

"What the devil!" It stopped turning. She pulled her finger back and sure enough, it started to spin. Again, she stopped it and again it spun, only this time faster. She was horrified -- *this* was the stuff of nightmares.

*

Sween returned to the great hall without Yule, and Kevin was surprised. There was no mistaking whose son Sween was. He had the same hair, the same blue-gray eyes and even his face resembled his father's.

The great hall was a large room and could easily hold dozens during celebrations. The ceiling was two stories high with small open air slits, but the light inside was not always good, so candles burned at intervals along the walls. More candles sat in holders on the table. Colorful tapestries hung on the walls and in a large stone hearth, a fire was lit in the mornings to keep the chill away, and not put out until night. An assortment of large and small weapons also hung on the walls.

A small back door opened into a room where food was prepared, and the stairs near the large front door led to a balcony on the second floor with more doors that opened into bedchambers.

Sween didn't have to ask what his father wondered. "Yule is taking Maree for a walk."

"Maree, I see. I wondered which lad would win her heart. She is very pleasing." His oldest son only shrugged. "Did you show him everything he desired to see?"

Sween sat down at the table and laid his head flat against the cool wood. "Aye."

Kevin knew what was wrong with his son. The boy drank far more wine than he should have the night before, and now his head was hurting. There was no point in talking to him when he was in that condition, not that talking ever did much good where Sween was concerned.

Kevin sat down at the head of the table and began to consider various problems that needed to be solved. He was laird over the MacGreagor Clan and had been since he was Sween's age. He didn't remember being a problem to his father, but then, his parents and all but one sister died in the plague. He made more than his share of youthful mistakes, and hoped not to die before his son was able to handle the responsibilities. Lately however, Kevin was beginning to wonder if that day would ever come. A year ago, Kevin made Sween his third in command, hoping it would inspire his son. It didn't. Sween always obeyed, but never took much of an interest.

Kevin forced his thoughts back to his duties. Soon, parents would be bringing their children for him to punish. This was often the most pleasant part of his day. It gave him a chance to get to know all of them and their parents much better. The littlest ones were allowed to climb into his lap, tell him what they had done wrong and hang their heads. It was never anything very serious and the parents did not bring the children until it was their third or fourth offense. He meted out their punishments and warned them never to do it again.

The rest of his day was filled with seeing that repairs were handled, hunters brought back enough food, riders were sent to other clans with messages, visitors were well received, and adult disputes were resolved. By night, and at the age of forty-seven, he was always exhausted.

*

Connor was Kevin's second in command and the two were the best of friends, although Connor was a good fifteen years younger. They were married to sisters, which made them brothers as well. As was his custom, Connor went to the Keep to see what Kevin needed him to do. He noticed Sween's normal morning position and rolled his eyes. Then he pulled out a chair and sat down next to Kevin at the other end of the table. "You look well rested."

"I had a good night. How are my nephews?"

"They are well. Justin runs off every morning to hear Maree's stories. Soon he will be old enough to give up the stories and learn to fight with wooden swords. Danny clings to his mother still."

"We appear to have most things under control today. Go home and relieve Rachel of your sons."

"I have a better idea. Rachel misses having the time to practice with her bow and arrows, and a morning without children would do her good. I shall find a lass to watch Danny and perhaps someday Rachel will love me again."

Kevin laughed and watched him go. Then he decided he had time before the children arrived to see what his youngest son, Neil, was up to. When he stepped out the door and onto the landing, he spotted Yule and Maree walking together down the road. He approved.

*

Yule enjoyed Maree's company very much. She was telling him a story about a particular MacGreagor elder, and she had his full attention. "What did she do then?" he asked.

"The only thing she could. She hid his belt and refused to tell him where it was. Without it, he had nothing with which to hold up his kilt."

"Did her husband give in?"

"He was a stubborn old lad. When he still did not agree to do as she wished, the next morning he could not even find his kilt." Maree enjoyed his chuckle for a moment and then continued, "The husband then looked at his shirt, which was now his only covering, and finally realized he had two choices; he could give in or deprive himself of sleep so she could not take his shirt. But..."

"He was an old lad who knew he could not stay awake."

She grinned, nodded and looked up at him. Would she ever get used to his magnificent eyes? "The old lad gave in, at last, and can you guess what the wife wanted?"

"I cannot."

"'Twas a simple thing. He was too old to fight, too old to hunt, constantly under foot and driving her daft. She wanted him to leave the cottage every morning and not come back until the noon meal...so she could have a few hours of peace."

Yule was delighted with her story and couldn't stop smiling. She would make a good wife, and if this was any example, she would forever be entertaining everyone he knew. He thought about kissing her, but she had only known him for a few hours and he decided it was far too soon. He stopped walking and so did she. "Unfortunately, I am here to learn from Laird MacGreagor and I should go back."

"I need to go back as well. I have three younger sisters and must help my mother with the noon meal."

"May I see you again later? I thought we might sit and talk. I believe I have a story you might like to hear."

She liked him. He was easy to talk to and he made her feel safe. He was not her first admirer, but the first to make her feel so special. "I would like that very much."

*

Laird Kevin MacGreagor and his wife, Anna, had two sons. Neil was four years younger than his brother, Sween, and he looked more like his mother with dark hair and blue eyes. Neil was a happy young man who rarely caused trouble and Kevin found him where he expected to, in the stable caring for and talking to the horses.

As soon as he noticed his father, Neil smiled. "Do you find it strange that the horse is so large, yet his legs are thin? I find it amazing that thin legs can carry so much weight and do it gracefully."

"You have your mother's love for them and the horses are aware of it. I do believe they tend to love you back." He walked to his own large stallion and rubbed the horse's nose. "As for thin legs, I have wondered the same. The legs sometimes break, you know. Perhaps someday we will learn how to fix them so we do not have to kill the animal."

"I hope so. Perhaps the English know how to do it."

"Perhaps, but sooner or later we hear what the English are up to, and so far nothing much is said about the care of horses."

Neil patted the side of a horse's neck and then lifted one of its legs to examine the hoof. "I have heard the king is a fair lad. Do you believe it?"

"If he is like his Uncle, he is a good lad." Kevin noticed when

Yule came into the stable and nodded to him.

"Many say the English cannot be trusted, but mother is English and I trust her," said Neil, letting go of the horse's leg.

"She is worthy of your trust. However, there is evil in every land. A wise laird rids his land of the evil, even if he has to kill to do it. It takes a great deal of courage, more so than to kill in battle, but he is wise to do it. Still, he must be certain he is not killing out of anger, but for the good of the people."

"For what crimes do you kill?"

"If a lad tortures animals, he will someday do the same to people and he must die. A laird gives him ample warnings first and if he continues to torture, the laird must execute him. The MacGreagor laird also kills those who harm lasses and children. Other clans do not hold to these standards, but the MacGreagors do and I hope they always will."

"But why kill these lads, Father? Why not just punish them so they will not do it again?"

"Once, when a MacGreagor beat his wife, my father whipped the lad, but let him live. The lad's anger was not abated and instead, grew into rage. A few years later, he beat his eldest daughter and nearly killed her. Had my father taken the life of the lad, the daughter would not have suffered such cruelty."

Neil picked up a sturdy wire brush and began to brush the horse's mane. Then he paused to ask another question, "What if a lad hurts another lad?"

Kevin folded his arms, leaned against a post and shrugged. "Lads normally do not hurt each other without just cause. They settle the dispute themselves and the laird is better off staying out of it if he can."

"I see." Neil went back to brushing the horse. "Have you ever banished anyone?"

"I have banished three lads. They were lazy and would not hunt to feed their families. However, a banished lad has nowhere to go and if he vows revenge, he is a danger to us all. A laird must judge the danger before he banishes."

Kevin turned to Yule and doubted the man was listening. "I see you have a lass on your mind."

"I was trying to think what I would do if a lad hurt Maree. I am beginning to understand your ruling," said Yule.

"In love already? I am not surprised; Maree is a very pleasing lass. A good lad feels a strong need to protect his mother and his daughters, but most of all, the lass he loves. Even after all these years, I am still relieved when Anna is safe in my arms. I could go daft thinking of all the ways I might lose her."

Kevin paused to consider what else he should tell them. "Most lasses are wise in ways a man is not. A lad thinks of how his decision effects today, but a lass thinks of tomorrow, next week and even next month. If you let her, she will teach you more than you are able to imagine."

"About what, father?"

"About all kinds of things, especially your followers. She sees when the people are unhappy or when they are unwell. For that reason, a lad must learn to listen to her. 'Tis not easy to admit we do not already know everything." He leaned toward his son and raised an eyebrow, "Do you think Yule is listening?"

Neil shook his head. "Does love always distract a lad that way?"

"Always and it never ends. I think of your mother constantly. I wonder what she is doing and especially if she needs something, but does not want to ask. They are like that, you know. Wives think we should not be bothered with such trifling things."

Yule was listening. "She needs new shoes. I noticed this morning when you introduced her."

"There, you have a good example, my son. She did not mention it, but I saw and requested new ones for her. They should be finished soon."

Neil hung his head. "I did not notice."

Kevin smiled and started to walk away. "You will. Someday you will notice everything there is to notice about a lass."

CHAPTER II

Steppen was starting to get bored looking at the backs of the cottages. Some had flowers, but most didn't. Instead, they had rocks upon which moss grew and got slippery when it rained. When she was just a child, she often tried to stand on the large, slippery rocks without sliding off. Maybe she still liked to, but she looked up at the sky and decided it would not rain.

The rain was a bothersome thing. Her brother said only the black clouds held the rain, but she knew that wasn't true. She'd even seen it rain when the sun was out. Once, she saw a curved line in the sky with all sorts of wonderful colors. She like it and hoped it would come back. Her brother called it a bow, but what did he know, he was only eight. Then again, it was the same shape as her father's bow.

Steppen suddenly stopped dead. Behind a cottage was a path that led from a door straight to the wall. What the devil was that for? She scratched her head and tried to figure it out. It didn't even reach the wall; it went to a bush in front of it. Perhaps the woman living inside gave her wash water to the bush. That might explain it. She was still scratching her head when she started to move on, but then that darn clump of hair fell into her eyes again, and she had to stop and swoop it away. When she got home, she would ask her mother to tie it back with twine. She was so excited first thing this morning, she forgot.

Suddenly, that same giant was standing right in front of her. "Are you back?"

Connor knelt down and stood two-year-old Danny on the ground in front of him. "I neglected to get your name."

"Oh that again. I have many names."

"I already heard, but I am interested in the one your mother uses when she calls you."

"Oh, mother calls me Steppen." She gave Connor her meanest frown. "I already know 'tis a stupid name."

"'Tis *not* a stupid name, 'tis very pleasing."

She eyed him suspiciously. "Are you that devil my mother warned me about?"

Connor was having a hard time containing his laughter. "I hope not. There is a lass on the path yelling your name."

Her eyes widened. "I forgot. I was supposed to be home for the noon meal!" She ran around the side of the cottage, and then up the path as fast as her little legs would take her.

*

Mungo and Sween grew up in the same clan, but had only been close friends for two years. Mungo had brown hair and brown eyes, was almost as big as Sween and was just as skilled with a sword. Yet Mungo was never thought of as handsome by the women and most paid little attention to him.

Sween normally did not have much to do, except stay in the Keep listening to Kevin, and that got boring months ago. He thought his father was much too gentle with the children, and vowed he would not even bother with the pests, once he became laird.

As he did on most afternoons, Mungo rode with him and Sween

chose which way they would go. Three weeks before, they happened upon two Ferguson women who were willing, and lately they usually drifted that direction. It was three hours on foot to Ferguson land, but half that by horse and they were always back by the time Kevin ordered the drawbridge raised.

Riding behind Sween through the trees, Mungo yawned. He enjoyed the drink as much as Sween and was also feeling the lagging effects. "I say we trade lasses, mine no longer excites me."

"Trade? Do lasses mind?"

"These lasses do not." He took a breath and marveled once more at how stupid Sween was. Anyone could have guessed the first meeting was arranged, but not Sween. Then, Mungo thought he was actually going to have to tell the simpleton what to do. Well, it would be worth it in the end. As Sween's second in command when the time came, all he had to do was supply the wine and women. That would leave him in control of it all, and Mungo cherished the thought.

"I do not wish to trade," said Sween.

"Careful my brother, she might hope to become your mistress someday."

"Why would that be so terrible?"

"Look around you; bonnie lasses live right under your nose. I will have the most pleasing of them all."

"If I let you, you mean."

Mungo looked away and rolled his eyes. Pretending loyalty to this man was never easy. "I heard your father talking to Neil this morning. He was teaching him how to be a laird."

Sween pulled his horse to a halt. "Did my father promise Neil he would be the next laird?"

"Nay, he did not say it, but 'tis clear he favors Neil over you."

"Neil is still a child and Father loves all children."

"How can you be so blind? Mark my words, he will name Neil before he dies and you will have nothing."

Sween urged his horse forward and thought the same thought he had countless times before -- Kevin would *not* choose Neil over him. He was the oldest and the people expected him to lead. Mungo was wrong; Neil would not be the next laird.

"Let me kill Neil and be done with it."

Sween had heard that countless times before too. "Not yet. If father names Neil and dies, then you can kill him -- not before."

"I do not understand your thinking. Why not eliminate the problem now and be done with it once and for all?"

He pulled his horse to a stop again and glared at Mungo. "If Neil is dead and the least bit of suspicion falls on me, Father would make Connor the new laird. The people love Connor and would gladly follow him. We must wait until *after* Father dies."

Mungo was surprised by such sound thinking. Perhaps Sween was not as stupid as he thought. Of course, Sween did not yet have wine in his stomach and that always dulled his mind. He would truly need to keep Sween drunk to have his way. "Then let me kill Kevin and we can have all we desire tomorrow."

"Nay, I will not order the death of my father. The people would hate me for it and we need them."

"How would the people know?"

Sween laughed. "When you drink, you have no secrets. If you kill Father, I would have to kill you to keep you quiet."

"Would you truly kill me?"

"If you killed my father, I would have no choice. Aye, you would die right enough, but I am fond of you and I would do it quickly." Sween was more like his father than he realized. He had just made sure Mungo knew who he was dealing with, just as Kevin would have. In the end, brute strength and cunning was the key to being a ruler. Sween felt he had the advantage in both areas and it was time to show it...at least to Mungo.

They rode in silence, which gave Sween time, to once more consider the idea that his father might appoint Neil the next laird. Neil was still young, but in only four years, he would be nineteen; the same age Kevin was when he became laird. It could happen...unless his father managed to die soon.

Kevin ruled with a heavy hand and Sween believed he felt it the most. The harder his father was on him, the more he resented it. Neil was hardly ever in trouble, but Sween couldn't seem to do anything right. He tried to please his father when he was younger, but gave up before he was seventeen. Now it was a question of how long his father would live. Kevin wasn't even sick and the truth be told, Sween could be an old man before Kevin died. The thought riled him to the bone.

*

The afternoon sun was warm and the air was fresh, when Yule and Maree sat down on a log inside the wall near the drawbridge. As usual, there was a steady stream of activity, with hunters coming home, men hauling water from the moat, and horses needing to be stabled for the night.

"Have you ever been to the Cameron Hold?" asked Yule.

"When the Fergusons attacked, we all went. But I was young, frightened and remember little except wanting to go home."

"I remember that too. Our lads had never seen so many bonnie lasses and spoke of it for months."

"Do the Camerons not have bonnie lasses?"

"We do, but we grow up among them and fail to notice as we should. Some MacGreagor lads prefer our lasses and we think them dim-witted."

She couldn't help but giggle. "Some of them truly are."

"We have those as well. Thomas died in the spring and Blair is our laird now. Do you know him?"

"I have seen him a few times. He comes to see Kevin, but we have not met."

"Do you know Bridget then?"

"I remember her red hair. She married Blair and relieved our lasses of much worry."

"How so?"

Maree folded her arms. "Bridget is very pleasing. She had the attention of all the lads and few noticed any of the other lasses."

Yule could see how that was possible. "Have you heard the rumor that her name is not really Bridget?"

A long time ago, the MacGreagors vowed not to tell anyone that Bridget's real name was Charlet. It was for her safety, Kevin said, so everyone agreed. The MacGreagors had not talked about it for a long time among themselves, but rumors will be rumors and some people will forever wonder.

Maree didn't remember ever having to lie before, but when someone's life depended on it, she was willing. "Well, first they said her father was really a Cameron. Then they said nay, he was a MacDonald. After that, everyone got confused as to who her mother really was. Does she have six brothers and four sisters, or eight sisters and two brothers?" Maree sighed. "I doubt even Bridget knows who she is by now."

Yule was pleased with her answer, but he didn't say why. "I believe Bridget misses the MacGreagors. I was hoping you would come to our hold and cheer her up."

"I would adore going to see Bridget. I do not know her well, but I will gladly tell her everything that has happened since she went away."

He found her answer exciting and couldn't wait to take her to his home. Her smile was warm, her attitude cheerful and she had beautiful eyes. Kevin was right; he was falling in love. Yet, her nearness was having an odd effect on him too. He could not seem to make his mind work properly. "The Cameron Hold is not as grand as this. We do not have a stone wall, a moat or even a large keep, but I believe you would be happy living there."

Maree glanced at him and then quickly looked away. Was he already thinking of marriage? She had not actually considered living somewhere other than with the MacGreagors. She knew other clans lived a far more rural life, especially the MacDonalds, but it never before concerned her. Yule seemed to be a good man, but would she ever be able to leave her beloved MacGreagor children? Perhaps she should be a little less willing to let him talk about his home. "You said you have a story to tell me. I confess I am not often the listener instead of the teller."

The log was not high enough for a tall man to sit comfortably, so he stretched his legs out and crossed his feet at the ankle. "There once was a laddie." He paused. "You may *not* ask questions."

"Very well, continue."

"The laddie was very lonely."

"Does he know the lonely lassie?"

"He does now, but you are getting ahead of the story."

"Do forgive me," said Maree.

"As I was saying, the laddie was very lonely and with no brothers, he had no one to play with."

She couldn't help herself. "He did not like lassies?"

"Nay, that came later. Tell me, what do you do when the children constantly interrupt you?"

Maree pretended to be insulted, "Surely you are not calling me a child."

He took her hand and brought it to his lips. "Do you know what I do when people interrupt me?"

"Not yet."

"I do not give back their hands." He carefully watched to see what she would do.

She slowly raised an eyebrow. "I believe my laird is watching you."

Yule drew in a quick breath, dropped her hand and stood up. When he looked around, neither Kevin nor anyone else was watching them. "You tricked me. I see now, you are far too clever for me." He smiled, offered his hand and helped her stand up. "Should I take you home? Will your father be concerned?"

She liked the feeling of her hand in his and didn't pull away. It was not as though letting him hold her hand was the same as giving him her pledge. What could it hurt to enjoy the company of a man for a little while? "I do not think Father worries."

"Then perhaps we might walk a little longer."

"We must, I have not heard the last of your story."

"True, but I have decided to wait for another day to tell the rest of it."

"I hope you do not forget the ending by then."

"I will not forget," he vowed.

*

She was too old for naps, yet when Steppen's baby sister slept and the little cottage got quiet, her eyes grew heavy and she fell asleep too. By the time she woke up, it was too late in the day to do much more exploring. Disappointed, she pouted all the way to the garden. Each day her mother sent her to pick herbs to put in their evening meal, and that was a chore. She hated chores!

She glared at a plant for a while and when she looked up, she spotted *her* Maree walking with that strange man. He even had a hold of Maree's hand. Nothing good ever came from a lad touching a lass, she knew that right enough. As soon as she got ten, she would show her brother a thing or two. Every time he touched her, it was to shove her out of the way.

As soon as the couple got close enough, Steppen sprang forward, blocked their path and put her hands on her hips with her thumbs going the wrong direction. "Who the devil are you?"

Yule smiled. "I am Yule, who the devil are you?"

She tried to make a fierce glare. "You gots the wrong color. Everyone knows a kilt is blue, not green."

"Some kilts are blue, but others are green and even yellow. I once saw a red one," said Yule.

"A red one? I do not like red ones," said Steppen, putting a hand on the back of her neck.

Yule was enchanted with the child and found it interesting Maree didn't scold her for being rude. "I was wondering. Would you like me to lift you so your neck will not hurt looking up?" When she nodded, he let go of Maree's hand and gathered the child in his arms.

Steppen was pleased with herself. She made that devil of a man let go of *her* Maree's hand. She sometimes used that trick on her father and it worked every time. She suddenly remembered her mother and looked down the path. For once, no one was coming for her.

Maree might have scolded Steppen on another occasion, but she wanted to see how he would handle a fearless child. Children could tell if a man was good or bad, and so far, Yule was passing the test. Good grief, Maree thought, she was actually considering him.

That pesky curl was down her forehead again and Steppen crossed her eyes. She forgot to ask her mother to twine it and all she could do was flip it back one more time. "I do not like green ones either."

"I see," Yule said. "There is a reason my plaid is different. I am a Cameron and not a MacGreagor. The color is how we tell who belongs to which clan."

Steppen frowned. "I heard of a Cameron once. I do not like

Camerons."

Yule couldn't come up with a good response to that and looked to Maree for help.

Maree took pity on him and touched the side of Steppen's face. "Did your mother send you to get herbs?"

Steppen rolled her eyes and wiggled until Yule let her down. "I have done it again!" She raced to a bush, grabbed a handful of leaves and ran down the path. Of course, they were the wrong leaves. She knew that. Her mother would send her back; hopefully before the green was gone. She was not finished with him yet.

*

Like Kevin, Neil was friendly, caring and knew the name of nearly everyone in the clan. Yet there were many MacGreagors, and he had not yet mastered his father's ability to remember which man married which woman, and which children belonged to whom. It was like a game to Neil and at the evening meal, Kevin enjoyed trying to trick him.

At thirty-nine, Anna was still a beauty who loved her family with all her heart. "Rose One had her baby today." Seated at the table, Anna waited while the serving woman put a bowl of food down in front of her, and tried to guess if Kevin or Neil would be the first to ask the name. She noticed Yule's perplexed look and explained. "There are three women named Rose in our clan, so we added a number to the back of each to tell them apart -- Rose one, Rose two and Rose three."

It was Neil who finally asked. "Rose One is married to Donald and she already has four children. What will they name this one?"

"Five children," corrected Kevin. "They are Celia, Dane, Daniel,

Marcus and Caral."

Neil grinned at his father. "Not Caral, Darrell. Father, you lose."

"Aye, but I am getting old. You have a young mind and you have the advantage."

"Now you make excuses," Neil shot back. "Confess it Father; I got this one right for a change."

Yule was enjoying the banter between them, and decided learning the names of all the members of the Cameron clan would become his goal as well. He glanced at Sween, who was half slumped over his food and clearly bored with the entire conversation. Yule found that perplexing. Sween would likely become the MacGreagor laird someday and he seemed to take no interest at all in his people.

Kevin turned his attention to his oldest son, "Sween, what remains for Yule to see?"

When Sween didn't answer, Yule spoke up. "Your son kindly showed me everything inside your hold. I am very impressed; 'tis all Blair said it was and more. I do wonder why you built a wall and dug a moat around your village?"

Kevin was not happy with Sween's manners, but decided to deal with him later. "'Twas my father's idea. He saw such a thing in England and wanted to make the place safe for the MacGreagor women and children. The clan was much smaller then and we have outgrown the wall. Many now live on the land outside."

"Do you think to build a second wall?"

Kevin took a bite of food, chewed and swallowed. He was still expecting his oldest son to take part in the conversation and not embarrass the rest of them, but Sween didn't say a word. He wanted to throttle his son. "I do not. We grow in number so quickly; we would forever be building wall, after wall, after wall."

Yule nodded and quickly swallowed his bite of venison. "Blair uses the same reason for not building a stone wall for us. He says expanding our wooden one does not require so much work."

Anna sighed. "Does no one want to know the name of the baby?"

Neil had a twinkle in his eye, "Mother, you want to tell it and we would not deny you anything."

"Anything?" she asked.

Kevin rolled his eyes, "Now you've done it. I have told you a thousand times not to say those words to your mother. Saying we would *not* deny her anything can turn our entire lives upside down."

Yule grinned. "I cannot wait to hear what she wants."

"Thank you, Yule." Anna patted Kevin's hand and made her demand. "I want a fence around the graveyard."

"Whatever for?" ask Kevin.

It was Neil who answered, "So the animals will not trample the graves."

Kevin narrowed his eyes. "You already knew what she wanted. You have tricked me."

Neil winked at his mother. "And far more easily than I hoped."

"In that case, you may build the fence for her."

Neil stood up and bowed, "At your service, father. I will begin it now."

"Now, when 'tis nearly dark? Sit down Neil, you are up to something and I want to know what," said Kevin.

"Very well." Neil sat back down. "I hope to ride your horse

tomorrow and..."

It was Kevin's turn to smile. "You may not ride my horse; you have a fence to build."

Neil's grin faded and his head dropped to his chest. "Mother...help."

Both Yule and Anna laughed, but Sween barely smiled. Yule said, "Kevin, I hope to take a ride myself tomorrow. I will take Maree with me, if you permit it."

"What say you, Anna? Should we let him fall in love with our Maree? How will we live without her?"

"I cannot imagine. She is..."

Sween finally had something to say, "She is a stupid lass who tells stories to the children."

Kevin was horrified and stood up. "You will leave my table -- now!"

Sween also stood up, "Of course I will, I always obey you." He shoved his chair back with his foot and stormed out the door.

Kevin watched him go, took a deep breath, slowly let it out and sat back down. "Yule, I..."

"You need not say anything, Kevin. The Camerons also have short-tempered lads. Tell me more about Maree."

Kevin liked this young man. He was wise enough to change the subject and turn an unpleasant situation into a pleasant one. He forced himself to calm down. "We love our Maree very much. She is very obliging and I worry she is sometimes too obliging. There are those who put upon her far too often."

"With so many MacGreagors, how do you know so much about

her?"

It was Anna who answered. "He hears it from me. I visit the wives and they tell me everything. Then at night before we go to sleep, I give him a full...almost a full accounting of all I have heard."

Kevin raised an eyebrow. "Almost?"

She leaned over and lightly kissed his lips, "You do not want to hear the rest, my love."

Kevin looked at Yule. "This is how my wife keeps me alive. I refuse to go to my grave without knowing all her secrets."

In less than eight hours, Yule had come to love and respect Kevin and his wife. They had a marriage every man dreamed of and he hoped he would be that fortunate. "I have another question; does Maree have a horse?"

Kevin didn't know and neither did Anna, so they both looked to Neil for the answer. "Like you said, father I have a fence to build so Maree can ride my horse...I suppose."

"I have a better idea. Sween will build the fence for his mother and you will ride Sween's horse with Yule and Maree tomorrow."

"Please father, my brother already hates me. I would much rather build the fence."

Kevin considered it. The rivalry between his sons was no secret and aggravating it always did more harm than good. Sween was prone to get even with Neil where Kevin couldn't see, and Neil never told on his brother. "You are right. Maree can ride my horse. I do not ride often and my horse could use the exercise."

"My horse," said Anna. "Your horse is too spirited for Maree."

*

Steppen tossed and turned in her bed. She'd hardly begun to do her exploring and after she stupidly fell asleep in the afternoon, her mother wouldn't let her go that far away again. Then, *the green kilt* disappeared before she got back to the garden to pick the herbs. After that, her father came home from the hunt and there was always something to do. Chores! It was the ugliest word she had ever heard.

Now she was having trouble going to sleep. Her bed was on the floor in the middle of her siblings and sometimes she got a wayward elbow or foot in her small domain. Tonight they were all asleep and none were fitful but her. She couldn't stop thinking about that thing with the hands. She would go back tomorrow and look at it again. Then she would find that awful man with the green kilt and make him leave her Maree alone.

CHAPTER III

In the morning, Kevin went to wake his oldest son, who was sleeping late as usual. "Get dressed; you and I will ride today."

Sween sneered, "I thought your knees hurt too much to ride."

Already Kevin was riled. "Get dressed!" He closed the door and went back to kiss Anna one more time. She was only half dressed after her bath, but he took her in his arms anyway. Her touch always calmed him and he couldn't remember a time he needed it more.

"He loves you, Kevin, I know he does."

"Perhaps, but he defies me constantly. We thought he would grow out of it. I have taught him all I know, but he does not listen. How can I leave the MacGreagors in his hands, when he cares for nothing but his own desires?"

She tightened her arms and put her head on his chest. She still loved the sound of his heart beating. "Perhaps 'tis my fault. Perhaps he believes I favor Neil over him."

"Neil is far easier to favor. He will be a good lad someday and I will be very proud of him. 'Tis our misfortune he was not born first."

"Do not be too severe with Sween. You have punished him relentlessly and it does nothing. Perhaps there is another way."

"Such as?" he asked.

She kissed his lips. "Perhaps 'tis time to simply ask him what makes him so angry."

*

Their ride began with both men keeping their horses at a walk, but Sween got his horse just a little ahead of his father's and Kevin noticed. He urged his horse to go a little faster in response and Sween did the same until they were racing down the road. Kevin thought to let his son win. He was indeed getting older and the jolting of the horse hurt his bones, but if he could make a change in his son somehow, the pain would be more than worth it. He decided not to let Sween win. He needed to make his son aware he was still laird and still strong enough to defeat him.

The road south took them past several cottages, a herd of cattle, hedgerows and a flock of sheep grazing on a hillside. Still they raced and at last, Kevin pulled far enough ahead to clearly win. He brought his horse to a halt and waited.

Sween was filled with such wrath when he caught up, he swung to the ground and pulled his sword.

Kevin was appalled. A man did not draw his sword unless he meant to use it. Even with his horse still dancing around, he stared at the rage in his son's eyes. "You intend to fight me? You would force me to kill my own son?"

"You cannot defeat me."

"I see, then you would kill your father and break your mother's heart."

Sween continued to glare at Kevin until the words finally registered. Then he blinked and looked down.

Kevin cautiously dismounted and pulled his horse's bridle down to force the brut to stand still. "What causes your anger?" Sween didn't answer so Kevin tried to think of another approach. "Is it your mother who disappoints you?"

At this, Sween's anger rose again. "You dare blame her?"

"She blames herself. When a woman greatly suffers during the birth of a child, 'tis not uncommon for her to favor the one she might have lost. 'Tis not something she can control and it does not mean she loves Neil more."

"I never believed she did."

"She will be glad to hear it." Kevin began to lead his horse back toward home, passing his son on the way. "When you were nine, you decided you no longer needed your mother's arms. That too is common, but when a laddie becomes a lad, he desires her touch again. You do not. Yet, your mother longs to have you hold her. Will you do it for her sake?" Kevin knew he was leaving his son behind, but didn't look back. He only stopped and waited to see if Sween would walk with him. "Lasses need the gentle touch of the lads in their lives and when you marry, you will find you need your wife's touch as well."

Sween finally shoved his sword back in his sheath and grabbed hold of his horse's reins. "I see, we ride so you can tell me to take a wife. You think a lass in my bed will calm my anger."

"What?" Kevin finally turned to face his son. "I would never have you take a wife unless you truly loved her. A marriage without love is no life at all."

"Then why are we here?"

"We are here so you can tell me what is wrong."

"Nothing is wrong. If it pleases you, I will go home, hold my mother and be done with it."

Kevin clenched his fist, and then made himself take a cleansing breath, before he did something he would regret. "That would be cruel even for you. She would feel your insincerity and it would hurt her much more than the lack of your embrace." Kevin narrowed his eyes, "And know this: she is my wife and no lad, not even my son, will ever hurt her again. I would sooner run you off my land than have you cause your mother more pain."

"There is no pleasing you, is there."

Kevin wanted to smash Sween's face in. He wondered for a moment if banishing Sween would not be, in the end, his best choice. Before him stood his own image, just as big, and with eyes that held a glare just as fierce. The only thing different was Sween's cold heart. Kevin didn't know what to do. He looked away and became distracted by the sight of Yule and Maree riding together up a hillside. It made him smile.

Sween saw what his father was looking at and did not smile. "I will have Maree."

Kevin was furious. "Maree is a good lass and I would be proud to call her daughter. But I would not have her condemned to life with an angry lad. You will *not* have her!"

There was nothing left for Kevin to do but walk away.

*

Neil didn't mind building the fence around the graveyard. It kept him out of Sween's way and that was a good thing. He paused for a moment to look at the place where his grandparents were buried. He never knew his father's parents, but remembered Anna's mother and stepfather. He loved them very much and was sad when each died.

The graveyard was a peaceful place in a clearing not far from the Keep. Through the trees, it was possible to see hillsides, other parts of the forest and still more clearings in the distance. Many MacGreagors came to the graveyard when they wanted a moment alone and Neil decided he would put logs just inside the fence so they could sit.

Dragging tree branches out of the forest, cutting the twigs off and then chopping the branches into equal lengths was hard work. He could ask for help, but time alone was also a luxury for a lad who happened to be Kevin MacGreagor's son.

He tossed a branch into the clearing and then stopped to watch Yule and Maree walk their horses up a hill. He liked Yule very much, and wished he had been chosen to show the Cameron how things were done in the MacGreagor hold. Of course, Sween was chosen instead.

Neil liked Maree too. He sometimes stopped to listen to her stories and wondered how she managed to make them up. Now it appeared Yule was about to take the MacGreagor storyteller away.

He noticed Sween was on his horse at the edge of the forest watching them too. Sween was never happy, but today he had a look of extreme hate in his eyes. Neil had seen that look a few times before. On one occasion, Sween had his brother on the ground. His foot was on Neil's shoulder and he had the tip of his sword against Neil's neck. Neil truly believed he would die that day. He reminded Sween their father would never make him laird if he killed his brother, and it worked. At length, Sween let him up.

Neil slipped back into the forest, untied his horse and mounted. Something awful was going through Sween's mind -- Neil could feel it.

*

Maree was happy to be away from the village and when they got tired of walking, she let Yule lift her back onto Anna's horse. They walked the horses at a slow pace and talked about all sorts of things. He was warm and wonderful to her, and she thought if she let him, he would be a good husband -- if she let him. Each time she thought he was about to broach the idea of marriage, she managed to change the subject. She was simply not ready to hear it yet.

She noticed Sween walking his horse through the forest, going their same direction, but didn't think it was all that strange. There were many MacGreagors and running into them was not unusual. Still, Sween seemed to keep the same pace and when she glanced at him again, he motioned for her to come. With his other hand, he held a finger to his mouth warning her to keep quiet.

She didn't care for Sween and he never paid attention to her, so his actions confused her. First, she thought it was a silly game and looked away, but then he did it again and she wondered if something was seriously wrong. Perhaps Kevin learned something about Yule's character and felt she was in danger. Still, something about Sween had always been disturbing. Then again, he was Kevin's third in command and she probably should obey. Yule was somewhat ahead of her and talking about an old friend, when Maree quietly guided her horse into the forest.

As soon as she reached him, Sween led her deeper into the trees before he finally stopped.

"What is it, what is wrong?" she asked.

He turned his horse around, moved it next to hers so they were face to face and took hold of her arm. "I will have you."

"What?"

"I said, I will have you to wife."

She was shocked. She tried to free her arm, but he tightened his hold. Maree lowered her eyes and tried to think of a way to reject him. He looked so mean, it frightened her.

"I will be laird someday and you will be my mistress. You will sleep in my bed, give me sons and you will be pleased to do it."

Maree said it, but just above a whisper. "I will not."

He slapped her face. "You will!"

She raised her eyes, narrowed them defiantly and spoke louder. "I will *not!*" Her horse started to rear up. She needed to get a firm hold on the reins, and didn't protect herself before he hit her again."

Sween's rage was complete. "How dare you refuse Kevin MacGreagor's son!" He was about to hit her a third time when someone suddenly grabbed him from behind, pulled him down off his horse and was about to cut his throat with a dagger.

Sween easily broke his attacker's hold. He hopped up, turned to see who it was and then jeered. "Neil, you simpleton, you hesitated. Father would be disappointed if he knew." Sween abruptly looked up and glared at Maree. "You disgust me and I reject you." He grabbed his reins and led his horse away.

Neil followed for a few feet and didn't take his eyes off his brother until he was sure Sween wasn't coming back. When he looked back, Maree was down off her horse. Distinct slap marks had reddened her face and when he opened his arms, she quickly went into them. He surprised himself. He watched his father comfort women often, but this was a first for him. He was taller than she and his arms were not yet as strong as they would be, but they were all he had to give and he was glad to do it.

She started to cry, but when she heard Yule calling her name she began to panic. "Do not let him find us." She quickly wiped the tears away and grabbed hold of Neil's arms. "Your Father will kill Sween for this, you know he will. Kevin forbids any man to hurt a lass."

"Sween deserves to die for what he has done."

"Aye, but would you have your father forced to kill him? I could not bear it and neither could you."

Neil pulled her close again and closed his eye. "You are right, but how do we explain your face? 'Tis red and might bruise."

Yule's shouts were getting louder, so she pulled completely away from Neil. "I will explain it. You shout for Yule, before he goes to Kevin and says I am lost."

Neil hesitated but she was right. What they didn't need was Kevin's men seeing the marks on her face. He cupped his hands and yelled, "Yule, we are over here!"

Maree had to think fast and there was only just enough time to come up with something before Yule arrived. She watched him dismount and then walk to her. To her surprise, he quickly examined her face and then took her in his arms. "You scared me, what happened? You were there and then you were gone."

"I am so sorry. I spotted a red fox and wanted to follow it."

"Then what happened to your face? Did you fall off your horse?"

"The horse started to rare up suddenly, and if Neil had not been there, I would have been thrown. I hit a branch."

Yule looked at her face again and then looked at Neil. "She has the mark of a hand. For whom does she lie?" He started to turn his anger on Neil, but Maree grabbed his arm.

"Neil just saved my life and if I tell you who did it, Kevin will kill him."

"Only if I do not kill him first. Who did this?"

Maree hung her head. "You cannot kill him either, he is Kevin's son."

Yule was stunned and looked once more at Neil.

Neil let out a long sigh and finally leaned his back against a tree. "If *you* kill Sween, it will start a war between our two clans. I am not strong enough to kill him in a fair fight and Maree is right, my father would feel duty bound to do it. I can think of nothing worse for us all."

"We cannot just let him get away with this," said Yule.

Neil sighed. "The MacGreagors have been letting him get away with things for years. They do it because they love our father and mother. They do not want to be the one to tell Father he has a brutal son."

Yule looked at Maree's face again, knew she was upset, but holding back her tears. "If she bruises, what do we do then?"

Maree let Yule take her into his arms again. She was upset, but determined to keep a clear head. "We can pray it does not bruise and wait to see before we decide. It does not hurt much now. I am grateful he did not use his fists."

"He would have killed you if he had." Yule tried to take deep breaths to quiet his anger. It wasn't helping.

They were all silent for a time, each lost in their own thoughts.

Neil would not forget this moment and someday, when he was older and as strong as Sween, he would make him pay. Maree was right; all they could do was wait to see if she bruised. Then he realized they had an even bigger problem. "Sween knows I will not tell, but he might think Maree will. She is in danger."

"Then I will marry her and take her home with me. 'Twas my intention anyway."

Maree needed time to think and there wasn't any. Getting slapped was one thing. Rushing into a marriage she wasn't sure she wanted was another. "Marry you?" she asked, taking a step back.

Yule took hold of her hand. "I hope to hear all your stories before I die." He realized she wasn't smiling and why would she be? These were the worst possible circumstances under which a man could ask a woman to marry him. He wondered if she thought he was asking because he felt sorry for her, or just wanted to protect her. He wanted to, but decided he would tell her how he felt about her later. "Do the MacGreagors have a priest?" When she nodded, he took that to mean she accepted his offer.

Neil was sick at heart and wasn't listening. What *could* they say if she was bruised? Letting her get hurt might make Kevin think less of Yule, and Neil liked the man. He lowered his eyes and prayed her red marks would fade soon. If she had no mark, Kevin would never know anything was wrong. All Neil would have to answer for was the lack of progress on the fence. After that, he would find a way to protect her from Sween.

Yule and Neil kept looking at her face, but the marks were not gone or they would say so. It was all too much and Maree's head was starting to ache. Anna's horse had wandered away and she wanted to go look for him, but Yule wouldn't let go of her hand.

"We do not know where Sween is," said Yule.

"But Anna's horse?"

Neil tried to comfort her with his smile. "Mother's horse will come when I whistle. Do you want to sit down? You do not look at all well."

Maree glanced around, found a patch of soft grass and let Yule help her sit. The thought that she might never be safe again weighed heavy on her mind. Maybe marriage to Yule was her only hope, but she wanted to marry for love. She might have been falling in love with Yule, but now even the thrill of his touch was gone. Sween had ruined everything. Why had she been so stupid? She should have known better than to let Sween trick her.

Neil crossed his feet and sat down beside her. He was relieved. The redness on her face was getting lighter and he didn't think it would bruise. "How can I make this up to you?"

She surprised Neil by leaning over and kissing his cheek. "Thank you for saving me. How did you know to come?"

"I saw him watching you and followed."

Yule was still standing and seemed to be in a world of his own. "I will need to build a cottage for you, but we can stay with Blair and Bridget until them. There is one empty cottage, but..."

Neil thought offering to go to the Cameron hold and help Yule build a cottage was a great idea. He despised having to endure the sight of his brother just now. Sween was probably already boasting to Mungo that he could get away with even this abomination.

They waited another full hour and at last, neither of the men could tell Maree had been slapped. Each of them breathed easier and before long, they were all at the graveyard. Yule and Neil talked about where to put the fence and how tall to build it, while Maree pretended to be interested. They acted happy and playful just in case anyone was watching, but they were just acting and soon, a tear ran down Maree's check

Yule quickly took her in his arms again.

Neil pretended to be embarrassed and walked into the forest to find another dead branch.

Maree tried hard not to give in to her emotions, but she was truly frightened for the first time in her life. She imagined a future with Sween hiding behind every bush.

When she trembled, Yule held her just a little bit tighter. "Does it still hurt?"

She wiped her tears away and took a forgotten breath. "My head is aching, but my face does not hurt."

For some reason, Anna felt a need to visit her mother's grave. Once Kevin told her about his ride with Sween, she needed to think and the graveyard was the most peaceful place she knew. Yet, when she walked up the path and spotted Yule holding Maree, she stopped. Something was wrong. Their embrace was not one of passion -- he was comforting her.

Had Kevin not just denied Sween's request to marry Maree, Anna might not have suspected anything. But she knew, somehow she knew Sween had caused trouble. She was about to turn and go back when

Neil carried a branch out of the forest and saw her.

"Mother, did you come to see me?" Neil said it a little louder than necessary and it had the right effect. Yule and Maree quickly separated.

"What's this? You have not yet finished the fence?" Anna walked to her son and hugged him. "You've had the better part of a day and I thought you much more able than this."

Neil rolled his eyes and put an arm around Anna's shoulders. "I am not convinced there are enough dead tree limbs in the forest to build it, and you know father will not approve the cutting down of more trees." He turned his mother so she could not see Maree wipe her eyes, and then pointed south. "Shall we build it that way or the opposite way to make room for more graves? Or will I be expected to keep extending the fence?"

"By the time that many of us die, I will not care where you extend it. May I tell you something?"

"Of course," Neil said.

"Your father loves it when I ask for things, but I am nearly out of ideas. Might you think of something from time to time?"

Yule said, "I would like to request something."

Both Neil and Anna turned around. "What?" they asked at the same time.

"Well, a MacGreagor wedding would be nice."

Anna was thrilled and threw her arms open to Maree. Maree's eyes seemed puffy, their embrace made Maree cry and Anna's heart sank -- something awful had happened. Maree was trembling, so Anna held her tight and let her stay as long as she needed. "Tears of joy, I

see. Sweetheart, you must dry your tears before your eyes get all red."
Then she sighed. "I confess I did the same thing when I finally
realized I would be happy. When do you plan to marry?"

"Before I go home, if Kevin allows it," Yule answered.

"Kevin has never stood in the way of love and I can see you love
her very much. I knew I loved Kevin and had not yet even heard the
sound of his voice."

Yule smiled, "I knew as soon as I heard Maree's story."

Maree knew she should say something. It was supposed to be a
joyful moment. "I will be sorry to leave the MacGreagor children."

Anna tried to ignore the lack of excitement in Maree's voice.
"The Camerons have children too, you know."

"I know, but I love these so."

Anna gave her a quick hug. "My dear, I love *you* greatly and
would do most anything for you, but you may not take the
MacGreagor children with you."

Finally, Maree smiled.

CHAPTER IV

Of all the things his father said that morning, Sween could only remember these few words; *I would run you off my land*. Sween's rage was finally gone. He had the reins of his horse in one hand with the other hand pressed hard against a tree. What had he done? He hit Maree and if Kevin found out, he might actually kill him. Banishment was the most he could hope for and that was as good as dead.

For the first time in his life, Sween was actually fearful. Kevin might not do the killing himself, but he could order it done. He might choose Connor and if not, there was always Blair Cameron or Shaw Ferguson. He wondered if they would kill Kevin's son. No, they would not and Kevin would not order anyone else to do it. Then he realized Kevin would never hurt Anna and killing him *would* hurt her.

Sween began to breathe just a little bit easier. He would be banished instead. An honorable clan would never have him once Kevin threw him out. Others, not friends with the MacGreagor might, but they would only use him for their own gain. No, Sween would be forced to go to England for refuge. His mother taught him English, so at least he could speak the language, but their ways were not his and he would hate it there. Being Kevin's oldest son would mean nothing to the English and he would be no better than a commoner.

He felt a twinge of guilt when he thought about his mother. She loved him and he never once doubted it. When did his feelings for her become so cold? He hadn't meant for that to happen.

Sween ran his fingers through his hair and gripped the top of his head. Perhaps he could go to sea. Perhaps he should even go now and save his father the trouble. He could always come back once Kevin was dead and claim his place as laird. He might have to fight Neil for it, but that wouldn't stand in his way.

Then again, there was always a chance no one would tell Kevin. Neil would not, but Maree might. Sween closed his eyes and tried to remember how hard he hit her. At least he hadn't closed his fist, he remembered that much. There was only one way to find out if he hit her hard enough to bruise her. He needed a good look before she went home.

He rode to the hold, slowed when he crossed the drawbridge, dismounted and took his horse to the stable. Then he waited inside. He didn't have to wait long. Just as she came over the bridge with Yule and his mother, Sween stepped into the doorway to get a good look. There wasn't a mark on her and she looked happy. He was greatly relieved. Obviously, she hadn't run straight to Kevin or told his mother. If he was very lucky, she had no plans to tell anyone ever.

He stepped back inside the stable and leaned against a wall. Maybe she wouldn't tell him now, but she might tomorrow or the next day. Sween knew what he needed to do and started to plan exactly how he could do it.

*

Maree was home with her parents by the time the servers brought the evening meal to the MacGreagor table inside the great hall. Yule and Neil were there. Anna's sister, Rachel, and her husband, Connor, joined them, complete with young Justin and two-year-old Danny. The only one missing was Sween and they decided to wait.

As he always did in the evenings, Connor gave Kevin a report on the day's warrior practice, the hunters and the amount of extra water they had inside the wall in case of fire. He was about to explain a problem with the stables when Sween walked in.

"I am sorry I am late." Sween walked straight to his mother and held out his hand. When she took it and rose, he wrapped his arms around her. "My father tells me I have been neglecting you and he is right. I do love you, Mother and I did not mean to slight you."

Anna had tears in her eyes and Kevin was dumbfounded. Rachel and Connor smiled, but Yule didn't look at Sween and Neil was quickly filling with renewed anger that had to be hidden.

As soon as Sween took a seat, the servers brought their meal, poured goblets of wine and Connor passed his toddler son to Neil.

"What am I to do with you?" Neil teased, kissing the child on the cheek. "I suppose you want my food." When the little boy nodded, Neil sighed and picked up his spoon. "You eat more than I do, you know."

Kevin spoke next. "Connor, you were about to talk about the stables."

"Please," Rachel groaned, "Not the stables while we eat."

Everyone laughed and Sween actually smiled.

Kevin wrinkled his brow.

Anna noticed too and her heart was becoming heavier than it had ever been before. Sween's new found behavior gave him away. He did have something to do with Maree's tears and Anna was sick about it.

In Sween's youth, she might have tried to bait him, but this was different. Whatever happened was far more serious than his childish defiance. She knew one thing for sure; she would never tell Kevin what she suspected.

They talked of Yule's marriage plans, of the fence around the graveyard, and of rumors floating within their clan and from other clans as well. And Sween seemed to pay attention, even nodding his agreement.

But Kevin was not a stupid man. He noticed that Yule never once looked Sween's direction. Neil seemed reluctant to do so too, though he was accustomed to pretending to be friendly at the table, even after taking a thrashing from his brother. Anna was behaving oddly too.

Yule's behavior distressed Kevin the most. Yule's jaw was set as though holding back a fierce indignation. Only one thing made a man that enraged; someone hurt Maree. No, Kevin MacGreagor was not a stupid man. He abruptly stood up and headed for the door.

"Is he unwell?" asked Yule.

Connor was quick to rise and follow his laird. When there was trouble, it was his duty to stay close to Kevin and protect him if necessary. Kevin was getting on in years, but Connor still had a hard time catching up. By the time he made it up the path to the cottage where Maree lived, Kevin was already knocking on the door.

Maree's father was pleased to see his laird and Kevin greeted him with a forced smile. "I hear we are to celebrate a marriage and I came to see if that is what the bride truly wants."

"Of course," said the man. "Come in."

"If you do not object, I would like to take her for a short walk," said Kevin.

Maree tried not to tremble. She knew this was coming, Kevin always made sure a woman was not being forced into marriage, either by the man or by her parents. Act natural, she told herself and walked out the door. She was surprised to see Connor waiting, but she smiled at him. "Kevin, I am very happy and I am not being forced."

He took hold of her elbow and walked her past Connor without saying a word. He wanted to make sure no one else could hear his questions, so he walked her all the way into the garden before he finally stopped. "Where did he hurt you?"

"Who?"

"You know who."

"Kevin, no one has hurt me."

He wanted to believe her so badly his heart ached. He could demand she not lie to him, but he knew the truth and didn't really want to hear the words. He wrapped his arms around her and whispered in her ear. "I am so sorry." Then he released her and stormed down the path.

Connor rushed to Maree and took hold of her shoulders. "Do not cry, not now. Your father will know something is wrong. Take very deep breaths."

She did as he said, until she calmed herself enough to speak. "I have never lied to Kevin before."

"You are truly the bravest lass I know. Did Sween force you?"

She was aghast. "Nay Connor, I swear it. Yule took me for a ride. Sween tricked me into the forest, demanded I marry him and when I refused, he slapped me twice across the face. You will not tell Kevin, will you?"

"Nay, I will lie too. We both love Kevin too much to let Sween destroy him."

"Neil is afraid Sween will do something to keep me quiet."

"Neil was there?"

She nodded. "He kept Sween from hitting me again."

"I see. Do not fret, you will live with the Camerons, you will never have to see Sween again and you will be happy."

When he started to leave, she grabbed his arm. "I do not want to marry Yule."

Connor closed his eyes and thought for a moment. "I understand, but you must keep pretending for now. 'Tis unfair to Yule, but I will talk to him when the time comes. Are you able to keep pretending?"

She nodded. "I will think of it as one of my stories."

"Good. Perhaps 'twill even have a happy ending."

*

Many years before, Kevin had three doors hidden in the wall, so the MacGreagors could go out when the drawbridge was up at night. During the war with the Fergusons, they were all able to slip out through the doors, swim the moat and hide in the forest. It saved a lot of lives.

The first door was behind a cottage and as soon as Connor got Maree back to her family he looked, but the cottage was empty. He went through the back door, walked to the wall and just as he suspected, the hidden door was open. He stepped through the passageway and listened, but he could not hear Kevin swimming in the moat and guessed he was already on the other side. Connor sighed, pulled the door closed behind him and went into the water.

It was almost dark and searching for Kevin in the forest was not without complications. It was a good thing they were not at war or they would both be easy targets. Still, he dared not call out just in case. He decided to follow the path toward Cameron land, and at last found Kevin. "She is not lying. She was with Yule and they did not see Sween."

Kevin sat at the base of a tree with his eyes closed, and it was a while before he finally opened them. "I took my son for a ride this morning and he misunderstood everything I said. He thought I wanted him to marry, so he decided he wanted Maree. I denied him. I told him I would never let her marry an angry lad."

Connor sat down across the path from his laird. "So you thought he hurt Maree to spite you?"

"I do not think it, I am sure of it."

"Perhaps you only expect the worst of Sween."

"He gives me little reason not to."

"Kevin, Sween is not that stupid. He knows what the punishment is for such a crime."

"That he does, but I doubt he believes I would kill him for his mother's sake. He is right, you know. I do not think I have it in me to kill him." Kevin bit his lip and shook his head. "If Sween has hurt a lass, he may do it again, and this time he could kill her. How do I live with that?"

Connor was not at all comfortable with lying and was glad Kevin could not see his face in the dark. "He did not hurt Maree, Kevin. You worry for nothing."

"I wish I believed it. How did I manage to raise an angry child? Where was my error? I raised both boys the same, yet they are so different."

"I saw no error in your treatment of Sween. He knows you love him, he must. I have two sons of my own and they are already very different. Perhaps our children are born to be who they become. Besides, we have an even bigger problem. How do we explain our wet clothing to our wives?"

Kevin couldn't help but roll his eyes. "Do you think they would believe we wanted to go for a swim?"

"We could try it. Rachel already thinks I am daft and 'twould not be that hard to convince them you are too."

"If Sween did nothing wrong, Maree already knows I am daft."

"She said that very thing after you left." Connor stood up and gave Kevin his hand. "Come with me, old lad, we have some explaining to do. I say we take up swimming in the moat after all our evening meals. 'Twill save us the trouble of walking all the way to the loch."

They made their way back through the trees toward the moat in silence before Kevin spoke again. "I have been meaning to ask you, how did your morning practice go with Rachel?"

Connor grinned, "She is still the best shot with a bow I have ever seen and...she still loves me."

*

In the great hall, Anna tried to make light of Kevin's sudden absence. She leaned a little toward Yule and said, "I believe my husband has a new love."

Yule looked shocked. "I would never believe that, Kevin spoke of his love for you just this morning."

"Oh, I have no doubt of his love for me, but a lad like Kevin loves many. Today, I believe his new love might be quite compelling and as you see, she draws him away in an instant. Did you not hear her?"

Yule shook his head. "All I heard was a horse."

Anna finally smiled. "Unless I am mistaken, we are to have a new colt." She enjoyed his relief and her sister's giggle, but when Sween laughed she looked at him. Then she quickly looked away.

Sween brought the goblet of wine to his mouth. She knows...or at least suspects, he thought. She wouldn't tell Kevin, that he was sure of. In the end, it would be his word against Maree's anyway. And, if he stayed with the MacGreagors, he would have to somehow convince his mother Maree was lying -- if he stayed. Going to sea was still an option.

*

"I could say you fell in the moat and I had to save you," Kevin said.

"*That*, they would never believe." Connor sat down at the edge of the moat and started to slip into the water. "You know, I think the cold water has eased my itch."

"Do you think Anna would believe I could stand mine no longer and jumped in?"

"I think she might. Where do you itch?"

"On the back of my legs, of all places. I have had the problem for years, though the older I get the worse it is. We have tried everything to relieve it. Where is yours?"

Connor waited for Kevin to come across the water and then helped him out. "My itch is around my waist where the belt holds my plaid. The wool causes it, I am convinced. Might I be allowed to go without a kilt for a day or two?"

"I would consider it, but Rachel would never agree."

*

After the evening meal, Yule wanted to find a quiet place to think. He walked down one path and up another until he spotted an old tree, went behind it and sat down. He was having a hard time controlling his anger, and sitting at the table with Sween was almost more than he could endure. He hated the man's smile most of all. Kevin was right; men who hurt women do not stop until someone stops them. Yule had seen this kind of thing before.

Neil was also right. If Yule killed Sween, there might be a war between the MacGreagors and the Camerons. On the other hand, no one would have to know it was a Cameron who killed Sween -- not if he was quick.

Yule spent the next hour planning how to do it.

He thought then about Maree. She was more than he could ever have hoped for. His feelings for her were glorious and maddening all at the same time. He wanted to be with her right now and could hardly keep from going to her door. Still, what she needed most after today was rest and he meant to see she got it. He wondered if she would cry and if her parents would get her to tell them the truth. He also wondered if he could marry her and get her away fast enough to save her life. Maybe he wouldn't stay a whole week after all.

*

Kevin got out of his wet clothing, dried himself off and climbed into bed beside Anna. "We retire early this night. Why?"

Anna snuggled close, put her head on his shoulder and started to draw circles on his chest with her finger, "Because I want you all to myself."

"Do you? Do you have worries, my love?"

"I only have one." She moved her body just a little closer.

He noticed and tightened his arm around her. "What might that be?"

"Well, my husband has an itch that makes him jump into the moat at night. Naturally, I approve of anything that helps him, but it confuses me. You said cold water hurts your knees."

Kevin smiled. After all these years, she was still able to trap him into telling her more than he cared to. This time, he could not let her do it. "Aye, but I have a wife who is willing to warm my knees when they are too cold."

"Like now?" She began to make her circles a little lower on his chest.

"Exactly like now."

She smiled and leaned back to wait for his kiss. What she desperately needed, was that glorious time when Kevin's love could make her forget about everything else.

Nothing soothed Kevin more than Anna's love and he needed it as desperately as she did. He would never tell her what he suspected, even if it took every ounce of his strength not to. He had to push the thought of Sween's crime out of his mind and there was only one way. Tonight and for the rest of his life, he would think only of making

Anna happy.

*

Thank goodness it was morning again and that spinning thing did not plague Steppen at all during the night. She was having a devil of a time with her little plaid and her mother was busy, so all she could do was wait until someone took pity on her.

She wondered where the green was and if he was holding her Maree's hand again. The thought disgusted her. She suddenly remembered she had to hurry or she might miss today's story. With urgent eyes, she tugged on her mother's skirt, but her mother ignored her. She tugged on her brother, Patrick's, kilt and then her father's kilt, but it was no use. Finally, the only one left was...he couldn't help her, he was only eight.

By the time Connor was dressed the next morning, he was so enraged all he wanted to do was find Sween and break his neck.

Rachel had been up for hours, feeding her sons and sending the oldest off to hear Maree's story. The two-room cottage was much like all the others, with a hearth in the corner and a long shelf along one wall in the first room, where the water bucket, food and eating utensils were kept. Weapons hung on the wall and with beds enough for two adults and two children plus a table with four chairs, the cottage was full but comfortable and clean.

"You did not sleep well," Rachel said.

He put his arms around his wife. "Did I keep you from your rest?"

"Not that much. Something is wrong; do you wish to tell me?"

Connor lightly kissed her lips. "'Tis too awful."

"Ah, then 'tis Sween." She left his arms and began to unwrap the cloth around yesterday's bread. Rachel broke off a large chunk and put it in a bowl. "I knew someday we would all have to deal with him."

Connor took a seat at the table and pulled the bowl closer. He took the bread, broke it in to pieces, dipped one in sweet cream and put it in his mouth. The cows were kept outside the hold and milk was plentiful, but not often cream. Unfortunately, he was too furious to notice the sweet taste. "I hoped it could wait until after Kevin died."

"Has he done something that awful?"

"He slapped Maree twice in the face."

Rachel's eyes widened. "Does Kevin know?"

"He suspected as much last night, but she lied to him and I think I managed to convince him nothing happened."

"And Anna, does she know?"

"I do not think so."

Rachel was suddenly enraged. "How could he do this to his mother? All her life she has thought of nothing but the rest of us. I swear I am tempted to kill Sween myself."

"As am I, but that would hurt Anna more."

"Then we must think of a way to stop his wickedness without killing him."

Connor finished his meal, kissed Rachel and picked up Danny. "If you come up with something, let me know. Meanwhile, go back to bed. You need to recover the sleep I deprived you of last night."

*

Just as Connor rounded the corner of the Keep with his youngest son perched on his shoulder, Neil came down the steps. "What are your plans for today?"

Neil shrugged. "I have no plans save to build a fence for my mother around the graveyard."

"Alone?"

"Well, I thought to ask Yule to help me, if my father allows it. I also hope Maree will plant a nice row of flowers."

Connor lowered his voice. "Will the two of you be enough to keep Sween away?"

"You know?"

"Aye and your father tried to get it out of Maree, but she lied to him."

Neil's heart grew heavy. "We all lie to him."

Connor shifted Danny to his other shoulder and walked with Neil toward the stable. "I could send a man or two if need be."

"Then we would have to think of a good reason and more lies. When does it ever end?"

"I doubt it ever will."

Neil stopped walking. "She has no mark, how did father guess?"

"I do not know, but because she has no mark, his guess is far worse. Kevin thinks Sween forced her."

Neil closed his eyes and bowed his head. "He did not force her; I stopped him before he could."

"Aye, but your father does not know that."

"Is there no way to relieve father's worry?"

Connor glanced at the Keep. "Smile and take Danny off my shoulder. Your father is watching from the landing."

Neil faked a laugh, took the boy and lifted him high into the air.

"My stupid, stupid brother. No doubt I will have to kill him someday."

Connor took the boy back, playfully slapped Neil on the back and headed for Kevin. He was halfway up the steps before he asked, "What wonderful chores do you have for me this day?"

"We appear to have most everything well in hand again this morning, but I will think of something, if you like."

"Did you notice the water in the moat was low?"

"I did notice that." Kevin opened the door and followed Connor inside. "What do you think causes it?"

*

Steppen was very upset. She finally got her mother to fix her plaid and hurried down the path, but Maree hadn't come out yet, and that meant Steppen would have even less time to see the hands and find the green.

She decided against waiting for the story, skipped on down the path and darted behind the first cottage. She turned the corner with an excited grin on her face...but as soon as she saw it, she stopped. The strange thing with the hands was not spinning. Steppen bit her lip. She must have broken it. She was nearly in a panic and turned all the way around to see if anyone was watching. What a relief, no one was. She gently touched one of the hands and when it moved, she held her breath. Maybe, just maybe she didn't break it after all. It stopped and Steppen stuck out her lower lip.

Yule saw the child go behind the cottage, followed her and got there just in time to see her turn back with tears in her eyes. "What is it?"

She grabbed hold of his leg and started to sob. "I broke it. I did not mean to, but I did."

"Broke what?"

She pointed at the hands. "That!"

"Oh, that." He knelt down and let her go into his comforting arms. "You did not break it."

"Nay?"

"I see no damage at all."

"But yesterday it turned."

"Aye, but yesterday we had wind. Today, we do not. 'Tis the wind that makes it turn."

She put her fists in her eyes, wiped the tears away and then smiled, "I think I like green today."

"I am pleased to hear it. Will you be alright if I leave? I have chores to do, you know."

She liked him right up until he said that word -- *chores*. She squirmed out of his arms, swatted his leg with her hand and ran away.

"What did I do?" Yule got no answer, shrugged, stood up and headed for the Keep. This morning he would watch Kevin deal with the wayward children, and then spend the afternoon with Maree. That was his plan anyway.

CHAPTER V

Kevin, Connor and Sween were in the great hall and Yule's second day with Laird MacGreagor started far differently. Sween was not hung over and was actually paying attention to his father.

"Connor," Kevin was saying, "send lads to follow the stream to the north. We must know if the MacDonalds build a dam again. Caution them not to go on MacDonald land."

"Aye."

Kevin continued, "I wish to send a word to Laird Cameron. Find a lad to take it for me."

Connor nodded. "I hear Neil builds a fence around the graveyard. Does he require help?"

Yule was about to volunteer when Sween spoke up, "I will help him."

Kevin studied his son's face. "You will help your brother? You have not offered to help with the work for a very long time. What has changed you suddenly?"

Sween boldly answered, "You have. After we talked yesterday, it occurred to me you might actually banish me."

Kevin stared into Sween's eyes. "Banish you for what?"

Yule held his breath and Connor's heart stopped.

"Lately I have known a lass. I was with her yesterday after the noon meal."

Kevin could hardly breathe. Was his son about to admit he forced Maree? Did he mean to see if his father would actually kill him? Just then another thought occurred to him. Perhaps Sween thought he would not kill him, but make him marry Maree to save her reputation. It would be yet another way to defy him and there was only one way to find out. "Is she a MacGreagor?"

"Nay, Father, she is a Ferguson. Her name is Jules and she is a...she is an arrangement."

Yule relaxed, Connor's heart started beating again, and Kevin felt like the weight of a thousand warriors had just been lifted off his shoulders. "Why would I banish you for that?"

Sween tried to look ashamed of himself. "I am not her only arrangement. If mother finds out, it will hurt her and you said you would banish me if I hurt my mother."

"How will she find out?"

Sween turned around and headed for the door. "I pray she does not, but you know how people talk and they tell her everything." He pulled the door open and then turned back. "I *am* sorry. I did not consider how it might hurt her. I will help Neil build the fence and await your punishment." With that, he was gone.

Connor stayed for a few minutes longer and then went to carry out Kevin's orders. Kevin took his usual seat at the head of the table and concentrated on being a better host to Yule Cameron. "What would you like to do today?"

"I hope to watch you with the children and then perhaps spend time with Maree," Yule answered, taking a seat. "Unless, of course, you would like me to take your message to Blair?"

"And take Maree with you?"

Yule grinned. "The thought has merit, you will admit. She should see what her home is like before we marry, and Bridget will be happy to see her. Maree can sleep at their keep for the night and I will bring her back tomorrow."

"If she has no objection, neither do I. My wife will gladly loan her horse again."

"What message would you like me to give to Blair?"

"Tell him my wife has a desire to see Bridget. We all miss her fiery spirit. Life here is not the same without her," said Kevin.

"I understand and just now I thank you for letting us have Bridget. She brightens all our days."

As soon as Yule was gone, Kevin looked up at the bedchamber he shared with Anna, and as he suspected, she was standing just inside the open door.

"Our son plays with us." She had been listening the whole time and if Anna was unhappy the night before, she was furious now. She walked down the balcony and then down the stairs. "We have closed our eyes to Sween's treachery long enough. I care not about the Ferguson lass, but I do care about Neil. He hurts Neil, you know he does and we look the other way. Neil has none to protect him save us and we neglect it."

Kevin got to his feet and put his arms around her. She was stiff in his arms and he could feel her tension. "We could banish Sween."

"And fear he hides behind every tree? What life would that be for Neil?"

"No life at all...for any of us."

"'Tis time, husband. This moment Sween goes to help Neil with the fence. I will see for myself this war between my sons."

"Then I will go with you."

*

Yule was eager to see Maree, but when he got to her cottage and saw the children still waiting outside, he was more than a little concerned. He carefully stepped around the little ones and knocked on the door.

Her mother answered, saw Yule, smiled and spoke in a hushed voice. "My daughter is not yet awake. Her excitement, you know." She spotted the children and turned her attention to them. "You are good children for being quiet and letting her sleep. You best go play now and we will see about a story tomorrow."

Yule watched them pout for a moment, then spring up and take off in different directions. "I would like to take Maree to see Bridget today and Kevin has agreed. Will you tell her?"

Just then, Maree peeked out from behind her mother. "I am awake and I agree."

"Good. I will be back for you after the noon meal. 'Tis a three hour ride and we will be there long before dark. You will spend the night with Bridget and I will bring you back in the morning." He smiled at Maree, nodded to her mother and left.

Yule was pleased. He wanted to be alone with her to tell her how he felt, and knew of a pleasant place along the path where they could stop and talk. Then again, the two of them alone would be an easy target for Sween, should he discover they were leaving. Perhaps he should take her north and then west instead of the usual path between the two clans. It would take longer, but it would definitely be safer. He headed to the stables to make the necessary arrangements.

*

Kevin stepped out on the landing and asked the parents to bring their children back later. He took Anna's hand and together they walked across the courtyard, and then over the bridge. They turned, crossed the meadow, and took the path through the trees to the graveyard. When they were near enough, yet still out of sight, they stopped to watch. Sween had his back to them.

Neil pulled a dead branch out of the forest and was surprised to see his brother waiting. "What do you want?"

Sween sneered. "I have come to help you."

"I see. Do you intend to actually work or just pester me while I work?"

Sween pulled his dagger and started to reach out, but Neil quickly jumped back. "Calm yourself, brother. If I do not have the branch, I cannot cut off the twigs."

Neil tossed the branch to the ground, and made sure his arm was out of Sween's reach when he did it. "But you would rather cut me."

"No more than you would like to cut me."

"You deserve worse."

Sween laughed and picked up the branch. "You will always hesitate; you are too weak to kill me."

Someday he would be strong enough, but even then Neil wasn't sure he could kill his brother. It was true; he always hesitated to hurt him even after one of Sween's poundings…but not for Sween's sake, for his mother's. "Where is Mungo, or have you finally rid yourself of that pig?"

"Mungo is a loyal lad."

"To you he is loyal; to the rest of us he is swine. He only uses you and you know it. I would be dim-witted to call a lad like that my friend."

"He will be useful when the time comes."

Neil walked into the forest. In a couple of minutes, he came back out and threw two more branches on the ground. "Mungo is of no use to anyone, especially you. You cannot lead if the people will not follow, and they will not follow you if they must deal with Mungo."

"I am Kevin's son; they will do as I command just as they do for him."

"They will laugh in your face." Neil saw Sween clench his fists and knew he was about to get hurt. "Why not draw your sword this time and finish me off? I am certain you can think of something father will believe."

Sween released his fists and mockingly smiled. "That would spoil my plan. I do not intend to kill you until after he dies."

Neil turned his back and once more entered the forest. "Now who hesitates?"

Kevin had heard enough. He turned and led Anna back down the path. Then he had a thought. "Wait for me here." He quickly kissed her forehead and then went back to the graveyard.

Sween was surprised to see him. "Father, have you come to see if my word is good?"

"Where is Mungo?"

"I...I am not sure. Most likely he is off to see Jules at the Fergusons."

Kevin glared. "He is to clean the stables. When he returns, see that they are clean before the sun goes down." Kevin started to turn away but changed his mind again. "He is to clean the stables every day. He might as well, he lurks there anyway." Kevin turned his back to his son and walked away.

Sween was furious. He grabbed a branch and began to chop the twigs off with vigor. He needed Mungo to do other chores for him. In fact, he sent Mungo to take care of a problem this morning, and he might not make it back anytime soon. Sween would have to clean up after the horses himself.

He could just imagine what Mungo was going to say about his new duty. Maybe they should both leave. They could go south to the border with England, where MacGreagors seldom go. They could hunt and live off the land until word came that Kevin was dead. Yes, maybe that was the answer. It was better than building a stupid fence or cleaning the stables.

*

Kevin and Anna walked back to the Keep in silence, but once inside the great hall, Anna went straight to the wall. She yanked her flask of arrows off the hook and put the strap over her shoulder. Then she grabbed hold of her bow.

Kevin covered her hand with his. "What do you mean to do?"

She turned to face him. "I intend to save our son."

"How?"

"I will shoot Sween."

Kevin had seen this fury in her eyes before and knew she meant to do it. Still, she would listen to reason once he calmed her, so he gathered her in his arms and cupped the back of her head with his hand. It took a while, but she finally relaxed enough for him to draw her close.

"He will kill Neil," she whispered.

He pulled away a little and looked into her eyes. "Do you really have it in you to kill your own son?"

"He has my father's evil. I had it in me to kill my father to protect mother and Rachel. If there is no other way to protect Neil, then yes, I have it in me to kill my own son."

He believed her. "But I love you too much to let you. 'Twould eat at your heart until you could no longer draw breath. We must protect Neil, but I must protect you, even from your own fury. We will think of another way."

"What other way can there be?"

"First, we must rid ourselves of Mungo. He will get the worst of chores until he leaves of his own free will. Then Sween will have only half the power."

She pondered that idea for a moment. "You will tell the other clans not to accept Mungo?"

"Aye, we will say he is a traitor and no other laird will trust him."

"You will need to give details."

"And you will help me think of some." Kevin was relieved to feel her completely relax in his arms and give her nod. The thing to do now was to out think Sween, and it would be good for both of them to put their energy toward that goal.

*

Great heaven above, today was swimming day. Steppen sighed her biggest sigh ever. There goes her exploring again. She was almost the oldest child learning to swim and still couldn't get it right. The men took them, with a couple of mothers along, in case the girls needed something only a mother could help with. Still, the men did the teaching. They were stronger than the women and could make sure the children didn't drink too much water.

Sometimes Neil went with them. Steppen liked Neil. He could lie on his back on top of the water and never sink. Steppen tried it every time she went swimming, but first her bottom would sink and then all that water would go up her nose. She hated that.

The water in the loch was always cold, but the men didn't seem to mind at all. They walked into the water with all their clothes on and seemed to love it. She didn't love it one little bit. She also didn't like the way her plaid stuck to her when it was wet.

She sighed another big sigh and went out the door of her cottage. She got in line behind the other children and started her march to the loch. They went down the path, across the courtyard, over the bridge, down another long path and then over to the rocks where they always sat to take off their shoes. She frowned all the way. Neil was not with them this time and if she somehow managed to float, he would not be there to see her. She was so miserable she could just sit there and cry.

Then she spotted the green and he was walking straight for her. "What the devil are you doing here?"

"I thought you might teach me how to swim," answered Yule.

"You do not know how?"

"We do not have a loch as fine as this one at the Cameron hold. Are you willing to teach me?"

"'Tis very hard." She let him lift her up and walk her into the water. She shivered just a little, noticed that he noticed, and decided she best be brave about it. Steppen straightened her shoulders.

"What do I do first?"

"It has something to do with your arms. You put one arm out and pull the water. Then you put the other arm out and do the same thing."

"What do I do with my feet?"

"You stand on them, of course. What else are feet for?"

"I see, but I have a question. When the water gets too deep to keep my feet on the ground, what do I do then?" Yule asked.

"Devil if I know, I am not allowed to go out that far."

Yule was having a horrible time keeping a straight face. "I say we kick our feet, do you agree?"

"We could try that." She was starting to like this green. He wasn't laughing at her like the other men did.

"I have an idea. You try it so I can see how. But I would not like letting go of you, so may I keep my hand under your stomach?"

Steppen thought that was a fine idea and quickly nodded. She carefully stretched out on her stomach and made sure his hand was under her before she started kicking her feet. Soon she added her arms and she was actually moving through the water. The green was right beside her the whole time, and she felt him change from using his whole hand under her stomach to just two fingers. Yet, that was enough to make sure he would catch her, so she kept right on going.

Suddenly, he wasn't touching her at all. She was actually doing it!

Steppen got so excited, she stopped and promptly sank. When Yule quickly lifted her out of the water, she hugged his neck. "Did I drink too much water?"

"I do not think so. Do you like swimming?"

"Maybe."

"Would you like to get out now?"

"Do you know how to lie on the water without sinking?" she asked.

"I do."

"Will you teach me?"

"Well, there is a secret to it."

"No wonder I cannot get it right. Tell me the secret, I promise not to tell."

Yule pretended to whisper in her ear. "You have to think about a feather and nothing else."

She was amazed and pulled back to see his eyes. "A feather?"

"Aye. You must pretend you are a feather. A feather cannot sink, you know."

She shifted her eyes and tried to remember if she ever saw a feather sink in puddles the rain made. No, she couldn't remember that ever happening. "Pretend I am a feather."

"Aye." He helped her lay on her back on top of the water. "Remember, you are not heavy, but as light as a feather. Close your eyes and think it. I will not let you fall." He kept his hand firmly under her back, watched her close her eyes and when she completely relaxed, he changed from his full hand to only two fingers.

Steppen was floating and her bottom didn't even sink. She was a feather and she liked being one very much.

*

Kevin's heart wasn't in it, but he let the children in and as soon as Yule came back from bathing in the loch, and changing into clean clothing, Kevin showed him the special way he handled the children. All the while, he was trying to think of a way to trick Mungo. Sween's constant companion had no living family and that eliminated at least one problem -- getting him out of the clan would not hurt anyone else. Slowly, an idea was beginning to form in Kevin's mind.

*

The horses were ready, the sun was bright and after the noon meal, Yule made sure Sween returned to help Neil build the fence before he went to get Maree. He seated her on Anna's horse and noticed she was armed with a dagger, a bow and a sheath full of arrows. So was he, plus he had a sword.

He mounted and headed them over the bridge. Instead of going west across the meadow, he led her toward the loch and then north through the trees behind the MacGreagor hold. No one, he was sure, saw which way they went.

They had ridden for quite a while and Maree knew she was being uncommonly quiet. She was glad he didn't want to talk about their marriage plans, and hoped he wouldn't bring it up at all during their three hour ride. However, she was excited to be going to see Bridget. In fact, she was excited to be going anywhere away from Sween.

Pretending to want this marriage really wasn't fair to Yule. He had done nothing wrong and deserved better. She wondered if she should tell him. If she didn't, he would tell the Camerons they were to marry, and then be embarrassed when she admitted the truth. Yes, telling him was the only honest thing to do.

Yule halted his horse.

When he didn't turn to tell her something, Maree knew something was wrong. Just as he did, she slowly studied the forest around them and listened for movement. She didn't see or hear anything, but when he turned his horse into the woods, she quickly followed.

Yule got them behind the tall bushes, slid off his horse, grabbed Maree and pulled her to the ground. Then he loaded his bow and watched. Not far from where they had just been, the blue plaid of a MacGreagor appeared. Yule rose up, took aim and waited. Yet when the MacGreagor continued on, he relaxed the bow string and knelt back down.

"Mungo," Maree breathed. "Sween sent Mungo to kill us."

"We must move," he whispered. He grabbed his reins, looked back to make sure she had a good grip on hers and then led them on foot up the hillside. He often looked back to make sure Mungo wasn't following and so did she. Not until they were safely on the other side, did Yule get them both mounted again. With her following, he began to thread his way through the dense forest.

Another hour passed before he stopped once more to look and listen. Satisfied they were alone; he turned to smile at her. "We are safe now."

Maree was trembling. "Where are we? Are we lost?"

"Nay, we are on Cameron land. He will not attack us here. Come, there is a small clearing ahead with a stream. We can rest there."

Sween was furious. The longer he thought about having to clean the stables when Mungo didn't get back on time, the madder he got. At least Maree would be dead by now and that was some consolation.

He finished cutting the twig off a branch for the fence, tossed it in the pile and bent down to pick up another branch. Suddenly, an arrow whizzed over his head and missed him by less than an inch. He quickly flattened himself on the ground and looked to see where it came from. It definitely came from the west but he could not see anyone. The Camerons lived in the west, but there was still considerable MacGreagor land before the border. He glanced north toward the Keep and saw no one, and then looked in the other directions to make sure he wasn't surrounded. He spotted Neil standing behind a tree, but the arrow hadn't come from that direction.

Neil grinned. "Someone wants you dead, brother. I wonder who it might be? So many hate you, it could be anyone. What a good joke that would be. You may actually die before father does."

"Silence," Sween demanded. He hopped up, ran for his horse, mounted and took off to look for his attacker.

Neil stepped out of the forest and strained to see who might have taken a shot. He would thank the man, if he ever found out who it was. He walked into the clearing and picked up the arrow. It was an ordinary arrow and anyone could have made it. He looked west once more, but whoever it was didn't show himself.

*

It was getting close to the evening meal and Steppen was hungry. She liked the green, until her brother said he took her Maree over the bridge. The green probably had her hand again too. Steppen huffed and vowed never to like the green again. Then she saw a sight she could not believe.

The door to a cottage was wide open and a woman sat on a chair inside. Normally, her father traded food for the plaids her family wore, and this was the first time she'd ever seen a woman making her own. The loom was little more than a square wooden frame, with the bottom in the woman's lap and the back of it leaned against a table. Small pegs dotted both the top and the bottom of the square and each had yarn tightly wrapped around it, which made evenly spaced vertical lines.

A ball of yarn was also in the woman's lap and with a large wooden needle, the woman drew the strand of yarn from one side to the other and then back again, until the bottom started to fill up. How she made that happen was not quite clear, but Steppen was fascinated. She inched inside and watched. Then she inched a little closer and when the woman smiled, she hopped to a short stool and sat down where she could see every possible detail. The woman was making cloth and it was a wondrous sight to see.

*

Maree was visibly shaking when Yule lifted her down from her horse, and he couldn't help but draw her to him. She didn't resist, but she didn't wrap her arms around him either. He decided she was too frightened to react to his touch. "Would you like to tell me about Mungo? Who is he?"

She pulled away, walked to the stream, found a rock to sit on and then watched the trees they had just come through. Maree was not convinced they were safe. "He is Sween's friend and he is liked even less than Sween. I wish Kevin would rid us of him, but Mungo manages to stay away from Kevin as much as possible. Usually, he lurks around the stables or goes off with Sween somewhere."

"Do you think he has it in him to hurt you?"

"I have not heard of him hurting anyone, but he would do it if Sween ordered it done. Everyone knows he hopes to be Sween's second in command someday. God help us when that happens."

He found another rock and sat down not far from her. "We could marry sooner. In fact, we could marry at my home and you would never have to go back. The Camerons will protect you."

"But I want to go back, the MacGreagors are my family."

"All lasses leave their homes when they marry."

"Aye, but..."

For the first time, he realized she had not actually accepted his marriage proposal. What was the matter with him? He was so caught up in protecting her, he had not asked what she wanted. He braced himself. "Go on."

She had to tell him, there was no other way. Maree took a deep breath and let it out. "I do not love you."

"I was afraid of that." He sat up straight and tried to force his hurt away. "I have rushed you into something you are not ready for. Please forgive me."

She felt sorry for telling him. She could see his disappointment and wanted to comfort him. "'Tis not you, 'tis Sween. I was beginning to...I thought I was." She looked down and tried to find the right words. "I do not know how to feel anything but fear just now."

He found in her words a glimmer of hope and thought maybe in time, she would get those first feelings back. "I am glad you told me. We have no need to rush into marriage. After all, I have not yet built a cottage."

She relaxed finally. "Aye, that would be good if you hope to take a wife."

"Indeed it would. It might take me quite a while and you will only be a few hours away. I could visit and we will see how you feel later."

Maree was so relieved, she reached out and took his hand. "Thank you."

CHAPTER VI

When a guard shouted to notify the Camerons someone was coming, Blair and Bridget went outside to see who it was. The tall wooden gates were open and when Bridget saw Maree, she was overjoyed. She remembered Maree and marveled at how much she had grown. She waited impatiently for Yule to help her guest down, and then hugged her. "You look wonderful, I am so happy to see you."

"And I you. I have a great deal to tell you," said Maree.

Blair's wavy blond hair hung down to his shoulders and his eyes sparkled when he slapped Yule on the back. "I send you to learn, you stay only two days and come back with a MacGreagor beauty. What should I make of it?"

"She wants to see Bridget, nothing more."

Blair watched his wife loop her arm through Maree's and walk her inside. "But you would like there to be more, am I right?" He grinned at Yule's nod.

The Cameron Keep was made of sturdy wood, finely polished on the inside of the great hall. A beautiful tapestry of gold and shades of green hung on the wall, the windows were wide, letting in ample sunlight when the curtains were opened, and the place was spotless. Unlike the MacGreagor keep, it only had one floor, but doors led to ample bedchambers and a stone hearth kept the rooms warm.

Bridget's long hair was just as red and her eyes just as green as

Maree remembered. "Yule said you miss us and I came to cheer you up."

"I miss all of you very much. You must tell me everything." But when Bridget heard Yule tell Blair there was trouble, she turned to listen.

"'Tis Sween," whispered Maree.

Blair offered his guest a seat at the round table and poured each of them a chalice of wine. He quietly listened to Yule tell about Sween slapping Maree and then frowned. "Everyone knew this would happen someday."

Bridget was almost afraid to speak for fear Blair would become enraged. "'Tis not the first time Sween has hit a lass, nor is it the second." Just as she expected, her husband was looking deep into her eyes and she could feel his tension.

"Wife, did he hurt you?"

"Nay, but I saw it. This is all my fault, I should have told Kevin. I could have done something, but I was afraid."

"There is more," Yule said. "Today Mungo followed us and I believe he meant to kill Maree. We managed to hide just in time."

Blair was repulsed. "They must both be stopped, but the Camerons can do nothing without starting a war."

"I could kill them both," said Bridget.

Blair stared at his wife. "Are you telling me you are accustomed to killing?"

"Nay, but I could. All MacGreagor lasses are taught to shoot. I have not practiced for a while, but..."

Maree narrowed her eyes. "I could do it. If I am caught, I will say 'twas an accident."

Blare looked at Yule and then studied the face of each woman. The women were dead serious. "You cannot kill two lads and say 'twas an accident."

"Aye, but if Sween is gone, Mungo loses any future power," said Yule.

"Nay," Bridget said. "We cannot kill Sween, he is Anna's son."

Yule nodded. "You just came to the same conclusion we did. No one can kill Kevin and Anna's son without hurting them. I have tried desperately to think of a way and nothing comes to mind."

"Could we wound him or cripple him so he no longer has the strength to hurt anyone?" Bridget asked.

It was Blair who answered. "Aye, but lads often die from a wound that does not heal. It would be the same as killing him, only his death would be slow and very painful. 'Tis a horrible thing for a mother to watch."

Maree stared at the chalice in her hand, "Besides, he could still get Mungo to do his bidding. The answer is to rid the MacGreagors of Mungo first."

Blair thought about that. "I have never killed a man because he *might* kill someone. He did not actually try to harm Maree today, he was only following you. 'Twould be unjust to kill him."

They were at an impasse and none could think of an answer.

*

In some ways the Cameron hold was different from the place Maree lived, yet the two were very much alike. Paths in all different directions led to cottages, children played, laughed and argued just as

MacGreagor children did.

The people were careful to clear the path for Bridget and treat her with the utmost respect. They noticed Maree's blue plaid and nodded to welcome her. The children did not come to her, but they did not shy away either. It warmed her heart and it was exactly what she needed.

"This is what I wanted to show you," said Bridget.

When she saw it, Maree smiled. Someone had built a little bridge over a stream and the workmanship was exquisite. "I have seen nothing like it."

"I doubt many have. The children love to play in the meadow, but the little ones could not cross without getting their shoes wet, so Yule built it for them.

Maree was amazed. "Did he? I am very impressed."

"Our people love Yule the way the MacGreagors love Kevin. He makes sure the elders have enough to eat, the children have good shoes and the lass with child is allowed ample rest. Before my son was born, I thought Yule would drive Blair daft fussing over me. But I love his caring ways."

"He sounds like a very good lad."

"He is indeed, but he is also strong when he needs to be. Blair greatly depends on him and so do the rest of us."

They turned up another path to see still more cottages. "Are you happy here?"

Bridget beamed. "I love Blair more than life and where he is, I will be also. I miss the MacGreagors, but these are my people now and I love them as well."

"Yule asked me if Bridget was your real name. The MacGreagors vowed not to tell and I had to lie to him." She expected Bridget to be concerned, but she seemed delighted.

"My dear, you have been tried. Yule knows my real name and he knows of the MacGreagor vow. He asked to see if you would keep it."

"I see."

Bridget stopped walking and took hold of her arm. "Yule would not have tried you unless you were chosen. Did he ask you to marry him?"

"Oh, Bridget, everything is so ruined. He asked, but only to protect me from Sween. I expected...I mean, I thought I would be in love before I married. Then everything happened so fast and I had no time to...I do not want Yule's pity."

"Pity? He did not ask out of pity. If that were his weakness, he would have taken any number of lasses to wife by now. Yule once told me he was waiting for a very special lass and he would know when he found her. He loves you, I can see it in his eyes."

"How can he love me, we have only known each other for two days? Do lads fall in love that quickly?"

"Some do, 'twould seem. But you are right, you need more time. It was eight days before I realized I loved Blair."

They walked a while longer and then went back. Once inside the Cameron Keep, Bridget showed Maree to the bedchamber where she would sleep. She made sure Maree had water and a basin so she could wash before the evening meal, and then she slipped out to talk to Blair and Yule.

She sat down between them at the table, looked at Yule and spoke in a soft voice. "She thinks you asked her to marry you out of pity."

Blair rolled his eyes. "How did you manage to muddy that up?"

"I do not know," Yule answered. "When I am with her I cannot think clearly. I meant to tell her how I feel on the way here, but she was frightened of Mungo and it did not seem the right time. Should I tell her now?"

Bridget shook her head. "Let her love you when she is ready. And you must not touch her save when necessary. Let her miss your touch. Give her time to wonder where you are when you are not with her. 'Twill happen, I am sure of it."

"What makes you so sure?" Yule asked.

"On our walk, she smiled at the lasses and the children, but she paid no attention to the lads. She is yours...just not yet."

"I pray you are right. How can I take her back tomorrow? I will go daft with worry over her safety."

Blair thought about that. "Aye, but if we keep her, Kevin will *not* understand and send a full count of lads to get her." He took hold of Bridget's hand. "My love, would you care to see the MacGreagor hold tomorrow. Perhaps we might think of something to do after we see Kevin."

Yule closed his eyes. "I forgot to give you Kevin's message. Anna wants to see Bridget."

"Perfect," Bridget said.

*

Before Sween took a seat for the evening meal, he dropped the arrow Neil found on the table in front of his father.

"Why do you bring me an arrow?"

"I thought you might like to know someone tried to kill me

today." Sween sat down in his usual chair at the other end of the table from the rest of his family.

Kevin took hold of Anna's hand and noticed Neil lower his eyes. Then he nodded to the servers to bring the food. "Did you see who it was?"

Sween shrugged. "I did not. I gave chase, but could not find the lad. Perhaps Neil knows."

Neil was quick to deny it. "I was in the trees and saw no one."

Sween glared at his father. "I demand a guard for my protection."

"I see. Why would someone want to kill you?"

"I do not know, father, I have done nothing to deserve it."

Kevin narrowed his eyes. "A lad does not try to kill another lad for no reason. Perhaps you might think a little harder. Surely you have offended someone."

"Why do you always assume I am to blame? I tell you, I have offended no one."

Kevin glanced at Anna and squeezed her hand. "I will arrange a guard for you tomorrow." He nodded his appreciation to the lasses who served them, let go of his wife's hand and began to eat. "Neil, how much longer will it take to finish the fence?"

"The work is slow, I admit," Neil answered.

"Then I will send two lads to help you."

Sween hadn't touched his meal and was incredulous. "You are not enraged that someone tried to kill me today?"

"Sween, I have loved you since the day you were born, but at whom should I be enraged? It may well have been an accident and you are uninjured. Bring me a name and then you will see my rage."

Sween's voice rose with his words. "I do not know who shot at me, father. How can I bring you a name?"

"I gave you a lad for protection and you seem to have lost him. Where is Mungo?"

Sween started to rise out of his chair. "I do not know where he is!"

"You do not know who tried to kill you and you do not know where Mungo is. Perhaps they are one and the same."

Sween stared at Kevin and slowly sat back down. It was something to consider and throughout the rest of the meal, he remained quiet and deep in thought. He sent Mungo to kill Maree. Why *wasn't* he back by now and why had word not reached them of her death? Indeed, where was Mungo? Perhaps his father was right. Mungo had not killed the woman and instead thought to kill him. But why?

"Son?"

"What?" Sween finally answered.

"The stables are not yet cleaned."

Sween got up and walked out the door.

*

Today, she saw the hands, the green, the woman making a new plaid, went swimming and didn't take a nap. Steppen couldn't remember being so tired, so when the baby went to sleep, she curled up in her father's lap. She only had a moment to practice being a feather before her little eyes closed. She did feel it, however, when her father kissed her cheek.

*

The hour was late when Mungo finally rode his horse over the bridge and into the MacGreagor courtyard. The instant he did, the drawbridge began to rise and four guards surrounded him. He noticed Sween standing in the stable watching and wrinkled his brow, but Sween did not come to his aid. There was nothing he could do but follow orders. He dismounted, walked up the steps to the Keep and went into the great hall.

When Sween tried to follow, the guards blocked his way. He watched his mother come out and head up one of the paths. Neil also walked down the steps and followed his mother. Confused, Sween went around to the kitchen hoping to get in the back way, but guards were also posted there. He was beginning to get a very sick feeling in his stomach.

Inside, Kevin smiled at Mungo. "Come, enjoy my wine. It occurred to me just today that you and I have not been the best of friends. I would hear about you and get to know you better. Come, sit down and talk to me."

Mungo was hesitant. The last time he had spoken to Kevin one-on-one was when he was assigned to protect Sween. That was more than two years ago. He cautiously sat in the chair next to Kevin with Connor sitting across the table from him. Connor was smiling too -- something serious was happening. "Kevin, what have I done?"

"Done? Nothing that I am aware of." Kevin poured a goblet of wine and handed it to Mungo. He filled his and Connor's goblet and set the pitcher down next to Connor. "In fact, I hear nothing but good reports of you from Sween."

Mungo needed that drink, brought it to his lips quickly and drank.

Just as quickly, Connor refilled the goblet.

Kevin raised an eyebrow. "There is that little matter of the Ferguson lass."

At last, Mungo began to breathe again. "Oh that. Sween wanted to know what 'twas like to bed a lass, so I..."

"You arranged it for him. I see." He waited for Mungo to take another drink. "My son will, of course, have to marry the lass. Will she make a good MacGreagor mistress?"

Mungo sneered. "She is a harlot, Kevin; she will not even make a good wife."

"Indeed? What then do you suggest we do?"

"Do? Why must we do anything?"

"Laird Ferguson believes my son has shamed one of his lasses. What say you to that?"

Mungo drank more wine and watched Connor fill his goblet again. "Ferguson has probably had her himself. She beds many lads and Sween was hardly the first to shame her."

"Have you had her as well?"

"Aye." Mungo was proud of himself. "I was the first."

"The first." Kevin sipped his own wine and sat back. "Then the Ferguson accuses my son wrongly. 'Tis you who must marry her."

Mungo nearly choked on his wine. "Me? I would rather die than marry her."

"I am deeply saddened. A MacGreagor does not shame a lass and then refuse to marry her." Kevin had Mungo right where he wanted him. He watched Connor take a drink to steady his nerves and thought he should probably do the same. It might be a while before they got

Mungo to tell them what they wanted to know.

Mungo finally sighed. "You are right, Kevin, tell the Ferguson I will marry her."

"Good, he will be happy to hear it. You have hardly touched your wine, is it not to your liking?"

Mungo needed little encouragement, took another long drink and set his goblet down just a little too hard. "'Tis the best wine in the Highlands."

"I agree. Tell me, where did you go today?"

Mungo had to think fast and it wasn't easy with his brain beginning to dull. "I was with her today."

"Then you do not know someone tried to kill Sween. I assigned you to protect my son, did I not?"

His eyes grew wide. "Someone tried to kill *your* son? I did not think that possible. Tell me who it was and I will kill him."

"We do not know who, and because you were with a woman instead of protecting him, you do not know who it was either."

He noticed Connor's smile was fading and Mungo swallowed hard. "I am sorry, Kevin, 'twas foolish of me and 'twill never happen again."

Kevin decided to reassure him. "You are forgiven. Once she is your wife, you will have no need to neglect your duty. We will have the wedding here and everyone will be glad of it." He raised his goblet. "I drink a tribute to you." Kevin touched his goblet with Mungo's and then with Connor's. He hardly sipped, but noticed that Mungo took several swallows.

"I am surprised, however," Kevin continued, "that you did not wait for one of our lasses. Once Sween is laird, you will no doubt become his second and could have chosen well for yourself."

Mungo could no longer hide his dread. "That too was stupid of me. She is not even pleasing and I can only hope she will not have me."

"Oh, I am sure she will have you and be glad of it. What lass would not want to be wife of Sween MacGreagor's second?"

Mungo buried his head in his hands. "I cannot abide my own foolishness."

Kevin noticed the sun was setting, took a candle out of its holder on the table and got up to light more on the walls. He did not speak for quite a while, to let Mungo keep drinking and to let the wine take effect. Finally he said, "Of course, there might be another way. You might claim someone else was the Ferguson lass' first."

Mungo's head was starting to swim, but he liked the idea very much. "Who?"

"Can you not think of someone?"

He tried, but no name was coming to mind. "Kevin, she has had so many I could name nearly every unmarried Ferguson and not miss the mark."

"Then 'tis settled. You will give me the name of a Ferguson and I will defend you to the lass's laird. Then you will be free to choose a proper lass when you are ready."

Mungo was so relieved, he drank a full glass in celebration. After that, his words began to slur. "Thank you, Kevin. I owe...you my life."

Laird MacGreagor finished with the candles and sat back down. "Naturally, I will want something in return."

"Any ting, just as."

Kevin took the goblet out of Mungo's hand and let his rage show in his eyes. "This shall be my command..."

*

Sween was beside himself with worry. Mungo had been inside with Kevin and Connor for hours, and he could just imagine what they were talking about. He paced, glanced at the landing constantly, neglected to clean the stables and finally sat down on the ground to wait. When his mother and Neil were allowed back in, he tried to enter as well, but the guards stopped him. Then Connor came out -- but not Mungo.

Well past midnight, it was clear Sween would not be sleeping in his own bed. He finally walked up the path to his Grandmother's empty cottage, went in, untied a flask of wine from his belt and began to gulp it down.

A mist was on the land when Blair and Bridget mounted their horses to accompany Yule and Maree on their journey back to the MacGreagor hold. Yule was about to help Maree up when he thought of something. "Bridget, could you loan her a plaid? If she wears a Cameron plaid, she will not make such an easy target."

Bridget quickly slid back down off her horse and grabbed Maree's hand. "That is a grand idea." The women were gone only a few minutes and when they returned, they were both wearing green Cameron plaids with long scarves to cover the color of their hair.

Blair nodded his approval and before he lifted Bridget, he kissed her passionately. Yule smiled when Maree looked away. She was embarrassed. He helped Maree mount and just as Bridget instructed, he quickly let go. For just a second he thought he saw a twinge of regret in Maree's eyes as he handed her the horse's reins. "Tell me if you want to stop. We are in no hurry." He waited for her nod and then mounted his own horse.

Yule was never far from her on the ride. When the way was wide enough, the men rode on the outside to keep the women safe, and often scoured the land looking for possible danger. When the path was narrow, Blair took the lead and Yule protected them from behind.

So far, their journey was uneventful and halfway there, they stopped near an overflowing creek. They drank their fill of water, let the horses drink and soon, Blair and Bridget began to take a walk.

"Would you like to walk?" asked Yule. He noticed her nervous glance toward the trees, so he lowered his voice. "We are on Cameron land still, and you are not supposed to know, but there are at least twenty Camerons seeing to our protection. Laird Cameron allows his wife to go nowhere without his guard."

She finally smiled at him. "He loves Bridget very much."

"Aye and she is a challenge." He offered his hand to help Maree walk over some rocks and then quickly let go. "She has a temper and she cares not who knows it. But she is never vicious and the people enjoy her outbursts. Blair enjoys it most, I believe. She calls him names."

Maree was horrified. "What sort of names?"

"They are never the same or in the same order, but her favorite is a horse's behind. There is but one name she is not allowed to call him."

"What?"

He lowered his voice even more and glanced back just to make sure Blair couldn't hear him. "She is not allowed to say he is worse than an Englishman." He enjoyed Maree's laughter very much and was glad to see it was back.

"What would he do if she called him that?"

"He loves her too much to do more than frown, probably. But she loves him too much to let it slip, so we may never know what he would do." Yule helped her step over a log and again dropped her hand.

She noticed and felt bad about it. Maree hurt him and she didn't know how to make him feel better. Besides, she once liked holding his hand and wondered if she would again. "Yule, I am sorry I hurt you."

"You have not hurt me. Are you cold?"

"Nay, but I thank you for asking."

"I brought an extra plaid to put over your shoulders. You will let me know if you need it."

She nodded. "I was wondering..."

"What?"

"Will you be staying at the MacGreagor hold as long as you planned?"

"I have not changed my plans. Kevin has much to teach and I am more than willing to learn. When we left, Kevin sent lads to see why the water was low in the moat. He thinks the MacDonalds have built a dam again and I am interested to see what he will do if they have."

"He will not start a war, of that I am certain," she said.

"Nay, none of us want a war with Laird MacDonald. We should

go back." He was encouraged, although he was afraid to let himself be. She wanted to know where he would be and it might be a good sign. He reminded himself not to touch her for the hundredth time, but he badly wanted to take her in his arms. He wanted to feel her close to him more than anything in the world.

"Do Blair and Bridget kiss like that often?" she asked.

"Constantly. At first, it made some uneasy, but we are used to it. In fact, many of the women expect their husbands to show affection more often now, and I have yet to find a man who is unhappy with the practice." Do not touch her, he kept repeating in his mind. He was about to go daft and decided to quickly change the subject. "The children will be glad to see you back."

"Aye and I will be glad to see them. I want to thank you for taking me to your home. Yesterday, I could not think of a story to tell them. I do not want to disappoint them, but..."

"I suppose *I* could tell them a story. My mother often told them when we were children, and I believe I remember a few."

"I am so relieved."

"Good. Then I will come and if you cannot think of a story, I will help. But you must remember to smile at me. I will know I am failing miserably if I do not see your smile."

She did smile and wondered how he could still be so wonderful after what she did to him. Bridget was right; Yule was a good man, a very, very good man.

CHAPTER VII

Steppen was back to exploring at last and decided to take up where she left off -- at the cottage where the strange path led to the bush. Yet when she turned the corner, the back door was wide open. She cautiously peeked in and saw a man inside. He was flat on his back on the floor and looked to be asleep.

She wondered if she should wake him so he could do his chores. Everyone knew chores started first thing every morning, especially for the men. Still, her father sometimes jumped straight out of bed when she woke him, and she couldn't be altogether sure this man wouldn't do the same. He might trample her. Getting trampled could still happen when a person was only six. They had to be twelve before that was impossible.

She wasn't supposed to go inside someone's cottage without being invited, she knew. Nevertheless, her curiosity got the best of her, so she took a step closer, then another and one more until she could see his face. It was Sween! What the devil was he doing there?

He began to move; she began to panic and nearly tripped over her feet getting out of the cottage. She flew out the door, around the corner and quickly flattened herself against the outside wall. She dared not even breathe.

Steppen could hear her mother calling and was glad of it, for the first time in her life. She hurried to the path, turned up the hill and ran into her mother's arms.

*

It was a pleasant afternoon when they crossed into MacGreagor land. Yule and Blair were even more vigilant and Blair ordered the guard out of the trees to surround and protect them. None saw any sign of Sween or Mungo.

Yet when Blair led them to the drawbridge, it was obvious something was happening. Most of the MacGreagors were gathered in the courtyard and that was not normal. It was the middle of the day and the people should have been hard at work. Instead, they seemed to be watching the door and waiting for Kevin to speak to them.

Blair led them across the bridge, put his hand up to stop the Camerons and remained on his horse at the back of the crowd. Bridget moved her horse up beside her husband and saw Yule move up beside Maree. The twenty-man Cameron guard filed in over the bridge, remained on their horses and took up positions behind their laird, which completely blocked the exit.

As soon as he saw her, Maree's father came to lift her down.

Maree quickly hugged him. "What is it?"

"We do not know, but it has something to do with Sween."

She thought she might pass out. As soon as Yule got down, she instinctively went to him, took his hand and moved close for his protection. She was terrified Kevin somehow found out what happened and Sween was about to die. She closed her eyes and lowered her head.

Yule was pleased she came to him, understood her fear and wanted to hold her. Yet it was more important to be ready to shove her behind him so she couldn't see. He glanced up at Blair. Both Blair and Bridget were still on their horses, staring at the door of the Keep and when it opened, Yule turned to watch.

Two guards brought Sween out and took him to the bottom of the steps. Then Kevin came out, followed by Anna and Neil. None of them looked happy. Kevin raised his hand to quiet the people, spotted Blair Cameron and nodded.

Then he began to speak, letting his powerful voice boom across the courtyard. "Mungo has been banished. He is a traitor to my son and he will never again set foot on MacGreagor land. If you see him, you are to kill him. I will request he not be given sanctuary by any other clan." He paused long enough to see Blair's nod.

Kevin then looked down the steps at his son. He knew what he had to do and did not hesitate. "This is my son, Sween, whom I love still. While Mungo has betrayed him, Sween has betrayed me." He saw his son start to argue and once more held up his hand.

The fury in Kevin's eyes began to increase with his words. "Sween has taken an oath to kill his brother when I am dead." He paused until the gasps of the people died away. "Therefore, he will live in the Olson cottage outside the wall." Kevin turned once more to look at his followers. "No lad is to hunt for him and no lass is to do his wash. He will not abide my protection and never again will he cross the bridge or come near his brother. No MacGreagor lass is to lie in his bed and no MacGreagor lad will call him friend."

Laird MacGreagor waited for his commands to sink in. Then he put his arm around his wife. "But for his mother's sake, no MacGreagor will kill him. If his mother wishes to see him, you will go with her for her protection, but you will not prevent her." Again he paused until every man nodded. The women looked relieved for Anna's sake.

Kevin had only one more thing to say. "When I die, you alone will choose the lad who will lead you."

He turned again to face Sween. "You will leave my home and not come back until the day I take to my bed in death. On that day I will forgive you and not before. Go now -- while my rage is controlled!"

Sween dared not look at anyone as he slowly made his way through the crowd. He didn't want to see the glares of the men or the sanctimonious smiles of the women. He had to stop a couple of times and wait for angry, reluctant men to move out of his way, but at last he reached the stable and a boy handed him the reins of his horse. He could feel every eye on him as he swung up and began to walk his horse toward the bridge. Then he waited until the Cameron soldiers parted. He sat there...saw no faces, endured no glares and allowed himself no emotion. Then he guided his horse across the MacGreagor drawbridge for the last time.

The silent crowd began to disperse and Kevin got a lump in his throat, but he dared not let Anna see. He watched his beloved son ride down the road and then took his wife in his arms. "He will be fine. You can always take him what he needs and see him often."

"I know." She took a deep breath and let it out. "You found a way to save us all, and I am pleased." She kissed his lips to soothe his soul.

Kevin released her and turned to his other son. "Neil, you will have protection until we see what he does. He will need a few days to control his anger...if that is possible. At least without Mungo, he will have ample time to think about what he has done."

"Father, you have stripped him of everything."

"Sometimes a lad must have nothing to appreciate the little he has."

Neil looked into his father's eyes. "I find I do not really hate my brother. Will you truly make him wait until you die before you forgive him?"

"I hope not." He ruffled Neil's hair and noticed his son no longer enjoyed the practice. Neil was growing up. "Meanwhile, we have guests." He waved Blair forward. "Perhaps someday we will see this as a beginning and not an ending."

Kevin finally noticed Maree and went down the steps to greet her. "You wear a Cameron plaid already? Have I missed your wedding?"

Maree smiled. "Not yet, my plaid got wet and I borrowed from Bridget." She hoped this would be the last time she ever had to lie to her laird.

It was Yule who spoke next, "Kevin, we have decided we do not yet know each other well enough to marry. We intend to wait a month or two."

Kevin studied Maree's eyes and understood. If Sween forced her, she would want to marry quickly to hide it. Yet Maree was willing to wait and he thought the fresh air had never smelled so sweet.

*

In the afternoon, Maree donned a clean MacGreagor plaid and waited for Yule to come see her. He did not. She hurried through the evening meal and waited again, but Yule did not walk up the path. At sundown, she decided to take a walk in hopes of finding him somewhere. He was nowhere to be found and at last, she went home and got ready for bed. He said he would come in the morning, but she wondered now if he would. She might have hurt him so badly, he was gone forever and would not come back. She put her head on the folded plaid she used for a pillow and closed her eyes. A single tear ran down her cheek.

*

He was a total mess. Yule tried to pay attention to Kevin's usual banter with his wife and son during the evening meal, but it was of little use. When Blair said something about another clan, he tried to concentrate, but even when Kevin reported that the MacDonalds had indeed built a dam, he didn't care. Once, when Bridget noticed his distress, she patted his arm and whispered, "Breathe, just keep breathing."

He smiled, but even that was nearly impossible. Was Bridget right? Was giving Maree time to miss him the best decision? He supposed it was, but how was he to keep from going daft missing her? Never in his life had he been so miserable. When the door opened, he quickly turned, praying Maree was coming, but it was Connor instead.

"Do you have a report?" asked Kevin.

"Aye," Connor answered. He walked closer and took the non-threatening pose. "The lads will take Mungo to the English border and set him free. They say he whimpers like a child. In the morning, word will spread of his treachery to all the other clans. We will not see him again."

"And my son?"

"Dermid is watching him. He went to the Olson cottage as you ordered and after he went in, Sween wept. Perhaps someday you will have your good son back."

"I pray you are right. Do we know yet who tried to kill him?"

"Nay, that we may never know. But if it was a MacGreagor I doubt they will try again. You said not to kill him for his mother's sake, and they will obey."

"And you? Would you like to join us?"

"Nay, I am going home to see if Rachel still loves me."

Kevin smiled. "If she does, we will all be at peace again."

Connor headed for the door, "Aye...if she does."

*

For Steppen, morning couldn't come fast enough. The green had brought her Maree back and she couldn't wait to hear a story. After that, she had naught to do, but finally continue her exploring. This time she would start at the garden and work her way down the hill. Even her plaid was cooperating and it was a sure sign this was going to be a wonderful day.

She slipped into her little shoes and was almost out the door when she remembered. Today she would stay until her mother had time to twine her hair and relieve her of that pesky lock. And to her surprise, it didn't take that long at all.

Finally, she was out the door and down the path. Six other children were waiting, all sitting down and watching Maree's door hoping she would soon come out. Steppen sat down beside her brother and folded her hands in her lap. Then she folded her arms and strummed her fingers. Still Maree didn't come out. What could the matter be? Two more children arrived and she glared when they tried to sit down right in front of her.

*

Inside, Maree wasn't ready and she didn't think she ever would be. If Yule didn't come it would break her heart. Still, she couldn't make the children wait forever. She took a deep breath and opened the door.

Yule was not there.

She sat down on the log and let each of the children take turns hugging her and kissing her cheek. They felt wonderful in her arms again and at least that was some measure of comfort. Now she had to come up with a story and the only one she could think of was the one Yule started to tell her. She didn't even know how that one ended.

"There once was a laddie who was very lonely."

Behind her she heard his voice, "Does he know the lonely lassie?"

She smiled and turned to look at him, "He does now, but you are getting ahead of the story."

"My greatest apologies."

"As I recall, the little lad had no brothers and therefore no one to play with."

Yule sat down beside her and wrinkled his brow, "He did not like lassies?"

"He might someday, but not yet."

"I think you are wrong, I think he likes one very much," said Yule.

Steppen was clearly annoyed. "Hey, what kind of story is this?"

Maree playfully touched the end of Steppen's nose with her finger. "I have not yet heard the ending either. Shall we let Yule tell it?"

"The green knows stories?"

"I do," said Yule. "You see, the lonely little lad decided to go to a place very far from home to find a friend. He rode his horse through the trees, up the hills and down again, until he finally found what he was looking for."

"He rode a horse all by himself?" Steppen's brother asked.

"In my story he did." Yule leaned close to Maree. "Do all the MacGreagors interrupt the stories?"

"Only when they think you will say 'twas a lassie the laddie found."

"I see. Aye, well that does change the story a bit."

"You will manage, I have faith in you." She grinned when he rolled his eyes.

"'Twas not a lass, 'twas a...wildcat. As soon as he saw it, the little laddie got down off his horse."

Steppen stood up. "I tell better stories than the green." She shrugged and walked on up the path. There were far more important things to do than listen to *him*. She was not alone, all the children were bored and began to wander away."

Yule sighed. "I do not have your way with words, I see."

"You still have me and I want to know how the story ends."

"As you wish. The little laddie couldn't find what he wanted until after he grew up. Then one day, he saw a bonnie lass who told wonderful stories to children. Shall I go on?"

"Do they get married someday?"

"I do not know yet. The lad has to wait for the lass to love him.

Do you think she might love him someday?"

She took a deep breath. "I think so. She missed him yesterday and that must mean something."

"He missed her too. Would you care to take a walk?"

"Only if you promise to hold my hand."

Yule stood up and gladly offered his hand.

Instead of starting to walk after she stood up, she turned to him. "The lassie wants to know what it is like to kiss the laddie."

His heart skipped a beat, but he did not kiss her. Instead, he gently touched the side of her face. "I meant to tell you how I feel, but there never seemed to be the right time. You are the special lass I have waited for. I want to marry you, have lots of children with you, hear your stories and love you the rest of my life."

She felt his arms go around her and closed her eyes to enjoy the moment. Then his soft lips were on hers and a surge of unfamiliar feelings raced through her whole body. His kiss didn't last as long as she wanted and she sighed when he pulled away. "I was afraid you had gone home. Promise you will not leave without telling me."

"I promise, and when you are ready, I will take you with me."

*

Steppen saw that kiss. She huffed, put her hands on her hips with her thumbs going the wrong way and knew what kissing stuff meant. The green wanted to marry her Maree and take her away. She would miss the stories, but soon she would be ten anyway. She could swim now and at ten, children had no need of stories. At ten, she could go across the bridge to play in the meadow and see what was in the forest. That was better than any old story and she could hardly wait!

*

For many years, the MacGreagors wondered who tried to kill Sween. Was it his father, his mother, his Aunt Rachel, Uncle Connor, Mungo, a woman he assaulted, or someone else who held a vendetta against Kevin MacGreagor's son?

Only one person knew for sure.

The bow was well strung, the arrow was sharpened to a fine point, the aim was exceptional and the shoes...the shoes were the shoes of a woman.

GILLIE

CHAPTER I

Mayze was not beautiful. Some claimed all MacGreagor women were beautiful, but Mayze thought most of the clan had not noticed her. She was painfully shy, happy to stand in the back of every crowd, and did nothing at all to draw attention to herself. Her hair was golden, not the light yellow most had. Her eyes were brown and her nose was acceptable, she supposed, but her eyes were a little too close together.

At age eighteen, she was still waiting for any man to notice her. She didn't really mind, but her mother sometimes got a pitiful look in her eye that drove Mayze daft. The eldest of seven children, there was always plenty to do and not much time to enjoy her true love -- which was walking through the forest in hopes of seeing a red fox or making friends with a wildcat.

Her mother did not take a new husband after Mayze's father died, although she often received offers. The men who wanted her brought food from the hunt, but with seven children already, her mother always thanked them and shooed them away with the back of her hand.

On her happier days, Mayze sometimes sang in the forest. She didn't know many real songs, so she just made them up. She sang about the sunshine, the animals and the glory of the forest right after it rained. Sometimes she sang about being in love, although she didn't know what that was exactly.

The solitude of the forest was always a comfort and she didn't want to go back, but there was trouble brewing in the MacGreagor Clan and everyone knew it. Mayze had turned to start back when she suddenly caught her breath. The man called Dugan was sitting on a log with a wildcat curled up in his lap. She stared at him. Although this one was not very large, most wildcats were much bigger than a house cat and could be very dangerous. She had never managed to get one to come that close, even when she tempted it with food.

Dugan scratched the cat behind its ear and the cat loved it. He knew Mayze was watching him...that was the whole point. The first time he heard her sing in the forest, he was drawn to her and searched the woods to see who she was. The sound of her voice was wonderful, and to him, she was the most becoming woman in the clan. He also knew she was shy and got nervous easily, so he had to find a way to entice her. The cat seemed the perfect idea.

His hair was a shade or two darker than hers, and when he finally looked up, his blue eyes sparkled. "Would you like to touch it?"

She was reluctant. She didn't want to scare the cat away and knew full well a wildcat could do some serious damage if it was provoked.

He understood her reluctance; it had taken him a good month to get the cat that close. "'Twill not hurt you. Come, the fur is soft and she will purr on a good day. Have you ever heard a wildcat purr?"

Mayze shook her head. She inched toward him, stopped and then inched a little closer until she could sit down on the log. She scooted closer...but not too close to him. Then she reached out and touched the cat's back. The fur *was* soft and the cat didn't seem to mind, so she scooted just a little closer and began to pet it. The cat liked her touch and soon began to make a strange sound. It was sort of like singing, except it was only one tone.

"I am Dugan."

"I know, you bring food for us sometimes."

"I did not think you noticed." Dugan was not as big as most of the Highlander men. As a boy, he knew he would never be a laird, never be given any important duties, and probably never do more than fetch for the more important men. He also knew his low standing might somehow keep him for getting a wife. MacGreagor men always seemed to outnumber the women, which meant the women could be very selective.

What he could do well, was hunt and he worked hard to improve his skill with the bow and arrow. His exceptional hearing and sight enabled him to excel and he soon gained a good reputation as a hunter. All the men were charged with feeding the widows and the children, so it was not unusual when he sometimes took rabbits or game birds to Mayze's family.

She abruptly stood up. "Thank you. I must go home, there is much to do and I have stayed away too long."

"Mayze, will you come back tomorrow? I would like to talk to you."

"About what?"

He was suddenly flustered. What did he want to talk about? He had to think fast, "Well, we could talk about sunshine and the way the forest smells after it rains." He was instantly afraid he had gone too far. Those were the things she normally sang about, and if she realized, she would know he listened. She might stop singing and never come into the forest again. Dugan held his breath.

"Will the cat come back?"

"I cannot promise you that, but I hope so."

With a slight nod of her head, she walked away and he released his held breath.

*

At 53 Laird Kevin MacGreagor was dying. He lived a good life, married a good woman, fathered two sons and managed to keep the clan out of as many wars as possible. He became laird at only 19 and during his lifetime, the clan steadily grew, until most lived outside the wall that surrounded the MacGreagor Keep. He had few regrets, did not fight death and believed in an afterlife where he would see everyone he loved again. Kevin had not been the same since his wife, Anna, died. A horse threw her and broke her neck some three years earlier. She died instantly and for that, everyone was grateful. It was his beloved Anna he wanted most to see again.

Connor was Kevin's second in command and did most everything during the time of Kevin's grief -- which never quite ended. Alone with him in the bedchamber, Connor knelt beside Kevin's bed and listened carefully to the last of his words. Kevin's eyes were dull, his hair was nearly white and his unfit body seemed shrunken. The man was so weak, Connor had to lean close to hear him. When Kevin finished, his second in command pulled back and nodded. Connor squeezed Kevin's hand, stood up, bowed his respect and then let

Kevin's sons enter the room.

When it was over and Kevin had drawn his last breath, Neil cried -- Sween did not. Sween left the Keep, mounted his horse, rode over the drawbridge and everyone supposed he simply returned to his imposed exile.

They could not have been more wrong.

*

On their shoulders, eight strong men carried the wooden box that held Laird Kevin MacGreagor's body. It was draped with a blue MacGreagor plaid and all the people followed. He was buried next to Anna in the pleasant graveyard where flowers grew wild, the wind whistled in the trees and a fence kept the animals out.

Laird Cameron and his wife, Bridget, Yule and his wife, Maree, wore green plaids and came to pay their respects on behalf of all the Camerons living on the land just west of the MacGreagors. Laird Ferguson and his wife Kenna wore yellow and did the same, representing the people in the land to the east. To the south lay the English and to the north lived the very large and sometimes hostile MacDonald Clan. No one came to represent either.

*

Neil MacGreagor was his father's son through and through, although his appearance was very different. At twenty-one, his stature was the same as his father's, but he had shoulder length, dark wavy hair and the brilliant blue eyes of his mother.

On the morning of the fourth day after Kevin died, the guests were gone, the people went back to their daily duties and Neil sat at the long table in the great hall with Connor. Beautiful tapestries hung on one wall of the enormous room with candleholders separating them. Weapons of various sizes hung along the opposite wall and high windows let in the light of day. A large door led to the outside landing and steps went down to the courtyard, while an inside staircase across the room went to a balcony where more doors led to bedchambers. A smaller door opposite the large one in the great hall opened into the room where meals were prepared for the laird and his family.

There was now only one to feed.

A fire burned in the hearth and several candles were lit, yet the room without Kevin felt cold and dank. It was Connor who spoke first, "What did he tell Sween?"

"He forgave him as he promised, but I am convinced my brother did not care. He at least hid his sneer and for that I am grateful. Father died in peace believing Sween would not kill me."

"But you know he will?"

"Aye, he will if I let him."

Connor leaned back in his chair and ran his fingers through his dark hair. "The people love you. As soon as you are laird, you can banish Sween and get him off our land. Your father should have done it years ago."

"I think the people will choose you to lead us."

"If they do, I will decline. I am thirty-five and I have grown tired in my old age. Today, Rachel still loves me but how long can that last if I am put upon constantly by the clan. Being a mistress can be lonely."

"Was my mother lonely?"

"Sometimes. She managed it well, but Rachel would not. Rachel likes having her family together and alone during the evening hours. To tell the truth, so do I."

"If the people choose me, you will be my second in command."

"I will advise you as often as you ask, but you must choose younger, far more fit lads to protect you. You will know who to choose."

Neil closed his tired eyes and bowed his head. "I hoped this day would never come."

"Kevin taught you everything he knew, yet you have doubts you can lead them?"

"I do not have his wisdom."

"You have more wisdom than you think. You will do very well."

"I hope you are right." Neil took a long breath and slowly let it out. "The time has come for the people to decide. We will ask for their decision tomorrow before the evening meal. Do you agree?"

"I do. I will tell them to gather in the meadow outside the wall."

"Good."

*

After Connor left, Neil walked up the stairs to the room on the opposite end of the Keep from his parent's bedchamber. The room was rarely used and sparsely furnished, but it offered more light than the others. Neil often went to that room as a boy, especially when he wanted to avoid his brother. It held the only window that looked out over the front of the hold and he pulled the cloth back. From there he could see the courtyard, the drawbridge, the road and in the distance, the loch and the surrounding forest. The people below seemed as solemn as he felt, but the hunters were coming back and men were hauling water in just as they did every evening.

He once asked his father why he did not sleep in this room and the answer was simple; it belonged to Kevin's parents and it was too painful to enter. Now Neil understood. He had not been inside his father's room since the moment Kevin took his last breath.

Neil dismissed the heartbreaking thoughts of his parents and turned his attention to the problem at hand. What would he do about his brother? From an early age, Sween was filled with anger and after Kevin discovered the depth of that anger, he sent Sween into exile. Sween wanted control of the clan and was willing to go to any lengths to get it, including killing his brother. It was not an idle threat and everyone knew it. For Neil, the six years after Sween's exile was a peaceful time, although he was not allowed to go anywhere without a guard for his protection.

In the beginning, Neil hoped his brother would change and they would be a whole family again. But the hurt in his mother's eyes every time she came back from a visit with Sween hardened Neil's heart.

Rarely did anyone mention Sween after their mother died. Sween was commanded to live on MacGreagor land and although his cottage was off the main road, it was not all that far away. His father probably knew more than he cared to say, but Neil never bothered to ask. Now he knew very little about Sween's life and wondered if that had not been a mistake.

He let the window covering fall back into place and walked across the room to look out the opposite window, at the meadow, more trees and the hillside. Several children were playing in the meadow and it made him smile. The responsibility for keeping those little ones safe was about to fall on him and already he could feel the heavy weight of the burden. He was the next generation of MacGreagor men and if not him, who? Never in his life had he felt so alone. It was so quiet in the enormous keep, he could almost hear his own heartbeat.

What he needed was a wife and children to fill his emptiness. So far, he had not met the one who captured his heart. He warned himself not to make a hasty decision simply to relieve his loneliness, but feeling the nearness of a woman, even the wrong woman, was something he needed desperately right now.

He stretched out on the bed, curled up like a child and let his exhaustion overtake him.

*

The next morning, Neil walked down the stairs to find Mayze waiting for him. She was the shy one, he knew, and he would remember not to overwhelm her. "Good morning."

She smiled. "Good morning. What will you have for your morning meal?"

Neil took his usual seat next to the head of the table where Kevin always sat. "I see you already brought my favorite. Thank you." She started to leave, but he cleared his throat to get her attention. "Will you sit with me this morning? I find the place unbearable when no one is here."

She nodded and chose a seat opposite him. Mayze always liked Neil. He was kind and knew not only her name but everyone else's. With so many in the clan these days, it was a skill to be greatly admired. If he wanted to talk, she would gladly listen.

"When mother was alive, she kept us well informed about what the people were doing. But we have not had a mistress these three years and I suddenly find I have little current knowledge. I was hoping you could help me."

She looked a little concerned, but slowly nodded.

Neil smiled. "Do not fret, I do not expect a full report. I most want to know about my brother."

"We are not allowed to go near him."

"I know, but there must be rumors, there always are." He took a bite of apple followed by a chunk of cheese and gave her ample time to answer. When she didn't, he looked her in the eye. "You and I were raised together. We have not been the best of friends, but I know which are your days to serve us, and I know you love walking in the forest. So do I. We are family and you must be honest with me."

She remembered to breathe and mustered all her courage. Sween was Neil's brother, after all, and she worried about saying the wrong thing. She finally decided now was not the time to hide it. "Of a truth, some say he has gone daft. He kills more meat than he needs and..."

"Go on."

"He kills viciously. He frightens us."

"Did my father know?"

"Aye, but he hoped someday Sween would change."

"I did as well. Mayze, what else do the people know that I do not?"

"In the beginning he went to the loch to bathe at night, but after your mother died, he does not keep himself clean at all. He has many lasses. We do not know who they are, only that they wear many different plaids."

"Has he hurt any of them?"

"I have not heard that he has, but how would we know?" Mayze tried to think of more to tell him, but there was no more. "What will you do with him? The people want him gone."

"I do not know. If I force him south, he might make an alliance with the English and north would be worse still. The Camerons will not have him and neither will the Fergusons. Besides, I may not be chosen to lead and then the decision will fall on another."

This time Mayze beamed. "You will be chosen. We will have no other and you will be a good laird."

"Do you really believe that?"

"I do, you are already a good lad."

"Thank you, you have comforted me greatly. I want you to come tell me if you hear more about Sween. One more question then you may go. Do you hate serving the Keep?"

"On rainy days, I love coming here. The larger we children grow the smaller our cottage becomes."

"But when the sun is out, you would rather walk in the forest?"

She nodded, slipped out of her chair and went out the back door.

He watched her go and sighed. "So would I. Walking in the forest alone is a pleasure I have not had in six years." It was true, Neil filled his days practicing his warrior skills, riding his horse, hunting, fishing and visiting families, but always with a guard to protect him from his brother.

Neil spent the rest of the morning trying to think who would make a good second in command and who he would choose for a third. Connor came to tell him all was set for the voting in the afternoon. He stayed for a while, gave his best advice and then left.

Neil paced, ate his noon meal and paced some more. He did notice when it became unusually quiet outside, but he dismissed it as the people gathering and talking among themselves.

CHAPTER II

Mayze walked out of the forest the day of her first visit with Dugan and didn't go back. The reason was Kevin's death. No one felt like doing much of anything and only time would console them. She did wonder what it would be like to talk to Dugan. He seemed nice, his smile was warm and he loved animals. In her mind, that was a very good thing. It was odd for a man to love animals and yet hunt them, but the clan had to eat and she supposed he had no choice.

Dugan, on the other hand, did wait for her in the forest the day after Kevin died. He didn't think she would come, but he waited as long as he could. Then he went hunting. The need for food didn't stop even during the time of mourning, and he hoped when he took her mother a rabbit or two, he might be able to see Mayze. The first time he arrived, Mayze didn't come to the door. The second time her mother got a sly look in her eye and invited him inside.

Mayze was sitting on the bed looking down. The other six children were sitting in a row beside her grinning, and looking like stair steps in size. He nodded to each as the mother introduced them, but Mayze still didn't look up and he realized her mother was embarrassing her. He turned to her mother. "Your husband was always kind to me and I respected him. 'Tis in his honor I bring you food." Dugan noticed her mother's smile fade and also noticed the relief on Mayze's face. He made his excuses and left.

Mayze was so grateful, she wanted to kiss him. Now her mother would not think he came to see her at all. She would much rather face her mother's pity than to feel herself on the marriage chopping block. Perhaps she might find a way to thank him for his thoughtfulness someday.

*

The moment of decision finally arrived and the people waited in the meadow. But when Neil rode across the bridge, flanked by his Uncle Connor, his Aunt Rachel and their three children, Justin, Danny and little Catherin, the people remained eerily quiet.

Dressed in a clean kilt and white shirt, with a strip of blue plaid over his shoulder, Neil wore new shoes with long leather straps that laced up to his knees. He stopped his horse at the crest of the meadow and looked out over the vastness of matching blue plaids. None of the people smiled and most did not even look him in the eye.

It was not until he heard the thunder of horses coming up the road that he understood the reason why. Sween was coming, with him the banished Mungo, and twenty men dressed in MacGreagor kilts, all fully armed and ready for battle.

Sween looked so much like Kevin, it was uncanny. He had the same blond hair and the same gray-blue eyes. He walked his horse up beside Neil, looked at the people and held up his hand. "I will be the MacGreagor laird and you will obey me."

Neil turned to glare at his brother. "Are you afraid to let the people decide?"

Sween sneered, "Not at all, ask them yourself."

Neil turned to once more look at the faces of the people. "Whom do you choose to lead you?"

Still the people did not look at him and then one man shouted. "Sween!" Another joined and soon the vote was unanimous.

Neil was furious. "What power do you hold over them?"

"No power at all. They are free to choose whomever they want, just as father commanded. 'Tis clear they want *me* and not you." Sween moved his horse forward until he could see Connor. "Gather your things, take your wife and your children and get off my land."

It was a full minute before Connor, the man Kevin trusted most, found the words to speak. He was also Sween's uncle, his rage was complete and he knew Rachel's was as well. "We do not need our things." At a slow pace, he walked his horse down the crest and into the meadow. The people slowly parted, but they said not a word. Neither did they look at them nor did they nod, and the women did not weep. With his family following behind him, Connor led the way through the trees and up the hillside toward Cameron land.

When they reached the top of the hill, they stopped to look back. The MacGreagors lived in a wondrous place where the rain kept everything green. The two-story stone building they called a keep stood in front of several cottages with paths between them and a vegetable garden in the back. A wall surrounded it all with a moat on the outside. New cottages dotted the grounds up the road and in the distance, they could see the loch they often swam or bathed in.

Rachel let out a long sigh. "I should have tried to kill him a second time."

Connor was shocked. "'Twas you?"

"I could not let him hurt his parents any longer. Then Kevin exiled Sween and I hoped that would be an end to it. I see now I was wrong."

"I should have killed him myself. It hurts my heart to leave Neil to face him alone."

"I do not understand. Why have the people turned on Neil?"

Connor took their young daughter out of Rachel's arms and settled her in his lap. Then he turned his horse and started down the other side of the hill. "No doubt he promised not to kill Neil if they chose him. They do it to save Neil's life."

Neil watched Connor and Rachel disappear from sight, knew they would go to the Cameron hold, and they would be safe there. Perhaps that was best. He turned once more to face his brother. "And what will you do with me?"

Sween sneered. "Nothing. You may even live in the Keep if you can stand to. You may come and go as you please and do anything you want."

"I do not believe you."

"As you wish." Sween turned his horse, rode over the drawbridge to reclaim his former home and most of his guard followed. Then out of the trees rode several women who also followed. The shouts of victory from inside came soon after and it made Neil sick.

Two of Sween's guards took up positions, one to Neil's right and one to his left. He ignored them, took one more look at his father's people and tried to understand what was happening. Still they did not meet his gaze and he could discern nothing from their faces.

Patrick stood at the front of the crowd and was the man Neil decided to make his second in command, once he was confirmed.

Even Patrick held his gaze down, but Neil knew he would hear his words, "Tell them I will not desert them."

He was about to turn his horse when he realized something and again studied the crowd. The women's clothes were wet. A man in the back bowed, but it was not a bow of honor -- it was the signal something was greatly amiss. Finally Neil understood. There were no children in the crowd and that meant Sween didn't just have a guard of twenty, he had an army big enough to hold all the children hostage.

With a slight nod, Neil turned to ride away from the Keep. When the two guards followed, he stopped and looked back at their foolish grins. "If you mean to kill me, do it now and get it over with."

"We are your protection," the first man said. "Sween wants you alive."

For how long, Neil wondered. He urged his horse forward. He needed time to think and if they were quiet, he could do that with or without them. One thing he knew for sure, he would no longer be living in the Keep. The very sight of his brother made him ill and he could just imagine what living with him would be like.

He was worried about the children and thought about riding around the hold to discover where they were being held. But he was only one man and what could he do? He closed his eyes and said a prayer for them. There was death in the air and he could feel it, so he prayed for them all.

With no specific destination in mind, Neil turned east toward Ferguson land and then north. He failed to notice the smile on the faces of his guard.

Dugan had only one thought -- as soon as Neil left and the crowd in the meadow dispersed, he headed for the special place in the forest and prayed Mayze would come. He paced for almost an hour before he heard rustling in the bushes and held his breath.

Mayze hoped he would be there too, and when she saw him, she was almost in tears. "Sween let all the children go."

"Good." He opened his arms and was surprised when she went to him, laid her head on his shoulder and cried. He couldn't think of a thing to say, so he just held her tight and let her get it out of her system. Rarely had he been given the opportunity to comfort a woman and he liked the feeling very much, especially since it was Mayze.

At length, she calmed down and stopped crying. "They are preparing the bodies."

"I know, the lads are digging the graves." He supposed the shock of the deaths had not yet hit him. All he managed to feel was anger mixed with his love for Mayze. It was an odd and almost overwhelming combination.

Finally, Mayze wiped the last of her tears away with a cloth. "Did you see the hurt in Neil's eyes? He felt so betrayed."

"What could we do, we had to save the children." Dugan urged her to sit down on the log and then joined her. He still wanted to be touching her, even if it was only to hold her hand, but he didn't think it was the right time.

"How many lads do you think Sween has?" she asked.

"I have no idea, a hundred maybe. We should count them when we can."

She frowned. "They brought their lasses too. They are very

disagreeable lasses and Sween demanded we give them our extra plaids to wear."

"Try not to fret, we will fight and rid ourselves of the swine. But first we must have a commander. When Neil comes back, he will lead us."

"*If* Neil comes back."

"He promised not to desert us; he will come back."

Mayze closed her eyes and hung her head. "Sween's first order was to remove all of Kevin's belongings and move his things into his parent's bedchamber."

"I am not surprised. He shed not one tear for his father, though the rest of us cried like babies."

"Do you think Sween hated Kevin?"

"He must have."

Mayze quickly glanced into his eyes and just as quickly looked away. "Sween makes Mungo his second in command."

"I expected that as well." The cat came out into the open and rubbed against Dugan's leg until he lifted it into his lap.

"I am frightened Neil will fight him and Sween will win. What will we do then?" Without even thinking, she began to pet the cat and then let it climb into her lap.

Dugan folded his arms. "Neil is a strong lad, he will win."

When she really looked at Dugan, she found a pleasant face and nice eyes. "I wish Connor were here, he could keep them from fighting."

"I wish he were here too. We flounder and the lads know not what to do." He studied her face for a moment and then looked down. "I fear something far greater than the brothers fighting."

"What?"

"We have never been so vulnerable. If the MacDonalds hear of our troubles, they might..."

"Do not say that." She stood up and dumped the cat on the ground.

He quickly stood up too. "I did not mean to upset you, but we must be on our guard."

Mayze glared at first, then sighed and finally calmed. "You are right. I just hate the thought of it. We have not been at war since the Fergusons attacked."

"I remember. I was only eight and wanted to help with the fight, but my father put a quick stop to that idea."

It made her smile. "God help us if we have to rely on eight-year-olds to protect us." She enjoyed his returned smile and then turned to go. "I should get back."

"So should I, I want to see what is happening. Will you meet me here again tomorrow?"

"If I can."

They walked together out of the forest. He felt protective of her and she felt protected. It was a new experience for both of them and each liked it.

*

Neil hardly remembered the sops were following him. He recognized neither and knew they were probably the dregs of other clans. As the sun moved farther west, he headed for the loch. He broke through the trees, slid down off his horse, dipped his hands in the cool water and drank. When he left the Keep that morning, he took no provisions, not even the usual flask of water.

He doubted Connor had any provisions either and wondered how they would manage the three hours it took to get to the Cameron hold. He missed them already and thought about following, but that might look like he was deserting his people. He knew only one thing for certain -- as long as the people who loved Kevin were on MacGreagor land, he would be too.

Neil sprawled out on a rock and rested. His guards got down, took up positions and pretended to be protecting him. It made Neil want to laugh. He would have asked whom they thought they were protecting him from, but he really wasn't in the mood for conversation.

Without looking at them, he sized up his guards. Taking them might not be all that difficult, especially if he wore them out first. At least he was well armed. For as long as he could remember, he kept himself armed and it was second nature to him. This day he was glad it was.

Neil got back on his horse and continued north.

He thought about actually having to fight his brother one-on-one and hated the idea. He would, if there were no other way, but it would be his last resort. Mentally, he counted the number of his father's warriors, the number of women and the number of children. Then he separated the numbers into how many lived inside the wall and how many lived outside. A plan was forming in his mind, and he...

Suddenly, thirty-two MacDonald warriors stepped out of the forest in front of him.

*

On the second day of Sween's rule, Mayze couldn't wait to be with Dugan again, and this time it was she who paced hoping and praying he could come. When he finally did and opened his arms to her, she didn't hesitate to go into them. Her knees were shaking and she could hardly speak.

He wanted to kiss all her fears away, but he just held her until she recovered her composure. "Neil is not dead, Mayze, Sween lies."

"How can you be sure? His guard came back without him and swore Laird MacDonald killed him."

"Aye, but they did not bring back his body."

She hadn't thought of that and began to breathe easier. "Where do you think he is, then?"

"I do not know. The guards looked like they had been in a fight. Neil might have fought them and escaped. We must believe that, we can think no other thought or we will all go daft."

She finally moved away. "Do the lads still want to wait before they fight Sween?"

"We must see to the safety of the women and children inside the wall first. Another twenty-five lads arrived just before I came, and God only knows what Sween has promised them in exchange for their loyalty."

"What if they keep growing in numbers? Can we still defeat them?"

"So long as we only have to fight Sween and his lads. Our worry is the MacDonalds. If Sween has formed an alliance, even with the help of the Camerons and the Fergusons, we will lose many a good lad and perhaps the battle."

She closed her eyes and shook her head. "Other clans want our land, why would Laird MacDonald be any different? He is forever trying to dam the water that feeds the moat."

"True and Sween is being stupid. Once the war was won, Laird MacDonald would have no use for Sween. He would die that very day."

"I will shed no tear for him...that I can promise." She liked being in Dugan's arms and wondered why she moved away. She hoped he would hold her again before she had to leave. "Have you heard Sween's latest edict?"

"Aye, the lads must bring food or wine before they will be allowed back inside."

"He holds the families hostage now, only inside instead of out. Is there nothing we can do?" she asked.

"There *is* something and I will need your help to do it."

"What?"

"We must make Neil our laird without Sween finding out. We will take a secret vote and confirm him. Then when Neil comes back, he will have full authority."

Finally Mayze smiled. "Yes, yes, that is the answer. What do you want me to do?"

If ever Dugan was going to be bold, now was the time. "First, I want you to marry me."

She stared into his eyes, then her smile turned to a grin and she went back into his arms. Before she realized what was happening, his lips were on hers and chills raced through her body. She had never imagined a kiss could be so thrilling. Soon her arms went around his neck and for the first time in her life, she loved and was loved by a man. Not just any man, the most handsome and caring man she could ever have prayed for.

When he thought he had kissed her longer than he should, he put his cheek to hers and held her tight. "Is that a yes?"

She giggled and nodded, but she wanted to stay in his arms as long as possible and wasn't ready to let go. "I am so happy. The world falls down around us and I am ashamed of how happy I am."

He reluctantly pulled away and took both her hands. "I feel the same. We will find a way to make our world good again and then we will marry, agreed?" He watched her nod and kissed her lightly on the lips. "You ask the lasses for their vote and I will ask the lads. Then we will meet back here tomorrow morning and compare. Be careful, I want nothing to happen to you. I will bring Patrick and he will hear our votes."

"I think Neil will choose Patrick as his second."

"So do I." Dugan kissed her one last time, took her hand and walked her back through the forest.

*

Some said Laird MacDonald was a witless man with few redeeming qualities. Laird for the last few years, he wore a red plaid, had dirty hair and an untrimmed beard. He was especially unkind to women and most stayed as far away from him as possible. Yet, it was the women who prepared his meals and served him. So when MacDonald warriors brought their prisoner in for the third time in two days, Gillie was there.

She tried not to look at the man. Looking at a man not a

MacDonald could get her in real trouble, and more trouble was exactly what she didn't need. It was not her first time serving the laird and it was all she could do to stay out of his reach. Everyone knew the serving women were often pinched, grabbed and sometimes touched inappropriately right in front of other men.

Yet when she walked behind Laird MacDonald, she took a chance and glanced at the stranger. He wore a MacGreagor plaid and she had seen him before. In fact, she once hid in the forest and watched him for nearly an hour. The thing she remembered most about him was the unusual friendship he seemed to have with his horse.

The horse was dark brown with a white mane and had no saddle or even a bridle. The man patted the horse's nose often, talked to him, and sometimes the horse nodded as though he understood. When the man moved to a new location, the horse followed and when the man stopped talking, the horse nudged him to get his attention.

She almost smiled at her memory and then realized she was too close to her laird. Before she could release the goblet of wine she set before him, Laird MacDonald grabbed hold of her wrist.

He looked at her with lust in his eyes. "I will have you in my bed later."

Gillie was mortified, but hid it well. She smiled sweetly and tried to pull her hand out of his grasp. "I will have your head chopped off later."

Laird MacDonald roared with laughter. "I like this one. She will serve me all week and if you are good to me, Gillie, I will give you the MacGreagor for a toy."

She quickly looked Neil up and down and then rolled her eyes.

"Some prize that is."

Again, her laird laughed, but he didn't release her and before she could stop him, he forced her into the chair next to him. "I cannot decide if I should kill him or let him entertain me for a few more days. What do you think we should do with the MacGreagor, Gillie?"

She suddenly had the man's life in her hands and a thought ran through her mind, but the time was not yet. "We should send him back before he stinks up the place."

"I see you do not know who he is," the MacDonald sneered. "He is Neil, Kevin MacGreagor's youngest son."

Even though he was unarmed, Neil hadn't taken his glare off of Laird MacDonald. He wasn't as worried about himself as he was enraged by the way the MacDonald was treating the woman. MacGreagor women were never treated with such contempt and he had not seen this before.

"I do not care who he is," Gillie was saying, her voice on the edge of a scream. "What I care about is the pain your hold has on my wrist. Kindly let go of me."

"If I do, what will be my reward?"

She knew what the MacDonald feared most was dying of a horrible illness, so she made one up. "I will not share my blue with you."

"Blue? What is blue?"

"They are spots on my skin."

The MacDonald couldn't let go fast enough, and with both hands he shoved her so hard, her chair fell over. She hit her arm on the table and then went sprawling across the floor.

Neil swore under his breath. He took a quick look at the lass called Gillie and noticed she was holding her arm. He guessed it was broken.

"Take him away, I will deal with him later," MacDonald demanded. "And order my bath. I have touched her, God help me I will die of the blue." With that, he stood and rushed out of the room.

*

The place they took Neil to this time was a one-room cottage with no furniture, only one window and one door. Four men stood guard outside the closed door and he knew they were there; he could hear them talking. Two were worried the MacGreagors would attack to get Neil back and the other two were hoping they would.

The first thing Neil did was examine the window to see if he could fit his large bulk through it. He could not. Then he pushed on several stones to see if the cottage was built weak enough for him to push his way out. That was not a possibility either. He finally sat down on the dirt floor to think.

When the MacGreagors heard, and they would soon hear, they would come for him even if his brother issued an order against it. That meant war and he dreaded the idea of anyone dying for his sake. He began to wonder why he was still alive. It didn't make sense.

CHAPTER III

The sun was setting, fires were being lit along the paths outside the cottages and Neil was still sitting on the floor trying to understand what was happening. If Sween planned this, how could he know Neil would go north after he left the Keep? He couldn't know unless someone followed and then told the MacDonalds where to find him. His so-called guards pretended to put up a good fight, but soon ran off and he was not surprised in the least.

But Neil didn't fight. There were too many and no point in dying any sooner than he had to. Now alone in the unfamiliar cottage, he tried to think exactly who his loyal followers were. Patrick was in front of the crowd nearest him, but unarmed. Still he thought Patrick would have been willing to fight without a weapon had Sween decided to kill him that day. Yes, Patrick could be trusted and so could the men who stood in the front of the crowd with him. He closed his eyes and tried to picture the face of each man. Then he heard a swishing noise.

Out of the corner of his eye, he saw the shadow of a woman quickly pass outside the window. And then he saw something fall inside. It was almost too dark to see, but when he went over and picked it up, he discovered it was a red MacDonald plaid. Someone was going to help him get out. He ripped off his blue MacGreagor kilt and began to pleat the red one. But when he was finished, he could not find the extra strip to put over his shoulder and he was worried about it. He wondered if the woman would drop it next and waited beside the window to see. But she didn't come back.

*

It would not be easy to tempt all the guards away from their post. Gillie had done it before and she knew just what to do, but the other soldiers were not guarding such an important prisoner as Neil MacGreagor and that time there were only two, not four. She took a deep breath, opened her shirt just a little at the top, slowly left her hiding place and walked down the path. In her right hand, she held a flask of wine and in her other, a flower. The side of her arm was bruised and had a lump, but her hand worked still and she guessed it wasn't broken. It sure was sore, however.

Gillie brought the flower up to her nose and pretended she suddenly noticed the four guards. She stopped a few feet away and smiled. "I can think of nothing a lass loves more than flowers."

"I can," muttered the commander. His eyes drifted from her lips to the exposed skin below her neck.

Neil heard her voice and recognized it. Gillie was outside and if he was lucky, her beauty would tempt the guards to look away long enough for him to slip out the door. He cautiously pulled it open a crack. Already the four guards were paying more attention to her than to the door they were supposed to be guarding. But he needed them to move a little farther away and hoped she could think of a way to do it.

Gillie batted her eyes, "What could that be?"

The commander smiled. "You know very well what I am thinking, lass."

"Perhaps I do, but you would have to marry me for that. The

problem is..." she slowly examined the face of each man. "I cannot decide which of you to choose. You are all very handsome. Nay, I cannot decide at all." She noticed the swell in their chests and was repulsed by it. Again, she smiled. "I have heard you can tell a lot about a lad by the look of his hands." She pointed at the one closest to the door. "May I see your hand? I promise not to hurt you."

The man chuckled, took a step toward her and reached out his hand palm up. Gillie took hold of his thumb and turned his hand toward the fire light. "Um." She wrinkled her brow. "Do you see this?" All of the men stepped forward to look and she had accomplished her goal.

Neil opened the door, quietly slipped out, closed it and hurried around to the back of the cottage.

"This line should go all the way around your thumb. It means, and I sadly say it, you would leave me a widow." The other men began to examine their own palms and it took several excruciating minutes to tell them what their thumb line meant and assure them they were not going to die anytime soon. At last finished, Gillie sighed. "I still cannot decide. However, I will reward your patience with this wine." She handed it to the commander, turned and walked back up the path. When she glanced back, they were still studying their palms and muttering to each other.

It seemed like forever before he saw Gillie's face in the dim light and felt her take hold of his hand. She put her other hand around Neil's neck and pulled his head down so she could whisper in his ear. "Pretend we are lovers." He nodded and kept her hand in his as she led him behind two more cottages and then into the open. He put his arm around her, felt hers go around him and casually walked by her side. They passed still more cottages, some with outside fires that lit up the night. Most of the MacDonald men were not wearing strips of plaid over their shoulders and he was relieved.

But then he noticed a man he thought he recognized. He could think of nothing else to do, so he drew Gillie to him and kissed her lips. With one eye partially opened, he watched until the man passed and then let her go.

Unlike the MacGreagor hold, the MacDonalds did not have a wall. Still, they had ample guards and she was taking him out the safest way she knew how. To get there, she had to take him all the way down the path to the end of the village and pray no one noticed.

He had to kiss her twice more and wasn't sure if the men he avoided were interested in him or in Gillie. If a man wanted Gillie, he might be challenged in front of witnesses, and that was the last thing he wanted to do, especially unarmed.

Gillie was worried about that too, so when she spotted a particular MacDonald who had been pestering her to marry him, it was her idea to kiss and not let the MacDonald see her face. She noticed Neil held her even closer that time and was starting to like getting kissed. What she wanted was freedom from Laird MacDonald and Neil MacGreagor had the power to give her what she wanted. If he liked getting kissed, then kiss him she would.

Finally, they reached the place where she could safely sneak him out. She went into his arms again, but not to kiss him, to whisper in his ear. "We are on a hill. If you try to go down standing up, they will see you. Lie down and roll." She waited for his nod, took his hand and pulled him through the bushes.

When she stopped and released his hand, he did as she said and rolled down the hill. It was a steep hill and he rolled quickly, but before he could stand up, he heard her coming and turned over to catch her. She was hurt, he remembered, so he let her stay in his arms until she was ready to move again. He felt her tremble and knew she was also frightened. Helping him escape could cost her greatly and he wanted to get them away as quickly as possible. Still, he waited.

She had a firm hold on his upper arms and wasn't ready to let go of him. She would have his promise first and it wasn't a request, it was a demand. "You *will* take me with you."

He didn't have to think twice about that. "Aye."

*

It was very dark. Gillie held Neil's hand and led him through the forest for what seemed like hours. They crossed a meadow and at last, she stopped. "We can rest here."

He felt her sit and he sat down beside her. "Where are we?"

"We are on Ferguson land." She heard him breathe a sigh of relief and she did the same. "I have never been so frightened in my life. When I kissed you at the last, it was to avoid Clone. He has been pestering me and I am sure he saw me. I feared he would try to follow us, but I doubt he could. He is not skilled at night. I have avoided him forever, it seems."

"You have done this often?"

"Escaped, you mean? Aye, quite often. You will take me with you to the MacGreagors."

"I will take you with me, but I am not sure I can go back to the

MacGreagors any time soon. I believe my brother wants me dead and he is their new laird." She didn't answer and he knew she must be disappointed. "I am friends with both the Ferguson and the Cameron. I can take you to either of them until the MacGreagors are settled." She still didn't say anything. "Gillie?"

"I am thinking."

"How is your arm?"

"Sore, but 'tis not bad."

"Good, we can sleep until morning. Move closer and I will try to keep you warm." He put his hand on her back, stretched out and waited. She didn't move away, but she didn't lay down beside him either. "I will not harm you."

"I know, I have heard a MacGreagor can get killed for such a thing. Is it true?"

"It is. We do not harm a child or a lass, and we especially do not force a lass."

"Laird MacDonald often forces a lass."

"Did he force you?"

"Nay." She was solemn for a moment and then giggled. "He is likely to have me slain now that he thinks I have the blue. He is so simple minded." Without really thinking about it, she lay down next to Neil and rested her head on his shoulder. He was warm and she didn't realize how cold she was until she felt it. She closed her eyes and quickly fell sleep.

Next to his body was a woman who had just saved his life. She did it to save herself, but he could find no fault in that. All she wanted in return was a better future and he was determined to give it to her. In fact, there was nothing he would deny her. She was shrewd, brave and he couldn't help but wonder if this was the woman he waited for. He finally closed his eyes.

*

The next day brought still more unfamiliar men into the MacGreagor hold, so Mayze stopped on a path inside the wall to watch. The grounds were becoming littered with horse dung and rotting food tossed away by the careless invaders.

The men were vile and so were some of the women they brought with them. They occupied all the empty cottages inside the wall, including Connor's and the one Dugan planned to take his bride to. When that wasn't enough, the women slept in the courtyard surrounded by men who smelled as disgusting as the women did. It sickened Mayze. Kevin protected them from more than any of them ever realized.

On the other hand, the drunkenness of the repulsive men gave her ample time to secure the votes of the women both inside and outside the wall, and if she could stand to walk through them to the bridge, she had much to tell Patrick and Dugan.

MacGreagor women were allowed to come and go as they chose, but they could not take the children with them, and getting in and out was frightening and tedious. Few of the women were brave enough to try, but Mayze had a purpose. She held her nose and prayed none of the men would wake up and try to grab her.

*

Patrick was a strong man with blond hair, a square face and dark eyes. He was indeed loyal and would gladly die to protect Neil. The eldest son in his family, he was unmarried, a good fighter and loved one sister more than the other, though he would never say so. Her name was Steppen, she was forever curious and a delight to everyone. But now that the best MacGreagor fighters were being kept outside the wall even if they brought offerings, he worried about her the most. Steppen had not yet learned to fear men for reasons other than battle.

He leaned against a tree and tried not to worry. Instead, he watched Dugan pace in the small clearing. "I never knew you to be a crafty lad, but you have proven me wrong. Secretly making Neil our laird is a stroke of brilliance."

Dugan was about to speak when he heard something, turned around and put his hand on his sword. He was relieved to see Mayze coming and went to kiss her.

Patrick was pleased. He liked Dugan and if he found a wife, Patrick was happy for him. He soon turned his attention to Mayze. "The lasses agreed?"

"Aye." She was embarrassed by Dugan's open show of affection and stepped away from him. "Was there any doubt?"

"Nay. When you go back, spread the word that Neil is confirmed. Yule Cameron is here and the Cameron will fight with us if we need them."

Dugan frowned. "The Camerons are not enough. I counted and Sween's men number two hundred and six. I fear we will see more before this ends."

"Where do they all come from?" Mayze wanted to know.

"From all over the Highlands, it seems." Patrick sighed. "We will start taking the families out, but just a few at a time so Sween does not notice."

Mayze clicked her tongue. "Sween is drunk and does not even know how many we are. He will not notice when half are gone."

"Not now, but the wine cannot last much longer," said Patrick.

"Sween's lads guard the hidden doors in the wall. How do we get the families out?" asked Dugan.

Patrick answered, "My cousin does not have much, but she has a powder that will make one guard sleep tonight. Then we can do the same and take more out the next night."

Dugan smiled and slapped him on the back. "If Neil is dead, you will lead us."

"Neil is not dead, Laird MacDonald has him."

The news upset both Mayze and Dugan. "Hell," breathed Dugan. "Now we must fight the MacDonalds."

Patrick shook his head. "Not now. MacGreagor lads cannot leave their wives and children in the hands of Sween and go off to fight. 'Tis unthinkable. We must find a way to get the families inside the wall to safety, rid ourselves of Sween and then we will see to the MacDonalds."

"You are right, what do you want us to do?" asked Dugan.

"Stay here. I will send someone to get the powder from my cousin and then I will find Yule and bring him back. He will help us make a plan."

*

When he woke up, Neil was on his side with his knees bent. Gillie had her back to him, she fit perfectly and both of his arms were around her. Her long dark hair was wrapped around to the front of her and spilled over his arms. It was soft, smelled of roses and he hoped she wouldn't wake up before he had time to enjoy the nearness of her a little while longer.

Gillie had not slept well. She was cold and his warmth felt wonderful, but there wasn't enough of it. Every time he moved, she woke up and adjusted herself accordingly. Twice, she had to move his strong arms to keep him from crushing her, touching her sore arm or putting his hands where they didn't belong. By the time the sun started to come up, she felt like she'd been in a battle. She was not reluctant at all to move out of his arms.

Neil slowly sat up and looked around. He wasn't familiar with the area and wondered if they really were on Ferguson land. He scooted around until the sun was in the east to get his bearings, then he got to his feet. He watched her go behind a tree and he did the same, then met her again at the edge of the meadow.

"How far into Ferguson land do you think we are?"

"Not far. If we go due south, we will find your loch."

"You have been to our loch?"

"I have been there often enough to see you there." Gillie took the lead and they began to weave their way south through the trees.

"And you never got caught?"

"Almost, your guards are very good. What happened to your horse?"

"He is around here somewhere. He got away when I was captured. Shall I see?"

She stopped and turned to glare at him. "Are you simple or do you play with me?"

Neil shrugged. "Simple, I suspect." He put two fingers to his mouth, whistled and waited, but the horse did not come. "He is probably home by now and too far away to hear me." She turned back around and for a moment, he didn't like her at all. Maybe she just woke up foul tempered and it would pass. He hoped so.

In another hour, she was far more pleasant and wanted to talk. "I am Gillie."

"I know, I heard Laird MacDonald say your name. What do you do, Gillie?"

"What every woman does, I suppose."

He found that answer odd. Most women liked to weave or had something special they did to keep from getting bored. They finally found a stream and stopped to drink. When he finished, Neil said, "Do you want to rest for a while?"

"Nay, I want to keep going. What is your home really like? We hear rumors of all kinds and it sounds like a paradise, but I do not believe most of it."

"We do have a good life. I guess 'tis because we love each other and care to make our lives happy."

She parted two bushes and stepped between them. "Your people do not argue?"

"Of course they do, they are no different from any other clan. But my father was a wise lad and he always found a way to resolve the differences when the people could not settle it between themselves."

Gillie stopped and turned to look at him. "If your brother dies, will you be the MacGreagor laird?"

"The people must decide that."

She looked up to make sure the sun was still in the east and then kept walking. "I have heard your father banished Sween, is it true?"

"Nay, he was only kept outside the wall." For a moment, he wondered how she knew his brother's name, but then he supposed all the clans heard about the MacGreagor troubles.

Gillie found a place to sit down. She lifted a foot, took off her shoe and began to rub a cramp.

"Would you like help with that?"

"I have done it often, 'twill pass. Will the people choose you if your brother dies?"

"I do not know."

Gillie stopped rubbing her foot, put her shoe back on and stood up. She smiled and then started to walk again. "I liked kissing you last night."

"I liked kissing you."

*

Yule Cameron wanted to see for himself what was going on inside the MacGreagor hold. It was here he found a wife and here he learned the way of the MacGreagors so he could become Blair Cameron's third in command. Now he was second and when Connor arrived with news of Sween's treachery, Yule insisted on being the one to come. He borrowed a MacGreagor plaid from one of the men living outside the wall, took his own flask of wine as an offering to gain entrance and boldly walked over the bridge. He soon spotted two drunken Camerons and had to control his rage and look away. Yule stepped around five sleeping people and then headed up the path. Once a place filled with children, he saw none at all and was glad the mothers were keeping them away from the disgusting sights and smells in the courtyard. Kevin would have...Yule could not think about that now.

He avoided looking at several men who seemed to be patrolling the paths and headed to the cottage he knew Patrick lived in. He didn't even knock before he entered and quickly closed the door behind him.

At first, Steppen was terrified and then she recognized the man. As soon as he opened his arms, she ran to him. But she didn't cry, she was too mad to. "Sween made Patrick leave. Father is crippled but they made him go anyway. Even my other brother was sent out and he is only thirteen."

"Where is your mother?"

"Mother had to go to the Keep to serve Sween and his lads. Is Maree safe?"

He held the twelve-year-old close. "She is very safe. Are you all alone?"

"My little sister is here. She is hiding. I used to call you the green, but I always liked you."

Yule stroked the back of her hair. "I liked you too."

"Two lads died this morning. They refused to leave their families and Mungo killed them."

"I heard. Try not to fret, the Camerons will help and we will get you out. You must be very brave until then, do you promise?"

"I promise." She hugged him once more and watched him go. Then Steppen went behind the bed to hide again with her little sister.

Yule was sick at heart. There was not an ounce of food inside Patrick's cottage and he suspected it was the same in all the cottages. He guessed Sween's men ate everything the hunters brought in and that thought made his blood boil. He glanced at the wall around the village and suddenly thought of something. Once more he opened the door to Steppen's cottage and closed it quickly behind him. "Steppen, I need your help."

She popped up and went to him. "What?"

"Tonight when your mother comes home, tell her..." He stopped to think for a moment. "Here's what we must do. After..."

CHAPTER IV

Patrick went back into the forest and gave Mayze the powder. "If you feel you are not brave enough to put it in the flask of one of Sween's men, find another to do it. Dugan, go on the hunt so you will have an offering. You can serve us better if you are inside to help Mayze."

Dugan nodded. "Where is Yule?"

"He went to talk to the families outside the wall. He has a plan to get food to the families inside. They are starving."

Dugan turned to stare at Mayze. "You have not eaten? How long?"

She hung her head. "Only two days."

"You should have told me?"

"How can I eat while my brothers and sisters go without?"

Patrick put a hand on her shoulder. "You need to keep your strength so you can help us. We count on you."

Dugan pulled an apple out of his pouch and handed it to her. "He is right." But she was reluctant to take it. "We are not leaving here until you eat every bite."

*

Late in the afternoon, Mayze avoided the grabs of two men, made it back across the courtyard and went outside the wall to meet Dugan. They held hands and sat close to each other on their favorite log in the forest. Neither cared that the cat had not come back.

She kept her voice soft so no one could hear. "He wants only the unmarried lasses to serve him."

"I heard, Mungo means to choose a wife." He suddenly caught his breath. "Has he sent for you?"

She nodded. "I am to go next week."

"I will kill him if he lays a hand on you."

Mayze knew he meant it and tried to quiet his fears. "He will not choose me."

"Why not, you are as bonnie as any of them."

She was shocked, thrilled and self-conscious all at the same time. "To you maybe. I will spill something on him and then he will reject me."

He grinned at first and then became alarmed. "You must not do that, he will strike you."

"Well, 'twould be better than having to marry him."

"If we were already married, you would not have to go at all."

"Aye, but Sween sent the priest away this morning and Mungo already knows I am not married. Besides, if I do not go, my mother will have to. She is unmarried still, you know."

*

From different sides of the same tree, Neil and Gillie peeked out. The man and woman sitting on the log were obviously too wrapped up in each other to notice. Neil knew who they were. He could trust them and he was happy to see both. However, he was wearing a MacDonald plaid and although Dugan was not nearly as big as Neil, he was quick and armed. Before he could stop her, Gillie stepped out from behind the tree.

Just as Neil expected, Dugan got to his feet and drew his sword at the sight of a MacDonald plaid. But when he saw it was a woman, he calmed down. "Are you lost?"

Gillie smiled. "Nay,"

"Are there others?"

"But one. You will be pleased to see him."

When Neil stepped out, Dugan's mouth dropped. "Thank God."

Mayze quickly went to Neil and hugged him. Then she pulled back to see his face. "You look tired and hungry."

"I am fine." Neil smiled to reassure Mayze and reached for Gillie's hand. "This is Gillie."

Mayze nodded and then turned her attention back to Neil. "Things are bad here. Sween has over two hundred lads; they are armed and have taken every spare plaid inside the wall." She looked him up and down. "We must get you out of that MacDonald cloth."

"I have one," Dugan said. "I have it hidden in the forest. I keep it in case I get blood on my clothing from the hunt. But 'twill take time to find one for the lass."

Gillie shrugged. "You can find me one later."

What they were wearing was not foremost on Neil's mind. Exhausted, he sat down on the log and rested his head in his hands. "Two hundred lads."

Dugan was quick to sit down beside him. "We held a vote and you are confirmed as our laird. What you say will be our command."

Neil noticed when Gillie sat down on the ground near his feet. "Tell me what is happening, Dugan."

"Sween has thrown the lads out, but keeps their families in. Patrick will be here soon and he will explain it. We have a plan to get some of the families out tonight."

"What happened before the people gathered to take the vote?"

"Sween spread the word that he meant to kill you in the courtyard and there would be a big battle, so we started taking the women and children out through the hidden doors. But Sween's lads were waiting in the forest and captured them. Some of the lasses fought, but...they killed three so the others surrendered."

Neil couldn't believe what he was hearing. He directed his question to Mayze. "They killed three *lasses*? Who?"

Mayze sat down on the ground at Dugan's feet. She was tired too, but hers was a different kind of exhaustion. Her emotions were nearly dull from all the heartache and worry. She wondered if she had the strength to get the names out and had to fight her tears. "They killed Victoria, Rose Three and Eppie. Eppie's oldest boy got badly cut and we do not know if he will…"

At the sound of someone coming, they all stood up and turned. Dugan pulled his sword and tried to shove Mayze behind him, but she pulled her dagger and wouldn't budge. Neil put his arms around Mayze from behind, took hold of the hand with the dagger and whispered in her ear. "May I borrow that?" Her bravery was short lived. She was happy to give it to him and even happier to move behind Dugan.

They relaxed as soon as they realized it was Patrick and five MacGreagor warriors. The men were so happy to see Neil, they had to control themselves to keep from shouting. Patrick grabbed Neil's shoulders and looked up to the heavens. "Thank you, God." He quickly released him and took a step back. "How did you escape?"

Neil pulled the woman out from behind him. "This is Gillie. She saved my life and you will protect her as you do me."

Patrick smiled. "Are you..."

"Nothing is settled." He took a moment to look over the men standing before him and was pleased. He trusted Patrick most, but Kessan, Loren, Walrick, Dan, Ronan and Dugan were all good men and loyal to his father. "Tell me what is happening."

Neil sat back down on the log and urged Gillie and Mayze to sit beside him. The men got comfortable on the ground in front of Neil and began to explain everything, while Dugan slipped away to find his extra plaid.

Mayze only half listened and wondered if she should go back, but decided to wait to see what Dugan thought she should do. They still hadn't resolved the problem of her having to serve Sween.

"Yule went inside the wall to look around," Patrick was saying. "'Tis worse than we feared. The families are terrified and try to keep hidden as best they can. We will lower food over the back wall as soon as it is dark and Sween's lads are drunk enough not to notice."

"I cannot believe Sween would do this. My brother is cruel but this is beyond cruelty. He has lost all reason."

Kessan spoke up, "Sween is drunk day and night. I doubt he knows what is happening. Mungo does it."

"We are about out of wine," Patrick continued. "The Camerons are bringing more, but we must decide what to do soon. If we let them get sober, they will be better fighters."

Three of the men quickly stood up, drew their swords and swung around. But it was Dugan and they breathed easier. Dugan handed the plaid to Neil, gave both he and Gillie an apple, crossed his feet at the ankles and sat down with the men. When he looked at Neil, he rolled his eyes. "You need a bath. You look like you rolled in the dirt."

Neil finally smiled. "I did."

"Will you kill Sween?" Dan asked.

"Nay, my mother made me promise not to and she was right. I do not want the blood of my brother on my hands."

"Then what will you do?"

"I do not know yet. Has Connor come back?"

"Nay," Patrick answered. "We do not believe he will until you are in command."

Neil nodded his appreciation to Dugan and bit into the apple. He glanced at Gillie long enough to see her greedily consuming hers. "Have you buried the lasses?"

All the men lowered their eyes and let Patrick answer. "Aye, we buried them this morning, but the boy does better and we think he will live."

"When you can, tell him I am proud of his courage. And tell the families of the lasses I know of their suffering. Perhaps 'twill comfort them a little."

"Finlay and Keith are dead also. They refused to leave without their families. They let us have the bodies and we will bury them tomorrow. And Cormick died this morning. His wife says his age got the better of him finally."

"I am sad to hear that as well." Neil finished the apple and tossed the core away. He noticed Gillie was also finished, got to his feet and offered his hand. "Mayze, take her to the loch and help her bathe."

Gillie took his hand, stood up, looked into his eyes and made her demand. "You will *not* leave without me."

He found the tone of her voice insulting, but he reminded himself she was the reason he was alive. Besides, she probably didn't trust him and there was only one way for her to learn. "You are safe on MacGreagor land. Go to the loch and wash."

It was clear she wasn't going to get the answer she wanted, so she reluctantly followed Mayze and disappeared into the forest.

Neil turned to the men. "I will need your vow of loyalty." Each man stood up, gave his pledge without hesitation and sat back down. "Thank you. Patrick is now my second and Kessan my third." Neil enjoyed the smiles of all the men for a moment and then continued. "Kessan, you will hear the pledges of the other lads. Dugan, you will lead my hunters. Choose your lads well; we want to control the food."

Dugan's chest swelled with pride. It was the highest honor he could ever have asked for and he couldn't wait to tell Mayze.

"Sween will know I have escaped soon enough, so tell the people...tell them a Ferguson loaned me a horse and saw me ride south of the loch. Say it is all right for them to tell Sween's lads."

Patrick found the possibility exciting. "Sween will send lads to look for you, and drunken lads too. We will be ready for them."

Neil ignored his comment. "Where is Yule?"

"Gone to get more wine."

"Good, we want to control that as well." The men couldn't seem to stop grinning. He studied their faces one at a time and wrinkled his brow. "What?"

Patrick answered, "You sound just like Kevin."

"'Tis good to have you back," Kessan added.

*

Mayze looked around to make sure she and Gillie were alone at the loch. She thought they would be, most of the women who were willing to try to get past the men in the courtyard had already come and gone. The men, she knew, would bathe at the other end of the loch and much later. She saw no reason not to bathe also, so they both stripped down and went into the cool water. Without the shade of the trees, she noticed Gillie looked awful. She had dark circles under her eyes and dirt in her hair. She also had other bruises besides the one on her arm. She wondered what happened, but was too shy to ask.

Gillie splashed water on her face and rubbed the dirt off. "Who do you think would win if the brothers fight?"

Mayze was mortified. "I hope not to find out. We loved Kevin and both are his sons." When Gillie submerged her whole head to wash her hair, Mayze sighed and started to get out of the water. Her constant thoughts of Dugan may have muddled her mind, but she didn't like this woman. She was pleasing to be sure, but there was something odd about her.

Gillie washed her hair, walked out of the water and began to shake the dirt out of her MacDonald plaid. "Is Neil married?"

Mayze was not happy with that question either, but she answered it anyway. "Nay. We should hurry, Neil cannot bathe until you finish and he needs a serious scrubbing."

Gillie laughed. "That he does. "'Tis all my fault, I made him roll down a hill."

*

The men gave Neil every detail they could think of concerning the clan, and then listened to him explain his escape from the MacDonald hold. When Neil lowered his voice, the men leaned closer. "Sween will not send lads to look for me; he will wait for us to attack."

Patrick nodded, "Then we must find a way to force them all out at the same time."

"Aye and that is what Sween will expect us to do. There is only one thing he will not..." When Neil saw Gillie; he got to his feet and nodded. "There you see, I did not leave you." He helped her sit on the log, watched Dugan go to stand by Mayze and then retook his place in front of the men. "Tonight you will take as many out as you can and drop food inside the wall as you planned. For my plan to work, we must get all the people out first."

"What is your plan?" Kessan asked.

"You will know soon enough." Neil looked at Mayze, "When will they run out of wine?"

"I do not know, but I can find out."

"Nay," Dugan said without thinking. He quickly bowed his head. "I am sorry, Neil."

"What worries you?"

Dugan hesitantly raised his gaze to meet Neil's. "She would have to go inside the Keep to find out, and Mungo is choosing a wife among the unmarried."

Neil rolled his eyes. "I can think of no worse fate than that for a lass."

No one was more surprised at her boldness than Mayze. "I can do it, Neil, Dugan worries for nothing. Mungo will not choose me, I am not bonnie."

Dugan started to argue, but Neil raised his hand to stop him. "Mayze, I value your willingness, but a drunken lad does not know the difference. Dugan is right, you must not go."

"I could go," whispered Gillie.

Neil turned to look at her, but he quickly dismissed the idea and turned away. "Mayze, ask whoever serves tonight to find out."

Mayze nodded and thought she should probably leave. The sun was beginning to set and if Sween put the bridge up as early as he had the night before, she might have to sleep outside. Still, she wanted to keep an eye on Gillie and if her suspicions were right, sleeping outside would be worth it.

"'Tis my turn to bathe," said Neil.

Patrick nodded. "We will guard you. There may be more lads coming to side with your brother."

Neil turned to Dugan. "Will the lasses be safe here?"

"Aye, hardly anyone comes to this part of the forest."

"Good." He looked at Gillie and then left with all the men following.

Gillie sighed and Mayze went to sit on the log not far from her. "What is it?"

"I dread having to spend another night in the forest. I much prefer a bed."

Mayze nodded. "So do I. Why do you have bruises?"

"'Tis nothing. Someone hit me, but that was days ago and I am healing."

"MacGreagor lads do not hit lasses."

"So I have heard. Would Neil hurt a lass?"

"I have known him for years and I have yet to hear an angry word come out of his mouth. Nay, he would never hurt a lass."

"No matter what she did?"

Mayze wrinkled her brow. "What do you mean?"

Gillie started to fluff her hair with both hands to dry it. "Well, sometimes a lass makes a mistake. I was wondering if Neil has a forgiving heart."

"Do you love Neil?"

"I am not sure. He is very handsome, but I hardly know him well enough to love him."

"Any lass would be proud to be his wife and Neil can have his pick. But he will need a very special lass," said Mayze.

"In what way?"

She definitely didn't like this woman. Gillie was asking how to win Neil's heart and Mayze wasn't about to let that happen. She saw the opening and decided to take it. "Well, the lass Neil chooses will be the MacGreagor Mistress. She will have to be stern with his followers and watch what they do and say. 'Tis her duty to see that everyone is dressed properly and clean. Clean is very important to the MacGreagor laird."

"I see."

Gillie got quiet and Mayze was beginning to feel just a little bit guilty for lying, but not enough to tell the truth. "We do not have extra plaids to keep you warm tonight. I am sorry."

"I will have the one Neil is wearing, 'twill be enough."

"Oh yes, I had not thought of that. Good then." Mayze was not sorry she stayed; she wanted to tell Dugan how she felt about Gillie. Neil looked at Gillie for a long moment before he went to bathe and remembering it now alarmed Mayze more than a little.

*

Neil glanced up at the sky, noticed how late it was getting and didn't even take the time to pleat his plaid before he started back. He didn't want Gillie to be alone and thought Mayze might have left her there. He was relieved when he saw both still together, so he stepped behind a tree and finished dressing while his men gathered in the small clearing.

Dugan smiled, offered his hand and helped Mayze stand up. "We need to get you back. I could find nothing on my hunt and will have to stay outside. Please do not let anything happen to you."

She glanced at the others, knew they were listening and was so embarrassed she wanted to disappear. But there were more important things to worry about. Mayze couldn't wait to get Dugan alone, took his hand and started off. "I will be careful." She was still talking as they walked through the trees. "You fret too much. Tomorrow, we should..." She glanced back, decided they were still not far enough away and pulled him until they were almost running. Then she stopped.

He thought she wanted to be kissed, but when she put her cheek to his and began to whisper, he listened intently. As soon as she finished, he pulled away and looked her in the eye. "They will sleep alone together tonight."

"You must go back and tell Patrick to stay with them. We cannot let her claim Neil has bedded her. She will force him to marry her, I am sure of it."

"She may claim it anyway; they were alone together last night."

Mayze had to think for a minute. "Well, there is nothing we can do about that. But we can do something about this and any future nights."

"Agreed." Dugan quickly kissed her and headed back. He was trying to think of a way to get Patrick alone when he nearly ran into him and three of the five men. Dugan put his head close to Patrick and kept his voice low. "Mayze doesn't like her and Mayze likes everyone."

Patrick's voice was even softer. "We do not like her either. We left two men with him; they will see him safe, even from her."

*

There was little left to do but sleep and they all needed it. Neil gave Gillie the extra MacDonald plaid, but before he moved away, she motioned him closer. When he bent down on one knee, she had a disgusted look on her face. "Dugan's pleats are crooked."

Neil had no idea what to say to that, so he just nodded and went to find a place to lie down. The last thing he needed to consider was Dugan's pleats and her words boggled his mind. He shook his head to clear his thoughts, turned on his side and tried to go to sleep. The guards were still standing and it bothered him, so he sat up. "Kessan, no one is going to attack us. Get some rest. There is much to do tomorrow and I need you at your best."

Kessan nodded and the place he found to lie down was right

between Neil and Gillie. She gave him a cold look, he noticed and was glad. Walrick moved leaves with his foot and made his bed on the other side of her.

Neil tried again to sleep, but his mind was racing. He thought of the war with Sween, but there was little to decide until he knew more. He remembered and said a little prayer for the hungry families inside the wall. Hopefully, they would be fed soon. Then he thought about Dugan's crooked pleats. Why the hell had she said that? She was a little odd, but he didn't think she was daft. Neil had to force himself to concentrate on something else so he could sleep. His mother once told him to think of a clear stream and pretend to watch a leaf float down it. He tried that.

*

Inside the wall, Mayze was chilled to the bone. She sat near the small stone hearth in her cottage, but they had little wood left to burn. Earlier, she talked to some of the other women about the wine and had a pretty good idea of when Sween would run out. Her mother was at the wall and her hungry brothers and sisters were wide awake hoping for something to fill their empty stomachs.

It seemed like hours, but when her mother finally opened the door carrying a large pot, the smell of cooked food filled the cottage. Mayze quickly grabbed bowls and filled them, and then she sat the youngest one on the table and fed her.

"I have never seen so much food," her mother whispered. "Thank goodness we have MacGreagors on the outside. Twelve families have been taken out and tomorrow night another twelve will go. Tell Neil we love him."

"I will." As soon as her sister was full, Mayze gorged on what was left. She hoped someone remembered to take food to Neil and *that* woman. Then she got the little ones into bed. She and her mother took off their plaids and covered the children. Another cold night would not kill her, Mayze supposed. Wearing nothing but her long shirt, she curled up close to her mother.

CHAPTER V

Neil woke to the smell of cooked eggs and meat. He couldn't remember a time when he needed food more. Gillie was already eating and so were Patrick and his men. He quickly sat up. "Did the food make it over the wall?"

Patrick hurried to swallow. "Aye, we are eating what is left now. The lasses cooked too much, but they will cook less tonight and we got twelve families out."

"How many are left inside?"

"I do not know. Maybe Mayze will know when she comes." Patrick took another bite and savored the taste. He hated to say anything that would hurt his laird, but if he did not tell him, someone else would. "Sween pulled your mother's tapestries off the walls and threw them out the window."

Neil was disgusted. "I am glad she is not here to see that."

"He is drunk, Neil, he does not know what he is doing. He loved your mother, I know he did."

"Just not enough."

They finished eating in silence and one of the men gathered the bowls. "What do you want us to do this morning?" he asked.

"Kessan, have you the lads pledges yet?"

"Not yet. I will finish that this morning."

"Good, try to keep a count and find two lads to take Gillie to the

Camerons."

"Nay!" She almost shouted it and alarmed all the men.

Neil slowly stood up and glared at her. "You will come with me." She was quick to obey and follow. He was furious by the time he got her far enough away to talk to her privately. "You are not to..." She was in his arms, her face was tilted up and her lips were more than he could resist. His kiss was gentle, but hers was so hard and demanding it shocked him. He grabbed both her arms and moved her away. "What are you doing?"

She smiled sweetly, "I am falling in love."

"I do not have time for that now. You will do as I say or I will never see you again. Do you understand?" He was surprised at his own harshness, took a deep breath and drew her to him again. He closed his eyes and held her for a long moment. "I want you out of danger. You will go to the Cameron hold and wait for me there. Agreed?"

She was reluctant but finally nodded. "You will bring me back?"

"I promise." He kissed her lightly on the lips.

"Do you love me?"

Neil sighed. "I am not likely to live through this war. Sween is ten times more cunning and stronger than I. If I somehow manage to survive, we will talk of love after." He took her hand and led her back through the trees.

Once they were both seated again, he remembered exactly where he left off. "Kessan, send someone to find two lads to take Gillie to the Camerons."

"Aye." Kessan nodded to Ronan, who quickly got up and left. "Do you want me to count the old and the youngest warriors?"

"Nay, I hope to settle this without a war."

Patrick looked alarmed. "Do you mean to fight Sween?"

"I do."

"But you said you would not kill him."

"True and I will not, but I can still try to shame him."

Kessan looked just as alarmed. "How will you get him to come out?"

"I know how to do it, but we can do nothing until the families are outside the wall."

When Dugan broke through the trees, he was breathless and could hardly speak. "Another fifty lads." He leaned over and gasped for air. "They bring almost as many lasses."

Neil stared at Dugan for a moment, and then ran his hands through his wet hair and stared at the ground. The men kept quiet to let him think.

While he waited, Patrick watched Gillie. She seemed happy and Patrick was worried about what Neil might have promised her. At least she would be gone for now and that would give him time to talk to Neil.

Finally, Neil resolved the questions in his mind and when he spoke, it was just above a whisper. "Sween has had six years to plan this and he knows he will never gain the loyalty of the MacGreagors. Somehow, the word of his success has gone out across the Highlands and I believe he means to let our people die and build his own clan."

No one spoke for several minutes. Each tried to come to grips with the possibility and it made sense. The families were starving and Sween was letting them. At last, Patrick spoke up. "He can kill the ones inside, but he cannot kill the rest of us."

Winded again finally, Dugan said, "But if the families die, they must know we would no longer supply food or wine. We could even keep them from getting to the water."

Neil shook his head, "You forget about the lasses they bring with them. We are MacGreagors and we do not let lasses die if we can prevent it."

Kessan bowed his head. "They have us then."

"But once they got hungry, the lads would surely send the lasses out," Dugan argued.

Patrick rolled his eyes, "Mungo would rather see the lasses starve. We must kill that scunner at the first possible moment."

Neil nodded. "I completely agree. Set archers to watch the windows. Perhaps they will get their chance. Tell them not to kill Sween, we need him alive."

Patrick took a deep breath and let it out. "This is worse than I thought, if the lasses bear children, this could go on for years."

"Aye," agreed Neil. He held up his hand to quiet them so he could turn another idea over in his mind. Without actually looking at her, he noticed Gillie was combing her beautiful long hair with her fingers and not paying attention. He kept quiet for a few more minutes and then closed his eyes. "I will challenge my brother. If he does not accept the challenge, we will have no choice. We will have to burn them out as soon as our families are safe."

Kessan gasped, "Burn our own homes?"

"Do you really want to live in them after the swine have used our beds? We will burn the place and build new."

"Even the Keep?"

"Even that. My father would approve and so would my mother."

"But the lasses would die," gasped Dan.

"We will start the fire in the back. The lads will run over the bridge first and the lasses will follow. Or perhaps they will use the lasses as shields. Either way, the lasses will be out."

Patrick wasn't so sure but Neil was their laird and he took a pledge to obey. He glanced at the other faces and they didn't look convinced either. He sure hoped Neil knew what he was doing.

*

Inside the wall, Mayze strolled up the path and noticed something very odd. She stopped to get a better look and when she realized her eyes were not playing tricks on her, she knocked on the nearest cottage door. As soon as Steppen answered, Mayze quickly went inside. Steppen's mother was sobbing and Steppen did not know what to do.

Mayze pulled up a chair opposite the woman and sat down. "What is it?"

"I almost did not get out. The lads kept..."

Mayze saw the look of horror on Steppen's face and interrupted her. "Listen to me, there is no one watching the door in the wall." But the woman kept sobbing and Mayze had to take a firm hold on her shoulders. "Do you hear me? Take the children and go outside the wall."

Steppen was instantly excited and could hardly contain herself. "Mother, we can escape now." She grabbed hold of her mother's hand and started to pull. Mayze pulled too and finally got the distraught mother on her feet and calmed down.

Relieved, Mayze opened the door and peeked out. She saw no one so she quickly ushered them around the cottage and to the wall. Steppen's mother pulled the hidden door on the inside wall out and let Steppen go through first to push the outside door away. Steppen helped her little sister and both eased their bodies into the water of the moat. They were finally free.

Before Steppen's mother headed through, Mayze grabbed her arm. "How much wine is left inside?"

"I doubt there is any. I think Sween is sobering."

Mayze put the door back in place and was about to go to the next cottage when she heard the shouts of several men in the courtyard. She crept down the path and found a place to hide so she could watch.

The people on horseback just kept coming across the bridge. She was not happy to see them and especially not happy to see more women in the laps of the men. Yet some women were smiling and others were not. The ones who were not seemed to hold their heads high with pride. The ones who looked happy cared not what they wore or even if their legs were properly covered. It sickened Mayze.

The distraction in the courtyard meant it was an even better time to take more families out, so she went to the next cottage and then the next to alert them.

*

Ronan came back to Neil's hiding place in the forest and brought two men to take Gillie to the Camerons. Neil nodded to each and then turned to look at her. A beam of sunlight through the trees lit up her face. Her hair glistened and her lips were so enticing, he wanted to kiss her. He went to her, but when she started to put her arms around his neck, he prevented it.

She saw no opportunity to argue and finally relented, but not before she leaned closer and said, "I love you." Then she walked away.

Neil watched her disappear into the forest and waited until he could not hear their movements before he turned to the men and whispered. "We must find a new place."

Patrick was relieved and nodded. Perhaps Neil wasn't falling under her spell after all. He had known women like her before and knew exactly what she was. Gillie often looked into his eyes and the eyes of the other men when Neil couldn't see. Her boldness was flirtatious, it made them all uncomfortable and he hoped never to have to tell Neil.

Ronan abruptly slapped Patrick on the back. "Mayze got your family out."

Patrick was so relieved, his knees went weak and he dropped to the ground. "How? Did she bring them through the courtyard?"

"Nay, Sarah saw them come out the hidden door and ran to get help. I do not know how Mayze manages, but there is a constant stream coming through the doors and there are people gathered on the other side of the moat to help the little ones out of the water."

Neil couldn't believe it. "Why would Mungo let them out so easily?"

Patrick wondered the same. "Perhaps 'tis not Mungo but Sween who frees them."

"My brother suddenly has a heart? He must be out of wine."

"Do you really intend to burn the place?" Kessan asked.

"Burn our own homes? Have you gone daft? Come, we must leave this place and find another." He started to lead them through the trees, but Ronan took hold of his arm, nodded and handed him a sword.

Neil carefully withdrew the sword from its sheath and studied it. "This is your father's sword."

"He would want you to have it. 'Twill honor our family if you wear it."

Neil nodded and shoved it back in the sheath. Then he tied the strings around his waist and adjusted the sword. "Do any of you have horses?"

Lorne nodded. "I have mine and I have your horse as well. Dumb stubborn animal it is too."

"Where?"

"This way." Lorne started south and the men followed. When they came to the path leading from the bridge to the loch, they cautiously crossed it and kept quiet until they were well away.

Neil turned to Lorne, "You have to pat my horse on the nose often."

"Nay, *you* have to pat him on the nose often. I will be glad to get him off my hands."

Neil chuckled. He stopped for a moment and looked back at his men. "I want you to know I had already chosen all of you as my advisors, except Dugan. Now I have him as well."

"Dugan is a better lad than I realized," said Kessan, ignoring the fact that Dugan was right behind him.

Neil suddenly thought of something. "Whatever you do, do not let them bury Cormick."

"Why?" Patrick asked.

"We need him." He didn't elaborate, dismissed the confused looks on their faces and let Lorne continue to lead them to his horse. When he saw his stallion grazing in the clearing, Neil's eyes lit up and the horse quickly came to him. He patted the horse's nose and hugged his neck. Then he gave the stallion a stern look. "You abandoned me."

The horse hung his head and everyone chuckled.

"I forgive you. Would you like to go for a ride?" This time the horse nodded, and Neil was thrilled to grab hold of his mane and swing himself up. He didn't forget to lean down and hug the horse's neck just as his mother taught him. He saw Lorne give his horse to Patrick and waited for him to mount.

Then Neil turned to look at the rest of the men. "We will meet back here. Kessan, send a lad to watch each door and the bridge. I want a full report on everything going in and coming out. Then set the archers and get the pledges."

He waited for Kessan's nod and then turned his horse north. He crossed the path to the loch again and kept going until he circled around to the back of the hold. Just as Ronan said, the people were coming out. He wanted to go to them, but they were being very quiet and he didn't want to cause a stir. He moved on until he came to a cluster of newly built cottages farther north.

Neil stopped and whistled. Instantly, the families came out and he began to walk his horse through them, touching their hands and reassuring them with his smiles. There were three women named Rose in the clan and to tell them apart, they put a number after each name:

Rose One, Rose Two and Rose Three, who was the youngest. When he spotted Rose Three's daughter, he quickly got down and opened his arms to her. She cried for her slain mother and he comforted her. Then he got back on his horse and looked out over the gathered people. "'Twill all be over soon, I promise. Make ready, there will be a battle. I wish it were not so and I will prevent it if I can, but make ready."

Neil saw the dread in their eyes and also saw their dread turn to determination. They would do as he asked and he was well pleased. For three more hours he rode from place to place, gathered the people living outside the wall and let them see he was alive. He gave them the same command and saw in each the same determination.

Finally, he and Patrick were alone in a clump of trees. Neil patted his horse's neck three times and closed his eyes. Patrick marveled at the love the horse had for Neil. At Neil's pat, the horse stood perfectly still. He did not shift his weight, stretch his neck to graze or even swat his tail. Like a stone statue, the horse let Neil relax.

Patrick let him rest too, though he was mindful to keep a close eye out for danger. Through the trees, he could see Steppen, his two brothers, his mother and his youngest sister outside the wall and safe. He remembered to breathe. At twelve, Steppen was starting to develop into a woman and Patrick feared she would fall prey to one of Sween's men. It was a worry he was happy not to have now. God help the man who laid a hand on his precious Steppen.

Patrick realized how tired he was too and wished he had Neil's ability to rest. Kevin taught Neil how to do that and when this was over, maybe Neil would teach him. The moment Neil raised his head and straightened his shoulders, it startled Patrick. "What?"

"Sween's lads will be wearing MacGreagor plaids."

"You are right, the battle will be ten times harder if we all wear the same. 'Tis a good thing you thought of that. We can mark ours somehow."

"How?"

"I do not know, but Dena will. This way." Patrick urged his horse toward the side of a hill.

"Who is Dena?"

"What? I am shocked to the bone. You do not know who Dena is?"

Neil tried hard to think who she might be. "I thought I knew everyone."

"Fret not, she is a weaver who came to live with her aunt recently." When they got to the road leading to the Keep, Patrick turned them south instead.

Just then, they heard shouts coming from the hold. Both quickly turned their horses around and raced toward the bridge. It wasn't hard to figure out what was happening. The bridge was going up and dozens of people were outside shaking their fists and shouting their rage.

When Kessan ran to him, Neil leaned down to hear his words above the noise.

"We got everyone out, save…"

"Who?"

"Agnes. Sween's lads got to her and…she is dead."

Neil closed his eyes and then sat up straight. He slowly lifted his gaze and stared at the only window in the Keep that faced his direction. Sween was watching him. His hair was unkempt, he wore no shirt and had no strip of MacGreagor cloth covering his heart. He did not look drunk.

For a moment, Neil felt that old familiar twinge of pity for his brother. How different life could have been for him and for them all. But now two men and four women were dead, and Sween would have to pay the price. He didn't take his eyes off his brother, but spoke to Patrick. "Go see Dena and get what we need, then meet me at Cormick's cottage. Tell Kessan to send the people away. Tell them the only noise I want to hear is that of the people inside. Sween will lower the bridge when we are gone and we need to know everything."

He saw Mungo walk up behind his brother and hit him on the back. The slug nearly knocked Sween out the window. Mungo was as unpleasant to look at as he had been six years ago. His hair and beard were too long, his clothing was wrinkled, his sneer was obnoxious and Neil could watch it no more, so he turned and rode across the meadow. He threaded his way through the trees and then up the side of the hill where he had last seen Connor and Rachel. Neil paused only a moment to look back before he quickly rode down the other side.

*

In the front of the hold, Lorne ran to Kessan. "He rides alone, 'tis not safe."

"Aye, but our horses are inside. Besides, he commanded us to watch the doors."

"Did we not take a vow to protect him?"

Kessan considered that. "Aye we did. Four lads can watch the doors well enough. We will borrow horses and find him." Lorne ran down the road and took the path to the nearest cottage, while Kessan told the people to move away, and then appointed another man to keep watch.

Five minutes later, they were both mounted on borrowed horses. They raced through the meadow and trees, and then up the hillside.

"Where do you think he went?" asked Lorne.

"He goes to tell Agnes' family," Kessan answered.

"Just like Kevin would have."

"Aye."

CHAPTER VI

Neil had a hundred things to do, but nothing was more important than being the first to tell children their mother would not be coming home. Her husband took it as well as any man would and kept his emotions under control for the children's sake. Agnes only went inside the wall to make sure her sister was safe.

Neil let the children cry for a moment and then got down on one knee and quieted them. "The time to cry is not yet. The inside families need your help, will you do it?"

Even the little one nodded. "Good. The children need a place to sleep and every family on the outside must help feed them and keep them warm. When this is over, we will all mourn together. Ross, you are the oldest. Go to the back of the wall and find Mayze. She will tell you which family to bring back."

They were being so brave, it broke his heart. But he stood up, nodded to their father and walked out. He prayed they would not also lose their father in the battle that was sure to come. As soon as he stepped out, he found Kessan and Lorne waiting for him. He was surprised and yet pleased they wanted to protect him. He got back on his horse and headed over the hill. "Have you a report?"

"Sween lowered the bridge again. How did you know he would do that?" Kessan asked, but Neil didn't answer.

When they reached the top of the hill, they stopped to look at the hold below. The land was still green and beautiful, but there were men and women inside the wall displaying their pleasures openly. Neil didn't want to see anymore, urged his horse down into the trees and headed for the back of the wall.

The people were all out now and there was a special woman he badly wanted to hold in his arms. Happy to see him, his followers shouted his name and touched his hand as he passed. Neil leaned down to touch as many children as he could and when he finally spotted her, he quickly slid down off his horse. She was right where she should be...standing beside Dugan.

He didn't open his arms and wait for her to come to him; instead, he went to her, wrapped his arms around her, kissed her cheek and swung her around.

Mayze smacked his arm, "Put me down, you brute."

He looked wounded, did as she demanded and then kissed her forehead before he released her. "When this is over, I will grant your heart's desire."

She quickly put her hand in Dugan's. "You are too late."

Neil approved and then his expression turned serious. "How many families are still without a place to stay?"

"Five, but the outsiders are still coming to collect them."

"And your family?"

"We will stay with Ronan and his wife. You heard about Agnes? I could not..."

Neil noticed a tear beginning to form in her eye and knew keeping her busy would take her mind off of Agnes. "You did the best you could. I need your help still, are you willing?"

"Aye."

"Get some rest and tell the others to do the same. We will have a peaceful night tonight. Then meet me at the new hiding place in the morning." He saw Mayze's nod first and then looked to Dugan. Once he also nodded, Neil got back on his horse. "I will need both of you to find something in the forest for me. Bring your noon meal; 'twill likely take all day."

*

Neil headed east toward Cormick's cottage and was pleased to find Patrick riding toward him. He stopped and waited for his report.

Patrick pulled his horse to a halt. "Dena has red dye. We can mark our shoulders with it."

"That will work." He urged his horse forward.

Patrick turned his horse around and pulled up beside him. "What do you hope to do?"

"For now we must wait to see what Mungo will do next. He may be so enraged at the loss of his prisoners, he will kill Sween for us and make himself laird. He will be easier to fight."

Patrick wiped the perspiration off his face and neck with a cloth. "Mungo probably plans to do that anyway."

They rode in silence down the narrow path and when they came to Cormick's cottage, Neil held up his hand; he would see the widow alone. Once inside, he walked to the table where the warrior's body lay washed and prepared for burial. He looked upon the face, closed his eyes and lowered his head for a moment. Then he did as his father always did and held the aging widow in his arms to comfort her.

Neil released her, urged her to sit and sat down next to her on the bed. "What I am about to ask is a horrible thing and I hope you will find it in your heart to forgive me. I will tell you alone my plan so you will understand, but I must have your pledge not to tell anyone. Do you agree?"

The widow wiped her tears off her cheeks and nodded.

"Good, this is what I need. We..."

*

Neil was exhausted and when he led his men back to the new hiding place, he quickly dismounted, hugged his horse and set him free to graze. Then he headed for the loch to swim and get clean again. The air was muggy and he hoped the rain would hold off for another day or two.

A thousand baths would not take away the hurt in his heart. He hurt for the families, for those who died, for himself and even for his brother. Then he hurt for what he knew was coming. He only swam once across and once back, but it helped. Patrick, Kessan and Lorne quickly bathed and just as quickly dressed. Then they all went back to the clearing to wait for news.

Neil finally realized he would be waiting for hours if he didn't do something. "Kessan, we need four more men to watch the doors and relieve those posted. Have them changed every two hours or so." He watched Kessan leave and then stretched out on the grass to rest. Flat on his back, he watched the wind push the clouds across the sky. "Patrick, when will Yule be back?"

"Soon, should I go find him?"

"Aye, tell him the families are out and show him where we are." While Lorne stood guard, Neil turned his eyes away and watched the clouds once more. He wanted to sleep and not have to think at all, but that was not to be. He tried to see every angle of his plan and imagine what his brother and Mungo would do to try to stop him. Then he tried to think of another plan in case the first one didn't work. But when Mayze suddenly broke through the trees, he sat up.

A completely drained Mayze dumped several plaids she'd gotten from the outside families on the ground next to Neil and then plopped down on top of them. "Dugan told me where to find you." She opened a bag, unwrapped a cloth and showed him a slab of cooked beef. "The people want all of you fed and fit. Do not argue with them, they are determined. I also have apples and cheese and..."

"Mayze."

"What?" She finally looked at Neil.

"I have never seen you angry."

"This is not anger, this is fury. How dare they try to starve the children! They took our extra plaids, the wood was nearly gone for our fires and we had nothing to keep us warm at night. And if that is not enough, they raped and killed Agnes. I tell you, Laird MacGreagor, I am furious enough to kill them all myself."

It was the first time anyone called him that and Neil couldn't help but smile. Besides, no one deserved to be comforted by his smile, more than Mayze. "I know a lad who would love to keep you warm at night."

Mayze suddenly realized she had been ranting and was embarrassed for a moment. But it wasn't long before her expression changed and showed her terror. "I nearly got slain. Mungo was yelling and coming up the path with his sword drawn. I only just got the last child out and closed the door in time. After I got out of the moat, my whole body was shaking and I wanted to scream. Maybe I did, I cannot be sure. Dugan had to threaten to toss me back in the water to calm me down." She paused to catch her breath. "It worked; I got mad at him instead."

Neil raised an eyebrow. "How badly did you hurt Dugan?"

Finally Mayze relaxed, "He will live to fight another day."

Neil didn't have time to comfort her or even talk to her any longer. Patrick and Yule came out of the trees. Neil got to his feet and locked forearms with Yule Cameron. "I am very happy to see you."

"I am very happy to see you are still alive." said Yule.

Neil released him. "I want you to meet Mayze. She saved all the people inside the wall today." He took the plaid she handed him and spread it on the ground for his guest.

Yule nodded to Mayze and sat down on the cloth. "What do you want the Camerons to do?"

While Patrick took up a position to stand guard with Lorne, Neil sat back down. "Are the Cameron's missing any lasses?"

"Two, how did you know?"

"By our count, there are as many lasses inside as there are lads, but no children. Lasses do not leave their children behind unless they are forced. I suspect Sween holds the women for ransom."

Disgusted, Yule closed his eyes and shook his head. "I spotted two of our lads inside and should have known. The missing lasses refused to marry them. This is a bigger mess than I thought. I must send someone to tell Blair."

"Aye, if you have lasses missing, then other clans may as well."

"But Sween must know the clans will come to fight with you."

"True, but if they hold the lasses hostage, who would dare attack? Have the Camerons heard anything about Laird MacDonald?"

"Only that he is furious you escaped. He blames a lass named Gillie. Is it true?"

"Aye, I sent her to your hold."

"When?"

"This morning."

"I am sorry, my friend, but we found two MacGreagors tied to trees on our way here, and the lass was gone."

Just then Kessan, Walrick, Dan and Ronan walked into the clearing. "They are hauling in all the water they can," reported Kessan.

Neil rolled his eyes. "I guess we know where Gillie went."

"You did not prefer her?" asked Patrick.

Walrick and Dan took up the posts of protection and let Patrick and Kessan join Yule and Neil on the cloth.

"I preferred her for about an hour. Before all this started, Mayze told me Sween had many unfamiliar lasses in his cottage, and the more Gillie talked, the more I believed she was one of them." Neil leaned over and slapped his second in command on the back. "I like to think I have a wee bit more wit than that."

Neil noticed everyone looked relieved, even Mayze. "What else is happening?" When none of them offered more, he was quiet for a moment before he said, "We will not let any more of Sween's lads in now that our people are safe. We will set a guard to watch the road and have warriors sleep in the meadow in case they are needed. See that torches are lit in the back near the wall so we can watch the hidden doors. If any come out, cut them down. And we will send someone to tell Laird MacDonald the families are out. Perhaps he will not think to help Sween when he knows. Then we will see to our evening meal and rest. Tomorrow there is much to do."

Dugan looked pale when he finally came to give his report. "Gillie is inside, she has betrayed you."

Neil nodded, "I know. They will be awake all of this night and every night waiting for a fire that will not come. By the time we are ready to fight, they will be spent."

Dugan sank to the ground in relief. "I did not want to be the one to tell you."

Abruptly, Neil's horse walked to the semicircle of seated men and Neil suspected he knew why. The horse lowered his head and as his mother taught him, Neil looked at the reflection in the horse's eye. There was a man behind him in the trees. Neil grabbed the horse's head, pulled himself up, drew his sword and spun around. "Do not make me kill you."

Dugan got Mayze out of the way while the other warriors drew their swords and went into the forest. Soon the intruder was surrounded, pulled out of the woods and forced to stand in front of Neil.

But Neil put his sword back in his sheath. "I wondered when we would hear from the Fergusons."

The man shrugged himself loose of his captors and wiped his sweaty palms on his yellow plaid. "You are a hard lad to find."

"That is good to know. Sit and tell me everything."

The Ferguson did as he was told and waited for the others to sit.

"Our Mistress Kenna is beside herself with worry. We have been watching for days and..."

"And our lads have not caught you?" Patrick asked.

"Of course not, if you were able to catch us, 'twould mean you did not teach us well enough."

Patrick bit his lip, "He has a point."

"Go on," said Neil.

"Laird MacDonald is raging mad. We thought he might attack, so Laird Ferguson and three other lairds went to warn him against it. Thirty-six lasses are missing from four clans. And 'tis worse, they have taken Laird Forbes' wife."

Yule rubbed his forehead. "I dare not think how I would feel if they had Maree."

The Ferguson warrior nodded. "We have had a devil of a time calming Forbes down. He wants to kill someone and I am not sure he cares who. Laird Ferguson wants to know how you plan to get the lasses out and what we can do to help."

Neil ran his fingers through his hair. "Tell the lairds they have enough food and water inside to last a few days and we will send more in if needed. The lasses will not go hungry."

"Laird Ferguson thinks with enough horses, we could pull the wall down."

Neil gave that idea serious consideration. "'Tis tempting. If we take it down in the back, we could force them out the front. However, I think my plan will work better. Tell the lairds I will meet with them at sunrise on the Ferguson side of the loch to explain." The Ferguson warrior was getting up to go when Neil thought of something else.

"Tell them not to attack. Sween's lads also wear MacGreagor plaids and they will not know which to kill."

"I understand. Tomorrow at sunrise." Neil watched the Ferguson walk back into the forest and then turned to his men. "How many horses do you think they have inside?"

It was Dugan who answered. "The first day or two they sent most of their horses out and we were not prepared to capture but a few. I do not know about the last fifty that went in."

"They are still in there," Kessan answered.

"How do they intend to keep them alive without hay?" Neil wondered aloud.

Yule Cameron answered, "They plan to stampede them out the front if we attack."

"Or eat them," Kessan put in.

Patrick shook his head, "How did they ever hope to win?"

"I doubt my brother seriously thought about winning."

"Gillie did," Mayze muttered. When Neil turned to her, she continued, "She asked me who would win if you fought Sween and then she asked if you would forgive her if you learned she had made a mistake."

"What did you say?"

"I told her I hoped you would *not* fight and yes, I thought you would forgive her. I asked, but she did not explain what she wanted you to forgive her for. I ..." Suddenly Mayze remembered what she did. "I tricked her. Gillie wanted to know how to win your heart, but not in those words exactly. I did not like her so I lied. I told her the MacGreagor mistress must make sure everyone was properly dressed hoping she would do something and you would think her daft."

Neil remembered now too. "So that is why she told me Dugan's pleats were crooked. She does not care who wins, she only wants to be mistress of the one who does."

Dugan was shocked and looked down at his kilt. "My pleats are crooked?"

Patrick ignored him. "She thinks Sween will win."

"I think she chose wrong." Neil reached over and took Mayze's hand. "I can see how tired you are. Dugan will take you back. In the morning, bring a pot to heat water and a bowl. If I am not back when you get here, find as many dead roses as you can."

Mayze wrinkled her brow but didn't argue. "I will do it."

"You will tell no one and let no one see you gather the roses. We cannot abide a mistake, do you understand?"

"I understand. Come future husband." She put out her hand, let Dugan help her to her feet and walked with him back into the trees.

"Lorne, tomorrow you will take a lad you trust and go to Cormick's cottage. His wife will give you what you need and a cart to bring it in. Keep it hidden in the forest north of the wall. Leave a lad there to guard it and come give me your report. Patrick will come with me to meet the lairds. Kessan, go to Dena and get her dye."

"What can we do?" Ronan asked.

"You, Walrick and Dan will get two carts and fill them with hay for the horses inside the wall. They must be hungry and we do not want them to trample the lasses trying to find a way out. Leave the carts in front of the bridge and walk away. When Sween's lads go out to get them, perhaps they will also let some of the horses out."

Dan nodded. "Done."

"There is one more thing I must ask of all of you. I need two lads willing to go inside the wall at night." All of his men volunteered and Neil was pleased. "I have not yet thought of a way to get Sween's guards away from one of the hidden doors."

Ronan was quick to make a suggestion. "We could cause some sort of distraction at the front."

"What sort of a distraction?" Neil asked.

Said Patrick, "We could use wine. They should be out and they would all go to the courtyard for that. In fact, they might fight over it."

Neil's eyes lit up. "Aye, they *would* fight over it."

Yule studied Neil's tired eyes and then looked away. "I would like to stay the night with you and see the lairds so I can give a full report to Blair."

"I will be happy to have you."

"In that case, I will send a rider to tell Blair our lasses are inside. I will be back."

*

Neil hardly slept at all, so waking up early enough was no problem. He roused Patrick and Yule, mounted his horse, waited for them to mount and headed for the loch. Already, the other lairds were there waiting and the sun had not yet risen.

With their guards far enough away not to hear, the lairds listened as Neil explained what happened, told them what he planned and why. Then he was ready to hear their suggestions.

Laird Ferguson was the first to speak. "We are with you. Your plan will work as well as anything we have come up with."

"They will still use the lasses as shields, even when they come out," said Forbes.

"Aye, but we can make them think we are as frightened of the plague as they are."

"Let them go free?" asked Laird Kerr.

"Aye and let them spread out. In smaller numbers, they will be easier to kill. The Camerons will wait on their side, the Fergusons on theirs and the rest will wait in the south. I expect most will run toward England."

Laird Forbes nodded. "'Tis a sound plan, but we will need time to gather our lads. What if they go north?"

Neil leaned a little closer and lowered his voice just in case. "What Laird MacDonald fears most is a plague. Once he hears, he will not attack nor will he let anyone wearing a MacGreagor plaid near his land. Sween's lads will be easy to hunt down."

Laird Ferguson agreed. "Forbes is right, we will need three days. What else can we do to help?"

"Three days?" Neil paused to consider that. "Cormick's body will not keep another three days and I hoped to use him to convince Sween's lads the plague is deadly. But perhaps we can think of some other way. We can use all the wine you can spare. There are two hundred and fifty inside, not counting the lasses, and they have exhausted our supply. The Camerons brought some, but 'tis not nearly enough."

Laird Ferguson asked, "Neil, suppose you tear the wall down so the horses can get out. We can better track the lads if they are on foot."

Neil nodded. "We have been worried hungry horses might

trample the women. We planned to give them hay today, but perhaps we should pull the wall down instead. They have several of our horses inside too and if they are still alive, we could use them. But 'twill not be easy, the wall is four feet wide in some places."

Patrick finally spoke up, "But 'tis only two feet near the stables and the wall is cracked in some places. Kevin always meant to have it repaired."

"Done then. We will do that today and wait until you gather your lads."

Laird Forbes was upset and having a hard time controlling his emotions. "Have you seen my wife?"

"Nay, but I have not yet met her. There is a hill from which you can see in and perhaps you can point her out. I will take you there."

"Wait here," Forbes said. As all the others lairds did, Laird Forbes went to his men and gave his orders.

Neil heaved a sigh of relief. "Patrick, go tell Dan and Ronan not to deliver the hay and tell Lorne not to collect Cormick's body. Let his wife get on with the burial." He watched Patrick and Yule leave and when they were ready, he led the lairds to the southern tip of the loch and then into the trees. Soon they were on the other side of the hold and on top of the hill.

In the early light of dawn, five lairds sat tall on their stout horses wearing plaids of different colors. Each of them was horrified by the squalor they could see inside the wall. Agnes' naked body lay on the top of a thatched roof. The gardens were destroyed, tree limbs had been broken and anxious horses wandered the paths or tried to grasp high leaves off the trees. Men and women alike lay half in and half out of cottage doors, some without clothing.

"I can bear no more," Laird Forbes muttered.

"Do you see your wife?" asked Neil.

"Nay, she must be inside. At least she is not the woman on the roof."

"Who stands in the window?" Laird Kerr asked.

"My brother. He knows the MacGreagors will not kill him." For a moment, he could see Gillie standing behind Sween so he looked away. "I promised my mother I would not order his death."

Laird Kerr started down the hill. "Your mother did not know he would do this."

*

Neil ordered archers to take up positions in the meadow outside the moat and men with iron bars and wooden mallets began destroying the wall. Twice Sween's men appeared at the top of the wall, but Neil's archers were quick to take their lives. As soon as holes were made at intervals and dirt was pulled out, ropes were threaded through and teams of horses across the moat pulled sections of the outside wall down.

More wall came down than expected each time, and most of it tumbled into the moat. The dirt filler between the inside and the outside wall was easy to clear away, and by the time the second outside section was prepared, two more of Sween's men were shot atop the wall. A gathering crowd outside the moat watched and cheered.

Neil often looked up at the Keep window hoping Mungo would show himself. Neither he nor Sween appeared. He let the people enjoy their small victory until he thought the horses inside might trample them once they were let out. Before noon, his men had several holes punched through the inside wall and it was weakened enough to topple over on its own. All they had to do was wait.

Yet when it didn't fall, two of the workmen standing between the wall and the moat decided to help it along. They picked up good-sized rocks from the crumbled outside wall, aimed at the ancient mortar holding the inside wall together and hurled them at the bottom. The wall began to sway but then it stabilized. Again, the men hurled rocks and as it started to fall toward them, they quickly got out of the way. Just as Neil hoped, the wall collapsed sending more rocks into the moat and a cloud of dust into the air. Finally, enough of the wall was gone for the horses to climb over.

Just before the mounts started out, the archers ran and so did everyone else until they were safe at the edge of the trees. At first, it looked like the horses would kill themselves trying to get out. Two were pushed into the moat and trampled, but the others made it across and managed to climb out of the water. In just a few minutes, the cloud of dust dissipated and it appeared there were no more horses left inside except those still tied up in the stables. There was nothing Neil could do about that.

The lush grass of the meadow tempted the hungry horses and most stayed to graze. That pleased the MacGreagors very much and they got ready to surround and capture them. Some men recognized horses left in the stable before Sween took control and heaved a sigh of relief.

Sween's men quickly gathered inside the wall, crouched down

and prepared for an attack. But the MacGreagors had no intention of fighting them -- not yet. Neil's men were ready, however, if the invaders came out.

Patrick stepped out from behind a tree. "They are out of wine. See how they hold their aching heads? Sween somehow managed to find every drunkard in the Highlands."

Neil spread his feet apart and folded his arms. "Dugan's hunters should be back soon. We will leave the meat and once the bridge is down, they will have two places to defend. 'Twill drive them daft when we do not attack."

"Aye, but they will sleep with their swords in their hands instead of the lasses. Of course they must also post lads to watch for fires." Patrick suddenly bit his lower lip. "Suppose we barter wine for lasses?"

"That is right dead brilliant. We might even dangle a flask or two out of reach."

"Like a mule tempted by a carrot he cannot reach. I would stay up all night to see that."

Neil glanced up at the window of the Keep, No one was there. "Send messengers to tell both the Fergusons and the Camerons of our success. Maybe we can get Laird Forbes' wife out. We could use an alliance with Forbes."

"Aye, we could. I think we might just win this war."

*

The next day, Neil sent most of the red dye back to Dena but saved some back. He realized red would not work since Sween's men could put the same mark on their plaids, but use blood to do it. Then he decided not to mark their plaids after all.

CHAPTER VII

Neil spent the morning showing Mayze and Dugan how to open the dead roses, take out the center without touching it and put it in the bowl. It was tedious work, but they had two days to do it and the more roses they could find, the better. Tomorrow they would steam the ingredient, let the bowl of rose centers bake in the sun and then grind them.

Neil decided to take a ride with Patrick around the outside of the hold to see for himself if all was going according to plan. At the back wall, he stopped to assess the situation. He was pleased to see that all his commands had been obeyed including guards near the once hidden doors. "Did we get the dead horses out of the moat?"

"Aye, last night after dark."

"Perhaps my grandfather's wall was not such a good idea. We might have lost many lives in this war."

"Aye," said Patrick, "but a wooden wall burns. Perhaps we should simply build more hidden doors others do not know about."

"Hopefully we will have time to consider that someday." He softly kicked the side of his horse, rode back around to the front and stopped not far from the missing section of the wall. A new shift of archers were ready, while other men stood between the moat and the outside of the wall, waiting in case Sween's men tried to get out.

Neil was pleased with their efforts, but was concerned about something else. "They might threaten to hurt a woman if we do not give them wine soon. Perhaps now is the best time to barter."

"I do not see the harm in trying." Patrick agreed. "But I will do it, you make a tempting target."

"As you wish." Neil stayed behind and watched.

Patrick untied a flask of wine from his belt, held it up and walked his horse through the archers. "A flask of wine for five lasses," he shouted. He waited for a long time before he heard an answer.

"Five flasks of wine for one lass."

Patrick recognized the voice. It was Mungo and he tried to spot him, but Mungo was staying out of sight. "Two flasks for three lasses."

Mungo's hideous laugh filled the air. "Five flasks for one lass!"

Patrick looked back at Neil. It would take a lot of wine to get all the women out, but it was a start. Then he decided an exception was in order. "We want the lasses you hold hostage, not your lasses. Agreed?" He suddenly realized he wouldn't know the difference, but Mungo didn't know that.

"Leave ten flasks of wine at the bridge and I will send two Kerr lasses out."

"Send the lasses out first and then we will deliver the wine." Patrick quickly rode back to Neil and then turned to watch. A few minutes later, two women made their way over the rocks in the broken wall and as soon as they could reach them, MacGreagor men pulled the women away from the opening.

The women had tears in their eyes, but after so many days inside, what they wanted to do most was bathe, so they quickly slipped into the water. Two of Neil's men went in with them in case they could not swim.

Neil nodded for the wine to be delivered and then rode around to meet the women after they got out. Neither woman was eager to get out. Instead, they submerged several times trying to wash their hair and cleanse their faces. Neil understood, got off his horse and offered his hand to the one nearest. "I am Neil MacGreagor. Come, Laird Kerr is at the Ferguson hold and he will be happy to see you."

He helped them both out and tried not to look too long at their bruised faces. "Can you tell me what is happening inside?" They both started talking at once, and so quickly he could hardly make out what they were saying. Finally, one got quiet and so did the other.

"We cannot go home, we have been shamed."

Neil closed his eyes. For a second, he wondered if Gillie was all right. Then he forced her out of his mind. "If Laird Kerr does not take you back, we will give you a home. 'Tis our fault this has happened."

Both of the women seemed relieved. It was a promise he would give twice more before the day was finished. He sent the women away with MacGreagor women to be fed and then sent a rider to tell Laird Ferguson. None of the women was the wife of Laird Forbes.

By nightfall, Neil's men, five Lairds including Blair Cameron, five second-in-commands, six rescued women, Mayze and more guards than any of them would ever need, were in a clearing that was far too small. And all of them intended to stay until the war was over. His horse wandered off and Neil wished he could too. It was impossible to think clearly. He made sure no one touched the roses or the dye and then started to rub his forehead. He finally realized his head was aching.

Blair Cameron took pity on the youngest laird among them. "You have dark circles under your eyes."

Neil took a deep breath and let it out. "I was not expecting to hold a feast quite this soon."

"Perhaps we should have the feast where Sween can see? I believe your father did that after he had the Fergusons trapped inside." Blair returned the first real smile he had seen on Neil's face in hours. "Your lads are tired, let me make the arrangements"

"Gladly. Perhaps tomorrow they will give us the Cameron lasses."

Blair nodded and then went to talk to his men.

Neil sat down next to Patrick and tried not to think about the bruises on the rescued women or what was happening to the women still inside. He repeatedly ran his fingers through his hair or rubbed his forehead. The image of Agnes' body on the rooftop kept flashing through his mind and he tried not to think about that either, but it was a struggle. He prayed her husband did not know.

Neil needed a body to make his plan work, but not hers and not the body of any other woman. They would have to do it without a body and hope the men inside the wall were sufficiently frightened. Then he wondered who he should send inside. If Sween's men caught them, he could well be sending them to their deaths.

*

On the morning of the second day, the small clearing was a buzz of activity. Messengers came to tell the lairds how close their men were and how much wine they were bringing with them.

Neil showed Mayze and Dugan how to finish the itching powder.

He made a funnel out of a leaf and poured powder into two empty flasks. Next, he chose the two men he would send inside the wall and had them practice flicking red dye so it would make tiny spots on skin. With any luck, the intruders would believe they had the same plague that killed Neil's grandparent's years before. A dead body would make it a lot more frightening, but...

He had to tell Laird Forbes three times why he was not sending in more food. Full stomachs needed more wine to get drunk, but the enraged Forbes was having difficulty accepting that excuse. All he cared about was his wife. Forbes sat with his head in his hands most of the afternoon. The waiting was unbearable for them all. At last, everything was ready and Neil finally got a couple of hours of sleep.

*

Late in the evening of the third day, the lairds hid in the trees near the bridge to watch as Patrick led a mule, with several flasks of wine tied over its back, toward the opening in the broken wall. He hoped Sween's men were thirsty enough to give him more women. "Five flasks for two lasses." Just as it had the day before, it took a long time for Mungo to answer. Patrick could hear swords clashing inside, but couldn't see what was going on. Aye, he thought, now they fight each other.

Finally, the noise stopped and Mungo's voice filled the air. "Five flasks for one lass."

Patrick shrugged. It was worth a try. "I will have ten lasses for fifty flasks, agreed?" The men inside the wall started yelling and before long, their shouts turned to curses. Patrick could just imagine them threatening to cut Mungo's throat if he declined and was trying hard not to smile. The MacGreagors wanted them drunk and they were way too willing to comply. Getting ten women out would be a bonus.

While the other men watched the wall, Neil watched the window, but Sween did not appear and he wondered if his brother was still alive. When he saw Patrick turn to look at him, Neil nodded to Kessan and then to Dan.

Each man led another mule draped with flasks to Patrick. Fifty flasks were not enough to get two hundred and fifty men drunk. But all the lairds were willing to part with as much as it would take, if it took every drop of wine in the highlands.

"Thirty lasses for one hundred and fifty flasks of wine," Patrick shouted. The men inside cheered and Patrick was sure they had just won the war. He got no answer back, but slowly, women began to climb over the rocks where MacGreagor men waited to pull them to safety.

Laird Forbes moved up closer to Neil, bit his lip and examined the face of each woman as she made it through the opening. Beside him, Blair Cameron hoped the women from the Cameron clan would be allowed out. He was disappointed and so was Forbes.

"Just a few more hours." Neil muttered. He nodded for Patrick and the others to take the mules toward the bridge and then watched the bridge lowered into place. He glanced again at the window. This time Gillie was there with Sween behind her. His arms were wrapped around her from behind and both were smiling. Neil turned away.

Once the bridge was down, the men slapped the rumps of the mules and made them run into the courtyard. Soon after, the bridge went back up, but not before they caught a glimpse of Mungo's bloodied body lying on the steps of the Keep. At least one debt was paid.

The lairds went to comfort the rescued women and then eat their evening meal. They each gave their men final orders and watched them leave to take up positions far enough from the hold to catch any men the MacGreagors missed. Then Neil stood before his men in the back of the hold. He thanked them for their loyalty, dipped his arms into a vat of blue die, moved away and nodded. One at a time, his warriors came forward and did the same so the other clans could tell them from Sween's men. Then he told them to rest. They were to be the first line and he wanted them fit.

*

In the darkest hour before dawn, Patrick, Walrick and Dan held the flasks of red dye and itching powder out of the water and swam the moat. Once the outside door was opened in the back wall, the men set it aside and then hoisted Patrick up.

He quietly stretched out on the top of the wall and peeked inside. The campfires were almost out, but there was a little light left. Just as he hoped, the posted guard was sitting with his back against the inside door, either passed out or sound asleep. Patrick pulled a rope out of his shirt, lowered one end to the men outside the wall and waited until they had a firm enough hold to support his weight. Then he eased the other end down on the inside, grabbed hold of it and slid down. With one hand over the man's mouth, he cut his throat and then pushed him out of the way.

He opened the inside door, let the other two men in and stood guard. In less than half an hour, the three completed their task.

Walrick and Dan pulled the dead man out, while Patrick kicked dirt over his blood and removed the rope. Then he went through the wall and closed the doors behind him. They crossed the moat, climbed out and headed for the front of the hold where Neil was anxiously waiting.

As soon as he saw them, Neil heaved a sigh of relief. So far, things were going far better than he hoped. One of the archers posted in the meadow across the moat from the broken wall looked at him and when Neil nodded, the archer smiled. The next move would be theirs. The ten archers were without blue dye on their arms so the men inside would not suspect anything had changed.

*

The sun was up and it looked like Sween's men were never going to wake. The archers were getting tired, the men hidden in the trees were restless, and Neil had just decided it was time to do something about it when he heard a shout inside the wall.

Then another man inside screamed. "Plague! We've got the plague!"

Neil watched his brother come to the window to look down in the courtyard and then heard other men shouting. A few seconds later, the bridge started to come down.

Sween bellowed at his men "'Tis a trick! Keep the bridge up!"

"Nay," a man cried out. He started to climb the rocks in the broken wall when one of Sween's guards grabbed him and pulled him back. The man looked up at Sween. "'Tis not a trick, see." He opened his shirt and showed his spots. Then he started scratching and the power of suggestion made others start to itch. Terror filled the guard's eyes, he quickly released the man and started to climb over the rocks himself.

Neil's archers outside the wall were ready. But instead of shooting, they got to their feet and began to run away yelling, "PLAGUE" as loud as they could. When the bridge came down, the path of escape looked clear to the men inside and they started pouring out.

Sween shouted over and over from the window, but it was no use. Most of the men didn't bother to grab a woman to use as a shield either. All they wanted was to get as far away as they could from the illness and just as Neil predicted, they ran in all directions.

The men who grabbed a woman found the screaming, fighting woman only slowed them down. One by one, MacGreagors with blue arms rescued the women and carried them to safety. Then they went after Sween's men. The hung-over, frightened men were quickly cut down and when they were dead, MacGreagors spit on their bodies.

*

With all the men gone from the courtyard, the frightened women still inside began to ease around the horse dung and garbage toward the bridge. But when Laird Forbes' wife saw her husband and the other three lairds start over the bridge to get them, she put out her hands and wouldn't let him come closer. "Plague," she shouted.

"Nay," he called back, starting to move closer. "'Twas a trick. There is no plague."

She didn't believe him and backed up.

"I love you; I would not lie to you. I have come to take you home."

At length, she bowed her head and tears started to roll down her cheeks, "I am dirty."

He gave her a comforting smile. "I know where there is a peaceful loch. Shall I show you where it is?"

She nodded and when he turned around, she and the other women followed him.

*

Neil did not fight beside his men. He could hear the clashing of swords, the screams of men in the forest and he waited until the sounds grew further away. The MacGreagors were good fighters and needed to exact their own revenge for the two dead men, the four dead MacGreagor women and the upheaval of their homeland. His interest was in his brother and the only other woman left inside the wall -- Gillie.

When he started over the bridge, he didn't notice how many people were following him. Patrick, Yule Cameron, Kessan, Blair Cameron, Dugan and Mayze were in the lead, followed by dozens of others who wanted to see Sween harshly dealt with. Each of them wondered what Neil would do and no one could guess.

Neil walked across the courtyard, pulled his sword and then looked up at the window where Sween stood watching. Older and stronger, Sween often hurt Neil when they were boys, and then ridiculed his unwillingness to hurt him back. But now, they were grown men, the brothers were of equal size and it would be a fair fight.

With his resolve set and his eyes fierce, Neil filled his lungs with air and bellowed, "Who hesitates now?" He saw Sween turn and then heard him running down the inside stairs. Gillie screamed, the huge wooden door opened and Neil prepared himself to fight. But he was not ready for what happened next.

Sween hurled himself off the landing and before Neil could react, his sword went completely through his unarmed brother's stomach. The plunge made them both fall to the ground and for a moment, Neil was too shocked to move. Gathering his wits finally, he pushed Sween off him, pulled his sword out of his brother and tossed it away. Then he looked at Sween's face.

But instead of contempt, Sween seemed at peace. He had just enough energy left in him to say, "Thank you."

With tears in his eyes, Neil wrapped his arms around Sween and held him while he bled to death. He listened to his last breath and when the death rattle finally ended, he carefully lowered his brother's body to the ground.

No one knew what to do, and when the women saw Neil's tears, they began to weep also. Patrick finally put out his hand and helped Neil up.

Neil had to take two deep breaths before he could talk, then he grabbed hold of Patrick's upper arms. "See that my brother is buried next to our mother." He waited for Patrick's nod, wiped his tears with the back of his arm and started to walk toward the bridge. But when Gillie shouted "Wait!" it made him look back.

Gillie was dirty, her clothes were torn and any other day Neil might have felt pity for her. But hours before she was in his brother's arms and now that he lay dead on the ground before her, she shed no tears. Neil turned to Patrick, "Get her off our land."

"Nay!" she shouted. "I made a mistake, can you not forgive me? I saved your life and I love you."

Neil remembered kissing her and felt ill. He turned his back to her and this time he said it louder, "Get her off our land!"

"Nay! I am carrying Sween's child."

Neil closed his eyes and just stood there. His brother's blood was still fresh on his body and in the midst of dozens of people, he felt all alone. He had taken on the weight of the clan's burdens and led them through their worst nightmare, yet he had no family left. Now there was a new life to consider and a child does not choose to whom he or she is born.

Finally, he turned to look at Gillie. "You may live in Sween's cottage." He nodded his command to Kessan and knew his third would take her there.

The crowd parted and watched Laird Neil MacGreagor walk over the bridge toward the loch to wash the blood of his brother off his body. Patrick followed, but he kept a good distance back and when he saw the freed women still there bathing, he ignored them and waded into the water, shoes and all, after his laird.

Patrick swam behind him to the other side and when Neil got out and found a rock to sit on, Patrick did the same. He remained quiet and watched Neil struggle to breathe and then shift his eyes from side to side in horror. He knew what Neil was thinking and wasn't about to let him suffer. "You did not kill him, he killed himself."

They were the words Neil needed to hear and at length, he closed his eyes and quieted his breathing, "You are right, I did not kill him." He leaned down and splashed more water on his face. Then he finally noticed the women on the other side had gone into the water fully dressed as he had and were getting out. "I never even saw them."

"You got them out alive and your father would be very proud."

Neil was not yet ready to smile, but he nodded. When he looked again, all five lairds were on the other shore watching him. He nodded to acknowledge their help and then watched them take their women away. "What day is this?"

"I cannot even guess."

"Do we know how many lads we lost?"

"Not yet, but Kessan will be keeping count."

Neil took a long breath and looked up at the peaceful sky. "We must burn the bodies."

"And if any are captured alive?"

"Lads who force lasses do not deserve to live. Besides, if we set them free, we will have to fight them again another day."

Patrick knew exactly what Neil meant. He would see to the executions himself. "What about Sween's women?"

"Take them to England and set them free. Warn them not to come back." Neil suddenly grabbed Patrick's arm. "Send someone to watch Gillie and make sure she does not harm herself."

"It may not be Sween's child. There may not even be a child."

"I know, see that no lad beds her in case she is lying. If there is, and after the child is born, bring it to me and when she is able, get *that* lass off our land." He paused to consider it for a moment. "The child may truly be Sween's and therefore 'twill have my father's blood. 'Twill become my son or daughter." The thought pleased him and gave him something to look forward to. A child would certainly help fill the emptiness in his life and deep down inside he hoped it was Sween's child.

Patrick sighed. "We have a lot to do."

"Aye, more than enough to keep us busy for weeks. Spread the word that the MacDonalds are not welcome on our land ever again." He stood up and started back into the water. "We will make a new life for all the babies born to us. We will live once more in peace, and I..." He stopped and turned back to look at Patrick. "I will be allowed to walk in the forest alone occasionally. I have missed that."

CHAPTER VIII

Seven MacGreagor men died that day and their bodies were taken to their families. But all the women and children were now safe and for that, everyone was grateful.

Neil slept in the forest the night his brother died and tried not to be too hard on himself. He had not killed his brother and he had to keep reminding himself of that. It was the first night in eight days he managed to sleep soundly through the night.

Farmers and herdsmen brought their carts and hauled Sween's men up to the top of the hill beyond the meadow. The few that remained alive were quickly executed and their bodies were thrown into the fire with the others. The stench of burning flesh filled the air for miles around and word of the war and the outcome spread quickly to all the clans across the Highlands.

Neil worked as hard as the rest of them, cleaning and clearing away the awfulness of the invaders. He started at the top of the paths and worked his way down, hugging the children, helping men change the straw in the beds and even sweeping floors.

He did not go inside the Keep and would not let the women clean it for him. They needed their lives set right first -- he insisted and they obeyed. So he spent more nights in the forest. The peace of the trees and the stars helped calm him.

For Neil's sake, his brother's body was also respected and laid out on the table in their grandmother's cottage. No one came to wash or see the body, not even Neil and when the wooden box was ready, Sween was put inside and the lid was sealed with tree sap.

On the third morning, the priest led the procession and all the MacGreagor dead were put in the ground, in the peaceful graveyard where flowers grew wild, the wind whistled through the trees and the small fence needed to be extended.

Neil did not cry, but he stayed after the others left. He sat on a log he had place there when he was fifteen and remembered the happy days when he still had a family. He stayed for an hour and then another before he was ready to go back. Then he walked the short path through the trees, crossed the meadow and went over the bridge. When he entered the courtyard, several women were gathered. He returned their smiles and wanted to hug them all. But they giggled and didn't seem to want to be hugged. "What?" he asked finally.

Mayze grabbed hold of his hand. "You will see. Come." She practically had to pull him up the steps of the Keep and when they reached the landing, she opened the door.

Neil stepped inside and was astounded. Everything was spotless. His mother's tapestries were on the wall again. Some of his father's weapons were missing and a few of the candle holders still needed to be repaired, but the filth was gone and there were fresh flowers once more on the tables. A warm fire burned in the hearth and the air smelled sweet.

He tried to look appalled, "You disobeyed me?"

Mayze rolled her eyes. She loved his smile and could have watched his face all day, but there was more to show him. She led him up the stairs and into the bedchamber with the windows on both sides. The bed was new and so were the plaids spread across it. New curtains for the windows were pulled back to let in the fresh air and the light.

He walked to the window, saw the children once more playing in the meadow and smiled.

She still wasn't finished and took his hand one more time. Then she opened the door to the bedchamber that once was Sween's room. Inside was a small wooden box for the baby to sleep in, a table, a chair and some toys. The women had even brought small plaids and leather belts for the child to wear.

Neil wrapped his arms around her and she was afraid he might shed tears of joy, so she quickly pulled away. "Please, I am about to become a married lass."

"I almost forgot. When are we to expect that?"

"As soon as Dugan repairs his cottage."

"You must come and tell me when it is decided."

"I have one more thing to tell you. We managed to recover some of your parent's things. We put them in your old bedchamber and cleaned the other one. Your grandmother's mirror is there and your father's sword."

"Thank you. Perhaps someday I will want to see them again." Neil walked her back down the stairs and admired his mother's favorite blue and gold tapestry. "I am surprised you managed to save that."

Mayze walked with him to the front door. "Sween did not look where he was throwing it and it landed on the heads of two MacGreagor warriors. They hid it."

"Remind me to thank them." Neil opened the door for her and followed her out. The women were still waiting and his smile could not have been wider. He stood on the landing with his legs apart and put his hands behind his back. "Thank you all very much. Mayze and Dugan will marry soon and we will have a great celebration." He waited for the cheering to stop, nodded and went back inside.

To his surprise, Patrick, Kessan, Dugan and his other most trusted men had come in the back door and were there waiting. "What could you possible want?" he asked.

Patrick walked to the head of the table and pulled out Kevin's chair. "Sit and be our laird. You have earned it."

Neil nodded and walked to the chair. As soon as he sat down, the men cheered and outside, a louder shout echoed. Neil couldn't stop smiling, "Do you know if we have a drop of wine left in the place?"

The back door burst open and women brought in trays of food, goblets, flasks of wine and had grins as wide as his. He watched his men sit down and he could not have been more pleased.

Mayze hugged Dugan and then boldly kissed Neil on the cheek. "One more surprise."

He shook his head. "No more surprises."

"Just one more."

Neil finally nodded and when he saw the front door open, he stood up. As soon as he recognized Connor, Rachel and their three children, he welcomed them with open arms. He made them sit at the table, and for a time, couldn't take his eyes off them. He still had a family after all.

The men began to tell stories of the battle, but Rachel objected, so they told funny stories and Neil watched them laugh. But he was only half listening. He thought about Gillie for the first time in days. He wondered if it was right to take a child from its mother, but decided he had months to figure that out.

He hadn't thought about his brother in days either and one thing was still stuck in his mind. If Mungo was coming up the path ready to kill Mayze, then it must have been Sween who ordered the guards away from the hidden doors. Maybe...just maybe...the good in Kevin's oldest son finally surfaced. Neil found some measure of comfort in that thought.

Gillie had come closer than any other woman to making him fall in love and he liked that feeling. Someday there would be a woman for him and she would be a lot like his mother. She would fill his life with love, laughter and children...someday.

*

Connor often glanced at Neil during their small feast. After the others were gone, he would fulfill his promise. The word was "hollow" and it was a secret word between the MacGreagor laird and the King of England. It was a word of love to some and the saving of lives to others. Connor could not guess if the word would ever pass between the two nations again, but at least each would soon be in possession of it.

Tonight Connor would obey Laird Kevin MacGreagor's last command and give the word to his son -- Laird Neil MacGreagor.

-end-

JESSUP

CHAPTER I

"The blade is made of the finest steel, but 'tis not the blade of the sword that brags of greatness, but the handle -- the handle is solid gold."

The young man gasped, "Solid gold?"

The old man leaned a little bit closer. He wore clothing as fine as any king with a blue tunic, matching shirt, stockings and pointed shoes. He had jewels on every finger, sat in a tall-back, carved oak chair and used his hands to cap the top of his cane.

As though they were not alone in the expensively furnished room with its highly polished table and its four-poster feather bed, the white-haired old man glanced around to be sure no one could hear. "They say the Highlander is dead, but he only sleeps. When you take the sword from him, you must be very careful not to wake him."

"A Highlander?" The young man pulled back and swallowed hard. "But..."

"Are ye scared, lad?"

He quickly squared his shoulders. "Nothing scares me."

The old man grinned. "I knew I could count on you. The King will pay handsomely for the sword and soon we will have wealth beyond belief. All we must do is steal the sword of Kevin MacGreagor."

*

Patrick MacGreagor pulled his horse to a halt and stared at her. The woman did not move. She was tied to a tree, her head was bowed, her auburn hair covered most of her face and there was blood down the front of her English gown. He watched her for several seconds and when she still did not move, he was sure she was dead.

Slowly, he examined the trees for danger. It wouldn't be the first time an enemy used a dead woman to make a man vulnerable. Blades were sometimes half buried in the ground and hidden under leaves, or swords were slingshot through the air as soon as the woman was cut free. It was a cowardly means of attack and honorable men never used such tactics, but not all men were honorable.

At Patrick's nod, Donny slowly got down off his horse and drew his sword. With the tip he cleared away the leaves and carefully took one step at a time until he was close enough to see her face.

There was nothing remarkable about the area except it just happened to be not far from where the Highlanders made camp for the night. It was also on the well-beaten path that those who wished to go north to Scotland would choose.

Jessup dared not even breathe and only looked at them once when they were farther away. She needed help desperately but not this kind of help. The men wore kilts with leather shoes laced up to their knees. They carried daggers, stout bows and arrows, and it looked to her they had swords longer from handle to tip than a normal man was tall. Their beards were thick, their hair was long and both had harsh looks on their faces.

They were Highlanders and every English woman knew Highlanders were beasts. At least that's what her Uncle always said. She grew up hearing horrible stories about how they killed their babies, ate the hearts of their enemies, abandoned their elders, and didn't even believe in marriage. She held her breath and prayed they would go away.

Donny's eyes widened, but his voice was just above a whisper when he turned to Patrick. "She is alive."

She would have screamed if she could have. But the blow to her throat made any kind of speech too painful. She could cry, however, and her tears soon gushed down her cheeks.

Patrick was shocked. He quickly got down and walked into the forest until he could safely come up behind the tree she was tied to. He looked closely but could not find any indication that the rope was attached to a weapon, so he drew his sword and sliced it in half. Then he hurried to get back on his horse.

Donny quickly pulled the rope off her, scooped her up and then lifted her into Patrick's lap. He swung up on his mount, turned his horse and quickly led the two MacGreagor warriors back the way they came.

*

One thing the MacGreagors were very careful about was the flow of water from their land into England. The lack of water could start a war and that was something the MacGreagors wanted to avoid at all costs. So when Patrick needed a few days away, Neil suggested he and Donny follow the stream south to make sure there were no problems.

The war between the brothers caused a great deal of damage inside the wall and the MacGreagors worked hard for months to get their peaceful lives back on track. The wall was repaired and the garden was replanted, although it would take another year at least to harvest the herbs and vegetables they depended on. Everyone was tired and needed a rest, including Patrick.

Patrick was Neil's second in command. He had a square face, blond hair and blue eyes. Donny, on the other hand, had a round face and green eyes. His hair was closer to brown than blond, and he was four years younger than Patrick. His youth was the reason Laird Neil MacGreagor sent Donny with Patrick. Donny could learn a lot from the clan's best fighter.

The ride to England normally only took two days, but there was no need to hurry and the men fished in a couple of ponds, slept in the sun, and swapped stories they'd heard of war and wild women, half of which neither man truly believed. No one lived on this part of MacGreagor land. Living close to the English was considered unpleasant at best and dangerous at worst.

As expected, the waterways flowing north to south into England were clear and the warriors were about to head back when they found the woman.

Jessup's pain was nothing compared to her fear. She was in the arms of a giant, he was speaking a strange language and her whole body shook. She tried to think of a way to be free of him, but he had his arm around her waist and it didn't look like he was going to let go anytime soon. Now what was he doing?

He thought her shaking meant she was cold, so he tried to make her turn until her back was to him but she went stiff as a board. She had more strength left than he expected and he finally had to put his arm under her knees and physically turn her whole body. Then he drew her as close to him as he could so she could absorb his body heat.

She thought about trying to hurt him and then thought better of it. She doubted he could feel pain the way real men did anyway, and she would probably hurt herself far more than she hurt him. He was taking her north at a full gallop and that could only mean one thing - certain death.

Then his warmth started to feel good. Before long, it felt so good Jessup couldn't help but snuggle a little closer. She wanted more of it and tried to wiggle her upper arm under his until he finally understood, lifted it slightly and let her. Then she rested the back of her head against his strong chest and her shaking began to subside.

He wanted to wrap his whole body around her and get her warm. First, he needed to take her further north and make sure no one was following. Then he could find out where she was bleeding and get it stopped. After that, he would see to her warmth and anything else she needed.

For just a moment, she wondered if the man who let her get so close and seemed to want to keep her warm, was such a beast after all. Then she wondered if there was such a thing as a good heathen.

That, she knew, was highly unlikely.

They were finally far enough away so Patrick slowed his horse. Then he lowered his head until his mouth was close to her ear, "Where are you hurt?"

His English startled her and she tried to sit up straight, but he held her fast against him. She couldn't speak and couldn't think of anything to do, so she relaxed and just shook her head.

"I do not understand, lass. You are bleeding so you must be hurt somewhere. Can you show me?"

Jessup thought about that for a long minute. This was odd behavior for a Highlander. If he meant to rape or kill her, why would he care where she was hurt? Then it occurred to her she might be able to trick him. She put her hand on top of the one he had around her waist and took hold of his finger.

Patrick knew what she was doing. He put the horse's reins in that hand and offered her his free one instead.

She sighed, although no sound came out. Then she took his other finger and first touched it to the cut on her forehead. She withdrew it and turned it up so he could see the blood. After he nodded, she guided his finger down to the hideous bruise across her neck.

When Patrick felt the lump, he realized if she could talk at all, it would be extremely painful. He thought about his little sister Steppen, and his rage began to build. He would kill the man who dared hurt Steppen and then leave her tied to a tree to die. This woman was not Steppen and not even a Highlander, but to the MacGreagors, all women were precious, and they would protect this one with their lives too. They would also kill the man or men who hurt her.

At last, they found the same pond they rested beside the night before and stopped. The men stayed on their horses until they were certain there was no danger and then Patrick let Donny ease her down, carry her to the edge of the pond and set her down on a rock.

Jessup tightly folded her arms as though she could somehow

protect herself by doing so. She refused to look at either of them and hoped they would just do whatever they were going to do and then leave her there to die. She closed her eyes.

When Patrick knelt down in front of her and started to brush the auburn hair off her forehead, she almost jumped out of her skin. "We will not hurt you, lass," Patrick said.

It was a trick. The Highlanders were famous for trying to get women into their beds by tricking them. That's why it was dangerous to be so close to the English border, although no one was ever quite certain where that border line was exactly. Now what was he doing?

Patrick pulled a cloth out of his belt, wet it in the pond, cupped the back of her head with one hand and held the cloth against her cut with the other. She winced just as he knew she would. Then he watched her eyes until she opened them again and he knew she had adjusted to the pain. He continued to apply the pressure for a few more moments and then carefully pulled the cloth away. The cut was close to her hairline, was deep but not long and the bleeding was beginning to stop. He renewed the pressure for another couple of minutes, removed the cloth again and at last, the flow of blood stopped. He quickly rinsed out the cloth and tried to gently wash her face, but she took it out of his hand.

Heathen, she thought, I can wash my own face. She washed it once, rinsed out the cloth and washed her face a second time. But then he had his finger under her chin. His touch was so gentle, it took her by surprise. And when she finally allowed herself to look into his eyes, she saw a kindness she did not expect at all.

He wanted to look at her neck and she resisted. But he increased the pressure under her chin until she decided she better let him look before he broke her jaw. Then his face looked pained and she suddenly wondered just how badly injured she was. Maybe she would never be able to speak again. Her brother would probably cheer the idea, but she didn't favor it. Jessup tried to clear her throat but the pain was excruciating.

He spoke to Donny in Gaelic, "'Tis bad. Someone hit her hard." Then he spoke in English. "Who did this?"

Jessup shook her head. She remembered something cutting her forehead and then someone covering her eyes. She felt the blow to her throat and the last thing she remembered was the smell of wood chips. The Highlander was asking another question.

"Do you have family?"

She nodded.

"Do you want us to take you home?"

She stared into his eyes. He was willing to let her go home? She looked away and then back again. What kind of heathen was this? He had the kindest eyes she had ever seen, he kept her warm with his arms, and now he was going to take her home -- a Highlander was willing to go into England just to take her home?

"Did you hear me, lass?" She was looking at him. She was also crying and he had no idea what to say or do. Was she in that much pain? Was she upset about going home? Was home the worst place he could take her?

Jessup didn't realize she was crying. Patrick reminded her of the father she lost to war when she was only nine. Without thinking, she began to touch Patrick's face.

Her touch made his heart skip a beat and he held still. He memorized her straight nose, her brown eyes and her wonderful face, while she traced his facial features with her fingertips. Too soon she realized what she was doing, stopped and looked away. He said the only thing he could think of, "I am Patrick."

Jessup slowly nodded and then glanced at Donny.

"He is Donny. We are MacGreagors."

She wrinkled her brow. Where had she heard that name before?

Patrick was concerned she might never be able to speak again. He tried to move slowly enough not to frighten her, but when she saw his hand move close to his dagger, she looked like she was going to panic. He tried to calm her by moving back a little and sitting down. That seemed to work. He untied a flask from his belt and offered it to her. "'Tis wine; 'twill help your throat." She didn't believe him, so he pulled out the soft cork and took a drink. Then he offered it to her again.

But instead of taking the flask, Jessup wanted to taste it first, so she wiped the extra liquid off his lip with her finger and then put it on her tongue. It was bitter, but she decided it was not harmful, so she took the flask, tipped it up and drank. It burned going down, but it did warm her and make her throat feel a little better. She tried to clear it again, but it was way too painful.

*

In less than an hour it would be too dark to take her home or anywhere else. Patrick built a small fire, while Donny used his net to catch three fairly good sized fish. He gutted them, wrapped them in leaves and then placed the fish next to the fire to cook.

Patrick didn't look directly at her, but out of the corner of his eye he watched her wash the blood out of the side of her auburn hair. She used his cloth to try to wash it out of her gown as well, but wasn't having a lot of luck. The woman looked at him often and then looked to see where Donny was. He realized she did it out of fear and tried to think of a way to quiet her worry. Then he realized if both of them were sitting down, she might understand they were not going to attack her.

Jessup began to breathe a little easier. Finally, both men were sitting down and at least she had a chance. She would trick them by thinking she just needed to go behind a tree and then she would run. Jessup slowly stood up. With her eyes glued to Patrick's face, she started to step toward the trees. He didn't move, so she went farther and then further still until she could barely see him through the trees. Donny was still there too and with her heart racing, she bolted into the thickness of the forest.

CHAPTER II

There was little left of the fire when Patrick decided to give up and go to sleep. Donny was wrapped in his plaid on the other side of the embers and everything seemed peaceful. So Patrick spread his extra plaid on the ground, stretched out on top of it and pulled it around him.

He was worried about her but it was not cold enough to freeze to death and he couldn't force her to be where she didn't want to be. He turned on his side, thought about her beautiful long eyelashes and fell asleep.

*

Jessup wasn't that far away. Running was one thing, running in the dark when she didn't know which way to go was something else again. The savage had not chased her and she was surprised by that. Perhaps he didn't mean to rape or kill her after all. It would be easy to do and God knows heathen had no reason not to, but still he didn't. He hadn't even tried to kiss her. Of course, it was possible Highlanders didn't believe in kissing.

She took a step closer. Donny left a fish for her, she noticed. He didn't seem to be a bad sort either. He was certainly quiet, and the quiet ones, she heard, were the most dangerous. But Donny wasn't much more than a boy -- albeit a very large boy. She took another step closer.

*

Patrick was a MacGreagor warrior and they were taught very young to know who was near them even in their sleep. The elders tested them often and when they failed the test, they had to go to the Keep and confess it to Kevin. It was the most embarrassing and humiliating thing that could happen to a young warrior.

In the end, the training saved lives, so when Jessup quietly approached the dying fire, Patrick opened his eyes just a sliver and watched. She was hungry, knelt down on both knees near the fish they left for her and was careful to watch for bones. But that wasn't the problem. She seemed to have trouble swallowing. He tried to think of a way to help her, but then she began to break off tiny bits that went down easier. It took a long time to eat and when she finally finished, she looked exhausted.

He moved. Jessup just barely caught the movement and got ready to run. But the movement stopped and she mustered her courage and dared to look closer. Patrick's eyes were open. Again he moved, slower this time, but instead of looking like he was going to grab her, he lifted the corner of his blanket and held it up.

She stared into his eyes and then looked at the blanket. It looked warm and it was not as though she hadn't touched him before. Still, it was night and he was lying down. Isn't that how most women got in trouble? She looked across the embers at Donny who was not moving, thank goodness.

She really didn't have any choice. It was Patrick or the cold. Jessup got to her feet, took a couple of steps closer and then knelt down on his blanket. She watched his eyes expecting him to grab her, but he didn't, so at last she turned, put her back to him and curled up. Then she felt him wrap his blanket around her. She would never get away from him now, she thought. A few minutes later, she was asleep.

*

According to the King of Scotland, Laird Larmont was a worthy warrior with a short temper who could be counted on to kill every man in sight for the slightest infraction. Of course, the King of Scotland himself had little dealing with the man - it was just too dangerous.

However, in the land of the Larmont Clan lived a woman who had, on more than one occasion, knocked the wind out of Laird Larmont. After the first time, he admired her and after the second time, he asked her to marry him. That was seventeen years ago.

Now his daughter was approaching the age of marriage, he was getting old and his wife could still knock the wind out of him. However, he gave her far fewer reasons to do it these days.

When it came to her daughter's happiness, his wife had her heart set on a laird and she was willing to settle for nothing less. Laird Larmont agreed and vowed to search all the Highlands for just the right man. To accomplish that goal he sent out an unlikely emissary -- a storyteller and his pregnant mare.

His name was Ewing Larmont and his mare's name was Clark. Of course everyone knew Clark was a man's name and one look at Clark's extended belly let the whole world know Ewing had a little trouble telling the genders apart, at least when it came to horses.

That, of course, was the idea. Ewing could tell a lot about a man by his sense of humor and the man who won his lovely Glenna's hand, first had to have a good sense of humor, and then the good looks of a

Viking, and after that, the courage to fight her father. Such a man did not exist and that suited Ewing just fine. So he set out like he was commanded and began his search, to find a son-in-law to be, for the fierce and reckless Laird Larmont.

*

It was not yet dawn when Patrick locked forearms with him and then waited for Donny to swing up on his horse. "Tell Neil I am well and I will only stay until I know she is safe."

"He will not be pleased when I come back alone."

"Tell him I ordered you to go back."

"Aye, but if you do not come in three days, I will be back to look for you."

Patrick nodded and watched Donny quietly walk his horse out of sight.

When she awoke, Jessup was wrapped in Patrick's plaid and her womanhood was still safe. She was amazed. Patrick, she decided, was a very strange Highlander. Then she smelled something. On the ground next to her were several chips of wood and the smell frightened her. She sat straight up and looked in every direction, but the danger was only in her head and soon she was able to relax and lay back down.

Several yards away, Patrick glanced at her just in time to see her fear and started to run to her. But by the time he got close, she was calm again. Worried he might frighten her more, he waited until she noticed him and then went to her. "Did something frighten you?"

Jessup tried to speak. Her throat was better, but what came out was rough and squeaky, so she grabbed the wood chip and handed it to him. He looked confused and when she motioned for him to smell it, he did but he was still confused. She realized he was thinking she was a wee bit out of her wits and shrugged.

He returned her smile although he was not at all convinced being afraid of a chip of wood was normal.

Never mind, she decided. She took the chip back and tossed it away. Once she could talk again, she would explain it. She sat up and looked at the pond. If it were not so cold and if she could get the Highlander not to look, she would take a bath and wash the blood out of her gown. But, it was too cold and the Highlander would look.

*

The man hidden in the forest watched them closely. The MacGreagor and the woman were not doing anything very interesting and there was no point in staying. At least he knew where they were and that would bring a good day's pay. As soon as the Highlander turned his back, Charles Corbit, the man who smelled of wood chips, quietly slipped away.

*

She could tell by the way he grabbed her hand, pulled her up and quickly yanked his plaid off the ground something was wrong. When he swung up on his horse and leaned down for her, she grabbed his arms and let him pull her into his lap. Then she tightly gripped the arm he had around her waist and tried to spot the danger. She didn't see a thing.

Patrick wove his horse through the trees. At each clearing, he galloped, and then slowed again through the next cluster of trees, sometimes doubling back and often randomly changing directions.

Her heart was racing and it wasn't until they were much farther away that she realized she was holding on so tight she had to be hurting his arm. She tried to speak her apology, but again her voice failed her.

Patrick knew he was probably holding her too tight and when she wanted to say something, he halted his horse finally and leaned his ear closer.

She touched the fingernail marks in his arm and hoarsely whispered, "I did not mean to hurt you."

He smiled, "I did not mean to hurt you. We can rest here." She nodded, but when he started to get down, she put her hand out to stop him.

She returned his smile once more, moved his arm away, turned and scooted away so she could turn and look up at him. "I am Jessup."

He folded his arms. "Jessup, who hurt you?"

She shrugged. "Too dark." She could tell he didn't hear her, so she put her arm around his neck and pulled him close enough to whisper. "He covered my eyes."

"Do you know why he did this?" She shook her head. When the horse shifted its weight, Patrick quickly took hold of her to make sure she wouldn't fall.

Her throat was throbbing, she really didn't have anything more to tell him, she was getting frustrated and a tear started to roll down her cheek. So when he put his arms around her and pulled her close, she let him hold her.

*

Glenna Larmont was a happy young woman with light brown hair that hung down her back. It was straight save for the sides that often curled around her face and showed off her soft blue eyes. She loved everyone, especially her father who acted fierce and reckless, and her mother who could knock the wind out him.

She had six brothers and two sisters, all younger. They lived in Stratsgory castle not far from the glen and someday she hoped to see a forest. The castle had long winding steps up the high cliffs and she often loved to sit at the top, look out over the ocean and watch the birds soar through the air, alight on the water and then take flight again. The land below her home was a lush green with enormous rocks and clear water inlets. But trees were rare that far north and a whole forest was something she couldn't imagine.

She wanted a husband ...someday, but not now. So she made a pact with Ewing before he and Clark left. Find for her the perfect husband - one that was in love with someone else!

*

Lady Jessup was destined to live without love her whole life. It was not a destiny she chose or even would have considered, but it was hers nonetheless. She was the daughter of wealth, the niece of still more wealth and the sister of one of the richest men in England, but in her mind her name and misery meant the same thing.

She had maids to do this and maids to do that. Doormen opened doors and closed them, gardeners grew the best roses for her and teachers of all skills and crafts came often to help her learn how to do this or that. But she had no real life. In fact, sitting on a horse in the arms of a man she did not know, in a forest she was not familiar with, was the closest thing to happy she had been in years.

*

Patrick was surprised she let him hold her. He put his cheek against the top of her head and just let her rest. Someone hurt her, wanted to hurt her still and she had to be terrified. But they did not shoot at her, so they must want her alive for some reason. His next thought was the most disturbing. They were using her for bait and Patrick interrupted their plan. That must be why they wanted her back.

He thought about sharing his suspicions with her, but decided to wait, she was already scared enough. Then he started to worry about her other needs. Letting her rest was one thing, but he had nothing to feed her. Reluctantly, he moved her away and untied the flask of wine from his belt. At least that seemed to ease the pain in her throat.

He let her drink and put the flask away. Then he decided he would feed her, let her rest and then take her home.

Finding food she could swallow was a problem. All he could think of was milk or cheese and the closest cow belonged to a Cameron. Fortunately, the MacGreagors were at peace with the Camerons and the cow wasn't all that far away.

*

Charles Corbit and the old man with the many rings on his fingers were just alike in the only way that mattered to either of them - they both worshiped wealth. The only difference was one had it and the other did not. Still, both were willing to do anything to get it. "I seen 'em with my own eyes. They stayed the night in the forest."

The old man enjoyed his seat on the stone bench in the garden. His weakened leg bones hadn't allowed him to walk in years, but on the mornings it didn't rain, two men carried him into the garden and left him there to smell the flowers and enjoy the sunshine. It became a convenient place for the lord of the manor to conduct his many financial affairs. "Did you tell Rupert you saw them?"

Charles stood before the Baron and nervously turned his worn-out felt hat in his hands. His baggy commoner clothing had patches upon patches over his knees and his elbows, and still the material was thread bare. "I had to tell him. He got me in a corner and threatened to have me executed. I told him there were two, but now there is only one Highlander. Rupert flew into a rage."

"I heard him. I will be glad when Jessup gets back; she is the only one who can quickly calm Rupert down. You did not hurt her, did you?"

Charles Corbit lowered his gaze, "I had to hit her once, but not hard. I meant to hit her in the head and knock her out, but Rupert put his hands over her eyes, jerked her head back and my blow struck her in the neck."

The old man slowly closed his eyes. "Tell me she did not see you."

"She did not. Rupert put a sack over her head so she couldn't see anything. I took it off her once I got her tied to the tree."

Lord Russell was not pleased to hear that, but he had more important matters on his mind, "The question is, will the MacGreagors attack just to save one man? Two would have been better."

"We could kill Rupert ourselves."

The old man glowered at Charles Corbit. "If that were possible, I'd have done it myself years ago. The king knows I hate the boy and will have me hung sure, if he dies by any suspicious hand. No, Rupert must be killed by the Highlanders or all is lost."

Charles finally dared to sit down on the edge of the bench near Lord Russell. "They might kill all of us."

"You fret for nothing, MacGreagors do not kill for the sport of it."

"But if the Highlanders kill Rupert, will the king go to war with them?"

"The king is weak and fears the Highlanders. He also favors Jessup. He knows she will be better off once her brother no longer plagues her. Then I will inherit all his wealth and you, you my friend, will have the MacGreagor sword."

"How do you know there is a golden sword?"

"I know because my grandfather had it made for Kevin MacGreagor's grandfather. All we have to do is get the Highlander in our possession and then offer to trade him for the sword."

*

Ewing Larmont was getting on in years and didn't really have much of anything else to do. He was of average height for a Highlander with long, slightly bowed legs and broad shoulders. His plaid was a multitude of colors beginning with dark green, a lighter green and then red and white stripes going up and down, and from side to side. The Larmont clan was small and except for the cow hides, milk and cheese they often bartered, the clan was of little consequence to the world. And that's just the way they liked it.

Of course, if the Vikings ever came back the Larmonts would be Scotland's first line of defense, which Ewing realized, would last all of ten minutes on a good day. Oh they were not cowards, far from it, most were as reckless as their laird. But when it came deciding time, they much preferred life to death.

He heard tell the Buchanan was unmarried and decided that would be his first stop. However, he was in and out of that hold faster than a bee sting, Laird Buchanan not only didn't want a wife, he didn't like storytellers and he especially didn't like mares named Clark. That suited Ewing just fine.

*

It took most of the day for Patrick and Jessup to reach the small, one-room cottage near the border between the two clans. It was made of stone and sod, the roof was thatched, chickens roamed freely and a very old horse stood alone behind a fence next to the cottage.

But when they got to the door, Arthur stepped out with his sword drawn. "You are not welcome on this land." He wore the green plaid of a Cameron and the years had been good to him, but he was clearly no match for Patrick.

Patrick felt Jessup's muscles tense and tightened his arm around her a little. "Why?"

She appreciated the gesture. They were speaking that strange language and she counted on his touch to tell her what to do. Still, she kept her eye on both the man in the doorway and the shiny, sharp blade in his hand.

Arthur glared at Patrick. "You wear a MacGreagor kilt and the Cameron warned us not to abide any of Sween's lads."

"Sween is dead and so are his lads. Neil is our laird now and I am Patrick, his second."

Arthur looked like the weight of a hundred horses had been lifted off his shoulders. "I am happy to hear it. I am an old lad and was not looking forward to fighting you. Come, you are welcome here."

Patrick nodded. "The woman is hurt and needs food she can swallow. Can you help?"

Arthur put his sword back in its sheath, moved closer and looked up at her injury. "The English did that, probably with a cane. They are such heathen. Can she talk?"

"Not much above a whisper. We found her tied to a tree on MacGreagor land."

Arthur sadly shook his head. "My wife would know how to help her, but she died two months back." He waited for Patrick to help Jessup down and then opened the door for them.

The cottage was indeed small, with one bed, two chairs, one small table and a loft with a ladder leaned against the side. Yet the old man kept it clean and livable. Even the straw in the loft looked as though it had been changed recently.

Jessup had never seen anything like it. Her home consisted of several rooms, expensive furnishings and people who constantly pestered her. She wondered if she could be happy in a place like this and then she looked at Patrick. When he noticed, she quickly looked away.

"Is she your wife?" Arthur asked in Gaelic.

"Not yet."

"There is a priest in the village just north of here."

Patrick smiled, "That is good to know. She has not eaten."

"Forgive me, I forgot about that." Arthur grabbed a cloth and unrolled a chunk of cheese. Patrick nodded his appreciation, set it on the table, pulled out his dagger and cut the cheese into small chunks.

He was relieved when she seemed able to chew it, let it melt a little and then swallow. It would be another slow meal, but they were in no hurry to go anywhere.

"She needs cleaning," Arthur pointed out. "If the English see her with you and bloodied, you will soon be a dead man. They are heathen to be sure, but they do not like anyone hurting their women but them. You can put her in my wife's extra plaid. She will not be needing it now." Arthur took a bucket and headed out the door. "'Tis milking time."

The old man was right, but getting Jessup out of her English clothing was not going to be easy.

She was still eating one small chunk of cheese at a time, and looking at the workmanship of a small dagger handle she held in her hand. When she felt him come near, she set the dagger down and slowly turned to face him.

Patrick was finding her harder and harder to resist. "He is Arthur and he will bring milk." She seemed to be saying something with her eyes, but he wasn't sure what. He didn't know when he decided it, but she was going to be his wife and right now he wanted to hold her. "Jessup..."

What was she doing, Jessup wondered. She could not live in a place like this with a man like Patrick. It would never, ever work. She forced herself to look away and break the spell his eyes seemed to have on her. Then she regretted it. He was so close and all she had to do was go into his arms and feel his kiss -- but who was she fooling? It wouldn't be fair to him and even worse for her. There were some things in life she just couldn't have and love was one of them. She moved back.

Patrick dropped his gaze and tried to remember what he was going to say. "You need to change clothing." She didn't seem to be listening. "Jessup, you need to wear this." He held up the Cameron plaid and tried to understand the faraway look in her eyes. "If you do not put it on, I will be forced to put it on you." She didn't move and he took a deep breath. He draped the plaid across the back of the chair and walked around behind her. Then he began to unbutton her gown.

She was petrified and thought about running, but he would have no trouble at all catching her, especially in a small room like this. She was beginning to tremble and forced the words out of her mouth, "No, please."

"I have no choice. I will not force you, I swear it. I am only changing your clothing." He let the gown drop to the floor. The blood had soaked through to her under clothing, but he could cover that up. He put a white shirt on her and then looked around for a woman's belt. He finally spotted it hanging on a hook, grabbed it and tied it around her. Then he knelt down and started to pleat the Cameron plaid, and tuck it under her belt just as he had a thousand times when his little sisters needed help.

She was beginning to breathe again. He was not undressing her -- he was dressing her just as he said and she finally looked down at the odd clothing. His hands were swift as he folded and tucked until he was finally finished and stood up. Then he was standing right in front of her and she finally had the courage to look at him again. It was a mistake.

CHAPTER III

"Will you marry me?" There, Patrick said it. It took every ounce of his courage and the look of shock on her face gave him the answer he feared most. "I should not have..."

She put her finger on his lips and shook her head. Asking was not what he did wrong. In fact, they were the most beautiful words she had ever heard. If only she could talk. She tried but her voice was raspy and now the words refused to form in her mind. He was so handsome and his arms were going around her just as she hoped they would.

She shook her head again to tell him 'no', but then she raised her lips to his. She couldn't help herself. His kiss was thrilling and she couldn't breathe. She lightly pushed him away, caught her breath, looked into his eyes and then melted in his arms. When he kissed her a second time, she knew the memory of his kiss was going to have to last her a thousand years and she wanted to completely consume every sensation and every emotion.

Four kisses later, Patrick couldn't remember if her latest answer was yes or no. Her word might have been no, but her lips were saying she wanted him as much as he wanted her. He stopped kissing her just long enough to say, "There is a priest close by."

A priest? She didn't think heathens had priests. Even if they did, she couldn't marry him. Before she was even born her life's path was determined and it did not include a Highlander, even one who made her heart race and her toes tingle. If only he would look away. His eyes were making her weak and she needed to be strong. What was he doing now?

Patrick wasn't about to let her change her mind. He swooped her up, carried her outside, put her on his horse and then swung up behind her. He headed his mount toward the village and then turned her in his arms so he could kiss her constantly. No way was she going to change her mind.

*

An hour later, they were married, although her "I do," was a breathless whisper, and she had to say it four times before the priest decided he heard it plain enough.

*

Ewing Larmont survived on his storytelling; one story for a loaf of bread, two for a full mutton meal and three if they offered apples or other rare delights. Along the way, he discovered if he looked hard enough, he could find all sorts of interesting things on the paths between the clans. That's how he found the felt hat. It was a pointy thing with a wide brim and it was blue, which was not at all his favorite color, but once the hat had a good washing it was presentable and kind of fun.

The land of the Geddes Clan was almost as pleasing as the Larmont's chunk of solid earth. It was comely in every direction with pristine water, grand mountains and moss covered rocks. The Highlands boasted of crisp streams and swells of hillsides, small villages, fertile farmland and some parts were dotted with herds of cattle or sheep. Ewing Larmont could not imagine a better home.

Some people were friendly and some were not, which suited Ewing just fine. Laird Geddes was unhappily married, grumpy and had no sons that would inherit his title. That suited Ewing just fine too, although he had hoped to find a husband for Glenna close to home so he could still see her from time to time.

Glenna loved his stories more than anyone else did and sometimes he made up fables about her, although he gave the little lass in the fable a different name. The older she got the more adult the stories became, but if Glenna noticed, she had the good grace not to let on. It was another reason for the old man to love her.

Finished with the Geddes, Ewing traded two stories for two loaves of bread and moved on.

*

What had she done?

Jessup wanted to walk off the edge of the earth and fall into oblivion. But she had no idea what corner of the earth she was in or which way to go to find the edge. She sat next to him on his blanket with her knees up to her chin. Patrick was still sleeping and she tried not to look at him. If she did, she might give in to the urge to climb back into his bed and back into his arms.

She loved him so completely, but this...this marriage was impossible. Sometime in the night, she got her voice back and she should have told him, but all she was able to say was how much she loved him.

Now, her heart was sinking into a great sea of desperation and all she could think about was how much trouble she...they were in.

Maybe they could hide. She could let Patrick take her to that place where the rest of the heathens lived, but how long would it be before the king ordered her found? As the king often said, she was the only real friend he had and he would not easily give her up. Would he send his men into the Highlands to find her? Probably so. She started to feel sick to her stomach. The King of Scotland would never allow the King of England to send men into his land to look for one stupid woman...even if that stupid woman was Lady Jessup Russell.

Besides, she loved the king far too much to just disappear and make him worry. He was, after all, the reason she managed to stay unharmed until now and naturally, there was that other matter. Jessup closed her eyes and thought about what she'd done. Her womanhood was no longer pure and the punishment for that would surely be death. She might already be with child. That thought almost made her smile. If she was, then she would be able to keep a part of Patrick with her until she died. On the other hand, his child would be cheated out of life just the way she had been. She quickly said a prayer: "Please God, do not let me be with child."

*

Patrick was not asleep. He heard her prayer and it was the first indication that all was not what it seemed to be. Why would a wife not want her husband's child? She did love him, how could he doubt that, but to not want his child was alarming. Maybe she was just frightened by the thought of giving birth. That must be it. He married her so fast, she didn't have time to consider all that married life involved, including the birth of children. Now all he could do was love her well enough to make her forget the worry.

Jessup thought about her brother. She'd been gone for two days and he would be completely out of control by now. Once before when she was gone, he managed to destroy half the crops in the valley and kill three men.

Good grief, she'd only known Patrick for two days and already she was his wife? How could she be so happy and so miserable at the same time? She let her eyes drift his direction and her heart began to ache for him. Would it be torment to be in his arms once more or torment not to? She gave in, curled up beside him and let him smother her with kisses.

*

There was a war in Jessup's mind and love was not even a contender, but by mid-morning it was the winner. She was on his horse, in his arms and so happy she didn't care anymore. For one day, she let herself be happy. She kissed him and loved him and did not think about anything but being his wife. He laughed at her often. Every time he tried to get the horse to move, she pulled on the reins to stop it and made her husband kiss her instead. They were getting nowhere fast and having a wonderful time doing it.

Finally he pulled her down, made love to her and then made her understand what she was doing. It was not safe. He needed to concentrate on the possible danger and she had to stop distracting him.

She pouted for a moment, promised to be good and then seriously considered his words. It really wasn't safe. Jessup straightened her Cameron plaid, let him lift her back on the horse and decided to be civilized, although she wanted desperately to prolong their precious time together.

Nevertheless, the time of their love was over and Jessup knew it.

While he concentrated on getting her home to the Highlands safely, she thought about how to get away from him. The longer they rode, the farther she would have to walk and the longer it would take to get her brother back under control.

At last, Jessup had a plan and was about to ask her husband to stop when they were suddenly surrounded by Englishmen.

Jessup recognized the men immediately. She folded her arms in a huff and cleared her throat, "Commander, how good it is to see you. You have come to save me, I see." Her husband's arm was around her waist and she intentionally relaxed so he would not become any more alarmed than he already was. Then she ran her fingers through the top of her hair to move it off her face and give her a moment to think. Patrick was not going to understand any of this.

"Lady Jessup, you were not easy to find. You are aware you are with a heathen?"

"Yes, but he does not speak English so he does not know he is a heathen. Did my brother send you?"

"Of course." The commander signaled to his men. In unison, the men turned their horses and forced Patrick to move until they were all headed toward England.

Jessup tried to keep her voice calm and airy. "How many has he executed since I have been away?"

The commander laughed, "Well, we did have to save the butcher again."

Patrick kept his face blank. He counted thirty men and although he could do some serious damage, he could not protect his wife at the same time. Their best chance would be to outrun them if he found an opening. If he didn't find an opening, the Highlander Patrick MacGreagor was about to see England and that was something he was not willing to do.

Jessup smiled at the commander. "The poor butcher, 'tis a wonder he stays with us."

"'Tis no wonder; your brother pays him handsomely."

"That he does. However, I should give you fair warning. I have grown fond of this Highlander and if anything happens to him, I will be very displeased. So much so, I will hide my brother's book for weeks, maybe even months, and no one will see their pay."

The commander looked horrified. "Even if your brother orders him executed?"

"Especially if my brother orders it."

The commander gave Patrick a once over with his eyes. "As you wish, but I see nothing special about him."

"Oh he is not special, he is just...unusual. I hope to teach him English. 'Twill be the feat to top all feats, do you not agree?"

"Then you do not want to ride with me?"

"His horse is as comfortable as any other and more so without the stiff saddle you like so well. I will stay with the Highlander for now."

*

Patrick was beginning to wonder exactly who this woman was. He really knew nothing about her, but then, she only started talking a few hours ago. Was her brother the King of England? It was possible, he supposed. Still, if the king's sister had been missing for days, this part of The Highlands would have been crawling with English soldiers long before now. And nearly every Highlander clan would have warriors headed this way thinking the English were preparing to invade. He really didn't think that was likely. No, she wasn't the King of England's sister. Still she had a brother who didn't sound harmless at all.

He tried to remember how many days it had been since he sent Donny back. After the third day, Neil would send men to look for him, but it would take them another two days to get this far and then how would they know where to look. Patrick wanted to see his wife's face but her back was to him. At least she talked the commander into letting her stay put. Not that he would have given her up, but he was pleased she found a way to avoid a struggle.

He had to admit her brother's men were good with horses. They kept him penned in even when the way was narrow. He kept hoping for the opportunity, but saw no chance to get away. The further south they went, the more anxious Patrick felt.

Jessup couldn't think how else to keep Patrick calm. She stroked his arm as often as she dared, but it was not enough and she could feel his tension increasing. Maybe she could talk to him in a roundabout way. "Commander, how long until we are home?"

"Another hour at the most."

"We really should not be bringing the Highlander with us." She felt Patrick tighten his arm but ignored him. "He probably has a wife and ten children waiting for him somewhere. You have children, Commander, you would not want..."

"Rupert said to bring you back and anyone we find with you."

"And you always do what Rupert wants?"

The commander looked at her suspiciously, "You know I do.

What are you asking?"

"I am pointing out that my brother almost always does what I want, and I will ask him to free the Highlander as soon as we are home, so why not save ourselves the trouble and set him free now?"

"I see. My lady, it will not work and you know it. I can only free him once Rupert agrees."

"And that is because..."

"He controls my pay."

"Of course." Her husband relaxed and she realized he intended to stay with her anyway. It was wonderful and awful all at the same time. She sighed. Didn't Patrick understand he could be about to die?

*

Laird Campbell proved to be a bit of a challenge for Ewing Larmont and Clark. First, Laird Campbell was not married and was not bad looking. He even had all his teeth. The man wanted a wife and thought a mare named Clark was the funniest thing he'd ever heard. He had blond hair, a good smile and his eyes were not set too far apart like some. If anything, they were a little too close together. And the more Ewing thought about it, the more he decided the eyes were way too close together.

Laird Campbell looked a bit like a Viking, he guessed. Of course, Ewing had never actually seen a Viking, but he could guess what they looked like the same as anybody. In fact, the Larmonts could still see the remnants of one of their long boats just beyond the water's edge where some claimed the Vikings originally landed. From the size of their boat, the Vikings must have been enormous.

The Campbell was close to Laird Larmont's requirements alright, however there was one problem -- the Campbell was not willing to fight Glenna's father. If the King of Scotland feared him, then the Campbell feared him even more. That suited Ewing, who was beginning to dislike him anyway, and after trading two fables for provisions, he was on his way again.

*

Once Rupert's men found the English road, the way widened and after several curves, the small band of soldiers and their captor came to a collection of small cottages situated around a nearly deserted courtyard and a large country manor. They crossed the courtyard and prepared to present their prisoner to their lord.

The house was much larger than the MacGreagor Keep with three floors, wide windows and polished stone steps. When the double doors opened, two men in scarlet tunics stepped out and held the doors open, while another man in a white tunic with gold trim and white stocking calmly stepped out.

"Well Jessup, 'tis good to see you again," the man in white said.

She could feel Patrick's tension and ever so slightly shook her head to let him know she was not in danger. Then she smiled sweetly and reached out her arms to the man in the doorway, "My beloved brother, Rupert."

He grinned and hurried down the steps. His shoulder length hair held a brighter hue of red than hers, his eyes were a solid green and freckles were splattered across his nose. He was about to reach for her waist when her foot caught him under the chin and nearly knocked him cold. He flew backwards, landed on his backside and quickly grabbed his jaw. "Jessup, why did you kick me?"

Patrick was shocked. She had grabbed hold of his arm so quickly he didn't have time to react and before he knew it, she kicked Rupert with the force of a man. He'd never seen a woman do that before and it pleased him. Maybe he didn't have to be so worried about her after all. He wanted to smile but he remembered to keep his expression stoic.

Her glare was red hot and her voice was becoming stronger by the minute. "I should have known you were behind this."

"Sister, 'twas the only way..."

"QUIET!"

Patrick quickly glanced around. Even the horses seemed afraid to move at her command.

She turned to the English commander. "Rupert is not surprised to see the Highlander. Why is that?"

With a little help from the doormen, Rupert finally got to his feet. "Sister that was the whole point."

"What?"

Rupert grinned from ear to ear. "I planned the whole thing. I am brilliant beyond compare."

"Brother, what are you talking about?" She looked at the commander who was now hanging his head. "He got you to kidnap a Highlander?" She waited for her words to sink in and the faces of her brother's small army to turn a putrid ash.

The commander was so upset, he could hardly speak. "No, my lady, I mean, well, yes."

"What did he tell you?"

"He said the Highlanders...took you."

"And what else?"

"Lady Jessup, a thousand pardons, but he said the king ordered you found."

Jessup shook her head. "This is the fourth time this year he sent you on a fool's errand. Do you never learn?"

The commander sheepishly nodded, "We learn, but 'tis for the pay."

"I swear you would kill your own mothers for the pay!"

Rupert was not dissuaded by her anger. "You will not spoil my fun this time, sister." He talked tough, but kept out of her reach.

"Look what they did to my throat." She raised her chin and then watched the grimace on her brother's face when he saw the bruise.

A tear came to his eye and Rupert truly looked upset. "He promised not to hurt you."

"He lied." She was still spitting nails mad and tried not to let her heart soften, but none of it really was Rupert's fault. None of it was her fault either. It just was...and there didn't seem to be anything either she or her brother could do about it.

Patrick was enamored. His wife spoke like a noble English woman, she kicked her own brother hard and had a command over men the likes of which he had never seen before. Who was this wonderful, exciting woman he managed to marry before she changed her mind? One thing was for sure, Neil MacGreagor was never going to believe this. An hour ago he could think of nothing but escaping, now he wanted to stick around to see what happened next.

Jessup was home and she knew her home was completely different from the one her husband lived in. She wanted to get him alone to explain, but that would take some doing. The poor man. She had not even allowed him to speak. His arm around her waist was more relaxed so at least she wasn't worried he wanted to kill someone. That was something she heard Highlanders could do in the blink of an eye.

She took a chance and looked up. He didn't seem upset and in fact, he seemed to have a sparkle in his eye. That was a relief. She finally let her brother help her down and then waited for Patrick. Once his feet were on the ground, he stood at least three hands taller than her brother

Rupert slowly looked from Patrick's chest up to his face. His mouth dropped open and his eyes widened when Patrick narrowed his gaze.

Jessup wasn't about to let the moment slip away, "Just imagine, brother, a whole horde of these coming down the road looking for...YOU!" She nodded an exaggerated nod at the gawking Rupert, took Patrick's hand and pulled him toward the doors. But before they were allowed to enter, the commander stripped Patrick of all his weapons, even the dagger his father gave him.

Patrick's fierce glare did not dissuade the commander and he was impressed. Not many men had that kind of courage and certainly not Englishmen. However, a commander who stands up to the glare of a Highlander, but cowers at the shout of a woman was a complete contradiction. It fascinated Patrick.

*

Patrick never guessed such things existed. The room was vast with a sweeping staircase in the center. Large needlepoint pictures hung on the walls and tables displayed silver bowls and jeweled goblets. One particular type of stone fascinated him the most. They were milky white, perfectly round, different sizes and imbedded in the side of the goblet. He had a thousand questions about those, but he would have to ask them later.

She took him to a smaller room where they could be alone, but she only stayed a second. "My brother is truly dangerous. He will not hurt you while I am here, but do not trust him." She quickly kissed his lips, slipped out the door and closed it behind her.

The room was less elaborate than the first, but still exquisite. The wooden walls were trimmed at the top with tiny gold leaves and tapestries of proud Englishmen hung on the walls. Patrick ignored those, but he did marvel at the throne. He'd heard the English king loved to sit in a high place and thought that must be what it was for. Of course the Scottish king liked to sit high as well, but he was worthy of such an honor.

What wonderful tales he will have to tell his sister about the odd belongings of the English. That reminded him of another English oddity -- they liked to build secret passageways. Then he wondered where his wife was exactly. He didn't like being away from her and thought about going to look, but she seemed to have control of the situation so far. Maybe he should trust her judgment a little while longer.

*

She took just enough time to quickly wash, brush her hair, dress in a clean gown with a high neck that covered her bruise and hurry back. She was far less worried about what she looked like than getting

Patrick out safely. But Patrick looked pleased to see her cleaned up and it touched her heart. She was about to tell him something, but Rupert was right on her heels.

"I suppose you told him all our secrets, sister."

"Of course I told him. Fortunately for you, the heathen does not understand English." She pretended to enjoy the moment and waited for her brother to stop laughing. "So tell me, why did you kidnap the Highlander?"

Rupert was careful to give the giant a wide berth as he made his way to the throne. He took a cape off the back of the overly large chair and put it on. Then he sat down and flared his cape open so the red lining enhanced his white tunic.

Jessup grinned. "You did that perfectly."

He giggled an odd childish giggle, "I practiced while you were away."

She tried not to look too serious. Her brother was far easier to manage when he was happy. "Rupert, I am so excited. You must tell me why you kidnapped the Highlander."

"I need him to get the sword."

"What sword?"

"Kevin MacGreagor's sword, of course."

Patrick pretended to be bored and wandered over to look at a tapestry. Why anyone cared about Kevin's sword was beyond him, so he easily dismissed the thought. If there was a hidden door it had to be somewhere in a wall.

She watched her husband's every move without actually looking at him and desperately wished she knew what he was thinking.

Somehow she had to let him see what he was up against. Jessup walked to the table next to the throne and lifted a jewel laden crown with the tips of her fingers. She had love in her eyes for her brother as she set it on top of his head. "I crown thee simpleton of the year."

Rupert roared with laughter, "You will not say that once I have Kevin MacGreagor's sword."

Patrick moved on to another tapestry closer to Rupert's throne.

"MacGreagor...why do I know that name?" Jessup asked.

"You remember, sister, Uncle Michael told us 'twas a MacGreagor who killed our mother."

"Of course he did, I had forgotten that."

Rupert leaned closer. "Kevin MacGreagor once killed ninety-three men at the same time and when he was finished, his sword dripped gold and not blood."

Patrick swallowed wrong and started to choke. As though she did it every day, Jessup walked over and pounded his back. As soon as he recovered, she filled a goblet with wine, took a drink for her sore throat and then handed it to him. She smiled when the sweet liquid did not suit his palate and he frowned. She took it back, watched as he quickly untied his flask and washed her wine down with his.

For a minute more, she watched her husband's eyes. "Rupert, you know swords do not drip gold." When she saw Patrick slightly nod, she knew he understood how deranged her brother really was and why he was so dangerous. She breathed just a little easier.

"Some do," Rupert countered.

"Well I have never seen one. Who told you about the MacGreagor sword? No, let me guess. It was Uncle Michael."

He instantly stood up. Rupert's nose flared and his eyes narrowed with his fury. "If you already know the answer, you should not ask the question. You know how I hate that."

Jessup quickly curtsied so low her nose was practically on the floor. "You are right, brother. I am sorry and it will never happen again."

Patrick was not pleased. His wife should not have to bow that deeply to anyone even her brother. Rupert was just a man and Patrick could snap his neck in a heartbeat. The more he thought about that, the more tempting the idea seemed. He walked to Jessup, took her by the shoulders and pulled her up. Then he looked long and hard into her eyes. He wanted her to know he had a limit and she had just reached it. But her reaction was one of sheer terror so he let go.

A second later, Rupert was standing next to her glaring at the Highlander. "Did he touch you, I could not see."

She quickly smiled. "Everyone knows not to touch me."

He put a finger on top of his head and pretended to wind himself up by turning around twice. Then he glared at Patrick, "You can only touch her to keep her from falling, but not if you are the one who pushed her."

It was getting impossible to pretend he didn't understand what Rupert was saying. And now Patrick had no idea what that meant. He did see, however, that it was his wife who was truly in danger, not him. At least he could reply with his eyes and his intense glare made Rupert start to back up. Patrick intended to make it perfectly clear -- it would be the last thing Rupert ever did if he hurt Jessup again. But then, was Rupert sensible enough to get the message?

*

Jessup had to get both men calmed down somehow. Her husband may not be happy, but he was not dangerous. Rupert was her biggest problem and he liked to talk about wealth, especially wealth he was scheming to get. "Dearest, who told you about the MacGreagor sword?" She waited until her brother turned his back and then gave her husband a pleading look. She grabbed his hand and had just enough time to brush it against her cheek before she had to let go.

Rupert slowly retook his throne and flared his cape a second time. He didn't trust her, so he waited just to make sure she wasn't going to answer her own question again. "Uncle Michael told it first, but later it was that other man."

Jessup was instantly alarmed, "What other man?"

"The one who hit you. If you must know, I held you from behind, but I did not know he was going to hit you."

"Was he the one who tied me to the tree?"

"He tied you to a tree?"

The one thing Rupert could not convincingly do was lie. His question was sincere and Jessup knew her overly susceptible brother was as much a victim in this as she was. When he started to cry, she went to him and wiped away his tears with her fingers. "Did you run away?"

He nodded. "I was frightened when you started to bleed. I can only touch you to keep you from falling, but not if I am the one who hurt you. I cut you with my ring. I had to let go. Mother made me promise, do you remember?"

"I remember." Jessup poured more wine in her goblet and took it to her brother. "Rupert, please tell me the name of the man who told you about the MacGreagor sword." She waited while he drank a sizable portion.

"I do not know his name. He talks to me when I walk in the garden and tells me all about the sword and its power. Once I have it, I will have all the riches in the world."

The problem with wealth, Jessup knew, was that the wealthy never thought they had enough of it. It always disgusted her. "Help me understand, why did you kidnap the Highlander?"

"To trade him for the sword."

"I see, finally."

Rupert changed from a pathetic babbling child to a strong older brother in seconds, "I thought of it myself, sister. I am the most brilliant man in all the world."

She stared at her brother for a long minute. "I see now that you are right. I also know that being brilliant makes you very tired. I suppose if you demand it, I will have to give you leave to go lie down."

"Oh sister, you are so good to me. Yes, that is exactly what I will do. I will rest until the evening meal." He stood up and lifted the crown off his head. Rupert set it on the table, took off the cape, tossed it back on the chair and headed for the door. "Do not play with the Highlander too long. The king will be here soon."

Jessup's heart sank. The last man she wanted to see right now was the king of England. She watched her brother close the door, but didn't move.

A second later, he opened it again and peeked in. "Did I catch you?"

"Not this time."

"Next time then." He laughed, closed the door and walked away.

Jessup slumped into her husband's arms. "I am so sorry. This is all my fault, I should have told you..." Patrick wouldn't let her keep talking. Instead, he was kissing all her worries away and she loved him dearly for it. How could a woman who was so entirely lost only three days ago be so madly and completely in love now? And how was she ever going to tell him she couldn't really be his wife and go to the Highlands with him?

She kissed him one more time and then led him to the hidden door in the wall. "I will make sure they leave you in this room. The king is coming and I will not be able to come back. The tunnel will take you outside the wall."

He wrapped his arms around her and held her tight, "What do you mean you will not be able to come back?"

"Patrick, I love you, but I cannot go with you."

He tried hard to let her words reach his brain. "You are my wife; your place is with me."

"I know, but you do not understand. If I go there will be a war between two very powerful barons and a lot of people will die. Please, you must go without me."

"Nay."

"Patrick, please."

"Nay, if you are staying then so am I."

She knew he was serious and no amount of talking was going to change his mind. "Alright, I will come back and go with you. But first,

I must talk to the king. Perhaps I can prevent this war without..."

"Without what?"

"'Tis not important. The king likes the night and will stay up very late, but I will come, I promise." She quickly kissed him and then pulled out of his arms. Jessup touched his cheekbone with her fingertip and looked into his eyes. Then she walked away.

He didn't like how that made him feel. It was as though she were memorizing his face so she wouldn't forget it. Did she just lie about coming back? He understood she loved her brother, he could see it in her eyes. But a woman leaves her brother and goes with her husband. All women do, 'tis the way of the world. Something more was going on here.

*

Ewing Larmont was suddenly in the grip of a dozen mighty warriors who were not the least bit interested in his stories. In the Forrester Clan there had been a murder, outsiders were definitely the most likely suspects and he was the only outsider they had seen in weeks.

But once he got through telling them about his mare named Clark, they decided a man that stupid wasn't smart enough to sneak into their hold, kill a man and sneak back out. He was soon absolved of the murder and eager to move on.

Crisscrossing all of Scotland was not an easy task and Ewing Larmont had no idea there were so many clans. He tried to remember which ones wore which colors, but it soon made him addle brained. Then he came across a festival held by a clan who joined with another clan and then a third. The festival was a sheer delight.

His first fascination was with a juggler and it was hard to pull himself away. The people all seemed happy, although a couple of times men of different kilts wanted to settle disagreements with swords or fists. Still, more often than not, the dispute was settled with a challenge to see who could throw a mallet the farthest, or loop a horseshoe around a peg in the ground.

There was only one thing wrong with the festival -- no one wanted to hear a story, and a storyteller could starve that way. So he traded his prized possession for food - his blue felt hat. He took the food, left the festival and found a place to sleep away from the clans.

He never heard a thing during the night, but when he woke up Ewing Larmont discovered Clark had given birth. What a beauty this new little stallion was. He had a black coat and a white mane, with white stocking feet and another patch of white right down the bridge of his nose.

There was something about the beauty of new life that made a man stop and consider, so Ewing decided a few days rest was a grand idea.

The colt stared at him with its big black eyes as if Ewing was the strangest looking thing in the world. And maybe he was. Soon enough however, the little one got a lot more interested in his morning meal. Ewing smiled. He hoped the look in the colt's eye was the beginning of a very special relationship just like the one Ewing had with Clark.

*

Laird Neil MacGreagor was not pleased to see Donny come back without Patrick. As soon as he heard the guard's whistle, he stepped out on the landing of the Keep and watched him ride alone over the drawbridge into the courtyard.

Neil spread his legs, crossed his arms and listened to the explanation with great interest. When he realized there was a woman involved, and a beautiful, one, according to Donny, he finally smiled. Then he ran his fingers through his dark, wavy hair. It was never safe for high-ranking Highlanders to be out in the world alone. It made them easy targets for any clan that wanted to take MacGreagor land, which in turn made the whole clan vulnerable. The murder of a second in command was a sure way to start a war and it wouldn't be the first time that happened. The clan was only eight months beyond their last war and certainly didn't need another. Then there was the possibility Patrick could get caught alone with an English woman and start a different kind of war. Patrick must be in love; he'd never done anything this foolish before.

It didn't take long for Neil to decide what to do.

First, he had to attend to some personal business. He went back inside the Keep, climbed the stairs, walked down the balcony and then stood for a moment outside the closed door. He knew what was in the room and was not eager to go in. It held all that was left of his parent's belongings -- his grandmother's hand mirror was inside and so was his father's sword. Still, the time had come to set aside his emotions and do what needed to be done.

Neil slowly opened the door and went in. He walked to the window, and then tied back the curtain to let in the fresh air and sunshine. He took off the sword that killed his brother and then strapped on the one his father always wore. If he was going to be away from home, he was honor bound to wear the MacGreagor sword.

CHAPTER IV

Servants had Jessup's bath prepared by the time she left her husband and went upstairs. She missed him already and the night ahead was going to be unbearable. She put on her favorite green gown and let her maid dress her hair, but she would rather have Patrick's hand all tangled up in her hair like it was ... only a few short hours before.

There was a big commotion when the king arrived. The people cheered and he waved his appreciation. Always before, she too rushed out to watch but this time she would rather be kissing Patrick. For one brief moment, she considered throwing caution to the wind and running to her husband. But that impulse soon passed. There were lives at stake and a lot more to consider than her own selfish desires.

She got a grip on her courage, walked out of her room and went down the stairs. Then she made her grand entrance into the dining room which was right next to the room where Patrick waited. But she tried not to think about that.

The King stood, took her in his arms and kissed her cheek. "You look amazingly more happy than usual, what brings this about?"

"I am very pleased. I hear you came to beg me to marry you."

Patrick heard her voice and walked closer to the wall. When she mentioned marriage to someone else, he was about to break the wall down, but then he heard laughter.

The king chuckled, "I hear the opposite, 'tis you who begs marriage of me!"

"Your Majesty, will Saturday do?"

He was dressed identical to the way her brother dared to dress when the king was not in attendance. He wore a white, gold-trimmed tunic with white stockings and a cape lined in red. Even his fashionable shoes, short hair, and two-layered linen doublet were the same, although no one was supposed to know what the king wore under his tunic. He had dark hair and laughing brown eyes and the King was still grinning, but pretended to look grief stricken, "Well now, I did agree to marry Catherin of Engals on Saturday. Are you free on Sunday?"

"Good heavens no, Sundays I go riding." She returned his hug and sat down beside him. "How foolish we are to have rejected each other all these years. We might have been quite happy together, you know."

The King brought her hand to his lips. "Aye, but we didn't have the heart to oft your uncle."

"Ah yes, Uncle Michael has ruined everything. I say we put him on a ship and not tell him how to get back to England."

"Great glory, why did I not think of that? Perhaps 'tis not too..."

The fun was over. Rupert walked in wearing a green tunic, bowed to the king and then took his seat at the table. Soon two men carried Uncle Michael in, chair and all, and placed him on the other side of Jessup.

Uncle Michael might have been an interesting man had he not developed an intense bout of self-pity when his legs no longer supported his weight. Now he enjoyed little delight except for his jewels. He had a new ring and was eager to show it off, so he made sure the new ring was on top when he capped his cane with his hands. He waited for the King to notice.

"Another new ring, Michael?"

As usual, Lord Michael Russell was too impolite to answer and instead, gave over his cane to his servant and got ready to eat. The men in Jessup's family were never in the mood to hear her spar with the king, although they never chided her in front of royalty. But if she dared attempt it, she would hear about it for days and usually she'd rather not.

However, on this occasion why not? If she got them all riled up, they might forget about Patrick. It would be worth it if she could spend another night with her husband...just one more night and it would be enough for a life time -- it would have to be. But to accomplish her goal, she had to be very shrewd. What she could not do was upset the king. "Your Majesty, the most fascinating news has arrived."

"Oh has it? My life is such a bore, I so long for something fascinating to think about. Do tell."

"Word has reached my ears that my intended has taken another lass to his bed."

If her Uncle Michael could have stood up, he would have. "What's this?"

On the other side of the wall, Patrick sat down hard in a chair. So that was the problem. Jessup was promised to some English pig and if she didn't marry him there would be a war between two barons.

The king didn't look at all concerned about her intended's infidelity. "Now Jessup, you know how men are. He is not yet married and he has certain needs. You understand."

She understood more than he thought, but the game had to be skillfully played or she would lose. "What sort of needs?"

The king glared at Uncle Michael. "You tell her."

"Me? I am not her mother."

"Neither am I," the king argued.

"Well if you would let them marry, neither of us would have to answer that question."

The king narrowed his eyes. "I do not prevent her marriage; 'tis your unwillingness to give up the land that prevents it. You know very well Lord Roy will not take her without a firm agreement."

It was the same argument the king and her uncle had been having since she was born. It was never resolved and that always made her happy. Lord Roy was a rich but disreputable man and she hated the thought of even being in the same room with him, let alone the same bed. By the time the king and her uncle gave up the argument, both would be far too tired to care where she spent the night.

Her plan was working. Now she needed to get dear Rupert in the mix so she would be rid of him for the night. "Your majesty, forgive me for interrupting, but I have a request."

"For you, anything."

"'Tis for my brother. He has not been sleeping well as of late. Have you a cure?"

Rupert looked confused at first and then he nodded to the king. "My sister is so good to me. She cares about all those sorts of things." He started to mutter to no one in particular just as he was prone to do during meals. Everyone was used to it.

The king leaned closer and whispered in Jessup's ear, "Have you considered knocking him out? A blow right under the chin might do."

"I tried that earlier, but it does not seem to work as well as it did when he was younger."

"Would you like a little help? I could ask one of my guards."

"Could you? I am forever in your debt."

The king grinned. "So you are, my dear, so you are."

She picked up her bowl of food and whispered in his ear one last time, "I am off to bed. Do enjoy your argument with Uncle for as long as you like." She winked, stood up, kissed the cheek of each man and then left the room.

Jessup couldn't wait to be in Patrick's arms again. As soon as the guards and servants were out of sight and it was safe, she opened the door, slipped inside the throne room and set the bowl of food down. It was so dark she wasn't sure he was still there and she started to panic. "Patrick?"

"Aye."

"Wait, I will get a candle." It didn't take her long to leave and then quickly come back. She set the candle on the table and then took the food to where he was sitting near the wall. She expected him to eat, but he set it down on a table and reached for her instead.

He pulled her into his lap, kissed her breathless and then pushed her back. "You are my wife. War or no war, you will come with me."

"What?"

"You used to be pledged to a baron, but now you are my wife."

He must have heard through the wall. Her husband was searching her eyes for an answer and she didn't have one. If only it were that simple. She started to explain, but then she realized he would want to argue and arguing with him would ruin their last night together. She smiled and surrendered. "I am your wife and I will go with you."

Patrick was relieved. He picked up the bowl of food, filed the spoon with juice and started to feed her. "You have not eaten all day."

He had to be hungry too, maybe even more so than she was. She couldn't remember the last time he had eaten. How could he possibly be wonderful enough to care about her that much? She let the juice fill her mouth, took the spoon away and fed him a large chunk of meat.

Between kisses they finished the bowl of food. Then she took his hand and led him to the secret panel in the wall. When it opened, Patrick marveled at the clever way it was built. Then he took the candle off the table, walked through the passage way and held the candle up.

Making sure she was behind him, he carefully took the stairs that led down to a tunnel entrance. Then he looked inside the tunnel to see if it was big enough for him to walk through. Just barely, he decided. The bottom of the tunnel was well worn and he guessed his wife often used this tunnel to escape her daft brother.

He cleared away a few cobwebs and was surprised at how long the tunnel actually was. He was sure they had already walked father than the courtyard was long. At last he came to a door. When he pushed out, it did not yield and so he tried pulling it in, but still it would not budge. His wife giggled and he smiled. She was waiting to see if he could figure it out. Then he realized it was a moving door like the one in the room so he lightly touched it in several places until well-hidden springs began to move the door to the side.

She had no doubt he could do it, but it was fun to watch him figure it out. What he would never guess was -- how to get back in. No one ever guessed that, not the king and certainly not her brother. It was something her father told her and it was the one thing in the world that belonged only to her.

Patrick expected more steps, but to his surprise, the opening was in the side of a hill not that far away from the house. The fresh air felt good, the moon cast its glow on tall, green grass and the clear sky was filled with millions of bright stars. He stepped out to look around, then he turned, took her in his arms and didn't care that the door moved back into place. When he finally released her, Jessup spread her brother's beloved white cape with the red lining on the ground and began to take off her clothes.

*

At first light, Laird Neil MacGreagor left Kessan in charge and headed south to look for Patrick. The three men he took with him were his best fighters and took an oath to protect their laird from the moment he became confirmed. They were Lorne, Walrick and Dan, and he went nowhere without them. Each was a big man with superior strength and boasted of throwing their opponents a full ten hands when riled. Not everyone believed that, but none were eager to find out first hand.

Hopefully, they would meet Patrick on the way and Neil's worry would be for nothing, but he had a feeling something was wrong. What he feared most was not being able to find Patrick at all. With the help of a full moon, they could ride long into the night. After that, it would be most of another day to get to the place Donny last saw Patrick. From there they would have to spread out and search every inch.

*

The next morning, Patrick could see her in the window of her third floor bedchamber. Her hair was done up in ringlets, her face glowed with color and her deep blue gown made the red in her auburn hair sparkle in the sunlight. As she had the day before, she made sure her high-neck gown covered the bruise. From the place just outside the tunnel where she took him the night before, he continued to stare up at her.

Without a word, she left him there and he wondered if it hurt her as much as it did him, but he didn't see how it could; It was her decision to go back inside without him. Maybe she didn't love him after all. Patrick only knew one thing for sure -- he had just lost his wife of less than three days and he had no idea why.

Once he found her gone, he tried everything he could think of but he couldn't get the hidden door to open. Now there was nothing more to do. He had no horse, no weapons and no wife. So he just sat on her brother's cape and stared up at the window. Jessup was not going home with him and Patrick had to make himself understand that. But his heart kept telling him she did love him. Maybe whatever kept her there was greater than her love for him. It didn't make it hurt any less, but it did help him understand. He wondered if there was anything in his life that would keep him away from her. That made him think about his sister, Steppen, and he was suddenly grateful he wasn't faced with that decision.

Then Patrick began to wonder just how unkind he had been to his wife. He wanted her to choose him, but maybe that was something she just couldn't do. He married her too quickly. He loved her, desperately wanted her and selfishly made her his wife without giving her a chance to think. Now she was stuck with an impossible situation and she was hurting because of his selfishness.

He closed his eyes and bowed his head.

The next time he opened them, the English Commander was standing beside him holding the reins to Patrick's horse. He hadn't even heard the horse let alone the man. His whole life had gone to hell and all he could do was roll his eyes.

"She wants the cape before her brother finds it gone."

Patrick just stared at him.

"Oh, I forgot you do not speak English." He started to make hand signals.

Patrick sighed and stood up. "I speak it well enough." He leaned down, picked up the cape and handed it to the commander.

"I should have known it was a game. Lady Jessup plays the best games in the whole world."

He was smiling from ear to ear and Patrick wanted to bash the man's head in. His wife was inside, he was outside and this was not a game! But he calmed himself. Maybe the commander could help him understand. "She plays games often?"

The commander took Patrick's bow off his shoulder and handed it to him. "She keeps her brother from killing people that way. The games keep him occupied, you see."

"Can no one else play the games?"

"'Tis complicated." The commander handed Patrick the sheath of arrows and then started to untie Patrick's sword from around his own waist. It was so long it was practically dragging on the ground. "We love our Jessup, do not think otherwise, but she was born to this and there is nothing anyone can do to help her."

"She cannot leave?"

"She cannot. The only way out for her is if her brother hurts her. Then the king would put him to death, but even if Rupert did hurt her, she would not tell the king. So you see, our lovely Jessup will never be free."

"She has an uncle, why is Rupert not his responsibility?"

"Because Rupert is more powerful? Rupert is the true lord, not Uncle Michael. Rupert does not know that and if he did, he could order the execution of his uncle. His uncle, on the other hand cannot order the execution of Rupert because he does not have the power. We are obliged to do as Rupert commands and then pray Jessup talks him into changing his mind before we actually have to kill someone."

"You are right, 'tis complicated." Patrick tied on his sword, moved it to the right place so he could draw it easily and then mounted his horse."

"You best be off now. Once Rupert finds you gone, he'll order us to capture you again. If you go west, I'll take the men due north so you can get away. Lord help us, we do not want a war with the MacGreagors."

*

Jessup watched her brother's commander take Patrick's horse and weapons to him. She saw him nod his appreciation and then had to move away from the window. The longer he stayed, the harder it was to keep from running to him. Maybe now he would go back to the Highlands.

She was so sorry she hurt him. What was she thinking when she said yes to marriage? She knew it could never work out. There was only one answer -- Jessup was the most selfish person in all of England. She just wanted to be happy for once. Now she was hurting a man who did nothing wrong and deserved better.

If he stayed, it would cost him his life. Even if she confessed to the marriage and was with child, she couldn't be with him constantly and sooner or later her brother's soldiers would kill Patrick. Her threat to postpone their pay would not be enough. If Rupert ordered the execution, which he would, they would obey. The only reason they saved the butcher repeatedly was because they liked to eat and did not like doing the butchering themselves.

She closed her eyes and leaned against the wall. "Please, my love, just go home."

*

The morning meal with the king did not begin until after most of the world started their afternoon. Uncle Michael was either still in bed or hiding and Jessup didn't much care which. Rupert had yet to put in an appearance as well. Sometimes being alone with the king was her only refuge and this day she was pleased to be able to let down her guard.

"My dear, last night you were aglow and this morning you are grim. Is there trouble I should know about?"

"Well, let me think. The pink roses refuse to bloom quickly

enough, the cat refuses to catch all the mice in the barn and I have eaten far more than I should."

"I doubt that, you have hardly touched a crumb this morning. Are you unwell?"

Jessup batted her eyes, "My heart is broken. My best love, who is also my king, rejected me again and I can scarce survive it."

He chuckled. "Oh you."

She sipped a goblet of milk, while he finished his meal. They enjoyed each other's company for a little while longer, and then she walked the king out the door and down the steps to his horse.

"Seriously, are you very unhappy?"

"Not very. I hardly do a thing, you know."

"Except keep your world in perfect order. I ask again, as I always do, has Rupert hurt you?"

"You know he would never do that, he promised our mother."

"He is daft, Jessup. Who can say what he will do? You must promise to tell me the truth or I will not be able to sleep nights."

"I promise."

The King kissed her cheek, mounted his horse and rode off with a full guard carrying polls with red banners behind him. They had no idea a Highlander was watching them.

*

She wanted to go to the window to see if Patrick was still there, but she denied herself. Instead, she went to the garden, found a stone bench and sat down to think. The weather was good, the sun was shining and the birds chirped in the trees as though there was nothing wrong in the world. But everything was wrong in Jessup's world.

She'd spent sporadic moments thinking about it, but now she needed to concentrate -- just how much danger was she still in? Who besides her pesky Uncle Michael had influenced Rupert? Who hit her and who tied her to the tree? Rupert said the man met him in the garden, but which man? Sometimes her uncle got rid of workers and brought in new ones to do the harvest or plant the crops. Sometimes the king took an interfering hand and replaced workers, and sometimes they countermanded each other and got so twisted up in the affairs of the manor, she didn't know the names of the people she needed to call on for something as simple as a bath.

So trying to guess who most recently influenced her brother was impossible. One thing was for sure, as long as Rupert believed Kevin MacGreagor's sword dripped gold instead of blood, she was still in danger.

CHAPTER V

Patrick was thinking the same thing. It was easy to guess the man with the banners and the escort was the king of England and any other day he might have been impressed, but Patrick was worried the king was all that kept Rupert from carrying out his plan. One imaginary gold sword, one missing Highlander and one daft brother meant his wife was probably still in serious danger.

He could ride back into the courtyard and surrender. It might keep Rupert from going off the deep end for a while, but it was just a temporary solution. No, there had to be a better way.

*

She always thought Uncle Michael was harmless, but now Jessup wasn't so sure. For Uncle Michael to fill Rupert's head with nonsense was one thing, but to have another verify the nonsense was not a coincidence, it was a conspiracy. It was time to have a nice long talk with Uncle Michael. She couldn't remember the last time she'd been in that part of the house. Uncle Michael was rarely there, so she never needed to be in his private quarters. She knocked and when no one answered, she opened the door.

Uncle Michael was sitting up in his bed counting the small, round pearls in his newest goblet. "Jessup, what are you doing here? I would offer to get you something to drink, but I am unable to walk still."

She ignored his haughty tone and pulled a chair up closer to the bed. "I have been meaning to ask you something."

"What?"

"Why did you tell Rupert a MacGreagor killed our mother?"

"Oh Jessup, you know how he is, some days he remembers and some days he doesn't. He kept asking and I just finally made something up, it means nothing."

"It meant nothing until this business of the sword came up. Whose idea was that?"

"What sword, my dear?"

She leaned forward and narrowed her eyes. "For years I have put up with your nonsense because it entertained my brother and kept him busy, but this time you have gone too far."

Uncle Michael turned his attention back to his goblet. "I do not know what you mean."

"You told Rupert to kidnap a Highlander and trade him for the MacGreagor sword."

"I told him no such thing."

"Uncle, my brother does not lie well enough to fool anyone, especially me. But you think you do." She took his beloved goblet out of his hand and threw it hard against the stone wall. The metal dented, a pearl popped out and then rolled across the floor. "Do not toy with me!"

He had never seen his niece that upset before and the man was visibly shaken, "Well perhaps I did say something." He picked up a little bell and began to frantically ring it.

She grabbed that out of his hand too. Just then, she heard her brother's old familiar shriek.

Rupert was furious and ran screaming from room to room. "My Highlander is gone! My Highlander is gone!" Then he ran through the courtyard, around the house and through the garden with his face contorted, "Jessup, I have lost it, the MacGreagor sword is gone forever!"

Jessup glared at her uncle, "I have not finished with you."

She slowly got up, walked out and started down the stairs. If the king had still been there, she would have shut Rupert up quickly, but the king was gone so she just let him rant and rave. The whole mess irked her to the bone.

When Patrick heard the blood curdling screams coming from the manor he was ready to ride into the courtyard, up the steps and straight into the house. Then it got quiet and he realized Rupert just discovered he was gone and the screams were coming from him.

Patrick mounted and quickly moved his horse inside a clump of trees. Just as he suspected, the commander and his men mounted and rode out of the courtyard. And just as Patrick also suspected, the commander did not take his men north like he promised, but west hoping to find him.

Patrick pulled his horse back out into the open and gazed at the manor. With the guard gone, he could easily go in and force his wife to come with him. Who would stop him? On the other hand, the MacGreagors never forced women to do anything. Besides, something told him that would be a mistake. The guards were not what kept her there, it was something else and until he knew what, he had to wait.

Patrick dreaded leaving her but he needed help.

*

Once Rupert was calmed down and napping, Jessup finally got up the courage to see if Patrick was still there. He wasn't and she felt like someone ripped her heart out. He was gone...he had actually gone back to the Highlands without her. She wanted him to -- even pray he would -- but now that he had, her heart was shattered into a million pieces.

In the silence of the bedchamber next to hers, Jessup put her head in a woman's lap and wept.

*

Keeping a close eye out just in case Rupert's commander decided to go north instead of west after all, Patrick hurried across meadows, through the trees and over the hills as fast as he dared go, and prayed Neil was on his way south to find him. For that reason Patrick stopped occasionally to whistle. When there was no answer, he moved on.

Night came, the moon lit his way and he rode on until both he and the horse were too tired. Then he stopped, whistled one last time and waited for a reply. None came so he spread his plaid on the ground and tried to sleep.

Sleep did not come easily. All he could think of was his wife being in the same house with her daft brother, who might not have hit her himself, but made it possible for someone else to hurt her. He imagined her too terrified to close her eyes and he was terrified for her.

Then he tried to get himself under control. Jessup had, after all, spoiled her brother's plan by taking Patrick outside and setting him free. Now there was no need to hurt her...until they cooked up another scheme to get hold of a sword that did not exist. At least they didn't know they had a Highlander's wife to bargain with.

He turned over and tried to get comfortable. It took a while, but he finally managed to fall asleep. When he woke up the next morning, Neil, Lorne, Walrick and Dan were sleeping in a circle around him. He couldn't believe it. For the second night in a row, he had no idea who was or wasn't near him in his sleep.

He turned to look at his laird and saw that Neil was not asleep, "Love is hell," he whispered.

Neil whispered back, "It makes a lad stupid, too."

Patrick couldn't help but smile. It was good to be back with his friends even if Neil intended to tease him for the rest of his life. They managed to surround him and even sleep by him without him knowing. "Aye, love makes a lad stupid."

He had no idea what day it was or how long it had been since he'd taken a bath, so he welcomed the chance to bathe in a nearby loch. He washed his hair, got out and felt almost human again. Lorne handed him a loaf of bread and a chunk of ham from home which was exactly what Patrick needed. Then between bites, he started to tell them everything that happened.

Neil tried to take it all in, but some of it didn't make a lot of sense. "She did not say why she cannot go with you?"

"Nay, she said she *was* going with me, but when I woke up, she was gone."

"Then she lied to you."

"Aye, but the fault is mine. I did not listen when she tried to explain. The commander said the only way for her to be free is if her brother hurts her and the king puts him to death."

"But her brother has hurt her," said Neil.

"True, but she will never confess it to the king. Rupert is daft but sometimes he is like a child. She loves him, I can see it in her eyes and she does not hold him accountable for her injury."

"Then who is accountable?" asked Kessan.

"I do not know and neither does she. During the attack, Rupert covered her eyes and she did not see who struck her."

Neil leaned against a tree and folded his arms. "Then it could have been anyone."

"Aye and whoever 'twas, is probably still in there with her." Patrick had almost forgotten to eat and took another bite of ham.

Neil thought about the decision he was about to make very carefully before he said anything. The five of them could probably take Rupert's English soldiers easily enough, but there would be blood and if Patrick's wife still did not want to come with them, then it would be spilled blood for nothing.

The more sensible solution, was to let the King of England take care of the problem. Contacting the king was not something Neil would do lightly and in fact, he never intended to do it ever. But if what Patrick said was true, Jessup was the king's friend and the two nations had a mutual interest in seeing her safely in the arms of her husband. At last, he made his decision. "If she will not tell the king Rupert hurt her, then we will."

*

There were few times in a king's life when mere words could frighten him, but when the messenger caught up, he stopped his guards and made the man repeat the message.

The word was "hollow" and it could only mean one thing. If he did not go and go immediately, there would be a war with the Highlanders. Sometime in the future he might enjoy such a war, but at present, he had all he could do to keep his barons from killing each other. The King of England turned his guard and rode back toward MacGreagor land.

Ewing Larmont's next stop was at a place he heard about from Laird Cameron. He didn't believe a word of it, but just in case, he followed the path to where the MacGreagors lived. Then from the top of the hill, he got his first glimpse of a place as close to paradise as he had ever seen. It was just like in his story about the glory of Land Esson.

The village was surrounded by forests but he'd seen plenty of trees by now. Still the green of the trees seemed to frame the village. The stone building was not as grand as the castle Laird Larmont and his daughter, Glenna, lived in but the wall and the moat surrounding it were mighty impressive.

Ewing also liked the idea that some lived inside the wall while others lived outside. It made for a change of pace in what could sometimes be a dull and boring life. There were no steps up the high cliffs like there were at his home. In fact, he couldn't even see any high cliffs, but there were plenty of birds to shoot if a man was good with a bow and arrow.

He watched for a time, saw the hunters come back and then saw the men haul in their nightly buckets of water. He got down off Clark, patted the nose of the colt and kept an eye on the group of men who walked over the bridge. They went down a path to a loch, stripped down and went swimming. In the land of Ewing Larmont, the lochs were far too cold to swim in and he marveled. Perhaps after dark, he would try that.

At last, he decided to mount Clark, ride down the hill, through the trees, across the meadow and into this interesting place the MacGreagors called home. But when he got to the meadow he was spotted, a guard whistled and several MacGreagors stepped out of the trees and surrounded him.

"What clan are you?" Kessan MacGreagor demanded.

"Clan Larmont."

"What do you want?"

"I want a husband for my laird's daughter."

Kessan laughed when two of his men stepped forward. "Take two, they are small."

Ewing did not quite get the humor since both were considerably larger than he was. "I will see your laird."

"Laird MacGreagor is not here."

"I see."

"Is he married? Does he look like a Viking...does he laugh? Is he..."

Kessan looked annoyed. "What questions are these?"

"My laird demands to know these things before he gives up his daughter."

Kessan crossed his arms. "My laird will choose his own wife whether her father likes it or not."

Ewing liked the sound of that. This laird might be worth

considering. He decided he would like to meet the man who would stand up to the Larmont. "When will Laird MacGreagor be back?"

Kessan shrugged.

"In that case, I will be back." He nodded, urged Clark forward and headed for Ferguson land.

*

In the same clearing where his father agreed to hide an English baby in the Highlands and the same clearing his grandmother used to meet the old king, Neil MacGreagor boldly walked out alone to face the new King of England, who also left his guard in the trees where they could not hear.

Neither man looked happy to be there, so Neil decided to get to the point. "Do you want a war with us?"

The king's complexion went pale. "Of course not. What has happened?"

Neil carefully studied the king. He was not fierce but neither was he weak. "There is a lie between our nations. Englishmen say my father's sword is made of solid gold and there is a plot to take it from us."

"Is there such a sword?"

Neil slowly withdrew his father's sword and handed it to the King. The only gold on it was a thin line of plating down each side of the handle.

"Who has told this lie and plotted against you?"

"The uncle of Patrick's wife and Patrick wants his wife back."

"I will deal with the uncle. Tell me who his wife is and I will..."

"She is Jessup."

The king's jaw dropped, "What? Jessup is married?"

"She is. She stood before a priest and married Patrick MacGreagor on Cameron land last week."

Neil expected the king to be furious or at least upset. He was not expecting to see the king's lips curl into a grin. "No wonder her cheeks finally had color. But that is wondrous news."

"You are pleased?"

"My friend, you have just solved a problem that has plagued me for years. Jessup, you see was pledged to marry one of my barons before she was even born. She does not like him and he does not like her, but her uncle will declare war if the marriage does not take place."

"But she is already married."

"Precisely and I cannot wait to tell her arrogant uncle. He is the same one who plotted to get your sword? How glorious. I am going to enjoy this immensely."

"Then you will send her out to her husband?"

"I will bring her out myself."

"We want the lad who hurt her too."

The king's grin quickly changed to a look of intense concern and anger. "Someone hurt Jessup? Tell me who and I will have him executed."

*

Jessup was wrong; the king did know how to get back in through the hidden door in the side of the hill. And once he showed Patrick and Neil, he didn't think he was going to be able to pry them away from it. Both men were captivated by the inner workings of the door and its multitude of springs. At last, he got them to follow.

In the scant light of a candle, they made their way through the long tunnel and then up the stairs. At the top, the king stopped, put his ear to the inside door and listened. All was quiet, so the king handed his candle to Patrick and pushed the place on the panel to make it move. The noise seemed excessive and each man held his breath until the king could step inside and verify the room was empty.

Just as Patrick had been, Neil was astounded by the display of wealth in the room, although he too ignored the tapestries of the noble Englishmen. When the king spotted the replica of his throne, he released the breath he was holding. "The boy likes to pretend, you see."

Patrick nodded his understanding and then held his finger to his mouth. Someone was coming. The men quickly pressed themselves against the walls and waited.

"My lady, you have not eaten all day," a servant was saying.

"I am fine, Millie, you fret too much." Jessup smiled, went into the throne room and closed the door behind her. The space had somehow become her sanctuary in the last few hours now that Rupert needed to nurse his hurt jaw. The king's guard had been a bit too helpful putting Rupert to sleep and like the child he was, Rupert was not taking it well.

She liked this room now because it held memories of her beloved Patrick and she felt close to him when she was there. It was almost as if she could feel him with her now.

Jessup didn't remember leaving a candle in the room and when she began to turn, Patrick's face was in front of her, his hand was across her mouth to keep her quiet and her eyes began to glisten with tears. Patrick had not left her. He slowly took his hand away and she was finally in his arms again with his lips on hers. A long moment passed before she realized they were not alone. Then when she spotted the king, she quickly stepped away from her husband and started to curtsey. "Your Maj..."

"You lied to me, Jessup. You promised to tell me if someone hurt you." He looked stern when he interrupted her curtsey, turned her around and unbuttoned the back of her high-necked gown. Then he turned her back around and pulled the cloth down to have a good look at her throat. He expected what he saw and he also expected the worry in her eyes, so he decided her comfort was far more important than his vow. "Do not be alarmed, I will not kill Rupert. But I will take away all his power. He will live with my cousin in the south of England where he cannot hurt anyone."

Her heart flooded with enormous relief. "Thank you."

"You may thank me later; I am not yet finished with this affair." The king went out of the throne room, through the entryway and waited impatiently for the stupefied doorman to open one of the large double doors for him. Behind him, Neil, Patrick and Jessup watched. Then the king stepped outside. "Commander!" he bellowed.

The doorman eased out behind the king, trying to understand why he hadn't seen him come in. But the king's guard was not outside and there did not seem to be an easy answer to the puzzle.

Taking what he thought was a well-deserved nap, Rupert's commander jumped up off the grass and ran to the king. "How did…?"

"Never mind all that." The king looked behind the commander, nodded and watched three highlanders come out from behind the trees. The MacGreagors walked their horses into the courtyard bringing Neil and Patrick's mounts with them.

He noticed the commander put a hand on his sword and the king glared at him. "Do not start something I will have to finish." He waited for the commander to drop his eyes, slowly nod and remove his hand. Then the king went back inside.

His next stop was Uncle Michael's bedchamber. He found the man sitting at a table playing a board game with a man the King had never seen before.

Uncle Michael gasped, "Your Majesty. I would bow, but as you know my legs..."

"Who hurt Jessup?"

The man at the table slowly rose up out of his chair and started to back away. Step by step, he backed right into Patrick.

The smell of wood on his clothing was overpowering and Patrick at first wrinkled his brow. Then he remembered how frightened Jessup had been of the wood chip that first morning and he finally understood. He spun Charles Corbit around, grabbed him under the arms and slammed him against the wall. "You hurt my wife!"

"Your...wife?"

CHAPTER VI

It was the first look Uncle Michael had gotten of the size of the Highlanders he so often made stories up about. He heard they were large, but really had no idea how large.

Neil walked to the table and leaned over until his face was only about two inches away. "You think to steal my father's sword?"

Uncle Michael's heart nearly stopped. He was physically trembling, his eyes were ready to pop out of his head and all he could do was utter something completely inaudible. However, he did manage to shake his head vigorously.

As soon as Jessup entered the room, the king wrapped his arm around her waist. "Do not look so frightened. I will not kill him either, though I would like to. He is your family and I love you too much to punish him that harshly. However," the king paused, let go of her and went to the table to look into Uncle Michael's eyes. "You will live on this property, but you will no longer use the title of 'lord.' I will send a man to oversee your expenses. Any wealth you obtain beyond that which you now have will go into my coffers, do you understand?"

Uncle Michael wasn't sure if he was more afraid of the king or the Highlanders, so he managed a weak nod to both.

Patrick still had Charles Corbit against the wall with his feet dangling and his head turning red. But when the king finished with Uncle Michael and patted Patrick on the shoulder, he let Charles

Corbit fall to the floor in a heap. Still, he did not leave until he had his say, "If you ever hurt a woman again, I will be back to kill you."

*

The king followed Neil out the door and down the stairs. "Tell me, how is my cousin, Charlet?"

"She does not exist, but if she did she would say she is very happy." Neil smiled, went out the door and mounted his horse.

*

Jessup didn't understand. When Patrick finished kissing her again and then brushed past her and went out Uncle Michael's door, she ran after him. He opened the nearest door and when no one was in that room, he went to the next one.

The king must have told him, Jessup thought. Her worst fear was about to come true and she tried to get in front of him. "Patrick, no."

He stopped, took hold of her shoulders and kissed her hard. "You are my wife and you are coming home with me."

She could not hold back her tears, "I cannot go with you. I cannot!"

He ignored her and continued on to the next bedchamber. "If you want to bring anything, get it now."

"No, I cannot go with you."

"You can and you will."

He started for the next door but stopped when she flung herself in front of him. "Please, you do not understand."

This time he put his hands around her waist, picked her up and set her down on the other side of him. "I understand more than you think." He opened the door and then caught his breath. The old woman sitting up in the bed looked like an angel. Her hair was pure white, her eyes were a pastel blue and her cheeks were the most beautiful pink he had ever seen on a woman. She immediately smiled at him.

"Hello," she said, "have you come to give me a hug?"

Jessup hurried around him into her mother's open arms and hugged her tight. "Yes, Mother, today you get lots of hugs."

"Thank you," she said."

Jessup looked pleadingly into her husband's eyes, but he ignored her. "What are you doing?"

He wrapped her mother in her blankets and then lifted the woman out of her bed.

Tears gushed down Jessup's cheeks, "No, no, please do not take her away from me. Patrick, please!"

He stopped and turned to look at her grief stricken face, "I am not taking her away from you, I am taking her *with* you."

"What?"

"The MacGreagors do not abandon parents when they are old and have forgotten who we are. She will live with us and you will care for her until she draws her last breath, just as I will care for my mother."

She was stunned. Uncle Michael swore Highlanders just left their parents somewhere to die. Jessup followed Patrick to the top of the stairs and watched him carry her mother down, across the room and then out the front door. All her life she believed a lie.

Outside, Patrick set his mother-in-law in Lorne's lap.

She smiled at Lorne, "Did you come to give me a hug?"

He did not speak English and had no idea what she was saying until Neil explained. Then Lorne smiled and hugged her.

"Thank you," she said.

Neil looked at Patrick and shook his head. "She is still not coming?"

Patrick shrugged and headed back inside. "Wife, where are you?" He noticed Rupert cowering behind a chair and the king trying to persuade him to come out. Jessup didn't answer, so he went back up the stairs and started opening more doors, until he found her. She was sitting on the edge of her bed crying.

"I love you," he said.

"I know, 'tis not that."

He sat down and put both arms around her. "What then?"

"When I walk out that door, I will be free finally. 'Tis a dream I have never dared dream and now I am suddenly frightened."

"Are you afraid of what will happen to your brother and uncle?"

"No, the king will see to them." She took a deep breath and brushed away her tears. "How did you know about my mother?"

"The King told us."

"How did..."

"Wife, we have a whole lifetime to talk. Will you come home with me now?"

She touched his face with her fingertips. Only this time she did not have to memorize his features and try to keep the memory for a thousand years. She was going to the place where all the Highlanders lived with her mother and the man she loved. At last, Jessup was going to have a real home.

*

Outside of Sween's cottage, Laird Neil MacGreagor swung up on his horse, took the baby out of Kessan's hands and carefully placed her against his bare chest. Then he wrapped his shirt around her and put his massive hand on her back. "Bury Gillie next to my brother." He waited for Kessan's nod and then took his daughter home.

The war with his brother was over, but in his family there were no winners. He took a deep breath, slowly let it out and looked at the top of the baby's head. She was a new life and offered him a new chance at happiness.

He once thought he loved the baby's mother, but that was not to be. Now Gillie was dead. There was no way to tell if this child really was his brother's, but she needed someone to love her and Neil needed someone to love. He would claim her and they would be good for each other.

When he reached the Keep, he carried the tiny baby up the stairs, wrapped her in soft wool and then laid her in the small box. Her bedchamber was the room Sween grew up in before he became consumed with anger. Now it would become a place of love and laughter again.

The child yawned and Neil smiled. She needed a name and he decided on one months ago. If the baby survived and was a girl, she would carry the name of a woman who loved Sween almost as much as their mother did. Her name was Leesil MacGreagor, she cared for both of Anna's sons when they were small and his daughter would be named after her.

Neil went to the room next to hers, brought back his grandmother's hand mirror and laid it on the table. Now it belonged to Leesil. Then he drew his father's sword and sat down on the bed. The handle was not gold except for the small strip down each side, but it was well worn. As a boy, Neil often admired his father's sword and now that he was a man, the weight of it felt perfect in his hand.

But this wasn't the only MacGreagor sword.

He set it down on the table and then pulled the bed away from the wall. With the tip of his dagger, he lifted a slat out of the floor and looked inside. Neil was the fourth generation to inherit the other sword and it was still there. He breathed a sigh of relief. A lot could have happened to the sword during the war with his brother, but it was safe.

He slowly took hold of the handle and pulled the sheathed sword out of its hiding place in the floor. Jessup's uncle was wrong -- the handle was not gold.

Neil slowly pulled the sword out of the scabbard, held it up and watched the long, golden blade glisten in the candle light. He smiled. Someday he would give this sword to his son, and if not a son, it would be Leesil's.

-- End –

GLENNA

CHAPTER I

Walrick MacGreagor still thought about her every day. Her name was Donnel, she was his twin sister and when they were five, someone kidnapped her. He especially thought about her on days like this when most of the MacGreagors had what they needed, no one was threatening war, water rights were not in dispute and the clan went about their lives trying not to be more bored than necessary.

Walrick, a stout warrior with dark brown hair and blue eyes was not Laird MacGreagor's second in command or even his third, but he was a worthy fighter, a valued advisor and a good friend. He often helped Kessan train the younger men, but on this day, he decided just to observe. So he chose a tree at the edge of the meadow, sat down and leaned back against it to watch the warriors sharpen their skills.

On a similarly mundane day fifteen years earlier, Walrick's father decided to take his family to their favorite meadow in the southern part of MacGreagor land. His mother prepared a noon meal, Walrick rode in his father's lap, his sister rode with her mother and they happily went off without a worry or a care in the world.

The twins were playing in the middle of a clearing and their parents were sitting on the grass, he remembered. His father had just kissed his mother, which made her smile, and even after all these years, Walrick could still see his mother's face. Then it happened -- she leaned over to kiss her husband back and an arrow meant for him suddenly pierced her heart.

It did not make sense to Walrick's father. The MacGreagors were not at war and it took several precious seconds for his father to understand what was happening. Realizing it was too late to save his wife, he raced to the middle of the meadow, managed to grab Walrick and get him to safety behind a tree. But when he went back for his daughter, Donnel was gone.

For hours, Walrick's father searched for her, beat the bushes and called her name. When all efforts failed, he sunk to his knees near his wife's body and let out a heartsick, wounded cry. That too Walrick still clearly remembered, and even now, it made him close his eyes and force the sound out of his mind.

MacGreagors searched the area for days, but Donnel was never seen again. They would have gladly gone to war to get her back, but Walrick was the only one who saw the colors the kidnapper wore and no one knew what clan those colors belonged to.

Nevertheless, Walrick couldn't help but believe his twin was still alive. He was convinced he would know if she was dead and he could still feel her in his heart. She was alive somewhere -- she had to be.

*

Ewing Larmont was on a mission to find the perfect husband for Laird Larmont's daughter, Glenna. The candidate had to be a laird, first; look like a Viking, second; have a sense of humor third, and be willing to fight Laird Larmont for her hand in marriage. The first three requirements were not so difficult to fulfill, but finding a man willing to fight Laird Larmont was not likely and perhaps not even possible. The King of Scotland called the fierce and reckless Larmont the most dangerous man alive and many believed it.

Nevertheless, the storyteller, Ewing Larmont, was sent throughout the Highlands to find such a man. Normally he was happy just riding his mare from clan to clan, making friends and telling stories to anyone willing to share a meal. But a few short weeks after his quest began, his life took on new meaning. He found himself to be the spreader of real news, not so real news, gossip, outright lies and advice even when he had no valid advice to spread.

Then he somehow became a seeker of truth. Parents who lost track of daughters after marriage to men in other clans wanted information -- what happened, they asked, to Sarah Buchanan, Mary Forrester or Julie Boyle? Finding the answers to these nagging questions captivated Ewing and to remember all the names, he made up poems that meant nothing to anyone but him.

By most standards, Ewing Larmont was considered an elder. He was 37, of average height, slightly bow legged and wore a green plaid with red and white stripes woven into it. His blond hair was turning white and his eyes had long since lost their twinkle. He survived on his storytelling; one story for a loaf of bread, two for a full meal and three if they offered apples or other rare delights. His favorite story was 'The Glory of Land Essen,' not because it was the greatest of all stories but because he could adjust it to fit many different circumstances.

It was in search of a meal that Ewing wandered into a friendly looking courtyard and encountered Laird Gordon's very skeptical son.

"The mare's name is Clark?" the lad asked for the fifth time. "But Clark is a lad's name."

"Aye."

"Then what do you call the colt?"

"Laura."

At age ten, the first-born son of Laird Gordon was completely puzzled. He stood with his legs apart and his feet slightly rolled outward. His arms were crossed just like a grown man and his frown was genuine. "You mean the colt will become a stallion named Laura? You best hide. My father will run you off, soon as he knows you are not right in the head."

Ewing laughed. "It has happened before, to be sure. But you see, I am a storyteller and most men enjoy a good story now and again even if they think I am daft. Tell me, does your mother yet live?"

"Nay, she passed at my birth."

"Ah, and has your father a new wife?"

"Not yet."

"Then I will see your father." Ewing announced it as if he had a choice. Three very large highlanders were standing behind the lad glaring at him and he was almost certain he would be standing in front of Laird Gordon sooner rather than later, willing or not.

The lad did not move. Instead, he admired the colt's black coat, white mane, stocking feet and the streak of white down the bridge of its nose. "You aim to barter this colt?"

"Nay, Laura is too young."

"My father will have this colt for me, you will see."

"I was afraid of that." Ewing dismounted, took hold of Clark's bridle and followed the boy and his guards into the center of Clan Gordon's village. The naming of his horses was to test the prospective husband's sense of humor and so far, the son failed the test. He feared the father would do the same.

*

For the first time in three months, Laird Neil MacGreagor got a full night of sleep. When he opened his eyes and realized the baby had not cried all night he panicked, rushed to the bedchamber next to his and threw open the door. To his relief, Leesil was not dead. She was wide awake, playing with her toes, listening to the sound of her own coos, and smiling.

Neil remembered to breathe. "You are going to be the death of me yet." Leesil could be any man's child, but she was looking more and more like his brother every day. Her hair started out very blonde, but it was beginning to turn dark like Neil's and it appeared she would have her grandmother's brilliant blue eyes. He vowed to love her no matter who she looked like, but it was a comfort when she began to resemble his family. Maybe she really was his brother's child.

Neil took off the baby's wet wrappings and put her in dry ones. Then he lifted her up and kissed her cheek. "You need a mother and I need a wife." As if it was a signal, Leesil began to shriek her hunger and Neil laughed. He carried her out onto the balcony and listened to her cries echo against the cold, stonewalls. She was exactly what his empty world needed -- signs of life.

The great hall was a large room with a new blue and white tapestry on one wall. A long table with chairs ran down the middle of the room with smaller tables along the walls. A large wooden door was at one end with a smaller one at the other end. A hearth burned continuously now that there was a baby inside and a man came regularly to see that it did not go out. Up the stairs, a balcony stretched from Neil's bedchamber on one end to his parent's old room on the other. Doors led to three other bedchambers in between.

Soon the great hall would begin to fill with people and Neil would be glad.

*

Victoria stood at the top of the stairs and looked down into the great hall. Neil was there with some of his men -- ignoring her again. Why couldn't he see she was perfect for him? Each time it was her turn to help in the Keep, Victoria made sure her hair was brushed, her cheeks were rosy and her eyes were bright. But if Neil noticed her at all it was just to nod his appreciation for something she did.

She turned and walked into his bedchamber. It was her turn to clean it and it was her favorite duty. She loved him. She had loved him for years and dreamed of the day he would put his arms around her. Dreams, it seemed, were all she had, but that was bound to change soon.

Victoria closed the door and slipped her hand under the plaids on his bed to see if she could still feel his warmth. Once they were married, she would feel his warmth every night and insist she be the only one to touch his bed. She would love him, please him and make him very happy. Why couldn't he see that?

She had a thousand ideas for improving his home to make it more comfortable. It seemed so dark and gloomy since the war, but Neil didn't ask for suggestions and she was far too shy to offer. She would just have to wait until after they were married.

*

Just as his father had, Laird MacGreagor spent the morning assigning cleaning duties to wayward children. He liked getting to know them and liked guessing which future warrior would marry which future woman. Patrick, his second in command was busy getting his wife and mother-in-law settled and Kessan was off training the new warriors with the help of the older ones. It was an ordinary day.

Too soon, the children were all gone and Neil was trying to decide what to do next when Kindel MacGreagor walked into the great hall. He stood as he always did when women entered. "What brings you to see me this fine day, Kindel?"

She meant to be bold and determined, but now that she was there, her courage vanished. "I am unhappy." That wasn't what she meant to say at all. "I mean, you are not...what I mean is..."

Neil knew Kindel never complained and he was taken by surprise. "What makes you unhappy?"

"I need you to help me." She abruptly hung her head, her brown hair fell into her face and her blue eyes misted over.

Neil gave her a moment and then softly brushed the hair away from her face, "Help you do what?"

A tear had already rolled down her cheek by the time she finally looked up, "Get a husband."

"Oh." He urged her to sit down and handed her a cloth to wipe her eyes. Then he retook his seat at the head of the table.

"I am not noticed," Kindel blurted out.

"I doubt that is true. Is there a particular lad who does not notice you?" He waited while she nodded her head. This, he knew, could be very dangerous. If the woman preferred him, he would have to reject her and that was not something he found pleasing. Still, he could not help her if he did not know who the man was. "Would you like to tell me who he is?" Again she nodded and he held his breath.

She quickly glanced around the empty room and then lowered her voice to just above a whisper. "'Tis Kessan."

Neil hid his relief. "Kessan is a good lad and he will make a good husband."

"Aye, but he is blind and stupid. I try, but he does not notice me." She suddenly got worried. "You will not tell him, will you?"

"I will not tell him."

"But you will help me?"

"I will try." He thought for a minute. He was new to the matchmaking duties of a laird and wanted to consider if they would suit each other. Aye, he thought at last, Kessan and Kindel would be a good match. "Can you find two others to go riding?"

"I can."

"Good. Tell them I will ask Kessan and Walrick to take the three of you tomorrow morning."

Kindel quickly stood up, kissed him on the cheek and rushed out the door. Neil smiled. He marveled at how easy it was to help others fall in love, and how difficult it had become to find a wife for himself. With gossip quickly spread and feelings easily hurt, he dared not show the least bit of favoritism to any woman until he was sure what he wanted. So far, he was not at all sure what he wanted. As he had several times in the past, he looked around the great hall and wondered what a wife would do to improve it.

*

Glenna Larmont was a happy young woman with light brown hair that curled around the sides of her face. She was tall, had blue eyes and looked very much like her mother. She also had six brothers and two sisters, all younger.

They lived in Stratsgory Castle in the north of Scotland with a father who was fierce and reckless, and a mother stout enough to knock the wind out of him when he needed it. The castle had long winding steps up the high cliffs and Glenna loved sitting at the top of the stairs with the wind in her hair watching the birds fly out over the ocean. That's what she loved to do, but on this day she was in her bedchamber having yet another unwelcome discussion about her future with her mother.

Glenna's clan offered everything a young woman could want -- except a forest. Her homeland was a lush green, held a collection of solid rock hillsides and many clear water inlets. But it had few trees and no forest. Yet wanting to walk through a forest was hardly a good reason to marry.

Mistress Larmont hugged her daughter. "Sweetheart, all women must take a husband. It is the way of the world."

"I know, but why so soon? I am not yet eighteen and I do not want to leave you."

"I felt the same, but I have been happy with your father. Happiness with a husband is different than it is with parents and I want that for you."

"Then you promise I will be happy?" Her mother hesitated and Glenna noticed. "That is what I thought."

"Daughter, you have two younger sisters to think of. If you refuse to marry, how will we ever find good husbands for them?" Glenna's mother walked to the window, moved the heavy drape back and looked out over the calm water. "Our clan is small and there are no lads suitable for you to choose from. For that reason, we sent Ewing to find a good husband elsewhere and you must agree to marry whomever he finds, 'tis the only way."

Glenna shrugged. Shrugging was not the same as giving in to her mother's wishes, it was just the end of yet another useless discussion on the subject. Glenna simply did not want a husband and God willing, she would get her way. Just to be sure, she gave the storyteller a requirement her parents did not know about; she required that Ewing find a man who was a laird, looked like a Viking, had a sense of humor, was willing to fight her father -- and loved someone else.

CHAPTER II

The Clan Gordon's village looked like any other with cottages, stables, followers and children. Laird Gordon's warriors were brave, his keep was ordinary and the women attending him were much like any other women. However, Laird Gordon did indeed look like a Viking. He had very blond hair, a stout mustache and beard, and he was an extremely large man.

Ewing Larmont had never actually seen a Viking, but he could guess what they looked like the same as anyone could. Ancient stories put them as blond with blue eyes, and the rest of his guess was based on the size of the sunken Viking boat the Larmonts had in their cove. It was very large and he surmised the Vikings must have been very large as well. He did know, however, that after they landed, Viking men married Scottish women.

"I will have your colt for my son," Laird Gordon announced. He stood with his feet apart and slightly rolled outward just like his son's. His arms were folded and his eyes were determined. The room was not large and seemed even smaller with twelve stout men in it. The walls were decorated with the skins and heads of wild boars and red deer. More skins covered the floors or hung over doorways.

Ewing tried to hide his fear. He did not consider himself a small man but Gordon was a full two hands taller. In a fight with Laird Larmont, that would come in handy but just now, Ewing could easily be crushed. On the other hand, cowering before such a man would be an even greater mistake. "Laura is not yet old enough to wean."

"Then you will live with us until she is." At his own mistake, Laird Gordon began to laugh. "Of course, Laura is not a she, she is a he. Never have I heard of a mare with a man's name and a stallion with a woman's name. You managed to confuse even me."

Ewing pretended to join in the laughter while he gave this man a good hard look. Laird Gordon had just met the first three husband qualifications; he was a laird, looked like a Viking and had a sense of humor. Aye, he might do. "I will barter the colt for your promise to marry Glenna Larmont."

Gordon abruptly stopped laughing. He sat down in his well-worn chair and glared at Ewing. "Tell me about this lass."

"She lives in the north. She is the eldest daughter of Laird Larmont and is of marrying age. She needs a husband and you need a wife. It will be a good match."

"Aye, but is she pleasing?"

Ewing took a moment to look around again. Except for the boastings of hunted animals, the furnishings were simple, the Keep was clean and Glenna's beauty would certainly brighten up the place. But then he noticed two women watching him. Neither looked happy and one slightly shook her head as if to warn him of something. He decided a riddle was in order. "Laird Gordon, is one rose lovelier than another?"

"Nay, they are all the same."

"Then who is to say if one lass is more bonnie than another? A lass is a lass."

Laird Gordon laughed. "True enough. When can I have this wife?"

"As soon as you fight her father for her hand."

"Why would I do that?"

"Because he requires it."

Laird Gordon shook his head. "To have this wife, I must kill her father? If I did that, she would hate me and a lass who hates her husband gives him a life of misery."

"Aye, but you would not be required to kill him. If you win, you will let him live."

"And if I lose?"

"You will die." A normal man would find this wife not worth the trouble, but for a moment Laird Gordon appeared to see it as a challenge and was actually considering the idea. Ewing held his breath.

*

It was an unusually warm day, when Kessan and Walrick helped three unmarried women mount their horses in the courtyard. As was the MacGreagor custom, women were not encouraged to ride without a guard and faced with another boring day, the unmarried Kessan and Walrick were happy for the diversion. Kessan was far more flirtatious, answered their questions and flattered the women with comments on their riding abilities.

Walrick tried to keep his mind and his attention on any possible danger, yet every time Kindel laughed, he looked at her. He had known her since they were children, but he hadn't realized how wonderful she really was until now. Her laughter sounded almost like music and if any woman could make him smile, he thought maybe she could.

However, a second later he remembered his missing sister, the death of his mother and his father's painful cry. Walrick was a strong man, when it came to a muscular build, and a warrior's mind set, but when it came to love he was still a frightened child. Never again did he want to hurt that badly and love opened him up to the possibility.

Walrick looked away.

Kindel thought she preferred Kessan, but she was beginning to think Walrick was more handsome. He actually noticed her and when she saw him look away, it oddly distressed her. She quickly brushed that emotion aside and suggested a game of skill to the other women.

Each of the women took turns shooting their arrows at a mark on a tree. Kindel was a terrible shot and her first attempt missed the tree altogether. She laughed it off, allowed the others to tease her mercilessly, and made the afternoon enjoyable for them all.

Walrick decided she needed more practice and it would be a good reason to spend time with her. Then he remembered he planned never to marry and dismissed the thought. Let some other man teach her. But he couldn't seem to keep from looking at her. He looked when she laughed, he looked when she spoke and he looked when she was quiet...to find out why.

By the time the men took the women back inside the wall, Walrick's heart was having a full scale war with his mind. He helped her dismount and even after his mind told him not to, he watched her walk away.

*

Mayze MacGreagor was the real hero in the war against Sween. It was she who got everyone to safety outside the wall and by the time Gillie died and Neil brought tiny Leesil home, Mayze was married to Dugan and with child herself. Various women had been chosen to serve Neil's needs, but Mayze liked being at the Keep when her husband was away with his hunters. Neil not only liked having her there, he liked letting her make decisions just as a mistress would. It took a burden off of him

The first few days, a wet nurse came to feed the baby, but Leesil did not like the woman's milk. She ate, when she was hungry enough and did not suffer, but when an elder suggested they try goat's milk, Neil and Mayze were all for it.

Other women came to help with bathing and dressing the child, but it soon became apparent the unmarried women had more in mind than just tending a child. Neil was pleasant, just as he always was, but none of the women pleased him when it came to choosing a wife and he was beginning to feel like a cornered rat.

It was for that reason he began to surround himself with all the unmarried men he could. Patrick had a wife and Dugan was married to Mayze, but Kessan, Walrick, Dan, and Lorne were unmarried as were several other men. He hoped he could make one of his men happy and not have to harshly turn away the attentions of any good woman. It did not seem to be working. Perhaps the men felt they could not be themselves around him, or perhaps Neil just didn't have the same skill as a matchmaker that his father had. Whatever the cause, the women paid him too much attention and the men paid the women too little.

*

Victoria did not like having all the men at the Keep when she went to clean. She liked it much better when Neil was alone with her. The men were always distracting Neil and how was he to notice her when he didn't even look up the stairs, except when Leesil fussed? It was infuriating.

Once, Victoria dropped something and he raced up to see if she was alright. She wished she had at least cut herself, but she was fine and had to admit it. He noticed her, but not in the way she wanted. His eyes looked the same as they did for all his followers without a hint of love...or even lust. She could not bear it and was careful not to drop anything ever again.

*

Ewing Larmont left the Gordon Clan without a husband for Glenna. He was relieved when Laird Gordon finally declined to fight her father and glad to be moving on. Next, Ewing wandered into the Blower Clan. He swapped news, told his stories and ate well for a few days. However, Laird Blower's first in command got it into his head that the harmless and loveable storyteller was trying to steal his wife. Ewing narrowly escaped by trading his colt for his freedom. He hated to give Laura up and thought about home more often than he had in weeks, so he set his mind to seeing the one place that reminded him of the real Land of Essen -- the MacGreagor hold.

*

Walrick thought about it for a couple of days before he finally got up the courage to approach Neil on the subject. Then once he firmly decided, he didn't even wait until the other men in the great hall stopped talking. "The lasses need more training."

His abrupt intrusion into Patrick's description of work that needed to be done in one of the vegetable gardens surprised all of them, especially Neil. "More training on what?"

"Some are not good shots and they need to be. If we are attacked, they must defend themselves and their children."

He was right, of course, and it was not unusual for Walrick to be overly concerned for the women in the clan. Sometimes he was positively obsessive about it, but Neil thought there might be another reason. Kindel, he remembered, had missed the tree on their outing a few days earlier and perhaps Walrick saw it as a good reason to spend time with her. "Do all the lasses need practice, or just a few?"

"I do not know. Perhaps we should test them to see which need more practice."

A very tactful answer, Neil thought. "Would you be willing to test the lasses?"

"I would."

"So would I," three other men said.

Neil smiled. "Done then. Arrange it to begin tomorrow morning in the meadow, and warn the lads not to laugh at those who are not good shots. Our protection is important and I will not have our lasses so upset they refuse to practice. Agreed?" He glanced around at all their nods. "Walrick, choose two to help you."

*

The next morning Neil dealt with three children who had not followed the rules, put Leesil down for her morning nap and then went to his upstairs bedchamber window to watch the women shoot in the meadow. It did not take long to see what Walrick was really up to. He tested Kindel and when she failed, he helped her load her bow and then helped her aim, but still Kindel missed.

As though he knew Neil was watching, Walrick turned, looked up at the window and when Neil nodded, he told Kindel Neil wanted to see her.

Walrick knew what was coming. He had seen this kind of thing before with one of the warriors. Men got angry, but she was a woman and he hated it when women got upset. Taking away privileges was never easy, but it had to be done.

Neil took a deep breath, went down the stairs and stood by the table to wait for her. Of all his duties, this had to be the most unpleasant.

"Have I done something wrong?" she asked as soon as she walked through the door. The worry was evident on her face.

"Of course not, but we must talk." He held a chair, waited for her to sit and then sat down next to her at the head of the table. Walrick, he noticed, took up a protective position behind her just as a husband would. There was no easy way to ask so he just blurted it out, "Kindel, are you going blind?" Just as he expected, she burst into tears.

"I do not mean to be. Every morning I wash my eyes, but it does not help. I want to be a wife and a mother, but if I cannot see..." She began to sob and Walrick put his hands on her shoulders to comfort her.

"You know we will not abandon you," said Neil.

"I know, that is what upsets me the most. I will be a burden on the people I love. If we are attacked, someone would have to risk their life to take me to safety. I could not bear it."

"The people love you and I promise we will not look upon you as a burden. Now that we know, we will do all we can for your comfort."

"What can you do?"

He wiped a tear off her cheek. "First, we can let the clan know so they can watch out for you. The children especially need to be careful so you will not fall and..."

"And they will feel sorry for me and get a pitiful look on their faces. I will hate it. Is there no way to avoid telling them?"

Neil looked at Walrick for help. "Well, we could..."

"'Twould help if we knew what she can and cannot see," said Walrick.

"Aye," Neil agreed.

Feeling a little more hopeful, Kindel wiped her tears and took two deep breaths. "I can see most things still. I cannot see to sew, but I can cook and clean, although my mother complains I do not get some things clean enough."

"Your mother does not know?"

"Nay, 'tis her sad look I fear seeing most."

Neil stopped to think for a moment. "You understand we cannot let you shoot anymore."

"I know and I am relieved."

"Good, then if you promise to tell me when your eyes get worse, we will not tell the clan just yet. But you must promise to let me know."

"I promise." She should have gotten up to leave, but she did not.

"Is there more?"

"Neil, I understand now that I must not take a husband. 'Twould be unfair to him and to my children."

"But if a lad loves you..."

"Aye, but if he knows I am going blind, how do I tell the difference between his love and his pity?"

*

Baby Leesil's favorite place in the world seemed to be on her father's bare chest. Neil did not mind at all, even when he got wet. But Mayze insisted constantly being held was not good for the child. She set Leesil's box on the table in the great hall in front of Neil, took the baby off his chest and settled her on the soft plaids where she could stretch, wiggle and contort her little face when necessary.

Neil discovered watching her was just as wonderful as holding her and finally nodded his approval. Then came that awful day when Leesil refused the goat's milk. Everyone panicked. Nursing mothers from all over the clan came to offer their milk, but Leesil was having none of it. Her stomach seemed to hurt, she screamed and even being held against Neil's chest didn't calm her down. After three hours, the worst of all thoughts crossed their minds - Leesil MacGreagor was about to die.

*

Ewing remembered the loch well. Being from the north, he rarely bathed in a loch and much preferred warm water in the old wooden basin his mother, and later his wife, heated water for. However, the MacGreagors did not seem to mind bathing in this loch and when he tried it on an earlier visit, he found it pleasing once he got used to the tepid water.

He had just submerged and come back to the surface when he

heard the baby cry. Ewing got dressed, led Clark down the path and then walked his horse over the drawbridge. In the courtyard, the distressed people were gathered and no one stopped him. So he threaded his way through the crowd, handed his reins to a boy, walked up the steps and gently pushed the huge wooden door open. Cautiously, he stuck his head in.

All he could see was the backs of several large men, but he could hear the baby loud and clear. He dared to take a step inside. Ewing was the oldest of a healthy brood and he was pretty sure he knew how to help, but the men in this collection were very large. He took two more steps, held his breath and cleared his throat.

At the sight of the stranger, both Kessan and Walrick spun around and drew their swords. "How the hell did you get in here?" Kessan yelled.

CHAPTER III

His eyes were wide, but Ewing was not about to cower. Instead, he boldly stepped closer and made the men part until he was looking at the Viking holding the baby. He knew instantly this was the laird he had been looking for. First, he needed to quiet the babe. "If you will let me, I will put that child to sleep."

Neil was nearly beside himself with worry, "She does not need to sleep, she needs to eat. She has refused everything."

"I see. In that case, if you will let me, I will feed her and then put her to sleep. She is exhausted."

"Feed her how? She refuses to eat."

Ewing looked around. He glanced at his worn and dirty kilt, then at Neil's much more presentable one. "I'll have that."

With a screaming child in his arms, Neil was not in the mood for jokes. He glared and started to lean forward as though he were going to stand up.

"I mean, cut me off a part of your kilt."

Kessan quickly pulled out a pleat, cut off a strip of his own plaid and handed it to Ewing.

"Good, now do you have honey?"

Neil settled back in his chair, nodded and Kessan went out the back door. Soon he returned and handed a small bowl of honey to the stranger.

Ewing folded the piece of plaid into fourths. "Get that flask of milk ready." He curled the folded corner, dipped it in the honey and put the tip of it on the screaming child's tongue. Leesil fought it at first, but then she stopped crying, tasted it and began to eagerly suck on the cloth. "When I pull this out, you give her the milk."

It worked. Leesil drank the milk until the taste of honey was gone. Then each time she began to cry Ewing repeated the process until the baby ate enough to sleep for a while.

Neal took a very long, deep breath and put the exhausted child in the box. "'Tis is a miracle."

Ewing nodded. "You have to mind what the goat eats. They get into the bitter herbs and it bitters the milk."

"I see," said Neil. "Tell me, who are you and how did you get in here without our knowing?"

"I am Ewing Larmont and I mean no harm. Your people are gathered outside and..."

Neil forgot about the people. They must be worried sick, he thought, and didn't stay to hear the rest of what Ewing had to say. Instead, he quickly walked out the door onto the landing. "She is sleeping." He smiled when the people began to cheer and he had to hold up his hand to quiet them. "Please do not wake her." They returned his smile, quietly left and then he went back inside.

"Your people love her, I see. Is she a special child?"

"Aye." Neil sat back down, glanced at his daughter and then reached for the flask of wine. "She is a MacGreagor and all MacGreagor children are special." He poured wine in a goblet and handed it to Ewing.

The more Ewing saw of this man, the more he liked. He was not only handsome; his people loved their children more than most. However Laird MacGreagor did not have blond hair. It was possible, he supposed, that some Vikings had dark hair...perhaps. He took a quick sip of wine. "Are you married, Laird MacGreagor?"

"Not yet, why do you ask?"

"I come from Stratsgory Castle in the far north where my laird and his mistress live with nine children. The eldest is Glenna. She is ready to marry and her father has sent me to find a husband."

"I see, I have not heard of these people. Tell me about the land of the Larmont?"

Ewing watched as the warrior pulled out a chair and nodded for Ewing to sit at the table. The seat was at the right hand of Laird MacGreagor and it was a great honor. Ewing held his head high and sat down. "The land of the Larmont is the place in the north where the Vikings first landed in Scotland. We live at the edge of a great ocean and under the waters of our cove lies the proof."

"Proof of what?"

"A Viking ship"

Neil smiled. "I would like to see that ship and the ocean someday. How many days would it take to go and come back?"

"I neglected to count. Perhaps five or six each way if one did not stop to see the sights. But there is much to see and several clans between our two lands."

"Perhaps we will see it someday."

"Perhaps you will collect a wife when you do."

Neil smiled. "The one you are sent to find a husband for?"

"The same. Her name is Glenna, she is pleasing and she will make you a good wife."

"I am surrounded by bonnie women and I have no desire to go elsewhere to find a wife. Besides, I love another and I could not leave her."

Ewing got even more excited. If Neil MacGreagor loved another, then he would also fulfill the last requirement -- Glenna wanted a husband who loved another. "Whom do you love?"

"I fear my heart will forever belong to Leesil." Neil glanced inside the box.

"The baby?" Ewing's grin was growing wider by the moment. Glenna did not say the one he loved had to be a fully-grown woman. Two more requirements and Neil MacGreagor would be the perfect husband for Glenna Larmont.

"Aye, this baby has my heart forever."

Ewing decided to change the subject. "Just now I am reminded." He paused to take another sip of wine. "In my travels I have received several requests for information. Mary Forrester's mother said she married a MacGreagor and she wants to know how her daughter is doing."

Neil frowned. "I know no Mary Forrester."

Lorne grinned, "Aye, you know her. Mary is married to Ossian who is my cousin. She will be very pleased to hear news of her mother. I will go get her." Lorne got up and rushed out the door.

"I am a happy lad when I can bring news to families," said Ewing. "Now, allow me to say I am a storyteller and a hungry one at that. In my travels, I trade a story for a meal. Are you interested?"

"You are welcome to eat with us but you need not pay. We owe you for helping us with the wee one. However, if you like to tell them, we will like hearing your stories very much."

"In that case, might I put my mare, Clark, out to pasture in your meadow?"

Ewing heard their gasps and knew he had the attention of every man in the room. He wondered if they would laugh or wait for their laird's reaction. They waited.

"Your mare is named Clark?" Neil asked at length.

"Aye." The seconds seemed endless. If he smiled, Neil would pass another husband requirement.

Neil smiled. "You gave your mare a lad's name?"

Ewing didn't have time to answer. Mary Forester MacGreagor rushed in, sat down beside Ewing and monopolized every moment of his time with questions about her family. He hardly had time to enjoy his meal.

*

Kindel and Emily served the evening meal that same night and as he watched, Neil noticed something more was going on in the room, other than the boisterous conversation between Ewing and Mary. There was a definite flicker in Walrick's eyes when Kindel came near. Perhaps he'd been right all along; Walrick was interested in far more than Kindel's eye sight. Kessan, on the other hand, boldly flirted with both women preferring neither one over the other.

"And two lads," Ewing was telling, "were thrown from the horse. Thank God neither broke any bones and each had but a few bruises."

"That is good news," Mary said.

Ewing ate his last bite, washed it down with the last of his wine and turned to Neil. "A fine, fine meal and I am very grateful. Now, shall we discuss..."

*

Mayze had eaten very little and hardly said a word, which was extremely unusual for her and everyone noticed except her husband. However, Kessan, the eldest of ten was pretty sure what that meant, so before Mary could slip out the door he pulled her aside and whispered in her ear.

Mary stood and watched Mayze making circles on her extended stomach for a time with her hands and then nodded to Kessan. Yep, Mayze was going into labor. Kessan almost didn't reach her in time. Just as she started to cry out, he scooped her up in his arms and grinned. "'Tis time!" He proudly announced it as though he were the father instead of Dugan. Grinning from ear to ear, Kessan carried her out the door.

Dugan, the smallest of all the MacGreagor men, was about to pass out. Walrick took hold of him under one arm, Lorne had him under the other and they practically had to drag him out the door. They hauled him down the steps, around the corner, up the path and left him sitting on a rock outside his cottage in a daze. Kessan took Mayze inside and soon the midwife went in to tend her. Then Walrick, Kessan and Loren hurried back to the Keep.

Dugan's friends cared and would be back to check on the expectant father later, but no one wanted to miss what was about to happen this night in the Keep.

*

Victoria loved these nights too and as soon as she and Neil were married, she wouldn't have to hide under the stairs for hours. After they were married, she could sit by him, enjoy the wagers, and then go up to bed when she got tired -- unless of course, she was the one giving birth.

Most women were frightened by the prospect, but if the child was Neil's, she was not afraid. Neil loved her too much to let anything happen to her. He told her so, right after...Victoria blinked twice. Something, a thought, was on the edge of her mind, but she could not quite grasp what it was.

*

In the great hall, Dan got the boards out while the woman cleared the bowls and the spoons off the table. Neil picked up his daughter and took her upstairs to bed. It would be a second miracle if she could sleep through this night, but wagering the sex of a new baby was the best of all sports and Neil had no intention of missing it even if it meant a fussy child tomorrow.

Kindel and Emily were also excited. Rumors always swirled about such nights as these in the Keep, but few women had ever seen one. As soon as the table was cleared, Kindle took Emily's hand and pulled her to the wall near the hearth. "If we are very quiet, perhaps Neil will not notice us and send us home." They sat down on a narrow bench and tried to disappear.

As soon as word spread that Mayze was in labor, the room started to fill up with men. The first thing Walrick did when he came back from taking Dugan home was look for Kindel. At first, he didn't see her, feared she was gone and started to get disappointed. But then he spotted her near the hearth. What he didn't see was Neil standing on the balcony above watching him.

Neil would have to send the women away soon, he knew. Betting men normally drank too much and were not always mindful of what they said or did. However, he wanted to watch just a little while longer. It was clear Walrick was watching her, but was Kindel showing an interest in Walrick? It was not that detectable, at least not yet.

The men formed two lines in front of the table. The first line was for those who made their mark on the baby boy board. The other line, a much shorter one, was for the men who wagered on it being a girl.

*

Ewing laughed with them, drank with them and enjoyed each of the men as though he were a member of the family. While he understood what the wagers were about, he could not quite make out what the winners would receive.

Seated at the table next to him, Neil explained, "The losers will do the work of the winners for one full week."

"I see, sounds like a fair wager to me. Do you wager with the lads?"

"I do not, but I do enjoy watching them."

Ewing smiled and stood up to stretch his legs. "Would you be interested in a small wager just between you and me? You can take whichever, a boy or a girl, and I will take the other."

Neil stood up too. "And what will the winner get?"

"If you lose, you will marry Glenna. If I lose, you will not."

Neil playfully slapped Ewing on the back. "And how will this

Glenna feel when she learns she is little more than payment of a wager?"

"She would not hear it from me and if you are wise, she would not hear it from you either. She is..." he paused intentionally to increase Neil's interest.

"Go on, she is what?"

"She is much more pleasing than most. Her mother can knock the wind out of her father and I suspect, Glenna will not let her husband get away with much either."

"Why does her father not let her choose her own husband?"

"We are a small clan and suitable lads are scarce. Besides, he prefers she marry a laird. She will make a good wife and mistress for any clan."

"Does she want a husband?"

"Nay."

"Still, her father will make her marry." Neil shook his head and went upstairs to check on Leesil. She was still asleep. When he came back out of the bedchamber, he once more stood on the balcony and looked down. Kindel and Emily were still there and Walrick did not seem brave enough to talk to them. But once he was back down the stairs, he asked Kessan to see them home and when he did, he thought he saw a measure of disappointment in Kindel's eyes. It made Neil secretly smile.

Tomorrow he would think of another reason to put the men together with the women. If anyone needed a husband it was Kindel and he could not think of a man more willing and capable of protecting a blind wife than Walrick. It would be a perfect match.

*

The wagers were all done and while some of the men went home, Ewing encouraged most to stay, get comfortable and listen to his story. "They called it the land of Essen," he began. "'Twas a place of golden goblets and silver plates, where pleasing lasses carried platters of every kind of savory food, up the steps to a castle twice more the size of..."

This, of course, was not the same version of the story he told to other clans. This version made the Land of Essen sound a lot like what Laird MacGreagor would see once he agreed to marry Glenna. It was a love story too, although most men denied wanting to hear about such things, most secretly did and Ewing threw in a great fight between two warriors over the pleasing woman to make it enthralling. A battle between two men was not that far from the truth when it came to Glenna, but Ewing decided the MacGreagor did not need to know that until much later.

Finally, Ewing ended his story. "They married, had many healthy children and lived a long life in the Land of Essen."

Neil raised his goblet in a salute. "You are a good storyteller. Have you more to tell?"

The room was already quiet and Ewing could not pass up the chance. "I do, but I am a man of many talents. I especially like a good wager and therefore I challenge you, Laird MacGreagor. If you lose this wager, you must make Glenna Larmont your bride. Will you take up the challenge?"

"You are a very persistent lad. What challenge do you have in mind this time?"

"Any challenge of your choosing, I am not afraid." He laughed and soon all the other men were laughing too. "Make it hard, make it difficult...make it impossible."

"Impossible?" Neil tried to think of something impossible. He looked at each of his men and none of them had any suggestions, but then he noticed Walrick was looking him in the eye. "What?"

"'Twould be impossible to find Donnel."

Neil studied the hopeful look on Walrick's face and quickly realized it was a wager he could not turn down. Only a very cruel man would deny Walrick the chance to find his missing twin sister no matter the personal cost. The clan would hate Neil for saying no and if by some miracle they could find Donnel, it would bring great happiness to have the lost MacGreagor daughter home again.

He had to say yes, but he needed just a little more time to think about it. He sat down and put his head in his hands. All eyes were on him, the room was completely still and Neil wondered what it would be like if he lost and had to marry a woman he had not seen and did not choose. It was true, Leesil needed a mother and he needed a wife, but … Impossible, he finally thought, it would be impossible to find Donnel and he was worried for nothing. "I will accept this wager."

*

After the wagering and all the storytelling ended, Ewing was offered a bed upstairs, while Neil and two other men went to help Dugan pace up and down the path in front of his cottage. Mayze gave birth to a healthy baby boy and made her husband a happy man. She also made all the men who placed their wagers on a boy very happy and the rest very sad. The men who bet on a girl were soon overwhelmed with work and as he usually did, Neil took pity on them and let them spread the extra work out over more than just a week.

*

Impossible was the word Ewing kept repeating over and over in his mind. How on earth was he going to find a girl kidnapped so many years ago? It truly was impossible and he did not hold out much hope. He was not that upset about it, however. Ewing liked his new life and if he never made it back to the land of his birth, he guessed it didn't matter. His wife was dead, he had no children and no one in the whole world would miss him.

He began his inquiry at the Clan Ferguson, told his story, enjoyed a meal or two, mounted his mare, and moved eastward to the next clan.

CHAPTER IV

After the war with Sween, Neil decided to build towers at intervals along the wall so they could more easily spot an enemy. The one nearest the bridge was finished first and men took turns watching day and night even when the bridge was up. Any time riders approached, the guards had a particular whistle that alerted everyone. A different whistle meant something awful was happening and the MacGreagors dreaded hearing that sound.

It was that terrifying whistle that interrupted Neil's evening meal. He quickly handed Leesil to a serving woman, raced out the door to the landing and looked up at the guard in the tower.

"KINDEL FELL OFF THE BRIDGE!"

Neil's heart stopped. He jumped off the landing and started to run. "WHERE?"

The guard pointed. "THE NORTH SIDE!" Neil panicked. If she fell off the north side, the current had her under the bridge by now. He jumped off the southern side and dove down.

Walrick was only one step behind him and went off the bridge on the northern side. He too dove down but it was dark under the bridge and he could not see her.

Neil's grandfather built the heavy bridge and it was wide enough for eight horses to cross side-by-side. Heavy rains in the north made the water in the moat run high, and Neil guessed there were three inches of air between the water and the underside of the bridge in some places but only two in others. If she found something to hold on to underneath, maybe ... He quickly surfaced and yelled, "RAISE THE BRIDGE!"

It seemed like forever for the aging hinges and chain to begin to screech. People poured out of their cottages and raced down the paths. Men coming back from the loch slipped into the moat farther downstream, while others inside the wall tried to help raise the bridge faster.

But time seemed to stand still and the movement was painfully slow.

They were running out of time. Walrick had been to the bottom of the moat three times and still didn't see her. He came back up under the bridge, tipped his head all the way back, gasped for air and dove back down. Each time, he had to fight the current and he knew she should have come out the other side by now -- if she were still alive. But she might have hit her head, her plaid might be caught on something and for the first time he admitted he loved her. He could not lose a mother, a sister and the woman he loved -- he would not survive it. Walrick took a deep breath, pushed his terror away and dove down again.

Neil couldn't find her either. She was stuck somewhere and if they did not find her soon, it would be too late. He surfaced and looked around hoping someone had her, but the men farther down were still diving and he couldn't see Walrick anywhere. The sounds of women crying mingled with the rushing water and the screeching bridge, but no man was shouting her recovery and Neil's heart was breaking. If she died it would be his fault. He should have insisted they tell the clan about her blindness so they could watch out for her. He was too soft hearted and if she died, he would never forgive himself.

*

Kindel was hanging on with the tips of her fingers to a board on the underside of the bridge. She too had her face turned up and was sucking in what little air there was between the top of the water and the moss covered wood. She told herself she had to get a grip on her fear. She was on the side of the moat near the wall and out of the swift current, but it was too deep to stand on anything, the wood was slick and her fingers were hurting. She thought someone would come for her soon and all she had to do was hold on. But that seemed like hours ago.

She decided if she was going to live, she would have to save herself. She took in as much air as she could and ducked down to look for the next place to grab hold and find air. For just a moment, she thought she saw Walrick's face. Then he had his strong arm around her and the bridge was going up. She wrapped her arms tightly around his neck and held on. Seconds later, he had her across the moat where the bridge was finally lifting and when he got her head out of the water, she gasped for air and then let out a frightened cry.

He was so happy to hear her cry he actually smiled. He made sure she was breathing well enough and then filled his lungs, "SHE IS ALIVE!"

She was indeed alive and Walrick was never going to let anything happen to her again. He let the water take them the rest of the way under the bridge, grabbed hold of Neil's arm on the other side and got her away from the swift current. He knew he should get her out of the water quickly, but he came too close to losing her and wanted her to stay in his arms just a moment longer.

Then Kindel refused to let go of him and tightened her grip around his neck. His embrace made her feel safe and she wasn't ready to give up that feeling. Neil brushed the wet hair off her face and asked if she was hurt, but she couldn't even let go of Walrick long enough to shake her head. She gritted her teeth and was never...ever going to let go.

It was the softness of Walrick's words in her ear that finally made her fear begin to subside. Later, she would not be able to remember what he said and it didn't really matter. He saved her and she would always love him for it. Patrick and Kessan were kneeling on the shore holding out their hands to her and at last, she let them pull her out of the water.

In the Kerr hold, Ewing Larmont found the wife of the Kerr so depressed over the loss of her newborn, he stayed only long enough to inquire about another child named Donnel. They knew nothing and were not in the mood for more questions or even a story.

*

It had become a habit for them and once again that morning, Neil and Walrick stood out on the landing of the Keep watching the women and children head for the loch to bathe. They were watching for a particular reason.

Kindel had a few bruises after her fall, but they were not bad and in a couple of weeks she was completely healed. Neil saw her coming down the path first and cleared his throat. Just in case she noticed them, neither man wanted her to think they were watching and pretended to be looking at something in the meadow.

When she came to the bridge, Kindel stopped and tried to gage exactly where the edge was. She decided the middle would be the safest and took a couple of steps to her right before she stepped on the wooden planks.

"Her sight is worse." Walrick finally said.

"Aye, she promised to come tell me."

"I remember."

"Have you asked her to marry you yet?"

Walrick was not surprised Neil guessed. "She has refused me."

"Why?"

"I am the only one who knows of her condition. She thinks I ask out of pity and not love."

"But you loved her before you knew. Have you told her that?"

Walrick rolled his eyes. "I tried, but she will not listen."

"There must be a way to convince her."

"If you think of anything, I will be happy to hear it."

Neil ran his fingers through his hair, "Suppose we put a rope along each side of the bridge so she will not fall off again? It might help ease her fear."

Walrick excitedly slapped Neil on the back and hurried down the steps. "'Twill surely ease mine. Sometimes you are brilliant."

He watched his friend hurry off to examine the bridge and think of a way to string the ropes. "If I were brilliant, I would be finding myself a wife instead of helping you."

*

The colors in the plaids of the Clan Forbes resembled the deep red and black ones Walrick remembered seeing the day his sister was kidnapped, but it was not a perfect match. Ewing wondered if perhaps over the years Walrick's memory dimmed or the color of the cloth changed. The Forbes wore plaids made of red and dark blue instead of black. Yet for the Forbes to live so close and still have a MacGreagor child without knowing it was not even remotely possible, and he almost didn't ask.

Laird Forbes listened to the story of Donnel's kidnapping and fondly remembered Neil. He owed Laird MacGreagor a great favor for saving his wife, who had fallen under the control of Sween and his men.

Forbes did not know of the woman Ewing sought, but he called forth all the elders. He charged them to search their memories to see if they, or any clan of their acquaintance, claimed an unfamiliar girl at the age of five, fifteen years earlier.

To Ewing's shock, the elders remembered just such an event. A woman lost her own child, went away, came back with a girl and claimed she was her dead sister's child. No one believed her. Shortly after, the woman died and no one knew to whom the child should be sent, so they kept her.

"Which clan?"

"This one," the elder answered. "The child is Allie."

No one was more surprised than Laird Forbes. It was a miracle. He led Ewing up a path to a narrow bridge over a waterway and pointed to the woman sitting on the bridge with her feet dangling over the side.

Ewing could not believe his good luck and wanted to take her home instantly, but frightening her would not do. He slowly approached and smiled when she looked up at him. She had sad blue eyes, a round face and dark brown hair. She looked a lot like Walrick and Ewing could not help but get excited. "May I sit with you?"

She did not trust him and glared, "Who are you?"

"I am the storyteller."

"Oh." She glanced down the path at her laird and when he nodded, she relaxed a little.

"If you will let me sit down, I will tell you a story."

"I do not care to hear a story just now."

Ewing was not going to be put off so easily, especially now. "I am very tired, if I am quiet may I sit with you?"

She finally shrugged and scooted over to make room for him.

"I believe you will like my story."

"You said you would be quiet."

"Aye, but you are very sad and this story will make you happy."

"How do you know I am sad?"

He ignored her question. "A long time ago, two children were playing in a meadow." He waited. He expected her to strongly object, but when she didn't, he continued, "They were with their mother and father and they were very happy. But someone hurt the mother and before her father could reach her, a woman took the child. The lassie's name was..."

Her mouth dropped and she turned to stare at the old man. "Was she called Donnel?"

"Aye."

"I thought 'twas just a dream." Countless times she'd tried to get the image of her dying mother out of her mind. Some days she thought it really happened and other days she was sure it was just a nightmare that would not go away. Maybe she was dreaming now. "What happened to the laddie?"

"His name is Walrick, he is your twin and he is looking for you."

Her eyes grew even larger, "Walrick, I remember that name. Will you take me to him?"

"Aye, he lives with the MacGreagors."

Tears finally began to stream down Donnel's cheek. "I could not remember the name of the clan."

"You were only in your fifth year."

"Five? No wonder I do not remember."

She suddenly threw her arms around Ewing. "Thank you so much. Will you take me? Can we go now?"

Ewing glanced back to see Laird Forbes' nod. "We will leave in the morning at first light."

*

It took three days, but when Ewing rode Clark down the road toward the bridge over the MacGreagor moat, it was obvious who the woman with him was. The guard whistled to signal visitors, Neil, Patrick, Kessan and Walrick came out of the Keep to stand on the landing and the clan began to gather in the courtyard. In shocked silence, they watched Ewing lead the way into the courtyard.

Walrick was so stunned, he couldn't move.

Neil finally walked down the steps and lifted her off her horse. "Welcome home. I am Laird MacGreagor and your brother has greatly missed you."

She nodded and looked at the faces in the courtyard one at a time. Everyone was smiling but she had yet to see the one face she longed for.

"He is up there," Neil whispered, pointing up the steps.

Once she finally spotted Walrick she smiled. She would know him anywhere. He still couldn't seem to move, so she went up the steps and just stood there looking into his eyes.

At last, Walrick pulled her into his arms. "I cannot believe it." He kissed her cheek and then stood back. "Are you well? Did they hurt you?"

"'Twas a lass who took me and she did not hurt me. I do not wish to go back, may I stay with you?"

Kessan grinned. He never thought of Walrick as handsome, but his sister was striking. "If you do not want her, she can stay with me." Everyone roared with laughter and Walrick promptly shoved Kessan off the landing.

The celebration began quickly and lasted long into the night. They danced and sang and laughed at Walrick until they were blue in the face. He had a silly grin on his face no one had ever seen before. Some of the women made sweet breads, while others took Donnel to the loch to bathe, and then brought her back wearing a new MacGreagor plaid. She was so overwhelmed with joy, she hardly knew what to do. She hugged Walrick often, that is, when he wasn't hugging her or staring at the face he never really believed he would see again.

Neil tried very hard not to think about his wager, but every time he turned around, Ewing was grinning at him. Like it or not, Neil MacGreagor was about to become a married man. He decided he best memorize all this happiness just in case he someday began to question how his marriage came about. He had a sinking feeling his life was about to become a nightmare.

*

Victoria had never been so furious and was actually thinking about killing the man called Ewing Larmont. She was glad Donnel was back, yes, and as the MacGreagor Mistress it would be her duty to make sure Donnel was happy. But that despicable Ewing was going to try to force Neil to marry someone else. She would not...could not allow that to happen!

But how could she get rid of Ewing? He was inside the Keep with Neil's men around him, all the people were celebrating and she was stuck pouring wine instead of sitting by her husband being served. Victoria had never been so enraged and could almost feel her body temperature rising.

She smiled, handed Ewing a full goblet and wished she had some poison to put in it. Then she thought about drawing her dagger and shoving it into his heart. No one would blame her once they realized she was perfect for Neil; she was sure of that. Still, it would spoil the fun and her husband would not be pleased with her so soon after they were married. They were married, right?

Ewing looked deeply concerned, "Are you all right, lass?"

Victoria stepped back, forced a smile and walked away.

*

Ewing was eager to get going -- Neil was not. He thought of all kinds of excuses to postpone the journey, but finally he had to own up to his pledge and set out. If he was a very, very fortunate man, Glenna would already be married by the time they got there, and he would someday laugh over the wedding that wasn't. At least the men would get to see the ocean.

It took several days to reach the land of the Larmont, mainly because Neil was in no hurry to arrive. They exchanged greetings with other clans along the way, pledged they meant no harm, saw evidence of the time when the Romans tried to take Scotland, admired the beauty of various lochs and gazed at the far off mountains, which were larger than anything they had ever seen.

Neil took all the men who wanted to go with him. He left Leesil with Mayze and left Patrick in charge of the MacGreagor Clan. His guard numbered twenty six men and they were all eager to see the sunken Viking ship.

They were all eager -- Neil was not. He desperately tried to think of a way out of his promise. But for a laird to go back on his word was unthinkable, so he tried to convince himself that Leesil needed a mother and perhaps this woman would not be so bad. Then he thought about missing teeth, dirty hair and greasy skin. It made him study Ewing far more closely. It appeared this man kept himself clean, at least. Maybe Glenna Larmont would not be so bad. Neil sighed. He'd been sighing a lot lately.

Ewing, on the other hand, was enjoying Neil's distress. And why not? His laird would be happy, Glenna would be happy, although not right away, and Ewing could get a well-deserved rest. Occasionally he remembered he had not exactly told Neil all he needed to know and the closer they got to Stratsgory Castle the more he worried about it. He had not mentioned that Neil would be required to fight Laird Larmont. On the other hand, it was too late now. Ewing would just have to deal with that small matter when the subject came up.

CHAPTER V

It was cold in the north on the morning they arrived. The men were wrapped in their extra plaids and each sat on his mount staring at the vast ocean. The waves were mesmerizing and when they crashed against the rocks, the MacGreagors did not mind getting wet at all. They might have stayed to watch the waves for hours, but their attention was soon drawn upward. Above the high cliffs sat a castle just like the one in the story Ewing told about the Land of Essen.

Ewing once thought he was happy carrying messages from one clan to another and meeting new people. But now that he was home, he realized he valued his old uneventful life even more. The MacGreagors, he decided, had seen enough of the ocean and he wanted this wedding over with so he could get on with his relaxing. Slowly but surely, he got them to the bottom of the steps someone long ago carved into the cliffs. "Welcome to Stratsgory Castle." He nudged and nudged until Neil began to climb the steps.

*

They had been at it for hours.

First, Ewing and Laird Larmont argued because Neil had dark hair and not blond. Everyone knew Vikings had yellow hair. At least Neil had blue eyes, Ewing repeatedly pointed out.

Glenna stood up and walked to a window. The day she dreaded most was here and she was not pleased. Her prospective husband's looks were passable, she supposed, although she had only glanced at him once. She listened a few moments longer and then turned to face her father. "I will not marry him!"

The large room on the bottom floor of the castle grew instantly quiet. It was pleasantly decorated in the red and white colors of the Larmont Clan with tapestries on the walls and large pillows scattered everywhere for comfort. Along one wall sat her mother, her six brothers and her two sisters. Along the other, Kessan and Dan stood with their feet apart and their arms folded watching. They proudly wore blue MacGreagor kilts with shoes that laces up to their knees. The rest of the MacGreagors waited outside at the bottom of the winding stairs where they could watch the ocean waves.

Neil stood in the middle of the room awaiting his fate. At first, he was offended to think she would reject him, but then he prayed she knew how to get both of them out of this commitment. If she did, he would be forever grateful. He quickly glanced at Glenna. She was not the beauty Ewing said, but her looks were passable, he supposed. At least she was clean, but he had not yet seen her teeth.

Glenna's father glared at her. "You will marry whomever I say." She put her hands on her hips and glared back. "He is not suitable, you said so yourself. Send him away and choose another."

Ewing quickly walked around behind her, leaned close and whispered in Glenna's ear, "He loves another, she is named Leesil." He expected her to turn and stare at him, which is exactly what she did. Ewing smiled.

"Daughter, if you do not marry him I will have him executed."

Kessan and Dan instantly stepped forward to protect their laird and just as quickly, Neil raised his hand to stop them.

Glenna slumped and finally looked at Neil. "He will do it too. Perhaps you can talk him out of this."

Laird Larmont grinned. "My daughter is tender hearted. She will marry you to save your life. Make certain you are worthy of her." He waited for some kind of reaction but Laird MacGreagor kept his face expressionless and Laird Larmont was impressed. An admirable man does not let his opponent know what he is thinking. He nodded for the Priest to begin. "You will fight me now. You are a strong man and 'twill be a good battle." The Larmont stood up and began to draw his sword.

"What?"

The surprise on Neil's face looked genuine which made Laird Larmont turn to glare at Ewing. "You did not tell him?"

Ewing trembled. "I meant to, but the subject did not come up."

"I will not fight you!" Neil insisted.

Laird Larmont shoved his sword back in his sheath and folded his arms. "You will fight me for my daughter's hand."

Neil was incredulous. "I will not!"

"You will, or you will not marry her."

"Fine, I will not marry her."

Ewing panicked, "But you made the wager and gave your word." By the time he realized what he had done, it was too late. He looked from Neil's disapproval, to Glenna's shock and then to the fierce anger on the face of Glenna's father.

Laird Larmont's voice rose loud enough for the men outside to hear, "You wagered my daughter's marriage?"

Ewing seriously considered leaping out the window, falling to his death on the rocks below and ending it all. But he knew he was right and decided to risk his laird's recklessness for Glenna's sake. "He is perfect for her. He is a kind man and his people love him. 'Twas the only way to convince him."

Laird Larmont's voice steadily got louder, which made Kessan and Dan take yet another step closer to protect Neil. "Did this man win or lose his wager?"

Ewing hung his head. "The MacGreagor lost."

Glenna's mouth dropped and she turned to face Neil. "Do you mean I am your penalty?" The room once more went deadly silent, except of course, for the whispering priest, who glanced at Laird Larmont often to see if he should stop.

Neil tried desperately to think of something to say to her but all he could do was watch her expression turn from shock, to hurt and then to anger. "Glenna, I..."

"Does Ewing speak the truth?" she demanded.

What could Neil possibly say? "Aye."

She did not smile, but the look in her eyes softened a little. "Thank you for not lying to me."

Laird Larmont could not have been more pleased. Ewing was right, the MacGreagor was the perfect husband for his daughter; he was more concerned about her feelings than his own destiny.

Neil closely studied her and was starting to admire this woman. She was not crying or exhibiting her anger, although she had good reason to. Instead, she kept her pride and her dignity well in check. Now that he had a moment to look at her, she was actually quite pleasant looking and she did have all her teeth. He was still watching her when she crossed over to stand beside him.

Glenna did not lean closer, did not look up at him and did not care if everyone heard what she had to say. "If I do not marry you, Laird MacGreagor, my father will kill you. And if you do not marry me, you will disgrace your clan. Am I right so far?" She waited for his nod. "We have but one hope left. My father requires you to fight him, but you have declined. Is that also true?"

"'Tis," Neil answered.

"Then I am pleased to say you do not meet all the requirements and therefore, I cannot marry you."

"Wait!" Laird Larmont took a step forward. "I have set aside that requirement."

She turned then to face Neil. "I thought he would. Do the lairds in your land force their daughters to marry lads they do not love?"

"Nay, we do not."

"And do you have a forest?"

"We do."

"Then to see this forest and for the sake of my daughters, I will marry you. I do not promise to love you, but I will be a good wife and I will accept your people as my own. However, if I am unhappy, you will bring me back, set aside this marriage according to the laws of the church and allow me to marry another lad. Do you agree?"

The priest started to object, but when he caught the look in the fierce and sometimes reckless Laird Larmont's eye, he thought better of it.

No MacGreagor ever set aside a marriage and Neil was not about to be the first. However, this mess was his fault and she should not have to pay for it with an unhappy life. The only way to prevent a dissolved marriage was to find a way to make her happy enough to stay. He quickly vowed to give that his best try. "I do."

The priest finished his blessing and with very little participation on the part of either the bride or the groom, they were married. There was no kiss and no congratulations, only quiet resignation.

Neil and his men followed Ewing and Laird Larmont down the steps in the cliff to the place where the Viking ship could be seen under the water of the cove. The MacGreagors were captivated by its size, the construction and the markings on the bow. Ewing made sure he stayed well away from Neil just in case the man had thoughts of ringing his neck.

But Neil just wanted to go home. He was tired, his men were tired and he missed Leesil. He had a wife now and that was going to take some getting used to. The sooner he got her home the sooner he could begin to make her happy, if that were possible.

His wife did not keep him waiting long and took little with her. He helped Glenna mount her horse, wrapped an extra MacGreagor plaid around her shoulders and nodded his appreciation to her mother for the packhorse loaded with food.

Then he let Glenna lead the way out of her village and saw the sadness of the people as they came out of their cottages to wave good bye. But instead of crying with them, she smiled and assured them she would be well. Just before they left the land of the Larmont, Glenna stopped her horse to look back. She waved one last time to her family standing high on the cliffs above and then nodded to her husband. Neil's guard quickly surrounded both of them and at last, they were on their way to the land of the MacGreagors.

*

During the first three days and nights that followed, Glenna was miserable. She wasn't used to riding for such long hours and even changing her position often didn't seem to help. The men gave her extra plaids to sit on, but with more than one or two she tended to slide off. At night she was too exhausted to do anything but eat and sleep.

None of them talked much while they rode and she understood it was for their safety. She really didn't feel much like talking anyway. Her husband glanced at her often and once she got over being so upset with him, she thought he was not all that unpleasant to look at. In fact, when he smiled, which had only been once so far, he might be considered by some as handsome. She had not smiled either, she realized.

Neil had no idea what to do or say. He thought about explaining the wager in an effort to make her feel a little less like his penalty, but the words he thought to say seemed so inadequate. The more gracious she acted the worse he felt. If only she would yell at him or hit him with something. But she did not. She hardly spoke at all except to ask for something she needed.

If she cried, he could try to comfort her, but she didn't even do that. Once she asked to be alone and he thought she might cry, but when she came back from her walk, her eyes were not red. His men did not know what to do either. Kessan finally took pity and offered to be at her side if she needed anything. She smiled at him, which was the only smile she granted any of them.

His men, Neil realized were feeling as badly for her as he was. They made sure she had as much privacy as possible and cared that she had enough to eat, but it was all any of them could think of to do. Glenna would have heard about the wager eventually anyway, but by then Neil would have had time to explain it and soften the blow. Now, it seemed, all anyone could do was wait and pray time would heal her wound.

Glenna noticed the MacGreagor men were more than attentive. They watched her every move and Kessan often asked what she needed for her comfort. She was beginning to like Kessan. He was her husband's third in command and as he explained, now that she was their mistress it was his duty to see that she was well taken care of.

She might have been surprised that her husband did not want to bed her that first night, but knowing he had a woman waiting for him explained it. There was hardly any privacy out in the open and she was grateful he did not demand it and embarrass her in front of his men. She would have to submit to him sometime, she knew, but hopefully not until they were alone. She also knew she was being too quiet, but couldn't seem to help herself. She lost her family, her pride and her dignity all in one short morning. Glenna wanted to marry for love and she was so disappointed she just didn't seem to be able to hide it.

*

Then on the fifth day, everything changed. They finally came to the edge of the forest and Glenna halted her horse. If she died right then, she would have been happy just to look at it. "It is Glorious!"

Her smile began to infect Neil and once he smiled, his men

released the breath they felt like they'd been holding all the way home. Neil did not speak...but he did look at her. When she smiled, she was as pleasing as Ewing said. Her eyes were as bright as the stars, her hair framed her face perfectly, her smile was glowing and her cheeks were a soft shade of pink. She was not just beautiful, she was magnificent.

Once she got started, Glenna couldn't seem to stop. She had a thousand questions about her new home and the people in it. The men enjoyed answering them and tried not to notice her questions were never directed at her husband. She tried to remember all their names and when she got it wrong, she laughed which made all of them laugh, even Neil.

She liked to walk the stiffness out after the day's ride and Kessan usually walked with her, surrounded by six of the other men. But this time when they returned, instead of sitting alone, she sat down on a plaid next to her husband at the campfire. "How much longer?"

He was surprised and pleased all at the same time. "Two days at most." Neil did not notice when the other men moved away to give them some privacy.

"Good, I do not think I can endure much more."

"You have been very brave."

For the first time, she smiled at him. "I will not ask you to take me riding anytime soon, I fear."

He returned her smile, "I am relieved. Some of us look more able to abide long rides than we truly are."

For a moment, she examined his face. "I very much wanted to marry for love, but you are not as unpleasant as I first thought. Perhaps we could be friends."

"I would like that. I promise I will try to make you happy."

She lightly touched the back of his hand with the tips of her fingers. "You will make me happy if you allow me a little more time." When she realized what she had done, she quickly pulled her hand away. "I do not mean to be unkind, but my heart is hurting still."

"I know, I never meant to hurt you."

Again she smiled. "I will recover, I promise. Tell me about your parents. I would tell you about mine, but you have seen them first hand."

He was happy about her request. He put his extra plaid around her shoulders and began to tell her all about Kevin and Anna, Connor and Rachel, and Justin and Catherin. An hour later, half of his men were asleep and when he looked, she was starting to doze off sitting up. Neil smiled; gently helped her lay on the cloth and made sure she was covered. Then he wrapped a plaid around himself, curled up close to her and fell asleep. For the first time in days, he felt like she might forgive him...someday.

CHAPTER VI

Once they were safely on MacGreagor land, Neil dismissed his men and let them ride on ahead to see their families. For Victoria, the news could not have been worse -- Neil was married. Her name was Glenna and the men thought she was pleasing. It made Victoria want to throw up.

At least the marriage was not consummated yet, or so she heard, and that gave her one glimmer of hope. Maybe Neil found his wife repulsive. Of course Glenna might make him bed her. He was a man, after all, and men were weak in that regard, but he would save his real love for her.

And then she heard about the vow; If Glenna was unhappy with the MacGreagors, he vowed to take her back and dissolve the marriage. This was more than a glimmer of hope -- this was the beginning of a plan.

*

Patrick raced across the meadow, threaded his way through the trees and hurried up the side of the hill that overlooked the MacGreagor hold. All that remained of the travelers for Patrick to greet was Kessan, Neil and Glenna. He was half out of breath when he moved his horse around until he could slap Neil on the back. "I am so happy to see you."

"I am happy to see you too. How is Leesil? I have greatly

missed...”

Glenna's new home looked just like the Land of Essen Ewing often talked about. It made Glenna smile. Not that she wasn't still mad at Ewing, but she understood better why he thought Neil would be the perfect husband for her. The hold was surrounded by forest, the Keep was large and the village was surrounded by a wall and a moat. She was so fascinated, she hardly noticed what her husband was talking about.

"Leesil is very well and has missed you too. I heard you took a wife," said Patrick.

"Aye, this is Glenna. Glenna, this is Patrick, my second."

Patrick nodded. "You were spotted on Cameron land and the people are waiting in the courtyard to welcome your wife. I am so happy you are home."

"Patrick that is the second time you have said that. Are their problems I should know about?"

"Only one. Three lads have asked for Donnel's hand in marriage, but Walrick will not let any of them near her. I fear they will fight soon."

"Walrick is a good lad," said Kessan, trying not to exhibit the swell in his chest. "I told him to save her for me."

Neil laughed. "Little has changed, I see. Glenna." She didn't answer and he had to say it again, "Glenna."

"What? Oh, I am sorry I was not paying attention. Your home is far more wonderful than I imagined."

"'Tis your home now too." He waited for her nod and then led the way down the hill, through the trees and across the meadow. The hooves of their horses clapped on the wooden bridge and then turned to thuds as they crossed the wide courtyard. The air smelled crisp and clean, birds sang in the trees and the people seemed truly happy.

A boy came to take her horse and she smiled at him. Neil dismounted, came around, lifted her down and she smiled at him. Then he took her up the steps and once they were on the landing, he turned them both to face his followers. "This is my wife, Glenna, and you will honor her as you do me." The people cheered, he smiled and she smiled at them. The women brought gifts for her including two MacGreagor plaids -- and Glenna smiled at them.

It was not until they were inside the Keep and Neil raced up the stairs to see Leesil that Glenna stopped smiling. His woman is here? She felt like she had been kicked in the stomach and when Kessan led her to a chair at the table, she was glad to sit down. She believed her husband was at least honorable, but he was going to humiliate her by going first to see his woman? And she lives in their home? Glenna put her head in her hands and closed her eyes. This was just too much for her to accept.

Patrick was afraid she was going to pass out. There were a lot of people in the room, they all wanted to welcome her and she had to be exhausted. He quickly sat down beside her. "May I pour you some wine?"

"Thank you." She tried to smile but her lips wouldn't move. "You are Patrick?"

"Aye, I am your husband's second in command." He poured, handed her the goblet and watched her down the whole thing like a seasoned warrior. She may look timid, he thought, but she was going to liven up the place. Patrick grinned.

"How long will my husband be with his lass? I am tired and wish to rest."

"His lass?" Patrick followed her eyes to Leesil's door and then looked back at her. "Leesil is not his lass, she is his daughter and she is not yet six months old."

"His daughter? Ewing said he loved another and her name is Leesil."

"Aye, but Leesil is not..."

Glenna abruptly grabbed Patrick's arm. "Please do not tell on me. My husband's people will think I am simple."

Patrick leaned a little closer. "Your secret is safe with me. My laird does not mean to neglect you and you look exhausted. I will take you up if you like."

"I can wait. I would not wish to embarrass him."

Patrick did not expect to like her, but Glenna already had his respect. She could handle it he decided, and probably needed it, so he poured her another goblet of wine.

Neil brought Leesil down, introduced his daughter to his wife and showed Glenna to his parent's bedchamber. He made sure the men hauled water up for her bath and asked two women to help her. Then he went to the loch to bathe.

When he came back, the great hall was quiet. Everyone had gone home except Patrick who reported that both his daughter and his wife were sound asleep. It warmed Neil's heart. Now there were three in his little family. He could not have imagined a more unlikely three, but they were his and he was glad to have the company.

Patrick promised not to tell, but his loyalty was to his laird and he felt Neil needed to know. "Ewing let your wife think Leesil was your kept lass."

Neil sat down at the head of the long table and closed his eyes. "No wonder she was so quiet."

"Is it true she heard about the wager?"

"Aye, she thinks she is my penalty. Already I have hurt her and I have no idea how to set things right. I believe she is on the edge of hating me and I do not blame her."

"Give her time, brother. I like her."

"I admit I like her too."

*

When Neil got up the next morning, dressed for the day and opened his door, he could hear Glenna talking to his daughter downstairs. He cautiously peeked around the corner and looked down into the great hall. Glenna was dressed in his plaid.

"I hope you do not think ill of me," Glenna said to the little girl, "but I do not know where a thing is. Dare we wake him?" She was sitting in a chair, Leesil sat on the table before her and she was letting the child touch her face. "Does he wake in a foul mood or is he the happy sort?" Leesil gurgled and Glenna moved her head back just as the baby tried to pinch her nose. "I can see you are not going to be much help. I forgive you, however." She kissed Leesil's cheek.

Afraid he would frighten her, Neil softly cleared his throat. Then he started down the stairs. "I normally wake up happy, and you need never fear disturbing me. The lasses will come soon. They will feed her and I will show you where everything is. Did you sleep well?"

"Aye, very well. I hope I did not spoil your evening."

"Not at all, I was tired also." He went to a small table, picked up a pitcher and poured both of them a goblet of water. "Glenna, I hate to put upon you so soon, but I was hoping you could help me."

She was surprised. "I promised to be a good wife and I will be. What can I do?"

He had been thinking about it half the night. The best way to handle an upset woman, he believed, was to give her something to do. But what? About midnight, an idea came to him. This morning, she already impressed him by making friends with his daughter. He had not expected that so soon and he hoped it was a good sign for their future. Now he wanted to keep her busy.

He paused to think of just the right words. Then he handed her the water and waited until she finished drinking. "A laird keeps a confidence for his followers, and we have one lass with a problem she asked me not to reveal. As my wife, I have made that promise on behalf of us both, do you agree?"

"I do."

She really looked quite wonderful for so early in the morning and he wondered if he was presentable. It was a long time ago, but his mother would have sent him away from the table for not being fit. He ran his fingers through his dark, wavy hair and charged himself to take better care in the future. "Her name is Kindel and she is going blind."

"How awful for her, what can I do to help?"

When the door opened and one of the women came to take Leesil to her morning meal, Neil nodded to the woman, but waited until she was gone before he continued. "Here is the problem, Kindel..."

Glenna was alone with him finally and she had a problem of her own to work out. "Neil, can we not have the wedding night now and get it over with?"

"What?"

"I know I must submit to you and I sincerely appreciate you not demanding it of me before now, but if we do not get it over with..."

"Get it over with? Do you think of it as a duty?"

She lowered her eyes. "We do not love each other, what else could it be?"

He studied her for a long moment and then sat down opposite her. "Glenna, you are not the only one who wanted to be in love before marriage. I made a mistake. I never should have agreed to the wager and now I have hurt you. What I want to do is set things right and somehow make you happy. Forcing you into my bed would do neither." He realized the discussion was uncomfortable for her now and changed the subject. "As I was saying, Kindel's sight is getting worse and..."

"I do not want to fear you. You will not force me in the night?"

"Is that what worries you?" He could tell by the way she was wringing her hands that it was.

"I will not force you in the night or in the day, I promise."

She examined the truthfulness in his eyes. She did not completely trust him, but Kessan did and she liked Kessan very much. She even liked Patrick. Maybe Neil would not be so bad once she got to know him. His promise was enough and she looked away. At least she got it said and out in the open. "I am sorry, you were saying about Kindel?"

"As I told you at Stratsgory, we do not force our women to marry without love. Walrick loves Kindel and I believe she loves him too, but he knows about her blindness and she thinks he has proposed marriage out of pity. She needs a husband to care for her and Walrick is a good lad. Would you be willing to get to know her? Perhaps she will tell you if she loves Walrick. If not, we will let her be."

"And if she does, then marriage would be good for her and I should encourage it?"

He tried to understand what her words meant. Did she resent his interference or was she agreeing with him? He didn't know her well enough to tell so he just asked her. "Do you disagree?"

"I am not well versed in affairs of the heart."

"Nor am I. That is why I need your help. Walrick loves her and who will care for her when her parents are gone? Yet if she does not love him..."

"I will ask her to walk with me. Does she see well enough to show me the forest?"

He smiled finally. "I believe she does. She promised to tell me if her sight got worse, but she has not admitted it. A few weeks ago, she fell off the bridge into the moat."

Glenna caught her breath. "Good heavens, she does need help. Perhaps she will tell me how bad her eyes are."

"Thank you, I was hoping you would help. I will show you where everything is and then I will take you to meet her."

*

At first, Kindel was thrilled that Neil would choose her to show his wife the forest, but once they crossed the bridge and started to wander through the trees, she realized what the real reason was. "Neil sent you to talk to me."

"Aye." Glenna loved every inch of the trees, the bushes and even the dead leaves that carpeted the forest floor. "He cares about you."

"Oh I know, he loves all of us just as his father did. He wants to know about my eyes, am I right?"

"He does. He said you promised to tell him if they got worse."

Kindel stopped walking and bowed her head. "Sometimes they are worse, but not all the time. I will tell him when they are worse all the time."

"Was it during one of those 'worse' times that you fell off the bridge?"

"You have been here less than a day and already you know about that?"

Glenna laughed, took Kindel's hand and guided her to a log. "I think that means he loves you most."

She bent down, felt the log with her hand and then sat down. "That is not true; he loves us all the same. If he loves anyone more, it is Donnel because she was away from us the longest."

"Who is Donnel?"

"He did not tell you about her?" Kindel wrinkled her brow. "I would have thought he would tell you about her first."

"Why?"

"'Tis because of her Neil married you."

Glenna wrinkled her brow. "You have managed to confuse me. Might you start at the beginning?" She should not have asked. Once Kindel got started, she couldn't stop. She told Glenna bits and pieces about Donnel, about Walrick, about the war with Sween and when she started on Kevin and Anna, Glenna decided it was time to stop her. "Kindel, 'tis too much to take in all at once. Will you walk with me again tomorrow?"

Kindel was suddenly embarrassed. "I have kept you and there are many others who want your attention." She stood up and almost fell over the log. Then she just couldn't hold back her tears another minute and when Glenna opened her arms, she went into them. "What am I going to do? I can hardly see at all anymore."

Her words were not a surprise to Glenna. Walrick and Kessan were standing not far away and Kindel did not even notice them. She helped Kindel sit back down. "In my land there is a lad who cannot see. But he is not sorry for his lack of sight, he is glad for his other gifts?"

"What other gifts?"

"Well, he claims God gave him finer hearing and I believe it. He can hear it in a voice when someone is ill and he can tell the difference between a baby's cry of anger and a cry of pain. He can also hear when riders are approaching long before they are seen. He is a valuable member of our clan and I do not know what we would do without him."

"But do the people have to care for him?"

"Sometimes, but most things he can do for himself. We do not let him go hunting, however." Just as she hoped, Kindel started to laugh.

*

"She was wonderful with Kindel, you should have seen her." Kessan sat down at the table in the great hall for the noon meal and then stood back up with Neil and Walrick as soon as Glenna walked in.

She went to the other end of the table, poured herself some wine and then looked at her husband. "Do I sit at this end?"

"Nay, you sit by me." He glared at Walrick who quickly moved down.

She nodded her appreciation to Walrick, sat down and sipped her wine. "The forest is even more pleasing than I imagined. Will I always need a guard when I go outside the wall?"

To Neil, she was becoming more attractive by the minute and he could not understand it. Maybe she was not changing, but his opinion of her was. She was also far more astute than he expected. "I did not want you to get lost and I was afraid Kindel would not be able to bring you back."

"And?"

Neil's shoulders drooped a little, "And 'tis not safe."

"Are we at war?"

"Not yet, but our neighbors to the north are not always friendly, so we are careful. I fear they would very much like to take my wife."

"I see." She smiled at the woman who served her and then began to eat. The mutton had not been cooked long enough and it was tough, but the men didn't seem to be having trouble with theirs. She did the best she could, but finally gave up and took the meat out of her mouth when no one was watching.

Neil noticed but ignored it for now. "Do you know how to swim?"

"We do not swim, the water is too cold."

"Then I will teach you. There are hidden doors in our walls so we can get out if we need to, but you will have to swim the moat. We teach all the children...that reminds me, Walrick, does Donnel know how to swim?"

"I do not know, I will ask her."

Kessan glared at Walrick, "Nay, I will ask her and if she does not know how, I will teach her."

Walrick started to rise up out of his chair. "You will keep your hands off of her. She is my sister and I will teach her."

Glenna was enjoying every moment of it. They reminded her of her father and his second. If she were at home and they got too out of hand, she would...She was not at home, she reminded herself and glanced at her husband. He was enjoying them too and when she looked, she thought he was actually a very handsome man after all. She quickly dropped her eyes before he noticed.

She wasn't eating and Neil thought that was odd. She ate very little in the morning and now nothing at noon? He decided to ask her later if MacGreagor food did not please her.

Glenna leaned a little closer to him. "Are there no lasses who can teach us how to swim?"

"Aye, but the lads have to be there for protection anyway." He hoped it wasn't true, but he suspected he was the one she did not want teaching her how to swim. "Would you prefer to have a lass teach you?"

"I would."

"Done then." She might be sitting next to him at the table, she might love his daughter eventually and she might be sleeping under his roof, but Glenna MacGreagor was making all the rules and it was clear Neil was not going to touch her until she was good and ready.

When she turned back to watch the argument, Neil took a bite of her mutton. Even he could not chew it and he spit it out. He stood up, took both their bowls and went out the back door. A moment later, he returned with a fresh bowl for her. He tasted it first and when the meat was tender, he set it down in front of her.

Both Kessan and Walrick were staring at him. "What is it?" Kessan asked.

"Her meat was uncooked." He watched them exchange glances and then sat back down and changed the subject. "Who among our lasses are the best swimmers?"

*

Patrick discovered that his wife could not swim either, so Glenna, Donnel, Jessup and their teachers headed to the loch in the afternoon. Then Patrick, Kessan, Walrick and Dan followed to protect them, and others wanted to watch. So by the time Leesil woke up from her nap, there was not another living soul in the Keep but Neil and he could not believe how empty the room seemed without Glenna. After her first days of silence, he was grateful for every smile she bestowed on them. It did not appear she was going to be selfish with her smiles and he was starting to look forward to them. He may not love her, but he was beginning to like her a lot more than he expected to.

Whether Glenna wanted him there or not, he decided to take their daughter to the loch to watch. Except for the guards, the courtyard was nearly empty and as soon as he turned down the path he could hear the laughter. He took two guards for his protection and then when he got closer, he decided to stand just out of sight at the edge of the trees to watch.

Glenna was having a horrible time learning, but she was not the main attraction. Jessup was so afraid of the water, she was yelling at her husband in English, which few understood, and nearly drowning Patrick. Patrick couldn't decide if he should keep trying to teach her or just let her kiss him, which was what she really wanted to do anyway. Neil laughed.

Donnel was quickly learning how to swim and three men, including Kessan kept trying to get Walrick away from her, but he was being brotherly and not letting any of them come near. She smiled and flirted while Walrick glowered and glared. It warmed Neil's heart and he decided an angry wife was worth seeing the twins happy.

Glenna spotted her husband in the trees holding Leesil and when his eyes lit up she followed his gaze to Donnel, whom she had only just met. She remembered Kindel saying Donnel was the reason Neil married her, but she hadn't really understood what happened. Besides, she did not want to know the details of the wager. It was over and done with and she was stuck with it. She turned her attention back to the swimming lessons.

CHAPTER VII

The next morning, Neil went to get Leesil before the child could wake Glenna. He changed her, took her down stairs and then stared at the bowl of eggs in the center of the table. He glanced up at Glenna's closed door and then shrugged. Maybe she asked for them.

"Good Morning."

He turned at the sound of her voice and was surprised to find his wife already up and coming in the front door. "Why were you outside?"

"I just wanted to stand on the landing and welcome the day." She smiled at him and hoped he was not going to be too upset. Some men were not good at controlling their temper and she had no idea how he would react. "The eggs were in my bed last night."

"In your bed?"

"Aye, neatly arranged under the bottom plaid." He did not look like he was going to lose control, so she poured them both some water and sat down. Glenna carefully held the goblet and let Leesil taste the water. "Fortunately, I noticed before I sat on them."

Neil felt his rage building. "I will see to this."

She gave the baby a little more water and then drank some herself. "'Tis a lass, you know. Could it be Leesil's mother?"

He suddenly realized how little she knew and calmed down enough to explain that her parents had passed. But his mind was racing. First, she could not eat the food and although the eggs might only be messy, what started as harmless could easily become dangerous. She needed far more protection...and inside her own home.

Glenna interrupted his thoughts. "Kindel needs a walking stick."

"What? Oh, I will have Walrick see to it."

The best way to handle an upset man, she knew, was to help him solve the problem. "Neil, I can sleep in the room with Leesil and as long as you and I are the only ones who know, I will be safe at night. As for the day time..."

"Why? Why would someone want to insult my wife?"

"Because I *am* your wife. Whoever she is, she hoped to marry you and now she is bitter. 'Twill pass."

"I will not let anyone hurt you."

He said it with such determination, it surprised her. Her father was very protective of her mother, but she did not expect that from a husband who did not love her. He also managed to keep his anger under control and that pleased her very much. If only she could stop feeling so betrayed still. It was not like her to hold a grudge. With eight brothers and sisters, a grudge in her family was a waste of time. But her dreams were so shattered and her heart just had not yet recovered.

For months, Neil didn't pay attention to who prepared his meals and who cleaned the Keep, but when the woman came to take Leesil to her morning meal, Neil tried to remember everything he knew about her. As soon as he realized she was married, he relaxed a little.

After the woman was gone, Glenna started to take pity on her husband. "You cannot taste my food, search every room before I enter and keep constant watch over me, 'twill make you daft."

He smiled. "If I am not already, you mean."

"'Tis enough we are both on our guard now. I refuse to let anyone keep me from getting to know the people and walking in the forest. If you let it disturb you, I will become a prisoner and I would hate that."

"You are right." He agreed for her sake, but as soon as she left to take another walk with Kindel, he and Patrick tightened the circle of protection around her, starting with four guards instead of two.

*

The eggs were unbroken and sitting on the table in the great hall. She expected to enjoy cleaning the mess out of Glenna's bed, but Glenna was smarter than she looked. Victoria narrowed her angry eyes and started up the stairs. She meant to force Glenna into Neil's bed. How could Neil know she was the superior lover he deserved if he had not yet been with his wife?

Victoria's plans were not totally suspended, she decided, just postponed. She would just have to think of another way to accomplish her goal.

*

It was the first time Neil noticed Victoria. She was always pleasant, he knew and loved taking care of Leesil, but would she want to hurt his wife? He watched her slowly climb the stairs and turn down the balcony toward Glenna's room. No, it couldn't be Victoria, she was married too.

*

"I have been thinking about what you said yesterday," Kindel began. She took Glenna's arm and was grateful not to have to worry about running into anything in the forest. Walrick walked close enough behind to catch her if she started to fall and she knew he was there. In fact, she thought today she would have a little fun with him.

"And what did you decide?"

"I decided my hearing has improved. For example, I can hear someone walking behind me. Is it your guard?"

"Unfortunately, yes."

"Why do you say unfortunately?"

Glenna stopped walking and put out her hand to touch the rays of sunlight shining through the trees. "I enjoyed far more freedom in my homeland and rarely had a guard. But I suppose I will become accustomed to it."

"Neil wants you safe."

"Aye, he is a very good lad."

Kindel looked disturbed. "Nay, he is not a very good lad, he is a great lad."

Glenna was not there to discuss her husband. She took the stick out of Walrick's hand and put it into Kindel's. "This is a special stick. 'Twill help you see after your sight is gone. Close your eyes and I will show you how it works." It did not take long for Kindel to get the hang of it and soon she was using the stick to feel her way around the forest.

When she got tired, Kindel felt for a log with the stick, leaned down to touch it with her hand just to be sure and sat down. "Thank you. I believe I will like this stick. Will you go with me to tell my mother and Neil?"

"I will be honored."

Kindel opened her eyes. She could faintly see the beauty of the white sunlight shining through the trees and took a moment to memorize it. "When I fell off the bridge, I really did not know how close I was to the edge. I thought I wanted to die until then, but after Walrick found me I was glad to be alive."

"I am glad you are alive too. You are a wonderful lass."

"Oh, I am not wonderful, but I am a lass and I have made another decision. I do not need a husband...but I want one. I have always wanted one."

Glenna glanced at the hope in Walrick's eyes, "Lads can make us miserable, but they can also make us very happy, I have heard. Are you in love?"

"I think so, it is hard to say. He is a very odd lad." Kindel was having a hard time
keeping a straight face. Thankfully, Walrick was behind her and could not see.

"Odd how?"

"You will not believe it. He asked me to marry him and when I said nay, he gave up. If he truly loved me, why would he give up so easily?"

Glenna rolled her eyes at Walrick, stood up and moved away. "What should he do instead?"

"He should kiss me at least once. How am I..." She felt him put his hand on her shoulder and step over the log. Then she stood up and let him draw her to him. She was finally in his arms again and they felt just as strong and as safe as they did when he found her in the water. Kindel hugged his neck and then whispered in his ear, "I am afraid you will have to do all the kissing once I can no longer see your face."

"I will not mind," Walrick whispered.

*

Glenna nodded to Kessan and with the other two guards following, left Walrick and Kindel alone in the forest. She would gladly give half her life to be in love like that.

She didn't want to go back to the Keep so she just kept walking through the forest with the men following. She knew her duties included getting to know more of the women, but she just wasn't in the mood.

The eldest of nine, her home always held a little one. She missed holding them and watching them grow. She wanted to spend more time with Leesil, but Neil had Leesil's day well organized and she didn't know where she fit in. Glenna didn't know where she fit in on any level of her new life. Someone wanted her gone and she wanted to be gone. All of it was just too hard. She didn't mean to, but she started to cry.

Kessan made the other two men stand back and went to her. "Finally you cry. I was beginning to worry about you."

She wiped her tears away and took a couple of deep breaths. "I am fine."

"You are not fine. You are angry and hurt and you have every right to be. But you do not understand and 'tis time someone made you listen." He knew he was being a little too harsh with her and quickly softened his tone. "Kindel is right, Neil is not a good lad, he is a great lad. He was willing to fight his own brother to save us."

Kessan could tell by the look on her face she was not impressed. He decided to take another approach. "Donnel is Walrick's twin sister and when they were five someone kidnapped her. Neil bet Ewing he could not find her."

Glenna was suddenly paying attention. She imagined his wager to be an insignificant one purely for sport. "That is what he wagered?"

"Aye. None believed Ewing could find her after fifteen years, 'twas impossible. But when he saw the hope in Walrick's eyes, Neil could not refuse to make the wager. You saw that hope yourself just a few minutes ago. Could you have denied him?"

Glenna hung her head. "So Ewing found Walrick's sister and Neil was committed to marry a lass he did not want."

"Aye and he would do it again. He would give up his own chance at happiness for any one of us. That is what makes him a great lad."

Glenna nodded, turned and started to walk again. She had a lot to think about. Neil said he wanted to marry for love too and now she understood. He was happy about Donnel, but as disappointed in how everything turned out as she was. She began to be ashamed of the way she had been acting. It was not just her misery, it was his too and she could at least try to put a smile on his face from time to time. She owed him that much for not being a beast and forcing her into his bed. Her life could be a lot worse.

She slowed down and waited for Kessan to catch up. "Tell me about this fight with his brother."

*

From time to time, Neil got word that his wife and Kessan were still talking. They walked through the meadow and the trees, up the hillside to look down on the village and then to the graveyard where the bodies of her husband's family and followers were buried. Kessan told her about the little fence and mentioned it had been extended twice since the day Neil began to build it for his mother.

They walked all the way around the moat, to the loch and back to the bridge; before Glenna was satisfied she knew most of what had happened. Inside the wall, Kessan showed her where all the hidden doors were and how to get back in. Then he showed her where the wall was torn down to let the horses out during the war.

She nodded to everyone as he introduced them and admitted she would not remember their names. They forgave her. She especially wanted to meet Donnel and when she did, she hugged her and welcomed her back. They had an odd sort of bond between them now and Glenna hoped they would be friends. By the time Kessan took her home, it was getting late and they were both exhausted.

She walked in, smiled at her husband when he and all the other men stood up and went to the table. She poured wine in a goblet and downed the whole thing. Patrick grinned and nodded at the other men as if to say, see I told you so.

She finished, wiped her mouth on her sleeve and saw the confused look on her husband's face. "Why so surprised, Neil MacGreagor, did you really think I could grow up around my father without being able to drink him under the table?" She quickly glanced at all the other faces. "When I get to know you better, I will challenge any lad here who thinks himself capable of out drinking me."

"I accept," Patrick nearly shouted. Then he looked at Neil to see his reaction. Slowly but surely, Neil began to smile.

Glenna continued, "Of course, you may want to put a bed down here so I do not fall over the banister. I tend to wander when I have had my fill."

"I am happy you warned me," said Neil.

Glenna poured herself more wine, walked to her husband and then turned to face the men. "Did he tell you about my father? If he did, he did not tell you the half of it. Even the King of Scotland is afraid of him. My father is the fiercest and most reckless man in all the world, but when my mother gets that look in her eye, my father takes off running." Glenna waited for them to stop chuckling and took a moment to appreciate Kessan's wink.

"The first time they met, my mother knocked the wind out of him. I would tell you how, but I might need to do that myself someday." Again she waited for them to stop laughing. "Father liked her the first time she did it and vowed he would never let her get that close to him again. The second time, he married her. Now he just takes off running."

Half the MacGreagors were rolling on the floor with laughter and Neil was delighted. His wife had put them at ease and the men began to joke with each other just like always. Then they started to make bets on who could out drink Glenna. Soon they were ignoring their laird and mistress completely.

She sat down, waited for him to sit beside her at the table and leaned closer. "I want more time with my daughter."

"What?"

"She is my daughter too, is she not?"

"Of course."

"Then I want to spend more time with her. She should be here with us now, crawling on the floor, getting into everything and wearing her poor father out. That is what babies are supposed to do."

"I did not think..."

"I know, I have come to realize I must tell you what I want, instead of waiting for you to guess."

"Good, I will count on you to do that."

It was the first time she really looked at him. His face was more than pleasant when he smiled. His eyes were warm and after all the things Kessan told her, she admired him very much. She did not feel love for him, but she did not feel resentment anymore either.

Neil leaned a little closer to her, "I was hoping you might like to brighten the place up a bit."

"Someday, but 'tis too soon. When I get to know the lasses better, I will ask for suggestions. Then they will not resent my changing things so much."

"How did you become so wise?"

She giggled. "I have eight brothers and sisters. Sometimes, wisdom is when you make others think what you do is their idea."

"Will it work on husbands?"

"I will let you know." At that, she genuinely smiled at him and he genuinely smiled back.

Kessan watched them from across the room. Ewing Larmont was right; they *were* perfect for each other. Soon they would know it too and now he could concentrate on his own problem -- how was he ever going to get Donnel away from Walrick long enough for her to fall in love with him?

Kessan sighed. Moving a mountain would be easier.

When Kindel and Walrick came in, Glenna left her evening meal to go with them to tell Kindel's mother about her blindness. Of course, her mother already suspected and she was glad Kindel was ready to admit it. Then they went back to tell Neil. He hugged Kindel and promised they would take good care of her.

Some of the men got a sad look on their face until Walrick glared at them. "She has agreed to be my wife, and if you pity her you will have to deal with me." He glared in all directions until Neil smacked him on the back to congratulate him. After that, Walrick grinned and kept right on grinning.

Kessan saw his chance and tried to sneak out of the room, but Walrick noticed and grabbed his arm. "I am taking a wife, not giving up a sister."

Kessan sat back down.

*

After the men were gone, Neil blew out all but the last candle and followed Glenna up the stairs. They both looked in on Leesil and he almost pulled the door closed until he remembered she was going to sleep in there. Just to be sure, Neil walked in, felt for lumps in the bed and looked all around. Then he smiled and went back to the door. "It appears to be safe. Sleep well."

"Neil, I am sorry."

"For what?"

"For judging you so harshly. I thought the wager was just for sport. You really did not mean to hurt me."

"I am sorry too. Ewing was not supposed to tell you about the wager. I wanted time to explain it, and then after you knew, I could think of no way to make you feel better."

She went to him and kissed his cheek. "You are a good lad and I am proud to be your wife."

He was so moved, he looked deep into her eyes, lightly touched the side of her face and then kissed her forehead. "Good night." He quietly closed the door.

Glenna did not expect to feel anything when he touched her, but her heart actually skipped a beat. She took off her belt and plaid, laid them across the back of a chair and straightened her long shirt. She wondered how it would feel to have his arms around her. Leesil began to squirm, so Glenna helped her turn over and then patted her back until she was sleeping soundly again. "'Tis good to have a daughter," she whispered.

Neil sat down on his bed. She really was all he could ask for in a wife. She was kind, thoughtful and good with the people. Already his men liked and admired her. And when she was not with him, he missed her.

What he wanted to do was go back into Leesil's room and take Glenna into his arms. But it was probably too soon. He removed his shoes, but he didn't go to bed. Instead, he went to the window, pulled back the drape and leaned against the wall. The half-moon cast its light on the meadow, the night was quiet and all he could think about was her kiss on the cheek. It pleased him very much.

She stood in the doorway of his bedchamber watching him for a long time. With the moonlight on his face, he was truly the most handsome man she had ever seen. His touch made her want more, but maybe it was too soon. She was about to turn away when he noticed her. Glenna was suddenly a little embarrassed. "I ..."

"What?"

She gathered all her courage and told him what she wanted. "I want you to hold me."

"I want that too." He opened his arms and let her come to him. At first, he held her like he would any of the women in his clan. But then he wanted to touch her hair and when she moved closer, he tightened his arms. Her touch felt so right and when she nuzzled his neck and he thought she wanted to be kissed, he lowered his lips to hers.

For Glenna, Neil's nearness was becoming more thrilling by the moment. His kiss was so tender at first, and then when it became more urgent, she realized she would not stop him. This was the kind of love she had always dreamed of and she never wanted it to end.

CHAPTER VIII

So, she has gone to his bed at last. Victoria stared at the undisturbed plaid on the bed in Glenna's bedchamber. Yesterday, she planned to go to Neil in the night and show him how much she loved him, but now Glenna would be there so she had to come up with another way. It only took a few minutes to think of an answer and she wondered why she hadn't thought of it before.

It was afternoon, Glenna was at the loch having swimming lessons, Neil went to watch the warriors practice and the baby was sleeping. It was time to clean but there was little to clean in Glenna's room.

Victoria peeked in on Leesil and smiled. Soon Glenna would be gone and Leesil would be her daughter. She glanced around the room and thought about how she would change it. Brighter curtains would immediately help. She turned to go and suddenly caught her breath.

"I did not mean to alarm you." Glenna touched Victoria's arm, looked in the box to make sure Leesil was still sleeping and then held the door open for Victoria. As soon as they were both on the balcony, she pulled the door closed. "You are Victoria?"

"Aye, Mistress."

"You need not call me mistress. I am Glenna."

"Thank you, Mistress."

Glenna smiled and decided to let it pass. "I would like to get to know you better. You do a very good job of cleaning and my husband and I..."

Her husband? Victoria kept smiling, but she wanted to scream ... Neil is my husband, not yours!

"Come, we can talk while I get out of these wet things." She led the way, opened the door to her bedchamber and began to undress. "What do you use to make the tables shine so? Where I come from we have…" Victoria seemed to be staring at, but not really seeing her and Glenna found it disturbing. "Victoria?"

"What?"

"Are you unwell?"

"Aye, I mean nay." She could not have planned this better. It was the perfect opportunity to get Glenna away from Neil and she could not pass it up. "My little brother is ill. I should not have come here today."

"I hope 'tis not serious. How can I help? Would you like me to go with you?"

The stupid woman was playing right into her hands. "I would like that very much."

Glenna tried to hurry. "You look dreadfully upset. Of course I will go with you. Find someone to tend Leesil while I dress. How far away do you live?"

"Down the road."

"Ask Kessan to get our horses."

"I do not have a horse."

"Then you can ride with me."

Patrick felt unsettled. Perhaps meat that was too tough to chew and eggs in her bed were only a way to make Glenna feel unwelcome, but both pranks seemed well thought out. Like Neil, he tried to figure out which of the serving or cleaning women might resent her, but Neil dismissed all the ones he thought might be guilty. He decided he should talk to Glenna and see if she noticed anything else. But when Patrick got inside the great hall, Neil was there alone. "Where is Glenna?"

"Victoria took her riding."

He was not sure why, but he was suddenly alarmed. "What?"

"Kessan is with them. Do not look so concerned, Victoria is married and she is harmless."

"Neil, Victoria is not married, her husband died in the war!"

The color drained out of Neil's face. He raced out the door, jumped down off the landing and ran for his horse. William was Victoria's husband and flashes of his funeral came to mind, but they buried many that day including Sween and Agnes. He remembered Victoria coming to him a few days later wanting something to do and he suggested she clean for him. After that, he hardly noticed her.

He heard Patrick yelling and asking which way they went. Neil looked up at the guard tower just long enough to see the guard point down the road. With Patrick right behind him, he rode swiftly across the bridge and headed south.

*

She tried to sink the dagger deep into Kessan's stomach and laughed at the shocked look on his face. But something was holding Victoria's hand and she couldn't thrust the dagger in. He was down on the ground, scooting away and she didn't have the strength in her one arm to stop him. Then she heard a horrible laugh and looked around to see who it was.

Glenna had her around the waist, but Glenna wasn't even smiling. "He said he loved me!" Victoria screamed. It was Glenna she wanted to kill anyway, so she tried to stand up and turn on her. But Glenna wouldn't let her move.

Kessan finally got out from under her and Victoria found that she was somehow flat on her back. But even with Glenna on top of her, she felt strong. The tip of her dagger was pointed at Glenna's neck and all she needed to do was...

For Victoria, everything suddenly went dark.

Glenna took the dagger out of Victoria's hand and tossed it away. She pulled herself up to a sitting position and looked at the still stunned Kessan. "Are you hurt?"

"Nay, I did not even see her coming. Are you hurt?"

"'Tis nothing serious." She touched the small nick in her neck and then looked at her finger. It was bleeding, but not much. Before she realized it, Kessan was holding a cloth on her neck to absorb the blood. "Truly, 'tis nothing to fret about."

"Neil will have my head if anything happens to you."

"Speaking of which..." She took over holding the cloth, and nodded at the sight of her husband's and Patrick's horses thundering down the road.

His wife was sitting in the dirt, Victoria was sprawled out beside her and Kessan was on his knees. Neil didn't bother to halt his horse before he slid off and ran to her. The cloth she was holding on her neck was covered in blood and he tried to keep the fear out of his eyes so he would not upset her.

Neil quickly sat down in front of her and looked into her eyes. She did not seem to be in a lot of pain. He was almost afraid to look, but he finally moved her hand away. The cut was small, but it was still bleeding so he pulled another cloth out of his belt and put pressure on the cut. Then he looked at Victoria.

"Glenna knocked her out." Kessan said. Then he watched Patrick retrieve Neil's horse and looked around to see where his was. They had just dismounted and were leading the horses up the path when Victoria screeched and then attacked him.

Neil looked at his wife again. "Did you break your hand?"

"Almost, and 'tis my drinking hand, too." She meant it as a joke, but her husband was not amused.

"You are coming home with me." He examined her hand, decided it was not broken, got back on his horse and then waited for Kessan to lift her up and put her into his arms. Neil held her close for a long minute and then whispered in her ear, "I cannot lose you, not now." He turned and took his beautiful and beloved wife home.

*

Glenna curled up in the bed next to Neil and let him cover her with his plaid. "Victoria's mind got muddled. She could not accept William's death, and when you told her you loved her the day she buried him, she misunderstood. She pretended you were her husband and that way she didn't have to feel the pain of losing William."

"Is she better now? Can we trust her?"

"I think so. She wants to visit her brother in the Ferguson hold for a while and I said she could if you agree. That reminds me; Walrick will not let Kessan get near his sister still. Kessan is hoping while Walrick is busy on his wedding night, we could..."

Laird Neil MacGreagor smiled. He had a family again finally and his home was once more filled with love. He was also still in the business of matchmaking and his wife was loving every moment of it. How much happier could a man be?

~ end ~

Coming Soon – Book 3 in the Viking series.

MORE MARTI TALBOTT BOOKS

Marti Talbott's Highlander Series: books 1 – 5 are short stories that follow the MacGreagor clan through two generations. They are followed by:

Betrothed, Book 6

The Golden Sword, Book 7

Abducted, Book 8

A Time of Madness, Book 9

Triplets, Book 10

Secrets, Book 11

Choices, Book 12

Ill-Fated Love Book 13

The Other Side of the River, Book 14

The Viking Series:

The Viking, Book 1 explains how the clan came into being.

The Viking's Daughter, Book 2

Book 3 is coming soon.

Marblestone Mansion (Scandalous Duchess Series) follows the MacGreagor clan into Colorado's early 20th century. There are currently 10 books in this series.

The Jackie Harlan Mysteries

Seattle Quake 9.2, Book 1

Missing Heiress, Book 2

Greed and a Mistress, Book 3

The Carson Series

The Promise, Book 1

Broken Pledge, Book 2

Talk to Marti on Facebook at:

https://www.facebook.com/marti.talbott

Sign up to be notified when new books are published at:

http://www.martitalbott.com